Francis Pryor was born in London in 1945. After studying archaeology at Cambridge, he emigrated to Toronto, where he joined the staff of the Royal Ontario Museum. Using the Museum as a base, he began a series of major excavations (1971–78) in England, at Fengate, on the outskirts of Peterborough. Here he revealed an extensive prehistoric landscape, culminating in the discovery in 1982 of Flag Fen, one of the best preserved Bronze Age sites in Europe. His books include his '*Britain*' series (for HarperCollins): *Britain BC, Britain AD, Britain in the Middle Ages* and *The Birth of Modern Britain*; two of which he presented as documentary series for Channel 4. He has appeared frequently on *Time Team* and has presented a number of programmes for Radio 4. *The Lifers' Club* is his first work of fiction.

The Lifers' Club

The Lifers' Club

Francis Pryor

unbound

This edition first published in 2014

Unbound
4–7 Manchester Street, Marylebone, London, W1U 2AE
www.unbound.co.uk

Typeset by GreenGate Publishing Services, Tonbridge, Kent
Cover design by Mecob

A CIP record for this book is available from the British Library

ISBN 978-1-78352-029-9 (special)
ISBN 978-1-78352-028-2 (trade)
ISBN 978-1-78352-027-5 (ebook)

Printed and bound in India by Replika Press Pvt. Ltd.

For Brian Fagan, the master of a good plot

A Sense of Place I

Flax Hole

One

The building shook. Windows rattled. Just outside in the quarry, five tons of stones smashed into a dumper truck. Next another, and another, then the turbo-charged diesel screamed into life, as the laden dumper pulled away, passing them close by. Mugs of tea rippled. But nobody in the stuffy Portakabin took any notice. For them, it was routine.

They were excavating in a huge gravel quarry in the Fens, about ten miles south-east of Peterborough. There was archaeology everywhere around them: Bronze Age burials, Iron Age and Roman farms, fields and houses. It had been a long project, but soon it was to end. And not before bloody time, Alan thought grimly. For weeks the rain had been pouring down. Outside, on site, the ground was wet and slimy. Lethal. Inside, water had seeped through the door and formed a little puddle, which slowly drained through a crack in the floor, where the doormat should have been. Condensation ran down the windows, two of which were boarded-up after an attack by vandals the previous week. But as site-huts went, it was pretty good.

Alan Cadbury and his twelve diggers were sipping hot drinks, their hard hats and Hi-vis waterproofs hanging, dripping on a row of pegs by the door. One or two read newspapers. No-one said much. They all just wanted to dry off for a few minutes and relax in the steamy warmth, while outside, in the gravel pit's washing plant, more stones thundered into yet another dumper, which revved-up and roared away, to shed its load round the back, in the flooded area quarried out the previous year.

Like two of the others in his small team of contract archaeologists, Alan was rolling a cigarette, which he'd light up as soon as he went back to work. He knew it was a nasty, stupid habit, and he'd tried to kick it dozens of times, but then a few hours, sometimes even a few days later, he'd find he'd lit another. So he kept them small, and as roll-ups went, this was very slim. More paper than tobacco. He'd only have time to grab a few quick drags while they walked across the quarry to their excavation. Then he'd have to stub it out when he reached the trench. Site rules. Radiocarbon contamination.

He swore under his breath as his last fag paper slipped from his hands. Carefully he leant forward to retrieve it from the floor. Earlier that rainy week, they'd put down thick layers of newspaper to absorb the worst of the wet. Thank God, he thought, as he watched his Rizla float down towards the puddle, it's landed on a dry patch. He reached out, leaning forward. As his fingers grasped it, his eye was caught by a story on a soggy sheet alongside it:

Honour killer at Blackfen?

Rumours are circulating that the so-called 'honour killer', Ali Kabul (25) is now at HMP Blackfen. The Governor's office was unable to confirm or deny this to our reporter. The victim, Sofia Kabul (16), was the murderer's younger sister who was killed at the family's business premises at Flax Hole Depot, Leicester, over seven years ago. The case caused a national outcry. Kabul was convicted at Leicester Crown Court last January and was sentenced [continued p. 32]

That's all there was. Alan glanced up to the top of the sheet: it was page 4 of the *Fenland Mercury* for two weeks ago. Rapidly he tore it off and read it again, frowning. Then he looked around on the floor for the rest of the paper, but it wasn't there. Nowhere. He sat back and sighed. Flax Hole, Leicester. Must be the same place. Can't be two Flax Holes – not possible. Memories started to flood in: another wet season, but winter and much colder. Two teenage kids, peering into the trench, eager to know what the diggers were up to.

Suddenly, another image flashed before him: the stuff of horror films. A young girl, lying in the trench, a faceless man piling soil on top of her lifeless body. He shook his head: stupid idea. Brain playing tricks on him: a waking nightmare. Stick to the facts.

Then his phone alarm went off. Back to work. He put the scrap of newspaper into his pocket.

'OK folks,' he said, rising stiffly to his feet, trying to inject some energy: 'Tea-break's over. Back to it.'

Nobody moved.

'For Christ's sake people, it's time we got back…'

Alan, they'd become good friends for the two years they were together on the course. By then Lane was already a successful career policeman, and it was his idea to do the MA, if only to find out what the new, and much-heralded, branch of forensic science could achieve. As he said at the time, there was little point in employing extra staff or consultants, if the police themselves had no idea what they could learn from them. But once he'd begun the course, he realised his lack of excavating experience put him at a big disadvantage. So he was delighted when he became friendly with Alan.

Alan was on the staff of the course and had been employed to oversee the fieldwork side of things. Although it was just a temporary contract it had come in the nick of time: he'd been out of work for a couple of months after failing to complete his PhD dissertation. People said he was pig-headed and should have made the changes the external examiner demanded. Instinctively Alan disliked the man: Dr Peter Flower. Posey and superior: every inch a clever academic and up with all the in-vogue trends, like post-structuralism. He wanted Alan to provide a 'relativist epi-overview'. He said it didn't have to be very long. He even pleaded with him. But no. Alan was damned if he would. And whose bloody thesis was it, anyhow: Alan's or Posey Peter's?

So he lost his grant and his postgraduate studentship. He was out of work. By then it was July and all commercial digging jobs had been filled. Frankly, the outlook was bleak and he was about to start stacking supermarket shelves when an old friend at Saltaire, hearing of his plight on the grapevine, offered him a temporary position on the Forensics MA course. To someone with Alan's experience there was nothing to it. Just the basics: trowelling, laying out trenches, section-drawing, soil-sampling, surveying, GPS – all familiar stuff. He didn't exactly feel stimulated by the course. Frankly he'd much rather have been out on a real site getting his hands dirty. But he had enough sense to know when to bite the bullet. Then he'd met Richard Lane and things changed.

Their lifestyles were so different: his chaotic, the policeman's organised and efficient. But as they worked and talked they began to grasp the point of it all. It wasn't just about clever scientific techniques. Arresting criminals. Bang to rights. That sort of stuff was fine on TV. No, it was bigger, more fundamental than that: why some things mattered and others didn't. Good and evil: basic stuff that makes us human. Why people did what they did. Every patch of land told a different story, and they were all about people. Best of all, they enjoyed sorting out the puzzle together.

Soon they were both working on various digs during vacations and on weekends. As they trowelled together on their hands and knees, Alan was surprised at the policeman's natural ability and he took much trouble teaching him the nuts and bolts of practical excavation. Rather to his surprise Lane too discovered that although Alan often operated by instinct – by 'feel' as he called it – he also had an extraordinarily tenacious analytical mind. He wouldn't let problems die. He was like a terrier and always managed to sort them out. And he was usually proved right, much to Lane's begrudging admiration.

After the course ended Lane tried to persuade him to train as a full-time police consultant, which he resisted out of that very same instinctive reaction. Lane tried to make him change his mind. But soon gave up. No, Alan was a hopeless case: he shied away from permanent commitment and didn't like the idea of working with non-archaeological material. He seemed hooked on the special appeal, the magic even, of old things and long-lost times. They stirred his imagination like nothing else and he couldn't set them aside. For Alan, past times held the key to the present, but at a more personal level than mere history; his work was a necessity, not a hobby or luxury.

Directly after Saltaire, Lane had been transferred to the Cambridgeshire force. In those days they maintained contact, although not closely – the odd drink at weekends. There'd been a series of unpleasant murders in and around Whittlesey, a small Fenland town east of Peterborough. Alan was able to advise them about Fen farms, Fen farmers and their hired help. He made several scene-of-crime visits, all of which brought in welcome consultancy fees. In the end they never caught the murderer, which didn't surprise Alan, who was far from certain that the killings were the work of a single individual. Yes, there were consistencies, but they were too obvious. Alan had the strong sense that something else, probably rather more sinister, had been going on. The press, on the other hand, were completely convinced – as indeed were the police – at least as soon as the first stories began to hit the headlines. Then it all fizzled out, not that anyone in the area seemed to care much. Life continued as before. Alan had been pissed-off, then he came to see that human beings can only cope with so much trauma on their own doorstep. Easier to turn your back, and pretend nothing had happened.

A couple of years passed. Alan and Lane kept loosely in touch: the odd phone call or drink when either of them was nearby. Then things got worse. Like the start of their friendship it was unexpected: Alan had always suspected that the police's approach to the Whittlesey murders was a result of political pressure from higher up. A case of political correctness, as all the talk at the time pointed to an immigrant gang. Several were known to be working in the region, but none had yet killed; their thefts were all about pink farm diesel, heating oil or scrap metal. Anyhow, one night, after a few too many beers, he told Lane as much. He knew as he said it, it hadn't gone down well. And he was right. Lane's eyes had said as much: OK smart-arse I bet you wouldn't have done any better – and at least I've got a career. So the scene-of-crime visits and police consultancies stopped, and that was that. Just eight years ago – shortly before the Flax Hole dig.

Alan fired up his computer and googled Richard Lane. It didn't take long to find him. An image of his old friend stared steadily out of the screen at him: Lane had been promoted to Detective Chief Inspector and was now with Leicestershire CID. Destined to be a high flyer, Alan thought as he stared back into the expressionless gaze. You've learned how to do a mugshot, he thought. Give nothing away, just stare down the lens. But there were a few signs: shorter sideburns, greying hair and just the hint of a double chin. Alan smiled: Lane's wife Mary was one of the best cooks he'd come across. Lucky sod.

To the world at large Alan's 'career' hadn't been flying at all. He'd managed to screw-up or turn down several offers of long-term jobs. He didn't want them. At least that's how he rationalised it. In reality he couldn't face getting on the ladder he'd seen so many of his friends start to climb. But it never went very high and they all ended up as project managers in commercial units, sitting in front of computer screens and talking to suited women in HR. They grew fat guts and endlessly droned on about how they missed 'being in the field'. Like hell, he thought: they couldn't have survived a month out in a gravel quarry in February. They'd lose weight fast: freeze their balls off.

So he'd drifted into being a freelance site officer, supervising one dig after another, winter, summer, autumn and spring. Not exactly high-flying, but he was proud of what he was doing, even so. He knew he was the best and enjoyed the challenge of surviving on his wits. It was like other things in life; he liked the danger, the ever-present and lurking precariousness of it. It was better than growing old.

Now he found he was standing in the bungalow's single empty corridor, looking down at the phone. The newspaper cutting lay beside it.

He took a deep breath, and dialled a number in Leicester. It barely rang before a brisk voice answered.

'Hello, Richard Lane here.'

'It's Alan…'

No response.

'Alan Cadbury?'

'Oh, hello Alan, it's been a while.'

'Yes, it has.'

Alan realised there was nothing for it but to get straight to the point.

'So, the reason I'm calling… Yesterday I read something in an oldish copy of the local rag about one of those "honour" killings. It seems the man that did it, Ali Kabul, came from Leicester.'

'That's right. It was a big case. You must have heard about it? Every newspaper, let alone TV and radio, was full of it.'

'No, sorry, missed it. The last few months have been a bit frantic. I've been digging everywhere. And you know what it's like, you don't see papers very often when you're in the field.'

'It was very high profile,' Lane continued, 'Not just here in Leicester, but nationally.'

Was there a patronising edge to Lane's tone, or was Alan just being over-sensitive? He pushed on regardless.

'The clip I saw mentioned the killing happened at Flax Hole Depot. That's the place off the Market Harborough Road, at the city end, isn't it?'

'That's right.'

'And there's a big café near it? Mehmet's, named after the owner?'

'Alan, something tells me you haven't got back in touch after all this time just to discuss the local geography.'

Alan tightened his grip around the telephone, resisting the urge to slam it back into the cradle and walk away.

'I think I must have been there when the killing happened.' Alan thought he could hear a sharp intake of breath. But when Lane spoke his voice was calm and professional.

'February 2002?'

'I was running a dig there. I'd set up a small contracting partnership with a colleague. We were part of a sub-contract for a larger job run by the City Archaeological Unit. Then, at the pre-planning stage, the City Archivist found documentary evidence for a flax-processing workshop complex there in the seventeenth and eighteenth centuries. Flax sites are rare in the east. So the project was delayed, while we did an assessment, followed by excavation. It turned out to be quite important.'

'Sounds fascinating, Alan, but I don't quite see how this is relevant.'

'The Depot was being completely redesigned, rebuilt and modernised by the owners.'

'The Kabuls?'

'That's right. And that's what I need to talk to you about. '

There was a pause. Alan could visualise Lane, slowly passing his hand across his face, the way he did when he was weighing up his words before he spoke.

'I wasn't involved in that case. Not the sort of thing I normally deal with. We've officers with more specialist knowledge who deal with crimes like forced marriages and honour killings. If you have anything to report then I suggest you contact...'

Alan cut in, he wouldn't be shrugged aside, not until he'd said what he had to say.

'It's nothing specific. More of a hunch.'

Alan thought, for a second, he could hear Lane swallow back a laugh.

'Ah, the Alan Cadbury hunch. I remember it well.'

There was a warmth to his voice, a softening. Less the formal police detective more the old friend whom he had knelt beside, in a cold, wet trench, both trowelling with fingerless gloves and frozen fingers.

'The thing is, while we were digging we were visited by two teenagers, both Turkish-looking. Both bright and intelligent. Brother and sister, I'd guess. They were also about the right age, and I'm fairly sure the boy was called Ali – although it was seven years ago and I never got to see him after the dig. I didn't find out the girl's name, but she was wearing a green school uniform.'

'That's the High School.'

'I'm sure I'd recognise her face if I saw it again. Very pretty. Her brother was good-looking too. Any chance you could get me pictures of them?'

There was a pause before Lane replied.

'I assume you have a good reason for all this?'

Alan reflected for a moment. Best not to give too much away at this stage.

'Yes, Richard, I think I do.'

'I can download them tonight, but I'd rather not trust them to email. Better if I showed them to you here. I'm on duty tomorrow, so why not come over Sunday afternoon?'

Alan had forgotten this about Lane. He took his time weighing up the evidence, working out the best course of action – but once he decided to act, that was it.

'To your house?'

'I don't see why not.'

'Great, Richard, that's really great. Thank you.'

But Alan was speaking into empty air, Lane had already hung up.

* * *

Alan put the phone down and looked out of the window. It was only mid-August and already the nights were drawing in. Across the open fields he could see a man with a pitchfork get out of an old tractor parked alongside a reed-filled dyke. Then he climbed into the dyke, reaching into the back pocket of his overalls. Alan knew what was coming next, as he'd helped his dad do the same thing hundreds of times when he was a lad. As he expected the flames soon appeared, fanned by a light evening breeze, licking along the sides of a dyke as the dead reeds and rushes caught fire: an eerie vision in the half-light.

Well, Alan thought as he folded up the newspaper article and put it back in his pocket, that could have gone worse. A lot worse.

Three

Alan was normally an early riser, but today he slept through to nearly nine o'clock. Still, he thought, it didn't matter: it was Saturday. Late last night he'd phoned his brother Grahame and invited himself over to the farm for lunch. It'd been a while since they'd seen one another and Alan always liked returning to the place where they'd both grown up. Their parents had been tenants of Lincolnshire County Council and Grahame had taken the lease on as soon as he'd graduated from Nettlesham, the Agricultural College in Witham Fen just east of Lincoln. Then the horrible accident happened.

Grahame blamed himself, but as Alan insisted, how could he have known what was going on, if Dad hadn't told him?

That was so typical of their old man, he just got on and did it. He was always fiercely independent. But this time he'd gone too far. He must have known he should have got help. It was always a two-man job: anything to do with baler repairs is dangerous. He knew that. They were constantly receiving farm safety leaflets from the Ministry and the NFU. Beware of balers. Always disconnect the PTO. Such a horrible way to go. Arm ripped off at the shoulder. Slowly. Blood everywhere. The two brothers had rushed to the screams. The air ambulance arrived, but too late. He died a thousand feet up, on his way to the Pilgrim Hospital at Boston. He'd always wanted to fly in a helicopter.

Their father's death brought the two brothers closer together. Alan was eighteen at the time and had just taken his A-levels. A few weeks previously the family had celebrated the news that he'd been accepted to read archaeology at Leicester. Grahame was about to graduate from college, but was then living on the farm, doing the practical element of his degree project. Together they supported their mother who, truth to tell, never really recovered from the shock. Anyhow, she withdrew from everything and there was nothing the brothers could do about it. They took her on outings and trips, anything to stimulate an interest in life. But nothing worked. Before their eyes she lost weight and in just six short years had passed away.

During these difficult years the two brothers grew much closer together. Grahame had even suggested that the two of them should run the farm together. He had discussed it with their County Council landlords and they were happy with the idea, but in the end Alan's instincts overrode what seemed, on paper, to be an excellent prospect, with a secure future. Laying aside the fact that he'd set his mind on archaeology, he also didn't want to be tied down. He couldn't bear the thought of being in the same place in ten, twenty, thirty, even fifty years' time. His life stretching before him like a well-lit road. No, it didn't appeal. Not even slightly. So he turned down Grahame's generous offer – and in their heart-of-hearts they were both relieved. But Grahame never forgot: he knew what he owed Alan.

Alan's imagination was about to revisit that terrible scene in the barn for the umpteenth time when his alarm went off. It came as a release. Time to get going.

After thirteen years as a professional field archaeologist Alan had developed a loathing for instant coffee. He hated the aftertaste and the headache it now always seemed to give him. So he filled his filter machine from a packet left over from the previous week. He smelled it. Lovely. Or was it? He thought he could detect a hint of diesel. That bloody stink – it was everywhere: the phone, his pyjamas, the stair carpet. And now the coffee. Still, he made a brew and drank it down black, as the milk in the fridge had gone off and he'd forgotten to get any more. No toast, but a packet of salt and vinegar crisps. As he munched his way through his makeshift breakfast, he was aware that something was niggling him. Blackfen Prison. Of course he knew the name only too well, as he'd been a young member of the team that cleared the site before construction began, and that must have been almost twenty years ago. But he'd also come across it quite recently – but where?

He opened the kitchen drawer that served as his erratic filing system of unopened bills and junk mail. He burrowed down through the strata of the last six months. There it was. A letter from Blackfen Prison with the words 'The Lifers' Club' emblazoned in big black type at the top of the page. It was an invitation, phrased slightly like a summons he thought, to come and speak to the inmates. He'd shrugged it off. But now… He folded the letter carefully and placed it at the top of the pile. One thing at a time, he told himself as he closed the drawer tight shut.

His Land Rover was universally known as Brutus. He'd bought it at a farm sale ten years ago, where it had cost him just £150. It was a macho-looking beast, with a canvas top, very knobbly tyres and huge steel helicopter suspension loops at each corner. During its life in the Army, Brutus had been the tender vehicle for a Rapier wire-guided anti-tank missile. It had been equipped with a dual electrical system, one for the missile and another for the vehicle. There was a control panel immediately behind the front seats' bulkhead, which Alan had removed, leaving a number of wires dangling free. He knew they were no longer live, but sometimes nervous people could be less convinced. Passengers were also made jittery by the fuelling arrangements, which consisted of two separate petrol tanks located directly under the front seats. To fill them you removed the bottom of the seat and undid a heavy-duty cap. Over the years Alan had grown used to the thought that he was driving around England sitting on top of two forty-gallon tanks of petrol.

The Ministry of Defence, in their wisdom, had equipped Brutus with a twenty-four volt electrical system. This made it almost impossible to buy replacement fuses, which long-ago had standardised around twelve volts. So if a fuse blew, Alan would try to fix the problem and then replace the fuse with a stout piece of wire. As a consequence of this, the electrics heated up – sometimes smoked – which also made passengers nervous. So nervous in fact that a year ago his insurance broker insisted that the electrics be rewired at twelve volts.

While this was being done, Alan also decided to have the petrol replaced by LPG gas, which the nice man who fitted it told him was both safer and cheaper. But there was a down-side. The only place where the gas tank could go was directly behind the seats, where the old Rapier missile control panel had once been. This made it rather up-front and visible;

again, some of his more nervous regular passengers didn't see this as much of an improvement. Even his mother, a sensible, pragmatic person, well used to dodgy agricultural machinery, simply refused to get in the vehicle at all.

Alan backed Brutus out into the road and headed west, towards Crowland Fen. The wind was getting up and dark clouds were gathering above the level horizon. It was still sunny at Tubney and soon the cab started to heat up. Alan opened one of the vents above the dashboard and took a deep breath as the cool air rushed in. In the distance he could just begin to make out the higher ground around Bourne and Stamford. Over there was the A1, heavy traffic, the east coast main line and the outside world. Out here it was very different. No traffic. Just the odd tractor and a few heavy artics fetching loads of bulk grain from outlying barns.

As he drove along the dead straight roads fringed with deep dykes on both sides, Alan found his eyes resting on those distant hills which were almost imperceptibly becoming better defined, less cloud-like and misty. Over there was England: Lincolnshire, Leicestershire, Rutland. That's where he'd been working back in February 2002. Flax Hole.

He found his thoughts returning to Ali, as they'd done a hundred times since he saw that newspaper story. Why had the lad made such an impression on him? Maybe because he was a contrast to the other diggers who weren't very inspiring. They'd landed the contract in late November and in those days the construction industry, and with it archaeology, was booming. Good, reliable and qualified staff were hard to find, but somehow he and Paul, his co-director, had managed to sub-contract half a dozen new Polish graduates from a large unit in Nottingham. The trouble was, they spoke poor English and tended to keep themselves to themselves. And of course the vodka, the ubiquitous vodka, didn't help much, either. So the social side of the dig had been dire. A terrible atmosphere: them and us.

Ali had been such a contrast to all this: bright, enthusiastic and with a genuine interest. Alan was suddenly hit by a visceral memory. He was back in the finds shed at Flax Hole. He had the finds laid out on the table in front of him, and was carefully piecing together the site sequence, object by object. Ali was transfixed. Alan handed him a Roman coin. Ali held it gently in his hand, as if he was scared he could shatter it with the slightest touch.

'How did you know?' asked Ali, quietly.

'They're quite common,' replied Alan, misunderstanding, 'when you've done a few digs, then you can easily recognise…'

'No, I mean, how did you know this was what you wanted to do? As a job?'

'Well, can you picture me in an office?'

But Ali was staring at him, intent. Alan saw, in that moment, this was important.

'I always loved old things. Museums, even as a kid. But after my first excavation… I just knew, I couldn't do anything else.'

'And your Dad didn't mind?'

'He could see it made me happy – so no, he didn't mind.'

'Even though you were never going to make any money from it?'

Alan grinned at him and shrugged.

'You never know, I might still find my pot of gold.'

Ali shook his head and smiled. Alan could see that the lad was a pragmatist, he knew that would never happen.

Alan took the coin and gently placed it back on the finds table. But what of Ali, would he ever find his own pot of gold?

In that moment, Alan realised that for Ali, family expectation was everything. He could not choose his own way in life without their approval.

He sighed heavily as the first ferocious gusts of a stiff thundery shower began to overwhelm Brutus's feeble windscreen wipers. As he slowed right down he found he was wrestling with the thought that the Ali he remembered was the same Ali in that newspaper story. But he couldn't accept it. It didn't make sense.

He pulled into a farm gate to let the shower pass. Ten minutes later, and Ali was still on his mind. Then the sun cut through and a 200-horsepower John Deere tractor with an immense disc harrow rig thundered by in the opposite direction. Together the sun and the tractor had managed to break into his thoughts. He took a deep breath and shook his head: no, even if Lane's pictures were of the Ali he'd known, he couldn't have done it. That was impossible. Absolutely impossible. He was more than convinced of that. And he also realised that it mattered to him, Alan Cadbury, personally. It wasn't only about injustice, although that was important. In his heart-of-hearts he knew he had failed Ali once. And he was damned if he'd fail him again.

* * *

Crudens Farm was just over a mile outside the almost deserted eighteenth-century village of Hostland. Like many Fen hamlets it was built on either side of a single, dead straight road. None of the original houses survived because their foundations had long ago cracked and sunk as layers of peat buried deep below the surface had dried and shrunk; this was the result of land drainage, which became increasingly effective after the introduction of steam-driven pumps in the mid-nineteenth century. So the earliest buildings were two double-fronted houses with 1885 date stones, close by the now deserted non-conformist chapel. The other four buildings were probably built in the 1930s and then there were two semi-detached council houses at the same end as Cruden's Farm. Grahame had bought one of them to house his two farm workers. Back in the 1970s there'd even been a small shop, but that had long since closed. The nearest pub was in Crowland, seven miles away.

As Alan approached the village from the east he could see the great ruined tower of Crowland Abbey in the distance. He adored that mysterious, evocative building. It wasn't a cliché to say that every stone told a story, because they did – even down to the reddened ones at the east end, burnt when Cromwell's soldiers lit a bonfire during the Civil War.

The Land Rover bucked as they crossed an old, steep-sided, 'cock-up' bridge which took the road across the West Level Main Drain. Alan looked down as he drove over. Nothing had changed. The two pill-boxes and the concrete base of a spigot mortar anti-tank weapon were still there. Grahame had always loved the wartime relics in the area and still made sure that local farmers looked after them. Alan smiled. For a moment he recalled his brother explaining earnestly how they had been built in November 1940, when everyone was expecting the Germans to invade. He was too young to know how to react to this, but could remember looking grave – which seemed to go down well.

Another heavy shower was building in the west as Alan turned into the yard. His brother must have seen him approaching, as he was out of the front door and walking across the yard when Alan pulled up near the back door. Like most Fen farmers Grahame and his family almost never used the front door, which was still reserved for special visitors, such as the vicar on his rare visits to beg money for one of his pet charities. Grahame explained that his wife Liz was away collecting their two kids from something athletic, healthy and open air in Wales. A few drops of rain were starting to fall, as Alan closed the back door behind them.

Grahame produced two bottles of his home-brewed bitter from the larder. He knew it was a particular favourite of his brother. They sat down – no, flopped, as only brothers can do – into comfy chairs in the sitting room.

For a few minutes neither brother spoke. They didn't need to. Then Grahame released some of the wind he'd taken in with his beer.

'It's been too long, Alan.'

Alan was only too aware of that.

'I know. I've been on some amazing sites.'

'That's no excuse. It's been almost a year.'

'Yes…'

Alan felt bad: Grahame was right, it wasn't an excuse. Because there wasn't one. Outside the storm had gathered pace. Lightning lit up the sky behind the ruined Abbey.

'So, what's up?' Grahame asked.

It was a quality that Alan had always admired in his brother: his failure to engage in pointless small talk. That, and his ability to read Alan like the proverbial book.

Alan took a deep swig of his beer, and then began.

'I don't suppose you remember, I was on a dig in Leicester, back in 2002…'

'What, that winter dig? Flax… Flax something, wasn't it?'

'Yes, Flax Hole.'

'Didn't you run it with that other chap?'

'Yes, I co-directed with Paul, Paul Flynn, Dr Paul Flynn, as he liked to be known.'

'Yes, I remember you said he was a pompous prick.'

'Did I? Perhaps that was a bit harsh.' He paused then continued, 'He was a bit of an oddball, but an excellent administrator. Thorough, methodical, good with the financial side of things.'

'So you had a lot in common, then?'

Alan shared his brother's grin for a second. Then he refocused. He had to get this right.

'You know how Dad always said; family must stick together, through thick and thin?'

'So that's what this is about? Guilty conscience because you've been too busy digging up bones to bother with your own flesh and blood?'

'No. I mean you're right about the guilty conscience…'

Grahame was leaning forward in his chair now, his teasing smile had vanished.

'Go on.'

'What if doing the right thing by your family, by their values, was… deeply morally wrong?'

'What's this all about, Alan? And what the hell has it got to do with Flax Hole?'

Alan pulled his wallet from the back pocket of his jeans. Carefully he unfolded the newspaper clipping and handed it over. Grahame read it twice, then looked up.

'This happened when you were there? No wonder you're spooked.'

'It's not that. I think I knew him. Ali.'

'And you're worried that he's going to be banged-up nearby?'

It never occurred to Alan that his brother might have deeper concerns.

'No, not at all. It's more serious than that. I don't think he did it.'

Grahame broke in.

'Of course you don't. You're too soft. You'd give Genghis Khan the benefit of the doubt if you could.'

'You didn't see them together, Ali and his sister. There's no way he could have killed her.'

'OK, but have you got any evidence that might help your case?'

'That's my problem. I've got nothing concrete to go on. Just a feeling, that's all.'

'Don't do anything stupid, Alan. Go to the police. They're trained…'

'Yes, I have contacted the police, or rather a friend there…'

'Don't tell me, Richard Lane. Your digging buddy?'

'Something like that. He's moved to Leicestershire. He's now quite grand: a detective chief inspector.'

'So what did he suggest – if anything?'

'He's going to find me pictures of Ali and his sister…'

'To make sure,' Grahame broke in, 'they're the people you knew on the dig?'

'They've got to be. It's too much of a coincidence.'

Alan could see the anxiety in his brother's eyes.

'You don't think I ought to be getting involved, do you?'

Grahame let out a short bark of laughter.

'And that's why you came to see me, so I could talk you out of it?'

Alan smiled. Even he could see the funny side. As if his cautious, caring brother had ever been able to talk him out of anything.

Grahame leant over, put his hand on Alan's shoulder for a moment.

'Just promise me, when it all blows up in your face...'

'You'll be the first to know, Grahame. You have my word.'

Grahame went into the kitchen and came back with two more bottles of beer. The brothers sat in silence, watching the storm rage outside the window, both lost in their own thoughts.

Four

The next day dawned sunny and the forecast was for twenty-four hours without any rain. This raised Alan's spirits as he climbed into Brutus for the journey to Leicester. It wasn't the greatest vehicle to drive in the rain: like all old Land Rovers the wipers were rubbish and the dashboard vents let the water in. The sliding window on the driver's side was also leaky and the heater was too feeble to de-mist the windscreen in rain or fog. All in all, it was good for combat and cross-country, but not much else. He put his tin of tobacco on the dashboard and helped himself to two cigarettes for the journey. He lit one and inhaled deeply. The rush of nicotine made him feel strangely relaxed.

He gently eased the beast into the prosperous outer suburbs of Leicester's eastern approaches. Brutus looked very out of place here, its chipped matte khaki paint thickly spattered with mud from the quarry site. The houses belonged to senior management types. Most of the cars were hidden away in garages, but a few were out in driveways. Some were being washed by youngsters, probably students on their summer vacations. Apart from the odd Jag there was barely an English car to be seen: just Mercs, BMWs and big Volvos. Alan hadn't visited Lane's house in Leicester before, but he'd printed a map off the internet which was propped on the ledge behind the steering wheel. The estate had been built in the late 1920s, probably shortly before the '29 stock market crash – and it had survived well. The gardens which had been laid-out in prosperous times were large, with mature trees and shrubs. The houses, too, were attractive, if very suburban, with big porches and fine bay windows.

He steered Brutus into a leafy cul-de-sac. Alan smiled, in Tubney they'd have called it a dead-end. Number 17 was halfway along, on the right. He drew up outside. As Alan stepped down to the pavement he spotted someone kneeling by the front door. She stood up on hearing his door slam shut. It was Lane's wife Mary.

She pulled off a pair of rubber gloves to reveal neatly manicured fingers, which she was wiping on her Head Gardener apron. There was a small trug of weeds on the path beside her. As the rest of the garden seemed entirely weed-less, Alan couldn't imagine where she'd managed to find any. She kissed him on both cheeks, then held him by the shoulders at arm's length, inspecting him, like a prodigal son.

'You haven't changed one bit, Alan. Your life seems to suit you.'

Alan was slightly embarrassed. He wasn't used to flattery. He should have returned the compliment, but instead said:

'I'm sure Richard's the same. It's about doing a rewarding job, I suppose.'

'I wish it was. He's just been put in charge of an internal reorganisation of the County CID. A thankless task. Lots of backbiting and politics and very little gratitude. And that's why he's not here…'

Alan's heart sunk.

'He was called out early this morning and should be back,' she glanced down at her watch, 'in about half an hour. He texted me ten minutes ago.' She picked up her trug and put it down on a bench in the porch, then opened the front door. Alan followed her in.

Alan could see at a glance that Mary was very house-proud. Everything was dust-free, neat and tidy, but the place had that slightly sad feeling of a home that once used to house children, who had now departed.

'How are the twins?' Alan asked, as they sat down in the kitchen.

'Both at uni. Jane's here at Leicester, Harry's at Sheffield.'

'And doing science, I assume?'

'Yes, they're loving it.' She paused while she poured boiling water into a teapot.

Alan remembered the twins well. Bright, enthusiastic ten year olds, they had inherited Lane's curiosity and Mary's easy sociability. They used to bring him 'finds' from the back garden: a rusty nail, a bottle top, a broken plant pot; all had to be subject to the most thorough forensic analysis over the kitchen table. And now they were all grown up, setting out on careers of their own. Meanwhile Ali was destined to spend his best years locked up. And Sofia was dead.

Mary placed a cup of tea in front of him, breaking his reverie.

'But you haven't come to see Richard about his kids, have you?'

She placed a brown envelope on the table before him. This was unexpected. Alan's pulse rate suddenly increased.

'Are those the pictures?'

'He said you'd want to see them as soon as you got here.'

Alan opened the envelope and tipped two colour photos onto the table. The young man's picture was a prison mugshot, complete with date, number and name cards. He stared blankly ahead, expressionless. The young woman smiled out of the photograph at him, her bright eyes a contrast with the dead gaze of the convict. The scarf covering her hair only accentuated her striking bone structure. She was beautiful. For a moment, Alan was overwhelmed by a sharp, surprisingly painful stab of grief.

Mary let him look at the pictures for a couple of minutes. Then she spoke.

'It's them, isn't it? The kids from Flax Hole?'

Alan was slow to reply, as if waking up gradually after a late night.

'No doubt about that. None at all.'

Alan looked up to find Mary staring at him intently. For a moment the thought crossed his mind that Richard Lane had deliberately stayed away for half an hour, to give his wife time to ask him the sort of questions women are better at asking than men.

'Had Richard told you why I wanted to see him?'

'I must admit it does all sound most intriguing. However, if you start digging around in an old case like this, it's going to put the county force in a difficult position…'

'But surely not Richard, he won't be affected – he didn't join them till much later, did he?'

'I know. But he has to work with the people who made the decisions. So you're going to have to make allowances for him.'

Alan's hackles rose. It was the same old story. Don't rock the boat. Don't upset the powers that be. He swallowed back his anger, for Ali's sake. For Sofia's. He needed Lane, and to get Lane on side, he'd need Mary too.

'I understand. But I can't just walk away as if nothing happened. I knew Ali quite well. I'm quite convinced nothing would have made him kill his sister. Nothing.'

'Not even family honour? I mean, you don't know what these Middle Eastern families can be like. Blood's a lot thicker than water out there, you know… Families are everything.'

'Yes, but the two kids are, were, very westernised. They had mobile phones. They went to local schools. And Turkey isn't the same as the Middle East…'

He tailed off. It sounded feeble.

'You obviously liked him,' Mary said gently.

'Yes I did. He was a nice kid and he just had so much… potential.'

Mary studied Alan closely. When she spoke, her words were quiet but insistent.

'The thing is, Alan, how do you know he wasn't putting on an act? The fact is he was convicted of murder. Maybe he had indeed killed his sister and needed to dupe someone like you who'd be a credible character witness in court.'

It wasn't what Alan had expected. Mary, who had always seemed so kind, so tolerant, pushed on with her argument.

'Richard told me the newspaper reported that the killing happened in 2002. So how come nothing happened for nearly seven years? To me that suggests an organised cover-up.'

Alan took a deep breath. Mary was just reporting the facts, as she saw them. As her husband, the policeman, had relayed them to her. Don't shoot the messenger.

'You didn't meet him, Mary. He was an open and honest lad. I just don't believe he was capable of that level of deception.'

Mary smiled and shook her head.

'He was a teenage boy, Alan. Deception is as natural to them as breathing, believe me.'

'There's bunking off school and then there's murder, Mary. Hardly the same thing.'

'But if it was an honour killing then presumably he was acting on instructions from senior members of the family. It wouldn't have been entirely his own idea?'

She was trying to soften the blow. Alan was having none of it.

'The trouble is, I still don't understand the facts of the case. All I've seen is that cutting. That's why I've come to see Richard. For one thing, an honour killing suggests fanaticism. He didn't seem to care about religion at all. I don't think he even went to Mosque on Fridays.'

'OK, so what did motivate him?'

Despite his mounting frustration, Alan had to swallow back a smile. Is this what happened when you spent twenty five years married to a policeman? Did the lingo of the job become part of everyday conversation?

'He loved history, old things.'

Mary smiled at him sympathetically.

'So that's what it's all about? The student that got away?'

For a second, Alan was back in the finds store at Flax Hole, placing artefacts in a sequence, with Ali, bright-eyed and enthusiastic, standing beside him as Alan explained how every object did indeed tell a story.

Alan shook the image from his mind and refocused on Mary.

'It's not that simple. His granddad was a wealthy business man. Ali was expected to follow suit. I don't think he had a choice.'

'Go on.'

'Towards the end of the dig he passed his driving test. His grandfather, Mehmet, bought him an old white Marina van with "Ali's Delivery Service" painted on the back. And that was that.'

'So he never even had the option of going to university?'

'Family came first. I think they saw it as a useful new branch of their rapidly growing business network. I should have been more persuasive, supported him in exploring other options.'

Mary gently took Alan's hand in hers.

'This isn't your fault, Alan. Can't you remember when you were that age? I bet you changed every few weeks. I know I did. One minute I loved my parents, the next I thought my mother was a possessive old bitch who was trying to relive her frustrated life through me... If I hadn't been able to escape to university, make my own life... '

As she spoke he felt his resolve stiffening. It seemed like something beyond his control. But he still chose his words carefully.

'It's hardly the same thing.'

'Isn't it? An intelligent young man, forced into a menial job by his family. He's going to be angry, volatile...'

'It's all conjecture, Mary. You've got no proof.'

'No, personally I haven't. But have you? The boy was given a fair trial. The law's started its course. He's locked up and'll be in prison for years. Let it be.'

And at that, the front door opened noisily. DCI Lane was back home.

* * *

Lane sat down opposite him at the table. No handshake, no small talk, just that steady even gaze.

'So Mary showed you the pictures?'

'It's them.'

'No doubts?'

'None.'

'We enlarged the girl's picture from a family snap. Take a look.'

Lane unzipped a leather file case and produced a copy of the original. Alan looked at it closely. At first his eye was drawn by the smiling face of the pretty girl, but then he found he was looking at two of the men beside her: her brothers Abdul and Little Mehmet. He remembered Abdul: a stern, ever dominant presence. And their younger brother: still just a kid, but bright and lively.

'Yes, that's her. And the old man on her right's Mehmet, the grandfather. That's Ali, and her other brothers, Abdul and Little Mehmet.'

'Again, no doubts?'

'No, none.'

Alan, who was examining the picture closely, asked:

'And when was it taken?'

'According to the case notes it was found in the attic, with some other stuff of hers, when we searched the house. As you can see, this is a copy. The original one has the date "July 17th, 2001" pencilled on the back. Probably in her handwriting.'

Alan examined the picture closely. Forensically. It had been taken immediately outside Mehmet's café and everyone was wearing their best, but nobody dared compete in magnificence with old man Mehmet, whose huge buttonhole of scarlet carnations clashed confidently with the crumpled silk handkerchief in his breast pocket. Behind this group, and at a respectful distance, were the slightly out-of-focus shapes of other suited guests.

He looked up and found himself wondering what Lane must be thinking. It was obvious from his expression and body language that he'd hoped the pictures would prove Alan's quest a wild goose chase. No policeman wants to see the Force proved wrong. Then, and as if to confirm this, Lane opened the conversation with what sounded like a government health warning. His words seemed somehow rehearsed and unnatural.

'There's one other thing you should know. I'm sure you won't go talking about this to the world, but do keep everything to yourself at this stage.'

'Good heavens, I wasn't planning to say a word.'

Lane brushed this aside, and continued.

'At the time the Leicestershire force managed to keep Ali away from the press and TV cameras. It was felt at a very high level that to make him into a monster would whip up prejudice and do huge harm to community relations not just here in the city, but right across the country. And like everyone else in the force, we in the CID did our bit to calm things down. And we also knew that notoriety would make it much harder for a very young man ever to reform.'

There was a short pause. Alan knew this was important. Now was the time to make a positive response.

'Yes, I agree. It sounds like you did exactly the right thing, considering the circumstances.'

Lane visibly relaxed and continued, his voice now lighter, more natural.

'Despite our earlier disagreement you might like to know that I don't always agree with high level meddling, but in this instance I think the powers that be were probably right.'

Another pause.

'Yes, I agree. But what I don't yet understand is quite simple…'

Alan hesitated. This needed to be phrased with care. There was nothing to be gained, and everything to be lost, by opening up old wounds.

Lane couldn't conceal his impatience.

'Go on,'

'Well, how was he found out?'

'Oh, that's simple: he confessed. He didn't take much persuading, either and it was a full and frank confession, too.'

Alan wasn't expecting this. He looked again at the mugshot. Was that blank stare guilt, or fear?

He was too involved, too emotional. If this were a dig he should spend more time thinking about sequence and contexts, less with the diggers. He must step back.

'OK, confession aside, let's look at the facts. Can we confirm absolutely that the crime – if that's what it was – did actually take place when the dig was under way?'

'Of course we can't be absolutely certain, but it fits with what we know and with the convicted man's confession, which talked about an empty warehouse. As we understand it, that warehouse was only empty while your people were digging.'

'Yes,' Alan broke in, 'something to do with Health and Safety. They were worried about things falling on us.'

Alan watched as Lane stood up and collected a folder from a desk next to the television table. He opened it. He showed Alan a black-and-white photo of a flight of stairs in the shell of a building. Alan shivered. God, that place was so cold. He remembered ice on the ground floor.

'Yes,' Alan said, 'I remember those stairs. Bloody lethal they were. The banisters had been removed for scrap when we got there. The place had been gutted. Our clients couldn't tear down the outer shell, as it was early Victorian and in the Conservation Area, but they planned to rebuild the interior entirely, leaving just the outside brickwork. I only went in it once, to see if it would do as a site store for tools and things. But you couldn't have made it secure. So we brought in Portakabins, as usual.'

'Then as soon as you'd moved off site, work started again?'

'Exactly. But there's something that puzzles me,' Alan said. 'The fact is, that none of the people who had worked on the dig were ever interviewed by the police. None of us were asked to give evidence at the trial. I know it was seven years later, but that doesn't alter the fact that we weren't called.' He paused for a moment, searching for the right words.

'Dammit, Richard, we're trained observers. You know as well as I do, that working on a dig sharpens your powers of observation.'

Lane was now nodding, Alan hoped in agreement.

'I agree, it's odd that none of you were approached. But did any of you see anything? *Is* there any fresh evidence?'

It was time to appeal to Lane's pragmatic side. To their shared history.

'The fact is, Richard, that site might still retain forensic evidence of some sort. Don't forget I know every inch of that place. We have hugely detailed plans, photos and drawings. We could reconstruct almost anything. But I'll never know unless I'm given the chance to investigate. Meanwhile I'm slowly becoming convinced – I'm not certain yet – but I think it quite probable that a young man is about to serve a long sentence for something he might never have done. And that's wrong. Very wrong. I mean, did he even have a motive?'

Lane nodded, and then slowly, carefully, drew another sheet of paper out of the folder in front of him.

'The girl Sofia was seventeen at the time.' Lane gestured to the notes in front of him. 'Ali killed her because she had brought dishonour on their family by proposing to marry a Sikh. We owe Ali's conviction almost entirely to the efforts of Sofia's fiancé, a man called Indajit Singh.'

'That's interesting. Is there anything there about him?'

Lane referred back to the notes.

'No, not that I can see; but that doesn't matter, because I know Indajit quite well. He's now a successful lawyer at the Crown Court here.'

'Could you put me in touch with him?'

'I could do, but I'd rather not. He's in India for the first time in his life – finding his family, he told me. To be honest, I think he struggled for years to cope with his fiancée's death. The last thing he needs now is to be reminded of it.'

Alan had to concede: he did have a point. But he wouldn't be so easily fobbed off.

'So how did he do it?'

'Apparently, he knocked her unconscious and then…'

'Not Ali, Indajit. How did he build his case against Ali?'

Lane held Alan's gaze for a long time, and then looked back at his notes.

'For a start, I don't think his evidence alone fingered Ali. More like somebody in the Kabul family. It was Ali's confession that put him in the frame.'

'But how did he do it?'

'Well, he's a lawyer and a damn good one, too.' Lane paused, then continued.

'To be honest, I've no idea precisely *how* he assembled the evidence, but he did and it took him the best part of seven years. Slowly and meticulously he managed to construct a watertight case for her "honour" killing by a member of the Kabul family. Everyone suspected the grandfather, as it's usually the head of the family who feels any supposed "insult" most keenly.'

'Presumably his evidence was strong, was it?'

'Yes, good enough to show that a crime had almost certainly been committed.'

'So he could have gone to the press had you not co-operated?'

'That wouldn't have been Indajit's style. But we also knew we couldn't just let it rest as it was. We had to intervene. To investigate. So somebody leaked…'

'In the police?'

'I assume so. It's a politicians' trick we all use. Advance information, call it what you like. Anyhow, somebody had informally let the family know that we were planning to arrest the grandfather.'

'That sounds a bit ill-advised.'

'Yes, I thought so at the time. But the top brass believed it would put him under added pressure. I think the local Force reckoned an arrest wouldn't have helped their reputation for integrity.'

'Which was real?'

'Oh yes, the Kabuls were highly regarded, still are.'

'Despite Ali?'

'Almost because of him. He was a bad apple, but he's seen as doing the right, the honourable thing, by confessing.'

'Meanwhile you were still in Cambridgeshire?'

Lane nodded, still deep in thought.

'So that was it?'

Alan could see Lane's memory was working overtime. He paused briefly, then continued.

'The thing was, Alan, we didn't have very much concrete to go on. Indajit's case was very, very persuasive and I still believe that events have shown he was dead right, but at the time we lacked the hard evidence to convict any single individual. There was loads of suspicion, but that wasn't enough to get a conviction. Ali's confession was exactly what we needed. Who knows, maybe the top brass had been right? Pressure on the family *had* worked.'

Alan sat back, thinking this over for a few moments, then asked the final question, the one he had been avoiding ever since he read the newspaper article.

'Did you find Sofia's remains?'

'No. And believe me we left no stone unturned.'

'I suppose having no body made it very much harder to build up a convincing case?'

'Oh yes, before Ali's confession, the family claimed she'd been persuaded to return to Turkey. But searches there revealed nothing. The trouble is, large parts of rural Turkey are still remarkably remote and un-modernised. Quite unlike the cities – places like Ankara or Istanbul.'

'So she could still be there – out in the countryside?'

'Yes, just possibly. But it's most unlikely. We'd surely have heard something by now. And besides, eventually, Ali told us where the body was. Is.'

'Where?'

Alan winced at the eagerness in his voice. He'd overstepped the mark, and he knew it.

'Any confession is confidential. It would be deeply unprofessional of me to…'

Alan held up his hands in a gesture of surrender.

'I'm sorry, I get it. It was a bloody stupid question.'

41

Lane began to place the papers back in the folder. Case closed.

Alan should have accepted it, but something made him try one last attempt to get his opinion across.

'The thing is, Richard, I've just got this gut feeling.' He closed his eyes to avoid his friend's intense gaze. 'It's just that I *know* he didn't do it. He couldn't have.'

Alan fully expected Lane to dismiss this emotional outburst. But when he met Lane's gaze again, his expression was softer, sympathetic even.

'If it's any consolation, he showed great remorse – or at least that was what several family witnesses claimed.'

He paused, before continuing.

'They agreed that Ali had been completely devastated by what he'd done.'

'And did the court accept all that?'

'Yes, they did. He was given a life sentence, with a provision that he could not apply for parole for ten years. I won't say it's lenient, but it's not exactly a stiff sentence, either.'

'No,' Alan replied, 'certainly not for a self-confessed killer.'

But, he thought to himself, ten years off the life of an innocent young man, that's a different matter entirely.

Lane held out his hand. Alan shook it.

'Good to see you again, Alan. Let's not leave it so long next time.'

'No, absolutely not.'

As Alan reversed out of the driveway, Lane and Mary stood at the front door, waving him off. The loyal couple, protecting their family unit from any unwelcome intrusion. He could almost laugh at the irony. Almost, but not quite.

Five

Alan wasn't going to give up on Ali, or be so easily fobbed off by Lane, he was sure of that. But he wasn't going to make any rash decisions either. So he did what he always did when faced with a problem. He would let it settle, and in the meantime, he would throw himself into his work. Now that the gravel quarry dig was over, this consisted of his upcoming lecture at Peterborough Museum.

Over the years he'd done dozens of them. They were part of the job and were often written into his contract. Some clients didn't seek publicity; others did. Generally the better ones liked to tell the world how well they'd looked after the archaeology they had subsequently trashed with their housing estate, pipeline or gravel quarry. To Alan's surprise, he discovered he enjoyed public speaking and was actually rather good at it. People liked his intensity and enthusiasm, even though sometimes he could be very indiscreet about the politics of the project, its funding, or the lack of it.

He could see from the faces around him that this particular talk had gone down well. It had been about recent research into the prehistory of the Fens and it included some spectacular finds of Bronze and Iron Age dug-out boats that he had helped excavate from an old course of the River Nene. He knew those boats would be a big draw, and they were. The people in the audience were smiling, but several were also looking contemplative. These were the ones he'd really reached and he knew from experience it was best to leave them alone for a bit. They'd seek him out later, often with a difficult question. As the purpose of the evening was to raise money for future research into the Fens, Alan had decided to make the talk slightly more detailed and technical than usual. And it seemed to have paid off.

The museum had provided wine and canapés in an effort to prise even more money from the audience. Alan and some local volunteers were moving from one guest to another, with plates of nibbles and collecting tins.

Alan had just refilled his glass and was about to resume his round, when a large middle-aged man in a dark suit stuffed a tenner in his tin.

'Let me introduce myself,' the man said, grasping his hand in a huge grip, 'I'm Norman Grant. I believe we have a mutual friend – Richard Lane?'

'Really?'

Alan couldn't conceal his surprise. Lane had made it clear that, as far as he was concerned, the case was closed. So what was this? Was he keeping tabs on Alan?

Alan studied Norman Grant. He seemed relaxed, friendly – eager, even.

'Do you work with him?'

'In a manner of speaking. I'm the Governor of Blackfen Prison, for my sins.'

Alan felt a lurch in the pit of his stomach. For a second, Ali's mugshot flashed into his mind.

'And Richard sent you here?'

'Not in so many words: he just told me the talk was happening. But he also knows that I am quite the archaeology enthusiast, no small thanks to *The History Hunters*, you know.'

The History Hunters was a very popular programme on terrestrial television, now in its seventh series. It featured a team of archaeologists who were given a day to research a site and then just two days to dig it. The research team were mainly university academics and the digging team would feature local professionals, led by one of a small group of Site Directors, which included Alan. Alan had been with the programme since its second series, and was now becoming quite well-known. Very often his heart sank when a *Hunters* fan approached, but certainly not now.

He was pleased at one level, but at another he was more confused than ever. Had he got it wrong? Was Lane offering him a lifeline here, a way into the investigation, without implicating himself or his Force? Either way, it was too good an opportunity to miss. Alan thought fast.

'Did Richard tell you I was on the original dig at Blackfen?'

'Before the new buildings were constructed? No, he didn't.'

Grant looked genuinely delighted. Alan pressed on.

'We found some fascinating stuff. It was an incredibly rich site.'

'Yes, I saw the report. Did you know the governor's office at Blackfen is sited precisely where you found the big aisled barn?'

He was referring to the largest building of the Roman farm exposed by the dig.

'Really? How did you work that out?'

'From your published plans. It only took a few tapes and a good modern map.'

Alan was impressed. He was also delighted because he knew from past experience that he could manoeuvre any discussion of a dig in any direction he wanted it to go.

'Tell me, Mr Grant...'

'No, please, it's Norman.'

That was a good sign. Alan pressed on.

'Norman, how many people in the prison know that it was built on the site of a Roman settlement?'

'Not many. The ones that do are mostly locals. Officers, that sort of person. They saw the coverage in the local papers. But many of the professionals who come in from outside have no idea at all.'

'And the prisoners?'

'No. I'd be surprised if even one of our inmates knew about it. But why?'

Excellent, Alan thought, he has no idea what I'm driving at.

'A few years ago,' Alan went on, 'I was contacted by a group from Blackfen, calling itself The Lifers' Club.'

'Yes, of course I know all about them. They contact loads of people in the area, and someone like you would be high on their list. Sadly most never reply. I suppose they're scared. Or daunted.'

'Should they be?'

'No, not at all. In actual fact I've got a lot of time for them. They're a group that's organised by the long-term prisoners themselves. It was their idea. These days they work closely with the Prison Education Service. No, the Club's been a great success.'

Alan was genuinely surprised, his day was suddenly getting a lot better.

'Why's that?'

46

'Because their ideas come from members of the group. Everything else in prison tends to be imposed from outside, by people like me. The Lifers' Club gives them a sense of independence, which is vital for their long-term self-esteem.'

'I'm sure it is. Besides, no matter what they've done, they're still human beings, aren't they?'

'That's what we hope, yes.'

Grant stiffened slightly. Alan could have kicked himself. Hadn't he learnt by now, stay away from the politics. Stick to what you know.

Alan forced a smile and pressed on.

'I have to confess, I was one of the refusers. I said I was too busy. To be honest, I rather regret being such a coward.'

Grant leaned in towards him, smiling again now.

'So are you now suggesting that you'd like to take up that invitation?'

'Well, why not? I'd hate to be seen as scared or indifferent.'

'Well, we'd jump at the chance to have you, if you're still interested.'

Now Alan had to hold back his excitement. He adopted his best, calm, professional voice.

'What do you think would go down well?'

'Something very general, with lots of slides. Not too academic, you don't want to scare them off.'

No, thought Alan. That's the last thing I want to do.

'Fine. I've got a general talk ready prepared. And will I get to know the names of the men in my audience?'

As he asked it, Alan flinched. That wasn't very subtle. But Grant hadn't noticed.

'If by that you mean, "will I be safe?" I can assure you that everyone will be security-cleared – that's a matter of routine

– but we'd normally only provide a list of names if your commitment was to be longer-term. In that case, both you and I would want to know who was attending and, of course, why.'

Alan's brain was working overtime. He had to grasp this chance, there may not be another.

'It's just that I was thinking that a simple one-off talk would be rather a wasted opportunity.'

'In what way "wasted"?'

'Well, it would be a shame to go to all the effort of gaining their attention and then just walk away.'

He paused, choosing his words carefully. Play the concerned academic. Don't make it personal.

'But wouldn't it be much better if we could then take the ones who showed genuine interest and do something more lasting, more worthwhile for them? Like an A-level course?'

'Now why on earth would you want to do that?'

Alan winced. He'd been too keen, too quick. But then he looked up to see that Grant was smiling at him: it was a joke.

'Don't get me wrong. We'd be delighted, but it would be a huge commitment.'

'One which I would relish, I think. If these men genuinely want to learn, to improve themselves, then it's my duty…'

Grant cut in, much to Alan's relief.

'Richard did warn me that you were an idealist, Mr Cadbury.'

'I'm sure he did. And please, call me Alan.'

Grant was smiling broadly now, and shaking Alan's hand.

'That sounds absolutely wonderful. Thank you so much, Alan. I'll have a word with the Club convenor when I return. I'll also mention it to the Education Service. I can't thank you enough. Splendid. Yes, splendid.'

* * *

A few days later, in the first week of October, Alan received an official envelope marked HMP Blackfen, in which was a letter from The Lifers' Club. It gave an address in Luton where he could contact the Prison Education Service and discuss his ideas. He wrote a letter to The Lifers' Club by hand and then phoned the Education Service.

Setting up the A-level course was hard work. He had to provide an outline which had to conform closely with the Examining Board's specification for their archaeology syllabus. In addition, he also had to specify how much 'contact time' he would have with each student; thankfully, however, the Prison Education Service were able to negotiate a way around the fieldwork and site visit requirements. It was well into autumn by the time everyone agreed on the study programme, which was now scheduled to begin on January 7th, with a general talk about the archaeology of the Fens and why it's so special, so much richer than what you might find on the dryland, at sites like Flax Hole. Maybe, Alan hoped, that might catch Ali's interest. After the talk, and as a special concession, the Governor had agreed to hold a tea and coffee reception for everyone attending. That way they hoped they'd get a good initial audience and with luck Alan could persuade sufficient students to enrol for the full A-level course, which would start a month later.

He was tempted to call Lane, to thank him. But his instinct told him to let it be. Lane may have engineered the introduction, but that might have been simply to enable Alan to hear Grant's version of events, the Governor's inside opinion of Ali and thereby persuade Alan to give up the case for good. Whatever Lane's intention, Alan doubted that he would approve of the outcome of the meeting. He'd wait until he had something to take back to Lane. Something that would force him to reconsider his opinion of Ali. Though what that might be, Alan had absolutely no idea.

Alan was aware he was taking a huge risk. If Ali's experiences over the past two years had embittered or radicalised him, he would be unlikely to want to take up something as seemingly marginal as an A-level archaeology course. For all Alan knew, he might indeed have become a religious fundamentalist, sitting alone in solitary confinement, resentfully planning mayhem against the West. But whatever had happened over the past seven years, he still hoped he could somehow re-discover the same breezy, intelligent person he'd known at Flax Hole.

In fairness to himself, Alan had thought long and hard about the implications of the new course. If, for example, Ali didn't show up, but sufficient numbers of other students did, then he was lumbered with over a year of lectures and numerous personal supervisions. And he'd have to follow through. He'd have to deliver. You can't raise people's hopes and then just dash them, on what would seem like a whim. Alan didn't rate his conscience, but even he didn't feel he could drop everything, just because one key student hadn't shown up. No, it was going to be a personal gamble. A very big one.

Six

Alan's heart sank as he walked across the damp car park. The finished building with its massive, black-topped security wall was far more depressing than he'd imagined nearly twenty years ago, when he'd helped dig the Roman site beneath it. To his left he recognised one of their old spoil heaps, which had been tastefully landscaped into a gentle tree-clad bank to protect visitors' cars from the biting north-easterly winds of early January.

The Home Office had chosen Blackfen because it was deep in the Fens, and like Dartmoor, any escaping prisoner would have to find his way through a cruelly exposed landscape: no rocks or savage hounds, but deep, water-filled dykes. As he made his way towards the Visitors' Entrance, he could see groups of tired, blowsy women with children clinging to their sides and baby buggies everywhere. They must be the prisoners' wives, girlfriends and families, he thought, as he approached the double glass doors. It was hard not to feel sorry for them: there was no laughter behind their eyes, which flicked restlessly from one person to another, as if expecting an assault. Nearly every woman was smoking, but not in the relaxed way you see in the outside world; instead, the smoke was sucked down deep, with hollow cheeks and tense, anxious expressions, while bent, nicotine-stained, fingers gripped the filters, as if for dear life.

There was a small queue at the main doorway. He had been trying to fix in his mind precisely where their trenches had been twenty years ago, when a voice from behind two thicknesses of glass sharply demanded his name, and reason for his visit. He fumbled inside the battered knapsack that held his notes and produced the authorisation letter from the Education Service, which he passed through a hatch in the wall next to the window. He heard it fall, and the faint sound of another hatch opening inside. Less than a minute later, the door to his right opened and a uniformed prison officer, complete with a Hollywood-style bunch of keys dangling from a chain at his waist, stood there, reading his letter.

He motioned Alan to come inside. The door slammed behind him. They were now standing in a large, modern entrance hall. Architecturally it was very severe, but then this was a prison.

'If you follow me, Mr Cadbury, I'll take you there; but it's quite a long walk. Would you care to visit the toilet first?'

Alan pushed the Gents door open and found the usual array of cubicles, but no urinals. He was surprised to see a prison officer standing on duty, next to the hand basins. There were rows of individual cubicles along two walls. He chose the nearest one and when safely inside did what he came to do. At first he was too busy feeling the welcome sense of relief to notice that two cameras were looking down at him. The first was in the cubicle itself, and the second in the ceiling of the room outside, high above his head. From time to time his eye was caught by the higher one as it moved from one cubicle to another, but there was no regularity. It wasn't on auto, but was being moved remotely, by someone, somewhere else. He found himself wondering whether he was being ogled by a pervert in HMP Central Toilet Control, somewhere miles away. It had a strangely inhibiting effect on him. Made him feel dirty. So breaking the habit of a lifetime (his dad had once told him, when an old ewe pissed into his boots, that 'urine, lad is sterile'), he washed his hands vigorously.

He rejoined his escort officer in the Entrance Hall. He was smiling.

'Unnerving, aren't they?'

Alan was in no doubt what he was talking about.

'Yes,' he said, 'a little intrusive.' He was aware that sounded ludicrously stiff-upper-lippish, but he continued. 'Are they everywhere?'

'What?'

'The cameras?'

'Yes, sir. Everywhere.'

'Even in the officers' section, in your own part of the prison?'

'Especially there, sir. Imagine what would happen if there was a hostage situation. You'd want the authorities to know what was going on then, wouldn't you, sir?'

Alan was speechless. He was quite right, of course you would. But the human cost of such security boggled his mind. He simply couldn't imagine what it must be like to have no personal privacy. You couldn't so much as pick your nose, let alone eat the bogey.

Perhaps it was a hangover from his childhood, but he also hated formality; he detested dressing up in smart clothes and being on best behaviour. Even putting on the tie he was now wearing was an unwelcome imposition, and he knew he'd tear it off as soon as he was back in the car park. That's why he liked the digging life: it was informality taken to extremes. He couldn't imagine what it would be like living the Blackfen life, whether prisoner or screw.

By now they were walking down a series of brightly lit, dead straight corridors. Sometimes he caught glimpses of the outside. It was a strange, almost night-time, world of blinding sodium lights and no horizon – all views being cut short by the vast block-built wall that both symbolised and enforced their confinement. That wall was immense. As he walked, he briefly closed his eyes, yes, he thought, you could probably see Chatteris, or Tubney out there, across the huge open space that was once Eastrea Mere. They could perfectly well have built a sturdy electric fence; at least you could have seen through it. Only then did he realise that the wall was about more than security. It was retribution. Punishment. Confinement. He had only been there for a quarter of an hour, and was already resenting its presence. Being a true-born Fenman, Alan loved the horizon.

As they made their way along the corridors, his escort had to unlock and open a series of metal doors, seemingly put there at random. Presumably, Alan thought, it was something to do with security. He waited while yet another door was unlocked. But this time the officer also opened a second door, on the left. It gave into a fairly ordinary looking modern classroom, with screen, projector, a green blackboard and a long desk, complete with a box of chalks, at the front. Alan looked around him. The room was still empty, but when eventually they came in, the class would be sitting on six tiers of continuous benches and narrow tables. At a pinch, Alan rapidly estimated, the room could have held about seventy.

The officer pressed a bell by the door and glanced at his watch.

'They'll be here in a couple of minutes,' he said

Alan wondered who 'they' might be. He knew it was a patently stupid idea, but he couldn't get mad axe-men and baby-eaters out of his brain. His mind was starting to race. To calm his thoughts he looked around him. He started to unzip his laptop case to connect it to the projector, when the officer raised his hand, to stop him.

'I'd wait, if I were you sir, we may not be in here.' His eyes were raised to the ceiling as he received a message through his walkie-talkie's earpiece.

He was right. Another officer took them to a classroom further along the corridor. This one was slightly smaller. Alan again started to unpack. But before he had managed to retrieve anything, the second officer cut in

'Before you unpack, Sir, I'd like to give you a tour of the security arrangements. Normally speaking there will always be two officers with you, but if there were to be an emergency call-out, you would need to be aware of what you can do for yourself.'

There were plenty of panic buttons, and not just around the lecturer's end of the room. By now, four prison officers had assembled in the room. Alan rummaged inside his bag looking for his notes, and as he did so, one of the officers slipped out and they could hear the sound of doors in the corridor being locked and unlocked.

While they were waiting for the projector, two of the younger officers moved towards the back of the room, presumably Alan thought, to be in place for the arrival of the prisoners. That left an older man with him at the front desk. Alan liked the look of him. He wore his hair less brutally cropped and didn't seem quite as hard-nosed as some of the younger men. Alan approached him.

'It's strange, I've done loads of lectures and to all sorts of audiences, but I don't think I've ever felt as apprehensive as I do now.'

'Oh, don't worry, Mr Cadbury, you'll be fine. They're not monsters, you know, despite what the press might have you believe.'

'You're right, of course. I know that.' He paused, 'But I suppose it's the surroundings. They don't help, do they?'

'It's the same for the inmates. But you'd be surprised how quickly they get used to the place. One of them once told me it's like a bad smell: after a few minutes you cease to notice it. It never goes away, but you learn to live with it.'

Suddenly, Alan sensed an opportunity amongst the small talk. He leapt on it.

'Do you know any of the men yourself, personally?'

The older man smiled.

'I should hope I do, sir. I'm on the long-term prisoners' welfare council and being the senior officer on J Block.'

'J Block?'

'That's where we are, sir. It's where we accommodate the Lifers. We try to make it a little bit more relaxed than the rest of the prison.'

'But hardly free-and-easy.' Alan added.

'Quite, sir. But some of these men will never get out. Others could be here thirty years, or more. It's only human to try to make their lives easier.'

'Yes,' Alan replied, 'what's the point of a short, sharp shock if you're in for life? I can see that. So do you get much time alone with the men?'

'Yes, with those who want to talk. A few don't. They're the ones to watch…'

Time was passing. Alan pressed on, eager.

'I'm having trouble trying to fix my audience in my mind and I do want to pitch the talk right. Each group is different. You might think that Women's Institutes are the same…'

'Jam and Jerusalem?' the officer interrupted, grinning

'Quite. But they never are. Take the ones around Cambridge. They're mostly academics' wives and very knowledgeable about certain things. Out here in the Fens they're different, but many are farmers' wives, so you can often learn a good deal of useful stuff about life in remote places. Lecturing, especially the questions afterwards, can be a two-way process.'

The officer thought for a moment before replying.

'These chaps have plenty of time to read. And many of them do. And of course now there's the internet.'

'J Block's on the web?' Alan was surprised.

'Yes, the whole prison is, but it's strictly supervised by Security and the Education Service.'

'As you might know,' Alan continued, 'I want this introductory talk to lead to an A-level course.'

'Yes, I did know that. If I were a bit younger I might have enrolled myself. It's on posters all around the jail. You wouldn't have seen them. The Lifers did them themselves.'

'Tell me frankly, do you think I've got any chance of getting an A-level group together, or will it flop?'

'Oh no, I'm sure it won't flop. There's quite a lot of interest here. *History Hunters* is very popular on Sunday evenings. We've DVDs and tapes of them in the Lifers' library and your programmes have been borrowed a lot in the past week. I can tell you, we're expecting a big turn-out.'

'Do you know any men who seem particularly interested?' Alan asked.

He held his breath while the officer thought. Alan could see he was mentally counting them.

'I reckon there are at least a dozen, that I can think of, offhand. Maybe more, as I don't know every man personally.'

'In the outside world most archaeological audiences tend to be a bit elderly and we're always trying to attract youngster people to join us. Will that be the same here, d'you think?'

Again the officer paused.

'You're right.'

Alan's heart sank at these words

'Most of them are a bit older, generally in their fifties and sixties.'

His words were cut short by the officer who had gone for the projector. He was now brandishing it triumphantly.

'Bloody hell,' he said to the man standing by Alan, 'had to go all the way to Room 6 to find this. I don't know what happens to these things. It's as if someone was nicking them.'

'What, in a jail? You must be joking?'

'Piss off, Fred,' he laughed at the other officer, 'but I'm sure there were half a dozen back in May. Now we're down to just two. Bloody ridiculous.'

They reeled out an extension cable and set up the projector. Alan attached his laptop and was about to boot the system, when one of the officers stopped him.

'Best go to the front,' he advised in a confidential tone, 'they'll be here any moment now.'

* * *

A red light started flashing over one of the three doors at the back. Two officers went across and stood either side of it, facing into the room. Meanwhile Alan had instinctively moved behind the desk, where he stood at the centre, with an officer at each end. He felt a distinct sense of trepidation, verging on outright fear.

As he stood waiting he could imagine what the scene would look like from a distance. He could see himself standing alone, with his left hand moving almost imperceptibly towards one of the panic buttons. But he knew he mustn't touch it. That would screw up all his plans. Then the double doors below the red light opened and the light went out.

Most of the prisoners would not have been out of place catching the early morning train to Waterloo, from somewhere in suburban Surrey. They wore their own clothes and were chatting in a relaxed fashion. A couple waved to Alan (he assumed they were the organisers of the Club) and they then distributed themselves across the benches, like any other group of mature students. After he had been introduced to the class by an education officer, Alan was about to begin, when the red light flashed again and another prisoner entered the room, accompanied by two officers. He sat in a reserved seat by the door. Unlike the rest of the prisoners, he was wearing handcuffs. Alan realised with more than a slight chill who he was.

It must have been thirty years ago, Alan struggled to recall the precise date, when this man had carried out a series of grisly murders, and had disposed of the mutilated bodies in an orchard behind his suburban house. The subsequent hunt for bodies was a scene of disorganised chaos and the public outcry that followed was a major factor behind the growth of the new science of Forensic Archaeology.

This last man sat down in his reserved seat, with an officer beside him. He stared at Alan with an unflinching, blank, emotionless gaze. Alan realised at once he was a psychopath – it was only too obvious. And he wondered why on earth he was here in a civil prison. Surely, he thought, he ought to be in Broadmoor, or a secure hospital somewhere? This man had taken the lives of innocent people, for his own satisfaction and pleasure. This is what a real murderer looked like. Nothing like the vulnerable young man in Lane's mugshot.

Alan shifted his gaze from the psychopath and started methodically scanning the rows, trying to spot Ali. On his right he could see the Governor's large form rise to its feet and start walking towards the front desk. Alan instinctively moved slowly towards the right, so that he could return to the centre when introduced. But his eyes continued to scan the rows, even as he stepped to the side. He knew he had to be disciplined about this. He was well aware there were too many people out there for him just to stare and hope one particular face would jump out at him.

Alan was shocked at how many black and Asian faces stared back at him from the assembled audience. His academic brain told him that, statistically, the percentage of non-white inmates did not match the percentage balance of the general population. So, what was this? Some right-wing papers might claim that ethnic minorities were violent for social or cultural reasons. Alan was more inclined to believe in a deep-rooted, prejudice within the police and judicial system. Not a deliberate or vocal prejudice, but a pattern of thought that was so deeply engrained in the subconscious of white Western society that neither judge nor jury would be aware of it. Yet another factor that would surely have affected the outcome of Ali's trial.

He could hear the Governor start his introduction:

'It gives me the greatest pleasure to introduce Mr Alan Cadbury, this evening's speaker. Mr Cadbury studied at the Department of Archaeology at Leicester University, and was instrumental in the excavations prior to the construction of Blackfen Prison, a site which I have done my own extensive research on, as a result of Mr Cadbury's initial findings…'

The old boy was now talking about himself to a large audience. With any luck, Alan thought, he should hold forth for a good five minutes. Maybe just time enough to check out everyone in the audience.

Row two.

Row three.

Row four. Who's that? Look up damn you. No, not him. Too thickset and squinting.

Row five. Yes. No. Too tall. Nose the wrong shape.

Alan felt the blood rush to his face as he realised that he, as much as anyone else, had a depressingly blinkered point of view. He had no problem distinguishing between the faces of the identikit white, shaven-headed muscle-bound prisoners. But the Asian men, at first glance, looked all the same to him. He forced himself to breathe. Slow down. Start again.

Row one…

Then slowly he became aware that everyone was suddenly clapping. Bloody hell, it was time to start. He walked to the centre of the desk and turned to the departing Governor.

'Thank you so much for that splendid introduction, Mr Grant,' Alan heard himself saying in what he hoped were ingratiating tones. 'I'll try to live up to your kind words.'

To his relief nobody seemed to have noticed he'd been miles away.

'Very well, gentlemen we've a small matter of twenty thousand years to get through…'

He had barely begun when some joker shouted out.

'Bloody hell Simpson, that's longer than you got!'

This took Alan completely off guard and he laughed as loud as anyone else in the room.

'Right,' he continued, 'I can see I'm going to have to watch what I say. A pity, that.' He paused. 'Now, the Governor told me to be sure to discuss the prehistory of oats and most particularly that of porridge.'

A bit heavy-handed, but it got a good laugh and with a throw-away query whether people at the back 'in the cheaper seats' could hear him clearly, Alan's talk had got off to a good start. But throughout, the psychopath's face remained immobile.

The atmosphere needed to be relaxed, if Alan's hectic overview of archaeology from the Ice Age to the twentieth century was to go down well. He knew that Ali had been fascinated by the processes of change he witnessed at Flax Hole. He was intrigued by how pits filled-in and how soils grew to cover old surfaces. So Alan discussed glaciers and how they had carved out the landscape of eastern England; how rivers and peats had formed the fens and how medieval farmers had left their telltale fields of ridge-and-furrow. And he linked all these to the ordinary things of daily life left behind by prehistoric communities, just as he had done that afternoon in the site hut in Leicester.

Anyhow, it seemed to have gone down well. Very well. As he showed the final slide of a Cold War microwave relay tower out in the open fen a few miles north of the prison, he glanced up at the clock. Damn, he thought, I've overrun. The Governor's introduction had dragged on for ever. There would be limited time for questions. And he needed time.

As the applause continued and the lights came up, the Governor approached the front desk. He nodded to one of the officers, who opened the double door to the left of the screen. A murmur ran round the room. All eyes were on the tea and coffee urns, plates of biscuits. The Governor raised a hand.

'That was an excellent talk – and I even learned quite a lot myself.' Polite laughter. 'But seriously, I think we've had a splendid session and Mr Cadbury deserves a warm round of applause.'

And he got one, plus stamping and piercing whistles. Again the Governor raised a hand.

'Now as you may know, Mr Cadbury has given this lecture as a sort of shop window to display the delights of archaeology. So I'm very keen that as many of you as possible enrol for his A-level course. And that's why we've organised a small tea and coffee reception.'

'What no porridge?'

It was the same joker. This time the laugh wasn't quite as big. The Governor smiled indulgently.

'As I was saying, please use the next half hour to ask Mr Cadbury questions, but as our time is limited, I must ask you all to be brief. Remember, if you come on the course, there'll be plenty more time to talk with him at greater length.'

He turned to the two officers standing in the open doorway, who moved to the side. The audience rose and headed into the reception area next door. Alan reckoned there were around eighty men there – seventy-nine now. The psychopath sitting on the back row had been taken away.

* * *

Alan and the Governor walked through to the reception and were met by a small queue of men standing to one side of table where the drinks and biscuits were being served. The Governor nodded to a member of the catering staff who poured them both mugs of coffee. Meanwhile Alan had been ambushed by a group of men, who seemed more interested in Craig Larsson, the charismatic presenter of *History Hunters*, than archaeology at A-level. And there was no sign of Ali.

Five minutes to go, and Alan was beginning to feel very depressed. The prospect of teaching an A-level course, without any interaction with Ali, was grim. And whilst the Lifers seemed, on the surface, polite and enthusiastic, he could tell they were on their best behaviour. There was an undercurrent of tension in the room, like a low-level hum of electricity, a sense of latent violence. Was he really cut out for this? Or was Lane right, was he just an academic idealist – good with rocks and dead things, but totally naïve when it came to the real world.

Alan's reverie was broken by a light tap on his shoulder. He looked round and there Ali was standing behind him, now fully six inches taller. The skinny youth had been replaced by a well-built young man. More than well-built, Alan reckoned he'd been at the gym. He looked athletic, with a short beard and closely shaven hair. A Number One haircut. But the eyes, that intense, intelligent gaze. That was still exactly the same.

'Remember me?' Ali asked quietly.

'Of course I do,' Alan replied. 'Ali Kabul. Best digger at Flax Hole.'

Alan saw a shadow pass across Ali's face, and then it was gone.

'Different life,' Ali shrugged.

Even though the room was full of men, all chattering away, Alan felt the silence stretch between them. And then, as if he was taking pity on Alan, who seemed to have suddenly lost all ability to make normal conversation, Ali continued:

'You still living out that way?'

'No. Haven't for a long time. Seven years ago I landed a big site near Peterborough and moved back to the Fens.'

'Moved back? So you come from around here?'

'Yes, I was brought up on a small farm near Crowland.'

'Good to be back home?'

'My brother has the farm now. I'm at Tubney.'

Ali was clearly none the wiser.

'It's a little village about ten miles away. Near Chatteris. I'm in a grim bungalow. Everything stinks of diesel. The place used to be owned by scrappies.'

Ali smiled ruefully.

'Sounds like you'd be better off in here.'

'Except that the Hat and Feathers is next door.'

'The what?'

'The village pub. They do excellent local ale. I drink there most nights.'

Ali's smile was neither hostile nor friendly.

Somewhere outside a loud bell sounded and men started to leave through a door on the other side of the room. Alan could have kicked himself. This might have been his only chance to talk to Ali. And what had he done? Just wittered on about diesel and his local boozer.

Ali glanced up at the clock on the wall, then said with some disdain,

'I'd better be off. Feeding time at the zoo.'

He turned to go.

Alan put a hand on his shoulder.

Ali spun round, immediately tensed. The instinctive reaction of a caged animal, or a man used to being challenged.

Alan released his grip, and looked directly into Ali's eyes as he spoke.

'Will you be coming, Ali? It would mean a lot to me and I think you'd enjoy it.'

He'd expected Ali to be pleased – or to have shown at least a positive reaction. But no, his expression gave nothing away. Alan felt chilled.

'What, like old times?' Ali replied, not breaking Alan's gaze.

'As near as I can manage. Without the mud and the trenchwork, obviously.'

Alan was talking too fast. His voice was shaking. If Ali noticed, he didn't show it.

'I dunno, I mean, all that digging around in the past. Hard to see the point of it now.'

Before Alan could reply, an officer appeared and took Ali by the arm, gently but firmly leading him away. Ali kept his head held high, his back straight as he was ushered out of the door. Alan stood stranded in the centre of the empty classroom. Echoing down the corridor, he could hear the sound of those metal doors slamming shut, one after the other.

Seven

The next day, Friday, got off to a bad start. Alan had a thick head – beer at the Feathers and whisky at home. Then he slept fitfully. He had dreamt he was back at Flax Hole. Fractured images came back to him as he lay in bed. Sofia was there. A man – he didn't see his face – was dragging her by the arm, throwing her into a trench, forcing her face down into the wet spoil heap and holding her there. Alan had been running through the mud, trying to reach her, but each step he took his boots were held tighter and tighter by the sticky wet clay, which sucked him down. And down. He was drawn further and further into the cloying earth.

He turned on his mobile and looked at the time: 08.06. Through the torn curtains he could see it was light, but gloomy outside. He didn't feel rested, but he knew he was awake and had things to do. Like finding work. He drank a lot of water and ran a bath. He lay in the warm water, and scrubbed himself clean, but that waking nightmare remained in the back of his mind. Then he lay back; tried to wallow. He wanted to, he had to think. That panicky dream meant something, he was sure of it. Of course she couldn't be buried at Flax Hole, that was ridiculous. But there was another memory, maybe a clue, bubbling to the surface of his subconscious, but still just out of reach. Then his phone rang. It was the Wake Up alarm: 08.15. He turned on the radio: news of a cyclone somewhere in the Pacific. He tried to regain his thoughts, while a voice said exciting things about tennis.

Then suddenly it came to him. The next step was so bloody obvious. Why didn't he think of it before? He jumped out of the tepid water, towelled himself a bit dry and hurried into the hallway.

He picked up an old notebook by the phone and dialled a number. It rang once, then a synthesised transatlantic voice offered him three options: press one for *The Museum Shop*; press two for *Reference Collections*; or press three for *PF Consulting*. He pressed three and a human being answered.

'Can I speak to Paul Flynn, please?'

'Who can I say is calling?'

'Alan Cadbury.'

A Chopin Nocturne cut in, played on what sounded like an amplified lute. Alan waited, almost holding his breath.

Flax Hole had been the first step on Dr Paul Flynn's fast track to fortune and notoriety. Paul's busy schedule meant that they had lost touch over the years, and they moved in very different circles now. Paul the businessman, always securing contracts with the big players of industrial development. Alan, the digger, hands-on in the trenches. Sure, Alan had thought him a pompous prick at times, but that was just Paul's social manner. He liked to be seen to be in charge and at the top of the pile. But Paul was also a perfectionist. He cared deeply about his research and the integrity of his work. That was something he and Alan had in common. It might just be enough.

Suddenly the music cut out.

It was Paul's voice.

'Alan, how very good to hear from you.'

He sounded genuinely pleased.

'I'm sorry, Paul, I've been shamefully out of touch, but I didn't want to interrupt your meteoric rise to pre-eminence.'

'Oh, for heaven's sake…' he said modestly.

But Alan could tell he was lapping it up. He always was a sucker for flattery. Time for some more.

'No, but seriously. I think it's time that archaeologists made more of an impression out there in the big wide world, and your enterprises have certainly done that.'

'Well, we've tried to offer value and *integrity*. That's the key.'

'Well, it's certainly worked. And nobody could possibly say you'd sold out to commercial interests, because you haven't. And look at all the employment you're offering to archaeological graduates.'

To Alan's surprise Paul was chuckling down the phone. He had a reputation for many distinctive qualities, but a sense of humour wasn't one of them.

'If I didn't know you better, Alan, I would think you were trying to butter me up.'

'I suppose I am. It's all a bit embarrassing really…'

'You need a job?'

To Alan's surprise, there was no underlying smugness in Paul's tone. In fact, if anything, he sounded sympathetic.

'Got it in one.'

'How about the first of February? With a recce sometime next week?'

Alan tried not to sound like he was biting Paul's hand off. Traces of cool must be retained in such moments.

'Yes, I can do that… I think…'

He paused and noisily turned a few pages of his address book. 'Yes… I can do that … yes, for sure. Where is it?'

'St Guthlic's Church at Scoby. The Parish Council want to install toilets. It's just outside…'

Alan broke in.

'Boston. Yes, I know it. A good early name and a good early church. But they can't possibly be on the mains drains out there, so presumably there'll have to be a cesspit too?'

'You're right. We've already done geophys along the pipe's length and it looks like you'll be dealing with around twenty stiffs.'

And some of them, Alan thought, are bound to be Saxon, because Guthlic was a local Saxon saint who'd lost an ear fighting off Viking raiders. In the Middle Ages that ear was permanently displayed at Crowland, Thorney and Lincoln, simultaneously. Alan loved the Dark Ages. The fifth to seventh centuries AD were a time when south and east England almost returned to prehistory, after the short Roman interlude. This was also when England re-invented itself and established its modern identity. One day he wanted to write a book about it, and a dig at St Guthlic's would give him superb material. He didn't find it hard to be enthusiastic.

'Paul, that sounds absolutely fantastic! Count me in. When should I come over?'

'I'm free on Friday morning. Say ten-ish. You could meet Harriet…'

'Do you mean Harriet Webb? As in, the brain with the bones?'

Alan knew her by reputation. Everyone did, but she was also notoriously unforgiving. She didn't suffer fools gladly.

'That's right, you'll be co-directing with her.'

And with that he rang off.

Alan leant back against the wall. He almost felt out of breath. It had all happened so fast. And so easily. He had a job working with one of the most highly-regarded bones specialists in the UK. And he would be focusing on a period of history he was passionate about. Alan was confident of his own credibility and he suspected that Webb's detractors were the sort of folk who resented high achievers. And she was certainly one of them, with a string of substantial papers to her name – many in prestigious national journals. In her case, the term 'up and coming' was spot on. Yet why did she choose to work for a consultancy hidden away in the depths of the Fens, when she could have walked into any of the best universities in the land? Money, Alan supposed. Paul certainly had a lot of it at his disposal – and that seemed to be the biggest motivator for most people, in the end.

He knew he'd have to tread carefully with Paul. They weren't co-directors anymore, and Paul would expect to be treated with all the respect that the head of a consultancy company required. He'd also have to find the right time to talk to him about Ali. Paul wouldn't be at all enthusiastic to know that a convicted murderer – however wrongfully accused he might be – was associated with one of his previous sites. It might reflect badly on the PFC 'brand'. But if Alan played it right, after a few nights down the pub with Paul, reminiscing about the good old days, who knows? The fact was, they'd worked split shifts at Flax Hole, Paul had suggested it halfway through the dig. So, Paul was essential to the investigation. He might just hold the missing piece of the puzzle. But he didn't know it.

* * *

Alan had spent every spare minute of the second and third weeks of January preparing material for his Blackfen A-level course. He knew the Guthlic's dig wouldn't allow him much time for anything else towards the end of the month, or in February, and he couldn't afford to have things go wrong. He had also become aware that, despite the Governor's personal support, some of the professional teachers in the Education Service resented an outsider breaking into their world and were keen to see him mess everything up. Then he'd be out like a shot. Despite his ulterior motive, Alan cared about his work. Now that he'd committed to teaching the course it mattered to him that he got it right. That the men who had signed up actually learnt something worthwhile.

And as far as the ulterior motive went... Alan tried not to read too much into Ali's parting words '*All that digging around in the past. Hard to see the point of it now.*' It could have been Ali's way of taking control of the situation. It could even have been a joke. One thing Alan was sure of, he wasn't going to give up on Ali. He'd drag him out of his cell and frogmarch him into the classroom himself, if he had to.

While he'd worked on his course notes at home in Tubney, he had time to reflect. Outside the winter was running its usual post-Christmas course. The cold, foggy windless 'dog days' that so often followed Christmas had given way to more active Atlantic weather, with strong winds, rain and increasingly snow, which blew off the huge open fields and accumulated in the roadside dykes.

Every morning local farmers towed cars out of the now hidden dykes, driven there by young lads from Peterborough, Spalding and Boston, more used to pavements and street lights than bleak open country. The going rate for removal of a boy racer's car from a dyke was £150 – and nothing said to the local Law. Most were happy to pay. Earlier that morning he'd taken the Land Rover to the village shop to buy milk and on his way back had come across two of the Campling boys and their 200-horsepower John Deere tractor. They were struggling to fix chains to a low-slung VW Golf, with drug dealer style darkened windows, which had been driven into the Old Fendyke Drain some time the night before. Alan stopped and gave them a hand. Once attached, the tractor's huge engine barely revved above tick-over, as it pulled the car back onto the road. As it came out, Alan chatted to its anxious owner, who was standing by, shivering in the north-easterly wind. He was pathetically grateful. He looked about thirteen. Alan wanted to put an arm around his shoulder: he was the typical posey 'young yob': 'all mouth and trousers', as his mother would have said. It was so easy to jump to judgement. Yet this crumpled youngster, far from his friends and starting to feel the chill winds of winter, was showing himself human. Funny, Alan thought, as he passed him an old wax jacket, you look like a dickhead, but you're not so bad. It was so easy to judge by appearances, but the truth always took time and effort to reveal. And you always knew it when you'd found it.

Back home Alan sat down in his one comfy chair. To hell with the computer. He'd worked too late the night before and was fed up with the bloody screen. He sipped his tea and leant back, looking up at the ceiling. Even the indoor spiders seemed to have gone to ground. Outside it was absolutely silent. Snow was starting to fall and the wind had dropped. Again, his thoughts returned to Flax Hole.

Slowly the realisation was dawning on him that he was involved with more than a mere puzzle. It was beyond that:

something to do with so-called basic values, Right and Wrong. Long ago Alan had abandoned faith, just as his father had done in the 1960s, when he too was a younger man. Alan was profoundly suspicious of people who proclaimed Morality. He was a secularist and he didn't support ideas like Good and Evil. They were too simple. Real life was far more complex. Although it had recently become unfashionable to be a relativist, he fervently believed that absolute good and absolute evil didn't exist; instead there were shades of good, of evil, of right and of wrong. And some instinct told him that the wrong, that the evil in this case was far darker and more absolute, than anything he had yet experienced in his own life.

He recognised too that the case would take a long time to sort out. He was aware he was an impatient man, and he'd have to be very disciplined with himself, if he were ever to get to the bottom of it all. He also had to acknowledge that he too had feelings of guilt. Partly about not supporting Ali and encouraging him to take a different path than the one that his family had dictated to him. But also, as his nightmare demonstrated, he also had a deep sense of responsibility for whatever had happened to Sofia. There were aspects of this case that worried him profoundly: they had to do with some fundamental attitudes to people from other cultures. He'd studied anthropology and he knew it wasn't a matter of simple racism; it was far more subtle and pervasive than that. And it also ran very deep. In fact he wasn't certain whether he was entirely unaffected himself. And that made it even more troubling.

The persistent ringing of the phone intruded into his thoughts. Alan pushed himself out of his chair and stumbled back into the hallway.

'Alan?'

It was the unmistakable brisk voice of Richard Lane.

'Richard, I meant to call...'

'I've just been speaking to Norman Grant. He told me about your visit to Blackfen. I don't know what you're hoping to achieve.'

'Well, a bit of academic stimulus never hurt anyone.'

'Please, Alan, don't insult my intelligence.'

There was a tense silence. Alan forced himself to break it.

'If I can talk to Ali, gain his trust over a period of time...'

'Then you think he'll retract his statement?'

Lane was not a man prone to sarcasm. Alan could hear an undercurrent of tiredness, world-weariness, in his voice.

'Richard, I'm not trying to undermine you or your colleagues. But I need to know the truth. You can understand that, can't you?'

Alan detected a long sigh down the phone.

'I accept that there's a possibility – a slim one – that Ali Kabul is innocent. However, to attempt to extract the truth from a convicted felon who has already made a full confession strikes me as astoundingly naïve.'

'It probably is. But I have to try.'

Another pause. Alan knew Lane would be weighing up the pros and cons. The risk and reward.

'Are you going to tell Grant?' Alan asked cautiously.

'No. At least, not yet.'

Alan breathed a huge sigh of relief.

'On one condition. Anything that Ali says, anything at all that's remotely suspicious, you report back directly to me.'

'Fine. Whatever you say.'

'I mean it, Alan. If I find out that you're withholding even the smallest detail I won't hesitate to blow the whistle.'

'I understand. Thanks, Richard. I do appreciate it.'

Then Alan realised he was talking into static noise. Richard Lane had hung up on him. Again.

Eight

It was Friday morning, an hour before dawn, and the Fens were at their most forbidding. Earlier in the night there had been a sharp frost, but sometime in the small hours a sea mist had rolled in from off the Wash and every twig, leaf and blade of grass was now covered in thick grey hoar frost. Alan was scraping it off the Land Rover's windscreen. The previous evening he had lifted the battery indoors and put it on trickle charge overnight, to make sure there were no starter problems now. To his relief, it fired first time. He listened to the engine running smoothly. Good old Brutus, he thought. He never lets me down when I need him.

Alan was steering Brutus rather gingerly across the frozen Fens in the area known as South Holland. He could feel through the wheel that his knobbly tyres, while providing excellent traction in snow and on wet grass, were almost useless on black ice. He was now driving through huge, flat, treeless fields which were as remote as any in Fenland. From fourteen or fifteen miles away he could just see the soaring tower of St Botolph's Church in Boston, known far and wide as the Stump. It had always amazed him that the tallest parish church tower in England had actually been built when the Black Death was laying waste the town's population. Religious people still regard it as a symbol of man's determination to conquer mortality. To Alan it was a Fenman's finger: a defiant, symbolic gesture to the Almighty for inflicting such a loathsome scourge on humanity.

The Stump was clearly visible to the south-east, when Alan turned off the single track road into the short drive leading up to Paul Flynn's base at Priory Farm. Like many older Fen farms, the house and outlying sheds and barns were surrounded by trees, partly to shield them from the bitter north-easterly winds, but also to give the family a little privacy. Then in 1942, when Lincolnshire – 'Bomber County' – became in effect a vast aircraft carrier for thousands of US and RAF heavy bombers, they'd built an airfield on the edge of the farm. One huge black hangar still survived, standing behind its concrete apron. As it did during the war, it dominated Priory Farm, but silently now, a dark and slightly sinister presence.

It had been a cold winter, but nothing could stop the aconites and snowdrops starting to poke through the thin grass around the tree trunks. In a couple of weeks' time, Alan thought as he coaxed Brutus over the frozen surface, this will be a superb display. Paul Flynn's farmhouse stood there in solitary splendour, defying the cold, unlit and alone. The upstairs curtains were still drawn close.

Alan knew that Paul had the reputation of a loner, a bit of an oddball. Alan had some sympathy for him and, even in the Flax Hole days, never joined in the gossip about Paul's lack of girlfriends – boyfriends even – and no discernible social life. Alan also enjoyed his own company. It didn't make him a freak.

Priory Farm made an ideal base for an archaeological business. Its remoteness gave security. The name was good too – and well merited, as the farm had been built close by the site of a long-abandoned medieval monastery, many of whose standing buildings had been bulldozed, when RAF engineers built the airfield's perimeter runway. There were other practical advantages to the place. Council Tax was very low; there were no parking problems and there was also plenty of space, where some of the dirtier jobs, such as processing bulk soil samples, could be done without blocking the drains. The old farm buildings, too, were sturdy. They'd been built in the 1860s, when farming was very prosperous. They had a cosy feel about them, a permanence that was so lacking in their modern steel-and-concrete equivalents. In the pre-dawn gloom, Alan could just about make out their shape, emerging from the darkness. They felt huge and strangely menacing.

He pulled over. He didn't want to start this new and crucially important phase of the project without thinking things through. It hadn't occurred to him that maybe Paul's friendliness had all been a front: that maybe he *wanted* Alan to work at Priory Farm – where he could keep him under observation. Or was that being paranoid? Why on earth should Paul be suspicious of him? After all they knew each other from years ago. But then… Paul had changed: he was far more controlling than at Flax Hole. He was also more corporate and Alan could see that PFC was now the centre of his life. He would never allow anything, or anyone, to threaten it. And the much-vaunted Harriet: what about her? Was she on Paul's side too? He turned the noisy engine off and leaned as far back in the stiff bench seat as he could. He shut his eyes and drank in the faint sounds of dawn: a wren's warning cluck, a rabbit somewhere in the leaf litter. Slowly his feelings of paranoia began to ebb away, but not completely: he had heeded their warnings. I will have to watch my step – and my back – he thought, as he restarted the engine.

* * *

Slowly Brutus came to a halt in the PFC car park, which held just one car. Alan parked next to it. He glanced down at his phone: it was seven thirty. He got out, slammed and locked the two front doors and tied the rear canvas flap down securely. It had worked loose somewhere out in Holland Fen.

The Archaeology Centre at Priory Farm had once been the feed store of the Victorian farm, and had been converted to offices, in 2003. Unlike any of the others, this office boasted a large bow window, which looked across to the few ruined walls of the Priory that had escaped the wartime bulldozers. Beyond the stumps of the medieval walls was a large concrete apron, where Lancaster bombers had once assembled before setting out for Germany. And out there, behind the apron, the massive black hangar was just starting to emerge from the night.

Alan walked across the apron to an old wartime single-storey building that had been converted into a canteen for staff working in the hangar. These days, the hangar was the home of Paul Flynn's two successful commercial enterprises, *Reference Collections Ltd*, and *The Museum Shop*. Both operations often had to work around the clock, especially if there were large orders to complete, and Alan knew there was always a good chance of a coffee in the canteen.

And he was right. On the far side of the room were two young Asian men reading copies of the *Sun*. He assumed it was their white van that was parked by the main hangar entrance, being loaded-up. He muttered 'Morning' to the men who stood up, ready to take their empty mugs back to the counter.

'No need to stand, when I enter,' he couldn't help saying.

'That's alright, Your Reverence,' the older man quipped back, without even a hint of an accent.

Alan took his mug across to a table by a window where he could keep an eye on the Archaeology Centre. As soon as anyone arrived, he'd head over there.

He had just sat down and was looking through his rucksack for the book about St Guthlic, when a quiet female voice behind him spoke.

'Do forgive me, but are you Alan Cadbury?'

Alan looked up.

'Yes, I am.'

'I spotted your Land Rover. Don't they call it Tacitus, or…?'

'It's Brutus, actually.' He paused. Somehow that name now sounded a bit childish.

She smiled broadly.

'And I'm Harriet. Harriet Webb.'

They shook hands.

'Paul tells me we're going to be working together.'

Alan got up to get her a cup of tea. As he waited while the machine spluttered and gurgled, he looked back at his visitor who was now busy with an iPad. He was surprised she could get a signal out here. His phone was only working intermittently.

Alan liked to look at people from behind. When you were face-to-face, eyes – yours and theirs – dominated everything. From the side, or from behind, you had time to observe body language, which could be just as, or no more, informative. Even when she was sitting down Alan could see she held herself very erect. Her posture was superb: shoulders back and relaxed, head held high, even when she was looking at her blessed iPad. She was much taller than average, slim and very elegant.

Most of Alan's archaeological friends had been brought up within the commercial sector. Like him, they had managed to get a university degree or diploma, but had then devoted their lives to digging; to travelling around following the work. But Harriet wasn't like any of these 'circuit' diggers. She'd never worked on the circuit, but had done very well at university. She knew what she was doing, and where she was heading. And she didn't even dress like a circuit digger. Unlike most of his female colleagues, she preferred a skirt to jeans, but even though she had excellent legs – and they were showing to particular advantage from where he was standing – she chose to wear her skirt just below the knees. Her heels were raised, rather than high.

He hadn't had much time to look at her when she arrived, but her face had struck him as attractive, if not actually beautiful. She had high cheek bones and full lips, painted a striking maroon colour. But that seemed to be all the make-up she wore. Her hair was long and dark, slightly reddish brown. He guessed her age at around thirty-five, or maybe a shade older. He was also fairly certain she was wearing contact lenses.

He brought her tea, and a small packet of digestive biscuits, over on a tin tray and sat down opposite her. Oddly, considering her fearsome reputation and his earlier suspicions, there was something about Harriet that made him feel relaxed, even safe. But he knew he must keep his guard up.

He looked at her eyes more closely.

'Yes,' she laughed, 'I am wearing contact lenses. Glasses get in the way on site, especially when I'm doing close work.'

Bloody hell, Alan thought, was I being that obvious? Better watch myself in future. Best to change the subject.

'So how long have you been working for Paul, Harriet?'

'Please, everyone calls me Harry.'

She didn't give him a chance to reply.

'I joined PFC just after he'd set it up, back in January 2004, but I'd already been working for *Reference Collections* since the autumn, September, I think.'

This puzzled Alan.

'I gather *Reference Collections* specialises in faunal remains – and that's Paul's own field. Why on earth would they want a human bones person there?'

'In those days there was quite a big market in human material, especially for hospital and medical school reference collections.'

'Really? Actual human skeletons? Where on earth did you get them from?'

'Mostly, I gather, paupers from China and people who've willed their bodies to science. But now various disease scares have finished that off. And not before time.'

'So what happens now?'

'Oh today it's entirely plastic replicas. We do over two or three dozen: male and female, various ages from babies to old men. We're importers from most of the big replica companies, mainly based in the States and increasingly in China and the Far East.'

'I didn't know that. Is it profitable?'

'You bet. Paul adds a two, sometimes a three hundred per cent mark-up. It's a nice little earner.'

'And your role in all this?'

'Very minor, which is why I spend nine tenths of my time over at the Archaeology Centre. Over here my job is to check through what the replica factories send back to us, to make sure it's what we – or rather our clients – ordered. And very often it isn't.'

'Doesn't say much about their quality control, does it? What, someone orders a baby girl and they send over an eighty-year-old man?'

'No it's rarely as obvious as that. Maybe a twenty-five-year-old woman is sent instead of a twenty-year-old man.'

'And you can spot that?'

Alan was impressed.

'Yes, although sometimes it can be quite difficult, especially if they get parts of the skeleton mixed up…'

'What, like a young man's legs with an old ladies' fingers?'

'Yes, that sort of thing. I certainly earn my keep when I'm checking replica bones.'

Alan nodded, quietly impressed. He could think of graduate students who'd have trouble distinguishing the skull of a twenty-year-old man from an eighty-five-year-old woman, let alone their finger bones.

They finished their teas. The radio in the corner started the 8 a.m. news bulletin. At the sound of the Greenwich pips, Harriet had leant over and wiped condensation off the inside of the window. She was looking out intently. Then she sat back.

'Ah, good, she's on time,' she said.

'On time?' Alan was puzzled. 'Who?'

'This month's work experience girl. I'd thought I'd give her a quick tour while I showed you over the place…'

'I didn't know I was getting a site tour first.'

'Yes, Paul phoned me last night. Thought it would be a good idea. And I agree.'

'So you decided to kill two birds with one stone?'

'Yes, but it shouldn't take long, I've done it dozens of times.'

Harriet turned to the door, which a young woman was now rapidly approaching:

'We'll do a quick tour through the hangar. Then you and I can nip round and see Paul in his office, about nine thirty. OK?'

'OK.'

Harriet looked at a note on her iPad.

'Her name's Sheelah, by the way.'

* * *

Most of the young people who Alan worked with were intelligent, but sadly Sheelah was an exception. As she walked towards them, he could see her body language was flat. And it wasn't just that she was a bit overweight, and was chewing gum. Her eyes were listless. He guessed her attention span was short. He could see at once she wasn't even slightly interested. He glanced across to Harriet, who raised her eyes to heaven.

'Oh no, not another one...' she muttered under her breath, while smiling a greeting.

They headed across the concrete apron towards the hangar. The white van, now loaded up, was slowly reversing out, and as it did so, another one, with a seemingly identical pair of young Asian men, drove across to take its place.

'They're busy today?' he asked Harriet

'Yes,' she replied, 'a big order for one of the Gulf States, I forget which. They're setting up a vast air-conditioned museum somewhere out in the desert. Part of a huge new leisure complex, aimed at tourists.'

'Why on earth would *they* want reference collections?'

Harriet smiled.

'No,' she replied, 'it's nothing to do with the *Reference Collections* side. It's a big contract for *The Museum Shop*. Twenty large display cases. Plus lighting, the works. I think we even did some of the designs. Paul's very excited. It's a big feather in his cap. He's already been out there half a dozen times. Word has it he's going to make a mint.'

Sheelah was looking more than usually lost. Alan turned to her.

'The Paul we're talking about is our boss. He's the man who set this place up. He's a specialist in the study of animal bones from archaeological sites.'

'What? Dinosaurs?'

It was Alan's turn to stifle a groan.

'No,' he replied brightly, 'mostly more ordinary domestic animals, like cattle, sheep and pigs. Then back in 2003 Paul had the bright idea of providing material for people setting up reference collections.'

Sheelah still looked blank. Then she asked her second question.

'What's a reference collection?'

Alan was visibly flagging. It was Harriet's turn to shoulder the burden.

'I look at human bones, mostly from old churchyards and I use collections – we call them reference collections – of bones from known people.'

'What, you know their names?' Sheelah was horrified.

'No, that would be horrible.' Harriet continued, 'these collections are mostly in universities, museums and hospitals and the bones are from people who have given their bodies to science. The point is, we know the age and gender of the individuals in these reference collections and also what disease killed them, if, that is, they died early. This helps me if, for example, the site I'm working on has produced a bone with signs of leprosy.'

'Yes,' Alan cut in helpfully, 'but you can do much more than that. If you find, say, a hip bone you can tell if the person was male or female and in certain cases whether they'd had children.'

'And if you find other bones,' Harriet added, 'bits of skull and teeth, in particular, you can work out, to within about five years, when that person died.'

They both looked at the girl. Nothing had sunk in. Harriet gave a barely perceptible shrug of her shoulders.

They entered the hangar through the main door, which was slowly rolling back to let the second white van enter. It had started to drizzle outside. A powerful arc light, high in the hanger roof, cut in automatically as the cloud cover increased.

They stood aside while the van backed in. Alan was impressed by what he saw: there must have been over a dozen large Portakabins stacked two, and in places three high, arranged along each side of the vast building. At the centre was a loading dock, stacked with pallets and stout wooden cases. Two forklift trucks were collecting more from somewhere at the far end of the building.

'Are all these… these…'

'Portakabins,' Alan suggested.

'Yes,' Sheelah continued, 'are all these Portakabins full of human bones?'

'Good heavens, no,' Alan replied, 'most of the *Reference Collections* business is actually animal bones and small botanical samples.'

'Seeds, pollen grains, that sort of thing,' Harriet added. 'Just think of anything a working university or museum might need, like samples of rocks, crystals, and of course fossils. Lots of fossils.'

Before Harriet could finish, Sheelah had started to wander off. It was as if she had no control over her legs. Maybe the brain-to-leg nerve had atrophied through lack of use. Somehow they had to keep her under control. Harriet caught her up, gently took her shoulder and pointed.

'And there's a vast storeroom at the back, as well.'

By this point they had passed behind the right-hand stack of Portakabins and were walking past a series of doors which led to further rooms along the main outer wall.

Harriet pointed at the doors.

'These are where the samples are prepared, catalogued and stored.'

Alan was surprised Sheelah hadn't asked what a sample was.

As they continued towards the back of the building, it started to grow much darker, and a lot colder. To their relief Sheelah shivered. Her legs took command again: they didn't like the atmosphere back here. So they headed her back towards the main doors. This time Alan and Harriet let her lead the way. They'd given up the unequal struggle. As they walked, Harriet kept up a running commentary.

'These Portakabins are where our museum display company, *The Museum Shop* prepare manikins, scale models and other things to go in display cases. Interactive graphics are the current big thing and they're prepared in that Portakabin up there.' She pointed at a smart, noticeably newer Portakabin perched right at the top, near the front. 'And over the back there,' she continued, indicating behind the Portakabins, 'is the Innovations Space where we do most of the development work for new products. Would you like to take a look?'

Sheelah was miles away. Harriet took a deep breath. It was Alan's turn to take up the burden. He tapped the girl on the shoulder to get her attention and pointed to a door set back in the outer wall and largely obscured by darkness.

'That's the BCA, the Biological Cleansing Area. It was the first thing Paul established when he moved in. It's where bones are cleaned for both reference collections and eventual display.'

His words tailed off. Sheelah was completely oblivious to everything they were saying. And now she was also doing something with a bright pink phone. She could have stepped into a snake pit without noticing. Then something snapped. He bent down and hissed in her ear:

'Please put that thing away and listen to me.'

Even Sheelah could see he meant business. She put her phone away and asked:

'What did you say it was called?'

'The Biological Cleansing Area. It's where we remove the flesh and fats from the bones.'

Her eyes were large now.

'What, like my mum, with sharp knives?'

'No, we can't use knives, as they'd cut and scrape the bones. So we put them into special tanks which we fill with maggots…'

Somehow Alan was determined to get through to this girl, even if it meant being blunt.

'What, live ones?' Sheelah asked, horrified.

'Yes, they have to be alive or else they wouldn't eat the flesh.'

'That's disgusting!'

She was now backing towards the main hangar doors, towards the light. Alan could see she was about to run.

'I'm only here because the college said I had to. They never said I'd have to work with live maggots.'

Alan started to explain that she'd be in another building entirely, but she refused to listen. Her brain had closed down. She turned on her heels and ran headlong towards the doors.

They watched her flee in silence. Then Harriet turned to Alan.

'Thanks a lot. She was going to be our assistant. And you don't need brains to wash bones.'

Alan tried to apologise, but Harriet wasn't having it.

'So now we're screwed. Thanks a bundle, Alan. I do hope you feel better.'

* * *

Alan knew he had screwed up, and no, he didn't feel any better. Harriet was walking alongside him, head down and frowning, as they entered the Archaeology Building and headed down the long corridor to Paul's office.

They knocked on the door and waited. Even though he felt cowed, Alan had never been a patient man. He was about to open the door, when Harriet restrained him.

'Oh come on,' he said under his breath, 'we haven't got all day to hang around in the corridor. Let's go in. He's probably just on the phone.'

'No, Alan,' she insisted, 'don't. It's not worth it. You've done enough for one day. Just wait till he says "enter".'

Alan would probably have ignored her, had the door not suddenly opened wide, and Paul stood before them. Alan was shocked. It had been nearly a decade since he had seen Paul, but he looked as if he aged much more than seven years. He was still two or three inches taller than Alan, but had grown, if anything thinner. His hair was receeding quite markedly now, and his pale neck seemed scrawny. But if he noticed Alan's startled reaction, he didn't show it.

'I'm so sorry to keep you waiting, but that was Piers Gabbit from Heskell Makepiece, and you know you can't trifle with him – or them.'

Neither name meant anything to Alan. He glanced at Harriet who for a fraction of a second seemed equally at a loss. Then they both nodded, sagely.

Paul shook Alan's hand.

'Good to see you again, Alan, glad you could come on board.'

'It'll be just like old times,' Alan said breezily.

'Well, yes and no,' replied Paul in somewhat formal tones.

'I'm kept rather busy by the demands of managing the company nowadays. I simply don't have time for the physical labour side of things anymore.'

The way Paul said it he made Alan and Harriet's job sound more like digging a drain than the highly skilled work of an archaeological excavation. But this wasn't altogether unexpected. Alan realised that Paul was pulling rank. Best to play along.

'Of course, but you're a natural manager, Paul. Your grasp of the admin and the funding issues at Flax Hole saved the dig, as I recall. I'd have been useless without you.'

It was a bit blatant, but Paul lapped it up. Harriet, however, only just managed to conceal her distaste.

'Well,' Paul continued, plainly more than a little pleased with himself, 'we all have our weaknesses, and our strengths of course. Talking of which, what do you make of this?'

On the table were maps and a geophysical plan of the churchyard at St Guthlic's. Alan immediately leant forward to examine the resistivity printout. The printout showed a wealth of detail below the churchyard's surface: he could see the outline of graves, pits and post-holes; also the foundations of the church and its tower's wall-footings.

'Phew,' he muttered half to himself, 'it's far more crowded than I'd expected. It's a good plan. Did you do it in-house?'

'Yes, six weeks ago, during a dry spell.'

Alan was impressed. It was a good piece of work.

'I like the look of that small group of graves there, near the tower.'

'Why's that?' Harriet asked.

'I've been doing a bit of reading,' Alan replied. 'The lower part of the tower's Saxon and I reckon there's a good chance that group might well be early burials. The graves are quite compact and they're all aligned precisely the same – just a degree or two south of true east-west.'

Alan knew that this sort of thing really impressed Paul, whose grasp of field archaeology wasn't very strong. He'd acquired a PhD from Cambridge, but it was all about animal bones: their nutrition, physiology and pathology. He could tell you everything about a pig femur, but ask him how it related to other aspects of the site and he'd be at sea.

Harriet was equally excited.

'The thing is, Paul,' she added, 'that it's incredibly rare to find earlier Saxon graves stratified within a later medieval cemetery. And it's even more unusual to get to dig them. With luck, we'll be able to get some fascinating data on the origins of the earliest population.'

'How fascinating,' said Paul. Alan noticed that he sounded genuinely enthused. It was good to see that the archaeologist in Paul still remained, despite all his commercial success.

Paul glanced up at the large and rather showy Victorian clock on the mantelpiece.

'And now to business,' he began briskly. 'First: budgets.'

He then mentioned a sum, slightly under thirty thousand pounds, which seemed to Alan improbably small because he also suspected that Paul would be looking for a high public profile, with plenty of press interest – and that could only be bought through expensive research techniques. Still, he knew better than to protest at this point. He glanced across at Harriet who was staring hard at him, and he knew he'd already said more than enough for one day. He remained silent.

Harriet, however, had no reservations in speaking her mind.

'That's very tight, Paul.'

'I'm aware of it; but if we'd bid any more, the job would have gone to someone else. I know that for an absolute fact.' At that he tapped the side of his nose, just like on television. Alan could see Harriet almost laughed. 'So we've got to make do with what we've been given. I'll sniff around for other sources of funding, especially when it comes to post-excavation. I'm sure we'll be able to raise some cash for radiocarbon dates, for example.'

Alan didn't share Paul's confidence and was starting to feel depressed. He'd held out high hopes for St Guthlic's and this was starting to turn into yet another routine cemetery excavation: a bone bash. A coffin chase. Call it what you like. But Paul was still speaking:

'OK. That's it. I'm afraid I've got a lot on my plate at this moment. I suggest you work on a detailed costed timetable and come back to me later.'

And with that, they were dismissed.

They headed down the corridor, back into the entrance hall, then turned left into Harriet's office.

* * *

Alan started to apologise about his earlier outburst, when Harriet stopped him.

'I agree, Alan, she was far more stupid than I'd expected and to be honest I rather doubt if she'd even prove capable of bones washing. But even so, if we're to work together successfully we must consult each other. Nothing is straightforward at Priory Farm. There are wheels within wheels here and you've got a lot to learn. OK?'

By now she was smiling. Alan nodded. He'd been forgiven.

'OK, Harry,' was all he said.

Alan was never much good at budgets and accounts, so he was relieved when Harriet volunteered to do an initial breakdown of her costs. Then they could have a discussion, and whatever was left over would be his to spend on the excavations.

Planning the layout of the Guthlic's trenches proved relatively straightforward: they would have to hand-excavate anything along the line of the toilets' foul water pipe, plus the entire footprint of the septic tank. The County Curator, the person who oversaw all commercial archaeological work in Lincolnshire, allowed them to remove the topsoil by machine, but all grave fillings and other archaeological layers had to be hand-sieved through 15mm mesh. Alan knew from bitter experience that this would slow things down seriously, especially if the weather was wet. Nothing was worse than trying to force sticky, wet, clay soil through a clogged-up sieve in wintertime. In fact, before all this business with Ali, that had been his abiding memory of Flax Hole. The wet sieves were the rolling sort, both of them mounted on heavy-duty steel tanks, fixed to stout wooden frames. The sieves themselves were pushed to and fro on trollies that ran on rails, welded to the tank tops. It was a messy business, with water slopping out at either end of the tank, as the trollies were pushed to and fro. And then they had to be emptied every couple of hours through a wide flexible pipe that drained into two big soakaways, one for each sieve tank. Not surprisingly, the wet sieve area was always awash with mud.

After they'd pored over the maps and plans, Alan asked Harriet whether she'd like to join him when he recced the site next week. But it turned out she still had pressing deadlines, which had to be met before the dig began. She also knew St Guthlic's quite well, as she only lived a few miles from it. For some reason Alan then asked whether she had ever gone there to worship.

'Good grief, no,' she replied, 'I'm not religious. Not even slightly. Why – are you?'

'No, not at all. Feels like a cop-out to me, placing your moral framework in the hands of some imaginary higher power.'

'I couldn't agree more.'

Alan was much relieved. He couldn't have coped if she'd turned out to be religious. Then, after a brief chat about finds storage, Harriet showed Alan the room that would be his office for the next few weeks. It was currently being occupied by Paul's principal project officer, who was working on tenders for new work – not that PFC needs it, Alan thought, as he looked around him. The entire building was a hive of activity.

Next they returned to Harriet's office, which was considerably larger than the one Paul had allocated Alan. The dominant feature was a long back wall, fitted from floor to ceiling with slotted shelving, on which were dozens of boxes marked with a site code 'CH', followed by the last two digits of the year.

'CH?' Alan asked out of interest, 'where's that? Cambridge Hotel, Cumberland House?'

She stopped him before the suggestions became sillier.

'No, Çatol Huyut.'

Everyone in archaeology knew about Çatol Huyut, an extraordinary site in western Anatolia, not far from Izmir. Everything was there, from early farming, to Classical Greek, Roman, Byzantium and finally the Ottoman Turks. It was the history of south-western Europe and western Asia in a nutshell.

Alan couldn't conceal his admiration:

'Which particular bones are you doing?'

'All of them.'

'What, everyone from Bronze Age to Ottoman?'

'Yes. It was part of the deal when I got my core funding from the Anatolian Foundation. They want to be able to compare between periods. And I don't blame them. It's the only way to work, nowadays.'

'And I suppose it's important for PFC too.' Alan was thinking aloud. 'It must be a big, prestigious project for them. Are there any British grants?'

'Yes,' she replied, 'The usual ones, the ERC, the Academy, the ARC.'

'Blimey.' Alan was impressed.

'Yes,' Harriet continued, 'Paul's certainly very keen on it. And he's helpful, too. Very helpful, in fact.'

They chatted for a few minutes, then Alan became aware she wanted to get on. She accompanied him out of her office. As soon as they were outside, Alan asked:

'So we'll do a recce next Tuesday. It's a shame you can't be there, Harry.'

He wondered whether she'd change her mind, but she shook her head.

'No, I'm sorry, but much as I'd love to, I'll be busy all that week and probably into the next as well. I've got a book deadline looming.'

Alan was impressed. He could see that Harriet, unlike him, was one of those people who could juggle multiple projects and still keep track of the facts. No wonder she had such a prolific reputation.

'What's it about?'

'The rural population. I'm covering the Vikings, but only just. My main interest is rather earlier.'

'What, Early and Middle Saxon?'

'Yes. After the earlier ninth century, things get rather muddled.'

'I should say so: raids, longships, rape-and-pillage.'

She gave him a quizzical, schoolmistressy look.

'Quite, Alan. I think we've moved on from that. But I'm still worried by the fact that Early Saxon times are still dominated by a few written accounts.'

Alan needed to redeem himself:

'Bede, Gildas, and the early Welsh sources?'

'Precisely,' she was warming to her topic, 'but we still lack a comprehensive review of the solid archaeological evidence for population change.'

'And most of that presumably, is bones?'

'Yes, it is. The book's called *Anglo-Saxon England and the Mediterranean World.*'

Alan was very impressed.

'And who's going to publish it?'

'I signed a contract six months ago with Humber and Potomac.'

'Harry, that's wonderful, congratulations!'

Alan was genuinely pleased for her. They were big and very prestigious publishers, based in London and Boston, Massachusetts.

'Yes, they even gave me a small advance too. But the deadline is next Christmas, January at the latest, and I'm starting to get a bit panicky.'

'Too much other work?'

'Yes, that's a problem. But there's just so much data. So much to write about. I've got to cut it back by at least a hundred thousand words.'

'And even the most idiotic of interns would have eased the load, right?'

'Well, as I said, that's probably debatable.'

Alan could tell she was trying to downplay the situation. It made him even more keen to put things right.

'Tell you what, consider me your replacement idiot.'

'I'm sorry?'

'Whatever you need. Cataloguing. Data analysis. Proofreading. I could even draft a chapter or two if that would help.'

Her reply was sharp and unexpected

'I'm sure I can cope, thank you very much.'

Alan could have kicked himself. Why didn't he think more about what he was saying? She had clearly taken his genuine offer of help as an attack on her ability as an archaeologist. He was beginning to understand how she had gained such a fearsome reputation.

Then he got it. Of course, how could he have been so clumsy?

'Harry, this is your field. I'd never presume or ask for co-authorship.'

Harriet fixed him with her gaze. She didn't seem convinced.

'Seriously, I'm a thirty-nine-year-old circuit digger. Do I look like I have grand academic ambitions? I didn't even finish my PhD.'

Harriet looked genuinely shocked.

'Why ever not?'

'Because my external examiner tried to force me to misinterpret key information in order to fit his own egotistical theories. So I quit.'

This obviously struck a chord with Harriet. Her whole body language shifted in an instant: from defensive to sympathetic. Alan pressed on, it was important that she understood exactly where he was coming from.

'I'm not Paul, Harry. I don't care about the prestige or the politics. I just care about the work. About getting to the truth of things.'

Harriet looked away for a moment. When she turned back to him Alan could see that she was blinking back a tear.

'You're absolutely right. I'm sorry, Alan, you must think me such an ungrateful cow.'

'Not at all. I'm sure that there are lots of people out there who would jump at the chance to take credit for your work. I'm just not one of them.'

'I can see that.'

There was a brief pause, then Harriet pulled out a sheaf of papers from the pile on her desk.

'If you can make a start on the post-Roman chapter, I'd be so very grateful. The thing is, I can't get to grips with the new ideas on Saxon Shore forts. Can you check I've got them right, as they must affect early migrations. I don't know, but maybe they encouraged, not deterred movement?'

Alan was listening closely. He nodded.

'I agree. It's certainly not straightforward – and people were moving around much more than we suspected, even twenty years ago. Leave it with me.'

Alan was about to shake Harriet's hand. But she would have none of it. Instead she kissed him on both cheeks.

'If we're going to be co-directors we can't begin our relationship with a handshake.'

She was smiling broadly.

As he walked across the car park to the Land Rover, Alan reflected on his eventful day. Apart from the incident with Sheelah, he thought he'd done pretty well. He'd managed not to rise to Paul's slightly patronising attitude. To be honest, although he'd never be so stupid as to say it directly, part of him felt sorry for the man. Paul looked stressed. He looked old. If that was what you got for running a successful consultancy business then Paul was welcome to it. Alan also realised that if Paul was under so much pressure then he'd have to choose his moment carefully if he wanted to bring up Flax Hole. This might be trickier than he thought.

Putting the Ali business to one side for a moment, Alan's gut instinct told him that his initial worries may have been misplaced. No, he thought, I'm going to enjoy my stay at Priory Farm with PFC. The St Guthlic's site was also looking good, and although he didn't want to get ahead of himself, the potential for discovering something very important about Anglo-Saxon origins was there: the early name of the church, its superb and remarkably high status tower and those intriguing graves at its foot, were all exciting Alan's instincts. And Harriet was not at all what he expected. She wasn't hostile, or anti-men as her detractors would have it. In fact she appeared remarkably forgiving. She was also smart and she spoke her mind – both qualities that Alan rated very highly indeed.

He had just climbed behind the wheel and was attaching his seat belt, when he felt his mobile vibrate in his trouser pocket. Somehow he managed to retrieve it without hitting the red button. He didn't recognise the number on the screen.

'Hello?'

'Mr Cadbury?'

'That's right.'

'March Fire Brigade, Chief Officer Clark here. I'm afraid we've bad news for you, sir. Your bungalow is on fire.'

Nine

Alan felt a rising surge of panic as he drove Brutus aggressively through what passed for rush hour traffic in the Fens: mud-splattered gang buses driven hard and fast, their passengers asleep or nodding-off in the back; tractors everywhere and small go-faster cars driven by young men with cropped heads and sticky-out ears. Two times he nearly smashed into gang buses that wouldn't pull over, their teenage drivers scared of the deep water-filled dykes alongside them.

As he drove, he thought about the bungalow he once called home. He didn't have many valuables. His laptop was nearly ten years old; his stereo system was a robust ghetto-blaster from his student days and what could only loosely be called his wardrobe were old jeans and second-hand shirts from local charity shops and could fit into a suitcase. But his library was another matter. Alan's extensive reference books ranged from *Teach Yourself Archaeology*, which his father gave him on his eleventh birthday, to the latest green hardback volume of the Danebury project, on research at Windy Dido, Cholderton, Hampshire. Alan loved all the scientific work which is such an important part of modern prehistory. Science was bringing the Neolithic and Bronze Age to life in a way that would have been impossible, even when he was a student. No, the thought of those books and that knowledge going up in flames was unbearable.

Most of the slush and mud that had melted during the day had vanished from the better travelled roads, but as soon as he turned off the main Boston–Spalding route, he found the smaller lanes were still very treacherous. A frost was making things worse and as he turned into Tubney it started to snow. He had expected to see blue lights flashing, but there were none. The roof of his bungalow had completely fallen in, the windows were broken and the front door smashed. There were a few thin wisps of steamy smoke still coming from deep inside the building. Alan leapt out of Brutus and was striding over to the shell of the house when he was intercepted by a uniformed fire officer with a clipboard.

'Are you Mr Cadbury?'

'Yes, I am.'

'I'm Chief Officer-Clark. I'm afraid I can't let you inside, sir.'

'You don't understand. My books…'

Clark gently but firmly held Alan back.

'The structure is unsound. We'll be sending in a team to secure it and retrieve what they can first thing tomorrow. I'll ensure that they prioritise the library.'

Alan looked up at this kindly bear of a man. He must have been in his sixties, at a guess. There was genuine sympathy and concern in his eyes.

Suddenly the enormity of the situation hit him. His home, which smelt like it oozed petrol from the walls, was – had been – a deathtrap. It would have taken the smallest electrical fault to set the fire off. If Paul hadn't called the meeting today, if he hadn't stayed on late chatting with Harriet. If whatever had caused this had happened on any other day, or in the middle of the night…

Alan felt his legs go weak.

Clark gently steadied him.

'Looks like you could do with a drink, sir,' he said as he guided Alan through the falling snow and into the Hat and Feathers.

As they entered the pub a couple of the regulars rose to their feet and patted Alan on the back. Four older men, who had remained at their table playing dominoes, raised their glasses to him.

They sat down at a round table in the bay window. Sandy the landlord came over and placed a large tumbler of whisky in front of Alan with a gentle, 'It's on the house.' Alan took a sturdy gulp and felt the back of his throat burn.

Clark took out a pen and noted the time on his clipboard.

'I'll try to keep this as short and painless as possible.'

Alan managed a weak smile.

'Firstly, the landlord here tells me that they can provide you with a room whilst you sort things out.'

To Alan's surprise, he felt his eyes prick with tears. Such a simple act of kindness. Clark looked down at his clipboard, allowing Alan a moment to compose himself before he asked his next question.

'I must ask, do you have any urgent medical needs?'

'I think the whisky's taken care of that.'

Clark gave him a brief smile and pressed on.

'So no prescription drugs went up in the fire?'

Alan hadn't thought of that.

'No.'

'And was the house insured?'

'Yes, it was.'

'That's good, sir. You'll need to inform your broker as soon as we're finished.'

Alan nodded, and gestured to Clark to continue.

'Now to the fire itself. We've isolated the cause to your electricity meter at the back of the property. A connection had worked loose and had ignited what looked like rodent nest-litter in the cavity, behind the plasterboard. It spread into the building through an enlarged cable feed access in the house wall. At that point flame damage was very extensive. Do you have any idea why that hole would have been enlarged?'

Alan had indeed noticed the hole because mice had used it to find their way into the house earlier, in the autumn.

'I assume the previous occupants of the house had drilled it through, probably because they needed a three-phase supply for their business…'

'Which they conducted on the premises?'

'Yes. They were scrap-metal merchants.'

Alan could see Clark's lips frame the words 'Bloody Dids', but no sound escaped.

'So do you think they did some of their work dismantling, and that sort of thing, in the house?'

'Without a doubt. The place stank of petrol and diesel when I took it over. And I could never get the smell out of the phone. It would probably still stink, if you could find it under all the rubble.'

'Doesn't surprise me. I've been doing this job for over forty years and those travellers, they're always causing problems. Start no end of fires.'

'What, deliberately?'

'No, usually by accident. Incompetence. Burning insulation off pinched cables, or setting cars and lorries alight when they're cutting them up. Mark you, it's not the real Gypsies who do it. They're fine. Good people. No, it's those travellers – Irish mostly.'

Alan had heard people say this dozens of times. He reckoned it went back to the 1840s when Irish labourers sought work in England, after the potato famine. Presumably, he thought, stories like this will be circulating about Poles, Latvians and Estonians in 2150.

Clark was referring to his notes again.

'It says here that the enlarged cable access through the wall had been blocked with painted wood, which burnt and allowed the flames into the kitchen. Can you throw any light on that, sir?'

Alan smiled.

'Yes, I can. I blocked the hole when mice broke in last September. Used a bit of old window frame I found in the shed. Oh yes, and plenty of filler. Not a very professional job, I'm afraid, but it worked. Until today, that is.'

'I don't think you could have anticipated what was to happen, sir. I'd have probably done something similar myself.'

'Thank you.'

'We were very surprised at the speed with which the flames spread through the property and my young assistant investigator made certain observations – none of them conclusive, mind – which might indicate that they had been encouraged in some way.'

'Are you suggesting I might have done it as an insurance scam?'

'My assistant investigating officer suggested that some flammable material might somehow have been introduced.'

'From outside? What are you suggesting – arson? I was up in Lincolnshire at the time. Lots of people can vouch for that.'

'Oh no, sir, I'm not suggesting that for one minute. But you know what these college courses are like: my assistant had just been on one and his head was full of all sorts of clever ideas. I think this was one of them.'

'Yes, you're right: it doesn't make any sense at all, does it? Why would anyone in their right mind want to burn down a grotty bungalow in a remote Fen village?'

'Don't worry, sir, I won't even mention it in my report. Best not cause any problems the loss adjusters might seize on. You know what they're like…'

The landlord appeared from behind the bar with a large basket of logs. He tossed a couple onto the fire and headed back. Alan rose to his feet.

'I know you're not allowed to drink on duty, but it's a horrible night. I don't suppose I could persuade you to join me in something from the bar? The beer's excellent here and Sandy stocks a fine selection of malts.'

'I know I shouldn't, sir, but it's my retirement party in two days' time, so I think we can allow ourselves to bend the rules on this occasion. And as you say, it's a very cold night. So yes, I'd love to join you in a nice peaty malt.'

* * *

Alan took his time at the bar. The shock of the moment was passing, but Clark's words were echoing through his mind. Arson? That would require a motive. A bloody serious motive, at that.

He returned to the table with a tumbler of water and two doubles of ten-year-old Lagavulan. He couldn't afford it, but what the hell. They touched glasses.

'To a happy retirement!'

'That's very kind of you, sir. Cheers!'

They both sniffed and sipped. Gorgeous. Clark was the first to speak:

'My own view,' he was now sounding very official, 'which you have confirmed beyond any doubt, and which will appear in the report, is that the spread of the flames was enhanced by petrol, fuel oil and diesel that appears to have been stored on the premises by the previous occupants. It probably soaked into floors, window and door frames. Possibly into the roof joists too, if they also made use of the attic.'

Alan took his time to respond. His reply seemed to come from miles away:

'Yes... Yes... That all makes sense.'

The fireman ignored him. He had found a hobby horse.

'Between ourselves, sir, I wouldn't be at all surprised if they didn't also have a nice little sideline pinching diesel and fuel oil from farms in the area. Many of the smaller farmers are only now starting to fit locks to their tanks. A few years ago there were easy pickings for light-fingered people, in many remote yards out in the fen.'

But Alan needed to discover more. He leant forward and asked confidentially:

'Between ourselves, what did you learn from your assistant investigating officer? The thing is, I work with many students and in my experience universities and colleges put so much trendy rubbish into their heads, they often can't think clearly. They can't spot the obvious, even if it's jumping around and about to bite them on the nose.'

As Alan had hoped, he had raised a subject dear to the fireman's heart.

'Oh, tell me about it! College courses! Loads of clever science, but not an ounce of good old-fashioned common sense. Frankly, it makes me sick. Those lecturers all draw fat salaries, but none of them could extinguish so much as a baby's night light. '

'That's a relief,' Alan said. It was time to add more fuel to the discussion.

'I thought the theoretical garbage was confined to archaeology alone...'

While he was saying this, Alan could see that Clark was sitting back in his seat, looking hard at him. Then he raised his hand. Alan knew what he was about to hear.

'That's right...' Clark said slowly, 'I thought your face was familiar. Haven't I seen you on *History Hunters?*'

Alan nodded and smiled.

'Yes,' he continued, 'I have. I'm a great fan. I never miss an episode and I watch them all again and again on the Past Times Channel.'

Alan was surprised it had taken the best part of a double malt to release the admission, but it was welcome, nonetheless. From now on it would be easier to get to the truth.

'Yes,' he replied, 'I've done a few episodes with them.'

He paused to take a sip from his malt. He didn't want the conversation to be diverted.

'But I'm interested that colleges seem to be the same everywhere.' He continued, took another sip, then asked, 'You mentioned your assistant had been to college recently?'

'Yes, he was on a two-year sandwich course. It finished a couple of months ago. My boss says he's going to be fast-tracked to the top. God help us all.'

'What did he think about the fire?'

'As I said, he reckoned some accelerant had been added.'

'Really? But how?'

'Mostly it's done from outside, through a broken window, or less commonly under pressure, using an aerosol or sprayer. They generally use petrol pinched from parked cars.'

'And he said there was evidence for this?'

'"Slight evidence" were his precise words, which in my view would be best and simplest explained by the earlier occupants storing diesel inside the premises.'

'But where did he…' Alan was groping for the right words, 'Locate, come across, the evidence?'

'The kitchen. Near and around the cable access from the meter box.'

For Alan that made plenty of sense. But he kept those thoughts to himself.

'Well doesn't that simply tell us, that's where they stored the fuel, stolen or otherwise? People in the pub have told me they didn't use the kitchen for cooking. They preferred their caravan parked outside.'

'It's odd that, isn't it,' Clark said, 'but I've heard of it before. Lifelong travellers would rather sleep and eat in a caravan and use the house as a secure store.'

'Yes,' Alan replied, now deep in thought, 'in a strange way it does make sense, doesn't it? You look after your livelihood. Your ill-gotten gains. Without the money from them you can't buy any food to eat at all, can you?'

Clark had stood up.

'No sir, you're right: it does make some sort of sense. And now I'd better be getting along. It's been a great pleasure meeting you, Mr Cadbury, and don't be concerned, my report will say nothing that might trouble you or your insurers.'

No Alan thought, it almost certainly won't.

But it wasn't the prospect of meeting the loss adjuster that was troubling him now.

* * *

Alan took another large whisky up to his room. He was in no mood for a night in the bar, being quizzed by well-meaning locals. He stood by the window, gazing out at the shell of what had passed for his home. The snow was falling fast now and settling on the exposed beams. The gutted structure was taking on the appearance of a lopsided skeleton. Without thinking he reached into his pocket and pulled out his tobacco and papers. Then his brain registered what his hands were doing and suddenly, staring down at the ruins of his house he resolved to stop smoking. And this time he was determined to succeed. He threw the papers, one by one, out of the window and flushed the tobacco down the toilet. He felt far better now.

The persistent ringing of his mobile phone broke into his thoughts. The screen flashed up the name: Richard Lane. The last thing Alan needed right now was another ear bashing. But he knew what Lane was like – he'd just keep on calling. Alan reluctantly answered.

'Alan, how are you?'

'To be honest, Richard, this isn't the best time.'

'I know. I was at work when the call came in about the fire. Are you at the scene now?'

Even in his exhausted state, this made Alan smile. Lane was a policeman through and through. He didn't really do civilian conversation.

'Not quite. I'm next door. At the pub.'

'Stay there. I'll be with you in half an hour.'

'I'm fine. There's no need…'

'Mary's sorting out the spare room as we speak.'

Again, Alan felt the beginning of tears. Again, he blinked them back. It took him a good ten minutes to talk Lane round and explain to him that the pub really was his preferred option for the evening.

When Lane was finally satisfied, Alan switched off his phone and closed the curtains so that he no longer had to look at those ghostly remains of his house. He was overwhelmed by Lane's simple concern and his generous offer. But it was impossible. Lane would see through him in an instant. He would know that Alan was hiding something, withholding information, the one thing that he had promised not to do. But the facts of the matter were too difficult, too potentially damaging, for Alan to share with anyone, let alone a police detective.

If it was arson, there was only one likely suspect.

He had spelt it out to Ali: the exact location of his home, he'd even bloody well told him about the diesel. He'd handed methods and means to him on a plate.

The question was, if Ali had talked, then who did he tell, and why?

And lurking behind that question was another, almost too disturbing to think about: if Ali was capable of ordering an arson attack, then what kind of man was he? The kind of man who could kill his own sister?

Ten

Alan spent the weekend fobbing off the concerns of the locals and further placating Lane. He was aware that he was coming across as dismissive, ungracious even, but he had no choice. Clark reported back to him on the Sunday. The fire had destroyed nearly everything, but two boxes of books on his bedroom floor had escaped unharmed. The boxes were charred, but the books inside were untouched. According to Officer Clark, books were almost fireproof, especially in boxes rather than on shelves. It was a small consolation, but better than nothing.

By Monday, Alan was back to old habits. He wasn't ready to properly consider Ali's involvement in the fire; it was too raw, too upsetting. So he threw himself back into his work with renewed intensity. It was his first paid day on the Guthlic's project and although he'd done a certain amount of background reading at home, he still needed to do more before he went on the site recce the next day. He spent the morning in the Lincoln Historic Environment Records Office, then after lunch drove to Priory Farm.

He walked across the entrance hall to his new office, which was next door to Harriet's. And as he had promised, Paul had sent him all the maps and plans they had seen with him the previous Friday. It could be a lot worse, he thought, as he looked around. It's far better than a site hut; it's warm, dry and well-lit. There were ample bookshelves and a modern-looking computer, which was hooked up to the PFC network. Yes, it could have been a lot worse.

He had planned to have a chat and a coffee with Harriet, but his eye was caught by the Guthlic's geophysics plot and before he knew it he had drifted over to the table and unrolled it. Automatically his mind had switched into dig director mode and he was planning the location of his first three trenches. An hour later there was a quiet knock on his door. It was Harriet.

'Fancy a coffee, Alan? I'm brewing up.'

'Oh yes please, Harry.' A coffee would go down very well. 'I'm sorry,' he continued, 'I meant to pop in earlier, but got snared by this plan.'

'It's going to be good, isn't it?' she said, looking down at the graves on the geophys plot.

'Yes, very. And I think it's fairly clear where the trenches need to go…'

Alan was thinking about relationships and inter-cutting graves. It was absolutely essential that they work out the sequence correctly, otherwise any claims that some bodies were earlier than others might sound a bit hollow. The more he thought about it, the more he realised that it was going to be a dig where chronology and sequence were all-important.

'Just looking at the geophys, Alan, makes me think we ought to be able to work out a pretty precise phase plan. Am I right?'

There was real anxiety in the way she asked this. Alan could see she shared his thoughts on chronology, completely.

'Yes you are, but it'll take really precise excavation. We can't afford to have any heave-hoes or passengers on the crew. They'll have to be good. Do you know the staff here?'

She nodded.

'I do. And I've already earmarked the people we'll be taking with us. So relax, they're all good.'

He was about to discuss trench locations, when her coffee machine began beeping.

Harriet's office was more lived-in and more comfortable than his. She even had three easy chairs, all covered with books and papers, and a coffee table. She cleared two chairs and they sat down. She studied him closely. Alan could tell she was choosing her words carefully.

'I didn't get a chance to ask you about it on Friday, but you mentioned you'd worked for Paul earlier?'

'Yes. A lot earlier and strictly speaking I didn't work *for* Paul, as much as *with* Paul. We were co-directors.'

'Like us?' she added brightly.

'I wish it was. No. We'd set up a contracting partnership in Leicester, as there was a lot of work there at the time. We rented a business unit out in the suburbs. It was cheap and clean, with plenty of space – nothing like as grand as Priory Farm.'

'That's interesting. I somehow can't see Paul setting up a partnership with… with anyone.'

This intrigued Alan.

'Why's that?'

'He doesn't empathise with people. He reasons and decides, if you know what I mean.'

Then she stopped. Alan could see she felt disloyal: after all she owed her living to Paul.

'I know what you mean, but I don't think he doesn't care. He's just an extreme pragmatist. That's what made us such a good team. He spotted that before I did, which I suppose is a kind of empathy in itself.'

'What do you mean?'

'Halfway through the dig at Flax Hole he suggested that we changed our roles. I became the hands-on field director, and he took over all admin. And I mean *all* admin. I barely needed to sort out paper clips. It was great, I got to do what I loved without any of the boring stuff.'

'I'm not entirely sure he did that for your benefit, did he?'

Alan could see that something was bothering Harriet. He gestured to her to continue.

'From what I understand, that Flax Hole dig was the beginning of the great PFC empire.'

This had never occurred to Alan before. But Harriet was right. It was directly after Flax Hole that Paul's big contracts started rolling in and he swiftly became a major player in the consulting world.

'You were a partnership and he just walked away and set up on his own.'

Alan shrugged.

'I suppose I didn't want to be tied down.'

'But did he even offer you the opportunity to come in with him?'

'No, but that was never the deal.'

Harriet bit her lip. Alan could tell that something was still bugging her.

'It's OK, Harry, this is just between you and me.'

116

'Yesterday, the minute you mentioned Flax Hole, he just seemed nervous. No, more than nervous. Shifty, I thought.'

'Did he? I thought he was just putting me in my place, you know, at the bottom of the glorious corporate ladder.'

They shared a smile.

'Anyway,' continued Alan, 'if he does have a guilty conscience let's use that to our advantage and see if we can squeeze a few more grand out of him for this bloody budget.'

Harriet laughed, and they returned to studying the trench layout.

* * *

The next day Alan made his recce visit to St Guthlic's. He pulled off the single track lane and parked Brutus in the small grass car park. There'd been a funeral recently and the wheelie bin behind the ivy-covered back wall of the sexton's shed was full of sad, wilting flowers.

He strode briskly across the churchyard and was relieved to see that the grid pegs set out by the geophysics team several weeks earlier were still in place. These were the pegs they had used to tie their survey area onto the Ordnance Survey map and Alan knew it would be essential to make sure that the excavation trenches could, in turn, be accurately tied into the geophysics. He'd been on sites where this had gone wrong – and they were chaotic. So those pegs were very welcome indeed. He counted them and could see without stretching a tape that they had been laid-out on a five metre grid. He pulled out his plan of the churchyard and started spray-painting the line of their first trench on the turf. Then the sun came out and even though it was still mid-winter he could feel the warmth of its rays on his back. He straightened up and admired his surroundings. At last, he was beginning to relax.

He could read the church's ancient stonework like a book. It had a fine Saxon tower, with distinctive long-and-short work, probably built in the earlier eleventh century. The nave, chancel and both transepts had been largely rebuilt in the earlier fifteenth century, at about the same time the vast tower of the Stump was going up across the fen in Boston. Like Boston, most of the money used to build Guthlic's probably came from the lucrative trade in wool and textiles that was then transforming so many churches in eastern England. His immediate practical concern, the new toilets, were to be housed in a small Victorian extension built onto the south side of the chancel.

Behind him the gate into the churchyard creaked. Alan looked round sharply. He was feeling jumpy after the fire, but it was only the vicar, accompanied by another man. After they had shaken hands, the Reverend Hilary Anstruther-Purse introduced his companion, who was wearing smart, new, tweedy country clothes, but was clearly not used to them. The man removed a glove to shake hands, but couldn't find an unbuttoned pocket to put it in. He was rather nervous.

He introduced himself as Alistair Crutchley and offered a handshake so warm and enthusiastic that Alan thought it would take his arm off.

'Good heavens,' he said, unable to contain his enthusiasm any further, 'I'm so glad to have met you, Mr Cadbury! I loved the show you did at Boston Haven. Wasn't that ship extraordinary? And who would have guessed there'd have been a slaving connection at that early date? Amazing. Quite amazing.'

Alan smiled weakly. He had thoroughly enjoyed the *History Hunters* excavation at this nearby site, where they had uncovered a seventeenth-century merchant ship. In fact, he would go as far as saying it was one of his favourites. But he really wasn't in the mood for a star-struck local.

'So you enjoyed it?'

'Oh, yes!' Alistair was smiling even more enthusiastically: 'I'd say so. It was first-rate. Absolutely first-rate.'

To Alan's relief, the vicar brought conversation to a halt with the suggestion that perhaps they should look inside the church.

'Most regrettably,' he said as he opened the door, 'we have to keep it locked at all times. We've had so much material stolen and we're so terribly remote. How far's the Hall, Alistair?'

He pointed towards a large wood across two enormous flat fields, where Alan noted the oilseed rape had been severely checked both by the frosts and by tens of thousands of pigeons, who roosted safely at night in the woods.

'It's just behind those trees,' Alistair said. 'Sometimes we walk to church in summer and it must take a good twenty minutes, door to door.'

'And of course the village is even further,' the vicar added, 'over a mile away.'

Once inside, they paused, so that Alan could enjoy what lay before them. It was an astonishingly fine building – and in an area famous for its churches. Alan may have had no time or patience for religion, but he could still appreciate the magnificent architecture.

They walked through the transept and into the chancel. The large perpendicular east window had been fitted with vividly-coloured Victorian stained glass. Along its base, ornate Gothic lettering proclaimed: *This window has been restored to the Glory of God, anno 1885, by Arthur Alistair Crutchley.*

'My great-great-grandfather,' Alistair said quietly, as they stared up at the window, through which the morning sunlight was now streaming.

Around them were memorials to other squires of the village, including the late medieval Lords of the Manor of Scoby who had survived into the eighteenth century. This was when they had demolished the old manor house and erected the brand new Hall.

'I know it's still rather unfashionable, but I do like Victorian stained glass. Particularly when the sun shines through it, like that. It's glorious, is it not?' said the vicar.

He pulled an envelope from his pocket, which he gave to Alan.

'Here,' he continued, 'these are the church keys. Keep them safe, then return them to me or Alistair when the dig's finished. They're the second spare set, so we won't be needing them in the meantime.'

And with that he left by the small door on the south side of the chancel. They watched him go, then Alistair turned to Alan.

'Funny thing,' he said, 'in my father's day the vicar was never given a key to that door. That was reserved for his – for the squire's family. He thought vicars must be kept in their place. Very old school.'

'When did things change?'

'Fifteen years ago, when father died and I inherited.' He was more relaxed now. 'Seemed all wrong somehow. I even handed the gift of the living to the diocese. I mean, why should we – the family – dictate who should be the next vicar, just because AAC said so.'

Alan interrupted him.

'I'm sorry, what's AAC?'

Alistair let out a small chuckle. 'Not what, who.'

Alistair pointed up at the window.

'Him up there: Arthur Alistair Crutchley. As I was saying, just because AAC had made a fortune in London and had then bought the estate, and with it the living, that didn't make him any better in the eyes of God. Quite the contrary, I'd have thought.'

Alan was quietly astounded. He'd got this chap completely wrong. When they'd first met, although they were both about the same age, Alistair seemed like he belonged to an earlier generation entirely. He would have expected him to take deference for granted. Yet again, an example of the cultural prejudice that we all carry with us, he thought. As with Alistair, so with Ali – it was just a different set of preconceptions, that's all.

* * *

Back in his office, Alan stacked his rescued books on his shelves. They still smelled strongly of smoke, but he had been assured it would eventually go away. He stood back. It was good, comforting even, to have them back with him.

Alan knew he had a decision to make. He hadn't started teaching the A-level course yet. All it would take would be a simple phone call to Grant. He could plead pressure of work, goddamit he could even plead the emotional trauma of the fire. But as he stood there, studying the remnants of his library he realised that he would do no such thing. Grant had informed him that twelve Lifers had signed up. The list of student names would be sent over to him in the next couple of days. Twelve men, locked away in that hellhole, wanted to learn and no matter whether Ali was amongst them or not, Alan wouldn't, couldn't, let them down. He had stiffened his resolve. He didn't know it, but lurking behind this altruistic motive was another, a purely self-centred one: Alan wouldn't stand for bullying. Never had, never would. If the fire had been arson, and if Ali was indeed behind it, then Alan would make sure he was called to account somehow. No matter their past history at Flax Hole; no matter the boy Ali had once been.

He scanned his shelves, searching out inspiration. One of the volumes was the standard work on the Anglo-Saxon settlement of south Lincolnshire, which he removed and took to his desk, where he unpacked his own laptop and opened his A-level lecture files. He worked away for about ten minutes, while munching on a chocolate bar – his lunch that day. He needed more information about Early Saxon cemeteries in the southern Fens, as he thought this could make a good special project for some of his students. Sadly, the book was no real help. Nor was the internet. He got up and knocked on Harriet's door.

He fully expected Harriet to send him packing, considering her looming deadlines, so he was surprised by her friendly greeting.

'I'm glad you came, Alan. I was getting so fed up. All I'm doing is ordering database entries by date, size, type and so on. It's driving me mad.'

Alan also hated that side of their work. But sadly it was part of the digital life. This time other, more archaeological, things were on his mind.

'Funny you should say that,' he began, 'because that chapter you gave me is having the opposite effect. It's making me think about all sorts of things, like the demise of the Classis Britannica and the start of a new, I suppose we'd call it privatised, marine and coastal economy in Late Antiquity. No wonder there was so much traffic across the Channel and the North Sea.'

'Yes, that's what I was starting to think…'

Alan continued – he had the bit between his teeth. 'I'd always thought that contact was concentrated around the western approaches – places like Tintagel. But no, just as much, maybe even more was happening over here. It's just that the historical sources don't discuss it.'

'And they don't cover places like Guthlic's either. No, I'm convinced that site could make a real contribution to the debate…'

'So can I read the next chapter too? I'm dead keen to see what the osteological evidence tells us about the Anglo-Saxon invasions.'

'Possibly,' she smiled, 'but you've also got to suggest a twenty per cent cut in the words.'

'Great' he said, 'I'll do that, but one good turn deserves another.'

'Yees…' she answered with mock doubt.

'I need to pick your brains. I want some basic info about recent Early Saxon cemetery sites in the Fens and East Midlands.'

'That's outside your normal period, isn't it? I thought the Bronze Age was more your field?'

'Yes, it is. But I'm trying to find some interesting special subjects for an A-level course I'm about to start teaching.'

At this point there was a knock at her door. Paul entered before Harriet had a chance to respond.

'Harriet, about your budgetary concerns. St Guthlic's is a relatively minor project as far as PFC is concerned and as such—'

He stopped short when he saw Alan.

'I see you've brought in reinforcements.'

Alan stepped in, eager to clear up any misunderstanding. If Paul had any residual issues with him, it wasn't fair for Harriet to get drawn into it.

'Not at all. I was trying to chase up some information on Pagan Anglo-Saxon burials…'

'A bit outside your normal field, aren't they?' Paul asked.

'Not in this instance. I'm teaching a part-time A-level course.'

'Oh really, a WEA evening class?'

Sod it, thought Alan. Now's as good a time as any.

'No. At Blackfen Prison, as it happens.'

They both looked at him. Those two words weren't often spoken at Priory Farm.

'A course for the warders?' Harriet asked, breaking the silence.

'No, it's for a group of prisoners. They call themselves "The Lifers' Club".'

Harriet was astonished.

'Are you saying they're all serving life sentences?'

'I imagine so,' Alan replied, 'but we don't get to find out about each individual prisoner. We're not permitted to discuss their criminal records. Our job is to reach the men who are there, whatever they've done. We take them as we find them.'

'How very noble of you,' said Paul. 'So long as it doesn't interfere with your work schedule here I suppose I can allow it. Now if you'll excuse us…'

Paul waved the budget papers at Alan, shooing him out of the door.

* * *

Half an hour later Alan was still staring at his computer screen. The title 'Lecture One' stared back at him, followed by a page of blank space. There was a knock at the door. It was Harriet.

'What on earth was that all about with Paul?' she asked.

'I think he suspects we're ganging up on him,' said Alan. 'I forgot he can be a bit paranoid like that.'

'It's not such a bad idea,' said Harriet. 'We could lock him up with the maggots in the BCA until he gives us a radiocarbon dating budget that is actually connected to reality.'

Alan shared a conspiratorial grin.

Harriet stepped forward and placed a folder on his desk.

'Anyway, I had a quick look through some old papers. Will this do for your A-level students?'

Alan liked the fact that she was so straightforward about it. They wanted to learn, and so as far as she was concerned, they were just students. Not criminals.

Alan opened the folder. It was just what he wanted: concise and to the point and everything tabulated: DNA estimates for Saxon incursions, evidence for new burial rites. The lot. As he flicked through he noticed that Harriet was sniffing the air and frowning.

'Alan, you old rogue, have you been having a crafty cigarette?'

'No, I haven't.'

'Well, there's a distinct smell of burning.'

'I know. It's the books. My house burnt down on Friday afternoon. These are the only ones that made it out alive.'

Harriet was astonished. She stood there, like a caricature, eyes round and mouth open.

'But Alan, that's terrible!'

'It was an electrical fault, happens all the time apparently.'

'And are you insured?'

'Yes, thank heavens, I am.'

'And are they being difficult?'

'No, they're not. Actually they're being very helpful.'

'And where are you staying now?'

'At the pub next door. It's fine.'

She listened to this at first anxiously, then with a look of exasperation.

'Alan,' she said in a tone of absolute authority, 'don't be so *utterly* ridiculous. You can't possibly co-direct an important dig from a room above a pub. The idea's quite absurd. No, I have a perfectly good spare room at my place in Mavis Startby. You will come and stay with me.'

And that was that.

Alan spent the rest of the day assembling Harriet's research file into a coherent lecture, adding his own personal touches here and there. The last thing he wanted to do was come across as lazy or fake. Just as he was clearing his desk, there was the familiar ping of a new email arriving. He went to his inbox: it was from Blackfen Prison. Student register. He opened the attachment. And there it was, staring out at him from the grid of the spreadsheet: Student number 8. Prisoner number 2957. Kabul, Ali.

Eleven

Harriet led Alan around her nineteenth-century two-bed house with the enthusiasm and efficiency of a professional archaeologist on a pre-dig recce. They had covered the lounge and kitchen. She explained that her only extravagance had been a reconditioned oil-fired Aga, which kept the downstairs rooms wonderfully snug in winter. Now they were doing the upstairs tour.

'I'm afraid I couldn't run to an en suite, so we'll have to share the bathroom…'

She opened the door and Alan glanced in. There were bottles and jars, coloured tissues in profusion, but no dangling underwear. It was feminine, but not oppressively so.

'And this will be your room. I think of it as the Fen room, as it looks across Dawyck Fen.'

'Which makes yours, I suppose, the Wolds room.'

'Yes, I hadn't thought of it like that. It's just my room, that's all. Anyhow, you've a basin. And do look out, you're near the immersion heater and the water can run scalding hot very quickly. I often hear guests yell in pain when doing their teeth.'

Alan gazed out of the window. The spectacular view had been swallowed by the night. Harriet was reflected in the darkened glass, standing a couple of feet behind him, smiling.

They'd only known each other a short time and here she was, opening up her home to him. He'd offered to pay rent but she wouldn't even consider it. He should be overjoyed but he wasn't. He was worried. Very worried indeed.

What if his worst fears were correct? What if he had been the victim of an arson attack? What horrors and dangers was he potentially bringing to Harriet's door? He'd been unbelievably selfish to even consider it.

'Harry, I've been thinking…'

'Sounds ominous.'

'I'm not sure this is such a good idea.'

'Why ever not?'

'You know, mixing the professional and the personal…'

Even as the words passed his lips Alan regretted it. He saw a flicker of embarrassment pass across Harriet's face, quickly followed by pure anger.

'Don't flatter yourself, Alan.'

'I didn't mean…'

Harriet cut him short.

'I'm a concerned colleague, offering you support at a time of need. That's all. If you find that too… compromising then feel free to book yourself in at the Travelodge down the road.'

She slammed the spare keys down on the bedside table and stormed out of the room.

Alan was furious with himself. Now he had two options: stay and endanger Harriet. Leave and create an unbearable tension between them at work and possibly undermine the whole project. Not just the St Guthlic's project, but Paul, Ali,

Flax Hole, everything that he'd been working so hard to get closer to.

He sighed deeply and sat on the edge of the bed, staring into the mirror on the room's neat little chest of drawers. Then it came to him. He might not be able to protect Harriet, but he knew exactly who could. But it would require him to be absolutely truthful, to tell him everything he knew, or currently suspected, only then could Richard advise him whether he, or more importantly, Harriet was in any danger. So he took a deep breath and rang Lane's home number, fully expecting Mary to answer, then after several rings the answerphone cut in. He left a simple message for Richard to call him back. But he didn't add: and please, please ring soon. But by now he was getting very anxious.

He slung his suitcase on his bed, unzipped it and pulled out the bottle of excruciatingly expensive red wine he'd bought as a house-warming present. He slowly made his way back downstairs, formulating a suitably grovelling apology and a promise to take on all her domestic chores for the rest of his natural life.

* * *

After a surprisingly amenable first night at his new home, during which Alan discovered that he and Harriet held two very important values in common – a passion for red wine and an innate inability to hold onto a grudge just for the sake of it – Alan returned to PFC in good spirits. He then spent all day making practical arrangements for the forthcoming dig: phoning diggers, contractors, plant operators, Portaloo hire, etc. He also had to be certain there were supplies of stationery, pencils, survey tapes and a good reliable dumpy level. Later on they could fix the trenches with GPS, but there was no need to have it with them all the time, as they could perfectly well use the existing geophysics grid. They were all essential, but not the sort of jobs he enjoyed much, so he was glad to get away at the end of the day. He was less pleased at the prospect of his duty-dinner that lay ahead. However, he'd been a circuit digger long enough to know that keeping the local community informed and involved was a vital part of any successful excavation.

It had been dark for two hours when he swung Brutus into a tree-lined avenue. Even in the headlights' glare he could see they were mature limes with trunks congested with young growth, which had recently been cut from the trees nearest the house. Their fresh, white scars were bright in his headlights' glare. Scoby Hall was an impressive, seven-bay Palladian mansion, whose colonnaded double front doors were approached by a sweeping flight of steps. He parked alongside Alistair's green Range Rover and walked up to the front doors. As he pulled on the heavy chain, he listened for a bell somewhere deep inside, but could hear nothing. Presumably, he thought, it rings below stairs, in the butler's pantry. There were tall, thin windows on both sides of the front doors and Alan saw Alistair scuttle across the wide front hall to let him in. He was slightly disappointed there was no butler. Alistair had taken off his tweeds and was wearing jeans and a baggy T-shirt. The front doors hadn't been locked.

Alan stepped inside and looked around him. He was amazed by the pictures, the gilded plasterwork and fine marble floors. And what was more, they seemed to be in good condition. Somebody cared about this place.

Once inside, Alistair took him through to the kitchen where they sat down to a high tea of butcher's sausages, dry-cured bacon (from the estate) and scrambled eggs, which was prepared by a rotund and very smiley middle-aged lady, who was introduced as Mrs Fowler. Alan suspected she might once have been Alistair's nanny.

Alistair took two huge mouthfuls of eggs.

'Claire thinks I eat too much fat, so this is our naughty treat when she's away, isn't it?'

He looked across to Mrs Fowler who was regarding him with a broad and not very conspiratorial smile. She addressed her reply to Alan.

'I can't see it does Mr Alistair any harm, can you, sir?'

'I agree,' Alan replied, when he had finished chewing a forkful of sausage, 'no harm at all. No, nothing but good.'

After the meal they took a flask of coffee up to the drawing room, where Alistair explained that his wife was away in London being a consultant headhunter – 'she usually hunts heads three days a week' – and the two children had returned to boarding school. So here he was, on his own, and feeling just a little lonely, Alan suspected. He was certainly in no rush to see his guest leave.

While they chatted about this and that, Alan's gaze was arrested by a remarkable full length portrait of a late Victorian country gentleman with a bushy beard, standing with legs slightly astride and grasping a shotgun, as if he intended to use it. The intensity of the man's stare was striking.

'That's AAC, of course…'

'Ah,' Alan cut in, 'I remember. The man commemorated in the east window.'

'Yes, him. It's by Grinterhalter.'

In the late nineteenth century the German artist was Court Painter and Alan knew enough to realise that he must have charged his sitter a fat fee.

'It's very good indeed. What eyes. They're remarkable.'

'Yes, you know how it is: some people say they follow you. To be quite frank, I don't like it much myself. I know it's very good and all that, but I can't sit facing it. That stare gives me the willies. Claire agrees. She wants me to move it out into the hall and I think I just might.'

By now they had risen to their feet and were standing facing the picture. Alistair pointed to a smaller portrait a few feet away to the right.

'That's his wife, Hermione. She almost certainly had consumption, which may have been one of the reasons they decided to move up to Lincolnshire, where the clean air was supposed to be good for the lungs. They had two children, including a son, my great-grandfather.'

He gestured to another picture of a young gentleman.

'He was far more prolific. Nine children: four daughters and five sons, all but one of whom were killed on the Somme.'

Below Hermione's portrait was a small pen-and-ink sketch of a young woman working at her embroidery. It was a very sensitive drawing and Alan leant forward to look at it more closely.

'That's Timothea,' Alistair continued, 'known in the family as Tiny. She had to be delivered by forceps, which sadly left her brain-damaged. But by all accounts she was a delightful person. She certainly had a special place in AAC's affections. Look...'

He took the picture down from the wall and handed it to Alan. On the back were two locks of hair: one very fine, auburn; the other darker and coarser, with a few grey strands.

They were tied by silk ribbons and sewn to the mount with the inscription: 'In fondest memory of Timothea, from her distraught father'. Alan was moved by this. He could imagine how he would feel in that situation.

'I suppose it's just a bit of Victorian sentimentality.'

'No,' Alan said pensively, 'I don't think it is... This is heartfelt.'

'She only survived into her mid-thirties and lived in a flat here in the Park. We call it the Granny Flat now, not that a granny lives there anymore, but it comes in useful when Claire has important clients to impress.'

By now they had finished their tea and Alan began to take his leave. But Alistair had more to say:

'Look, as you can probably guess from this place, I'm not completely short of cash. I was in banking for eight years, but managed to get out before it all went tits up. And Claire still earns a tidy sum, hunting her heads. My real love in life is history. Not just the family stuff, but the bigger picture. Who we are, why we are, how we got here and all that. So if you'd let me, I'd love to come down to your dig and help out. I'm sure you must have odd jobs to give a keen volunteer like me? Things that nobody else wants to do?'

'If you wouldn't mind helping with finds, that sort of thing?'

'Fine. Just the ticket. But look, I really don't want to cause offence by saying this, but I'm determined it must be done properly. To high standards.'

'No offence taken. PFC has an excellent reputation, and can assure you we will do the best we can with the resources made available – if that doesn't sound too horribly corporate.'

'Don't worry, I'm used to it. But still, you get what I'm driving at?

Alan nodded, he could tell that Alistair was passionate about his subject.

Alistair continued, 'So do you know if your people can afford expensive things like radiocarbon dates?'

Alan was impressed. Alistair clearly knew his stuff.

'That hasn't been confirmed as yet, but rest assured I'm working on it.'

'And have you done geophysics?'

'Indeed we have, yes.'

'And did you detect bodies?'

'No, not bodies.'

Alan was teasing him. And it worked: Alistair's face fell.

'Oh, I was rather hoping…'

'No, you don't understand, geophys can't detect bodies. Radar can sometimes, but not ordinary geophys. But it can detect graves.'

'And are there any?'

'Yes, lots. And some of them look quite early.'

'But we'll need radiocarbon to prove that, won't we?'

'Yes, we probably will.'

'Well,' Alistair said, almost rubbing his hands with delight, 'I promise, you can count on me for them.'

'That's very generous. Carbon dates don't cost too much these days, but some of the other diagnostic tests can sometimes prove very expensive. A few cost hundreds, even thousands…'

'Oh, don't worry about that.' Alistair sounded almost dismissive. 'Go ahead. Run the clever tests, then send me the bills. I'm sure the estate accountants can find ways of writing them off against tax. They're very good at that sort of thing, you know. I'll contact our agent tomorrow.'

'That's extremely generous, Alistair. Are you sure you mean it?'

'Of course. So what happens next?'

Alan pulled out his diary.

'Right,' he said turning the pages, 'we're machining on Monday and Tuesday. I don't want people around then, as you wouldn't be insured with the digger there and everything. But from Wednesday you'd be very welcome to join us. Wear a stout pair of boots and something waterproof.'

Alan couldn't believe his luck: a rich volunteer with time and money on his hands. At last they'd be able to do some proper research. Things were looking up.

Twelve

Alan had been a fully qualified digger driver for about ten years and normally he liked to do all the delicate work himself. And nothing is more delicate than working in a churchyard. He'd done it many times and was aware that it's possible to drive an excavator disrespectfully, with a loud blaring radio and spoil heaps dumped anywhere, regardless of graves and tombstones. But he prided himself on doing such jobs in a manner that could only be described as reverential. In churchyards he always worked at half revs and never shook the bucket to dislodge a lump of stuck clay; instead he would shift it quietly, with a spade.

The reason he wasn't driving the machine was that PFC had entered into a long-term agreement with AK Plant, the company who gave them, so Paul insisted, *very* preferential all-in rates. And those rates included 'an experienced and fully qualified operator'. So Alan was to act as 'banksman' – the man who stands outside and looks behind the bucket, the driver's only blind spot. After eight hours on site, Alan knew that the banksman's job could be demanding, but in many respects it was the most important on the dig: let the bucket scoop two inches too low and something vital could be removed and lost forever. So you could never afford to let your concentration slip. Not for one minute.

When Alan arrived at St Guthlic's, the digger driver was just finishing the routine morning grease-up. He was a young man, probably in his early thirties, Alan reckoned, but there was something odd about the way he stood, as if his legs had been shortened by disease when a child. Alan shook his hand and made a remark about the weather they were to expect, but it got no response. Instead, the driver pointed at himself with the single word:

'Kadir.'

At which he nodded and smiled. Maybe Alan failed to conceal his astonishment, because he then added, 'Very good driver. Very, very.'

Alan's heart sank. That was all he bloody well needed: a complex site and a digger driver who didn't speak English.

Then a splash from a puddle in the car park signalled the arrival of Paul. Alan smiled at the driver and said 'Me, Alan' in an attempt to mend relations. Then he hurried across to Paul, to vent his frustration and anger.

As they walked back to the digger Paul explained that he had especially asked for Kadir, as he was by a long way AK Plant's best driver.

'Fine,' Alan broke in, 'but if he doesn't bloody speak English, he could be the best digger driver in the world. It makes no fucking difference!'

He couldn't believe Paul's complacency which had to be all about saving money. Put simply, AK Plant did a good deal for their clients.

By now they had reached the digger and to Alan's amazement Paul greeted Kadir in Turkish. He could see from the driver's frown of concentration that he wasn't fluent, maybe even a bit halting and hesitant, but he could make himself understood. He then explained to Alan how he was to use signs to show precisely what he wanted done, while Kadir looked on, nodding in appreciation.

To Alan's astonishment Paul's suggestion worked very well indeed, and yes, Kadir, was a brilliant driver. Not only could he work precisely, and to within millimetres, but he could also differentiate between soil colours and could manoeuvre the machine superbly, by just using the front and back buckets – something that Alan found almost impossible, and very dangerous; several times he had nearly turned the digger over. So disaster had been averted; but still, he did think Paul should have alerted him in advance.

The machining had gone well, but they had overrun slightly. The weather, too, had held. It was now late on Wednesday morning. They had just finished the last of the mechanical work and the digger was heading across the graveyard back to the car park. Alan paused and looked around him. The trowelling-down of the machined surface along the line of the foul-water trench was now well advanced, and the dark outlines of some ten graves could clearly be seen on the clean, stripped ground surface.

Never one to miss an opportunity to pick up a trowel, Alan jumped into the main trench and joined the three people trowelling the surface. One of them was Alistair whose technique rather reminded him of DCI Lane all those years ago. That morning Alan had been trying to push all thoughts of Lane to the back of his mind. He knew he mustn't be diverted from the task at hand, but he was also very concerned that Lane hadn't returned the call he made that first night at Harriet's. He was acutely conscious, too, that he ought to have spoken to him, if just to reassure him that he was doing fine, after the fire. But he was still nervous about being subject to Lane's forensic questioning. He resolved to do it once he'd seen Ali, once he'd got some answers, perhaps.

In the meantime, Alan focused on Alistair. He could see that the professional diggers had done what he'd asked them to do and had quietly taught Alistair the arts and subtleties of trowelling – that most difficult and fundamental of archaeological skills. He also knew they would have contacted him very quickly, had their pupil not been any good. But Alistair was a natural, and his trowelling was both fast and clean.

He knelt down next to Alistair, who moved over slightly and for a few minutes they worked, in rhythm, together. Alan had always loved trowelling and he began with enthusiasm. Then he found his mind wandering back, once again, to Ali, Lane and Harriet and the trowel in his hand became less firm and decisive. He was suddenly aware that Alistair was trying to engage him in conversation. He hadn't heard a word.

'I'm sorry, Alistair, I was miles away. Can you say that again?'

'I saw those graves in the geophys plot,' Alistair began.

'What, the ones at the foot of the tower?'

'Yes, them. Somebody said they'll be important when we get to them. That sounded rather intriguing.'

'I know, with luck we'll start them next week. There's something about the way they don't respect the precise shape and orientation of the tower that I find fascinating.'

'Yes, I noticed that too, but I thought no more about it.'

'Of course one can never be certain, but when you get such seeming misalignments they often indicate that the two features cannot be contemporary.'

'But the tower's still standing, and it was built in the late tenth century…'

'Which can only mean,' Alan explained, 'that the graves are earlier. I would guess they could be Middle Saxon, even earlier. And of course that's very important as they would then pre-date the Viking invasions and could potentially give us important new information about the origin of the earliest English population.'

By this point Alistair had laid his trowel aside and was staring wide-eyed at Alan. There was a short pause. Then, very quietly, Alistair spoke.

'As I said, Alan, if you need any financial help, just ask. This sounds absolutely fascinating.'

Once again, Alan couldn't believe his luck: a wealthy volunteer who instinctively knew how to excavate. Then he found his mind drifting yet again back to Ali and the bungalow. The same doubts. The same fears. He took his bucket to the spoil heap, emptied it, then returned to the trowel-line. Alistair hadn't noticed him get up – he was so deep in concentration. Dammit, Alan thought, this is stupid. I'm in a trench, doing what I love, with people I respect. Mind over matter.

And this time it worked: the rhythm of the trowelling, the peace, the occasional slight comment, 'blimey, that was a big worm', calmed and focused his mind on the job at hand. For about an hour there was quiet, as everyone concentrated on their work. Then the archaeologist working at the southern end of the trench, close to the sexton's shed, called across to Alan. Her shout was loud, urgent. Alan almost jumped out of his skin. What the hell? He got out of the trench and walked rapidly to where she was standing and waving one arm.

He had more or less expected the first real action would be from here, where there'd been some modern disturbance – lumps of cement, tiles and brick rubble, probably dumped there when the estate builders were constructing the fine sexton's shed. In fact 'shed' wasn't the right way to describe what was in effect a small garage-sized brick and mortar building.

Alan stopped and looked down. He wasn't very happy with what he saw. Perhaps, he thought, we might have machined a bit deep, but that rubble would have taken an age to have shifted by hand. And anyhow, you can often do more damage when tired and careless after working all day with a mattock, than with a machine. Paula, one of PFC's most experienced diggers, had carefully removed all the remaining builders' debris and had just trowelled a short distance into the underlying sub-soil to expose a clean surface. In the process she had come across fragments of very thin bone. At first, she told Alan, she thought they came from a burrowing animal, maybe a rat, fox or rabbit.

'But then,' she handed Alan a piece of bone, 'I found this.'

Alan took it. One glance was enough. In his hand was a wafer thin skull bone of a very, very young baby.

Alan handed the tiny bone back to Paula, and knelt by the side of the trench. He looked down sadly at the pathetic little scraps that had once been a human being. Nobody likes digging the remains of young babies. It's not just the emotion, the tragedy – although that enters into it – but they also present some formidable practical challenges. For a start, the bones are so tiny and very, very, fragile. They can easily be snapped, even when working with a toothpick and fine paintbrush. He stood up with a sigh. Paula was staring at the grave – for that's what it had to be – with a serious expression. Alan thought he knew what was worrying her, but even so he asked:

'What's up?'

'Horrible, isn't it? Of course I'll do it, but I'm not too keen on digging neonates…'

She used the slang technical term to avoid saying 'babies'.

'Yes,' Alan agreed, knowing full well why she felt as she did, 'Yes, they can be very tricky. I've always tried to steer clear of them myself.'

He paused, then doing his best to sound cheerful, suggested: 'I know, let's be decisive. It's time for a cup of tea, but first I'll give Harry a ring. We need her out here.'

'D'you think she'll dig…' she was seeking the right word, 'Dig…it?'

Alan felt the same: somehow 'him' or 'her' seemed inappropriate.

'Yes, I'm sure she will. She likes to do the tricky stuff herself.'

Alan had started to pull the phone from his pocket, when they heard the now familiar creak of the churchyard gate behind them. They both looked up. Talk of the devil, he thought, as he pushed the phone back. Harriet had just arrived, together with her graduate student, Amy. Alan beckoned with his arm and they walked straight over.

Harriet stepped into the trench and bent down to examine the bones.

'Hm, that's a little bit unusual, but not unheard of.'

She was thinking aloud, but Alan needed to know.

'Unusual? What's unusual?'

He was impressed with her professional attitude. She was interested in the bones for what they could reveal about the site and she had the strength and experience not to let her emotions get in the way, unlike poor Paula.

She had started to excavate, but very, very carefully, using a dentist's toothpick, which she drew from a roll of tools in her shoulder bag.

'These bones have been constricted,' she continued, half to herself, 'they're wrapped...no...they've been pushed into something. Maybe a bag?'

There was a pause while she investigated further. Then she looked up.

'That's not so common in most later Christian burials, where even young babies are properly laid-out. Of course medieval babies were always swaddled...'

She bent down again and continued working for a few minutes in silence, then Amy asked Alan in a quiet voice so as not to disturb Harriet, who was now working with a magnifying glass, very close to the ground, 'But surely we're just outside the graveyard. That's the churchyard wall, isn't it?' She pointed to the low stone wall beneath which the contractors would insert the foul water pipe when the dig was finished. 'Wouldn't that explain why it's bundled-up, too?'

'Yes it would. At least I think it...'

Alan hesitated. Something was wrong. A thought had struck him. He turned round and headed back to the Land Rover, where he kept the maps and site plans.

Alan knew that in medieval, and as recently as Victorian times, the Church's attitude to the burial of unbaptised children had sometimes been very harsh. Especially to bereaved parents. Sometimes the more humane priests and vicars would contrive to baptise a dead or dying child, even when still inside its mother's womb, provided they could lay a finger on it and pronounce the magic words. This sounds extraordinary to modern ears, but without baptism, a child was not allowed to be buried in the holy ground of a graveyard.

From time to time contractors working close by churches still found little bundles of bones pressed up close to the stones of churchyard walls, as if hoping to catch a trace of Divine Grace, which might somehow manage to filter out through the stonework. In the past, people believed that without that Grace, which previous canny Popes had decreed only the Church could dispense, a child could never enter heaven. Far worse, without the Church's blessing, a stillborn child could never be reunited with its parents in the afterlife. And in an age of faith, such denial of Grace would have been unimaginable mental cruelty. It was the ultimate moral blackmail and the Church had continued to profit from it for centuries... Alan took a deep breath. He had to suppress his anger.

He laid the plan of the churchyard out on the Land Rover's bonnet. And then suddenly it struck him. He could have kicked himself. How could he have missed it? The sexton's shed had been built along, and immediately inside, the line of the medieval wall. That meant that the Victorian wall, probably re-using stone from its medieval predecessor, had been built about five metres into the graveyard. He walked briskly towards the perimeter, at the point where the Victorian diversion rejoined the older line. He pulled away some ivy and brushed aside the dead leaves and roots. One glance was enough. The join was obvious: the new stonework and the harder mortar of the later masonry was clear to see.

He stood back for a moment, thinking about the implications of this. At first it seemed to explain everything.

But did it? The more he turned it over in his mind, the more doubtful he became.

As Alan returned to the trench, Alistair came up to them with a tray of steaming mugs of tea. He had fitted into their small team as if he'd been working with them for years. Having successfully managed her escape from the dead baby, Paula had appointed herself tea lady and had dispatched Alistair who was plainly itching to see what had been found.

'Presumably it's medieval, buried just outside the churchyard?'

Alan smiled. Alistair knew his stuff. Who could blame him for making the same mistake as the rest of them?

'Yes, Alistair,' Alan replied thoughtfully, 'it could be medieval, for all I know,' he paused, 'but it's certainly not outside the churchyard...' He broke off, frowning, then continued: 'nor is the septic tank, come to that. And I wouldn't be at all surprised if we don't find a load of bodies when we clear the ground for that.'

He then produced the plan and explained about the diversion of the churchyard wall.

'But why do it? Why bend the wall?' Alistair asked.

'Presumably,' Alan replied 'to allow the insertion of that rather grand sexton's shed.'

'That's typical of my great-great-grandfather,' Alistair said, smiling broadly, 'if he'd put the shed over there, closer to the road and on unconsecrated ground, it would have been on estate land. And he wasn't going to part with that for nothing, even to the Church, was he?'

Alan didn't believe this for a moment, but he decided not to say anything. In his experience when someone suggested a simple motive, like miserliness, he was always suspicious.

Any man prepared to build such a grand shed wouldn't mind parting with a few square feet of ground. It would all be part of his display of wealth. No, he thought, it didn't add up. What ought to have been an obscure corner of a country churchyard was now starting to look interesting.

But he didn't want to upset Alistair so he dodged the question – for now, at least.

'Still, your distinguished ancestor did do Guthlic's proud. I don't think I've ever come across such a fine sexton's shed in a parish church before. Certainly never seen one with a coat of arms above the door. That's the sort of thing you find with abbeys or cathedrals. It's very smart. Very smart indeed.'

'Yes, AAC liked his coat of arms,' Alistair added, 'he used to put it everywhere. It's terracotta, of course. Made in Stoke-on-Trent by a firm called Bearstows. The estate accounts show he bought two batches, amounting in all to half a gross.'

'Seventy-two?' Alan wasn't quite certain how many were in a gross.

'That's right. He put them on all estate buildings: cottages, farm buildings. You name it. We've still got almost a dozen unused ones, up at the Hall. Each is individually numbered and marked with the maker's stamp on the back ...'

Their chat was suddenly interrupted by Harriet, who hadn't stopped working on the bones.

'Bloody hell,' she said in a very audible whisper, 'there's another one.' She looked up to Alan, as she spoke. As she moved her head he could distinctly see the pale hip, or was it the shoulder, bones of another infant, in the dark of the trench below her. He took a deep breath, but said nothing. There was nothing to say. He could see by Harriet's look that she agreed with him. She resumed excavation.

Alan remained at the trench edge, deep in thought. A group of babies argued against a medieval date and their shallow burial suggested they were far more recent. And what about the diversion of the churchyard wall, how did that fit in? All his archaeological experience told him that there had to be a link. Maybe more facts might help him, but sometimes they had the opposite effect: they obscured. No, he knew in his heart of hearts that now was the time when things would be clearest. He leant against the wall and the clammy damp of the cold stonework against his legs gave him a sharp chill. He flinched. But when his thoughts resumed he discovered that he suddenly understood the connection between walls and bodies, bodies and walls... and family honour.

A Sense of Place II

Blackfen Prison

Thirteen

The next day Alan was driving back to Harriet's across a frozen fen, on a cold winter's afternoon. Even though it was barely mid-February, the sun, when it did manage to appear between rainclouds, had begun to acquire a little warmth. But not today, which had been dank and overcast. Bloody miserable. By rights, Alan ought to have been feeling optimistic. After all, the two babies were an unusual discovery: puzzling and unexpected. But there was something about them that he found profoundly unsettling. The way they were found, bundled into a bag. Behind this, there lurked another thought: had this also been Sofia's fate, to be broken up and discarded?

He'd set his mobile to silent, as Brutus was too noisy to hear a ringtone anyway. And now it was vibrating in his shirt pocket. Rapidly he pulled into a field gateway and answered. It was DCI Lane. At last.

'Hi Richard, I've been trying to get hold of you. We need to talk. It's about Ali.'

'Great minds and all that,' replied Lane. 'Norman Grant phoned me last night. They've been having security problems…'

Alan's heart sank at these words.

'Oh no, Richard,' he broke in, 'don't tell me tomorrow's cancelled.'

'No, relax, Alan,' Lane continued, 'It's just a heads up. It looks like our friend Ali might be smuggling mobile phones into the prison. No concrete proof as yet, but we're looking into it at our end.'

Oh that old scam, Alan thought. But Ali, why was he doing it? He suspected it was about more than just making money.

'I thought the authorities had said they were going to stamp it out?'

'Supposedly yes, but there are ways and means. Anyhow, it would seem there's a turf war inside Blackfen...'

The signal out in the Fens can be terrible and now the line was breaking up.

'What, for control of the phone supply?'

'Among the prisoners, yes. There's also tension among the staff between outside security consultants, who are backed by the Governor, and the in-house people. So nobody seems to be talking to anybody.'

Alan had little time for internal politics, either from the inmates or the staff. He cut straight to the point.

'So how will it all affect me?'

'Indirectly, from what Grant said. They're having to tighten up on everything. Especially on any opportunities for one-to-one communication between inmates and outsiders.'

'In case phones get smuggled in?'

'Yes, that's the idea.'

'So how on earth am I going to get to speak to Ali? I *must* see him face-to-face.'

'I agree. I'll see what strings I can pull.'

'Great, thanks, Richard. But there's something else…'

'I'm sorry, Alan, this line is terrible. Let's catch up tomorrow evening when you're done.'

'I'm not sure it can wait…'

As he spoke, Alan became aware that the line had died. He looked at the screen: no signal. Had Lane heard him? No telling.

And then the truth of the matter hit him. It was obvious, how could he have been so bloody stupid? If Ali was behind the mobile phone scam, he could easily communicate with the outside world. Ordering an arson attack was simply a matter of, quite literally, pressing a button.

* * *

Nine hours later, Alan was back on the road. He pulled wearily down on Brutus's heavy steering wheel and drove into the prison car park for the second Lifers' Club session. All the way across the South Holland fens he'd been trying to work out his options. Any sane person with a modicum of self-preservation would simply walk away. Scrap the entire course. He could easily pretend to Grant and Lane that Paul had read him the riot act about taking time off. Of course this would be a big white lie because, as ever, Alan had been at pains to insist to Paul, like all his other clients, that he would be working for PFC as a freelance. But Lane and Grant wouldn't know that. At all events, he thought, it was an option, but one of last resort – a nuclear one. Before he took that drastic step he needed to see Ali again. He wouldn't challenge him directly, he wasn't that naïve, no matter what Lane might think. But he'd find a way of bringing up the subject of the fire and see how Ali reacted. That is, provided he was allowed to talk to him at all.

Once inside the prison, he was assigned an escort officer. On his previous visit, the officer had been friendly and they had chatted away amiably. But not this time. Now the man was taciturn. They also seemed to be taking a different route to the classroom used in the previous session. Maybe, Alan wondered, they'd been allocated a new place, because the A-level course audience was going to be smaller than the introductory slide show. He suggested this to his guide.

'No, sir,' he replied, 'Administration have decided that we're to be in a smaller facility. More secure. Better camera surveillance.'

This didn't sound good. Alan was dubious:

'But it is a proper… a proper classroom, is it?'

'So they tell us, sir.' This carried the implication that whatever 'they' told the staff was of little worth. He continued: 'But it's what we've been given.'

The conversation had ended.

After what seemed like an interminable trek through identical brightly lit corridors, they arrived at a classroom. Alan looked around him. It was a small space and the seating wasn't raked, like for the previous session, neither were there any windows. It felt claustrophobic and airless. The acoustics were flat, too. It would be hard work addressing an audience here, even a small one. But what the hell. Resigned, Alan went over to the projector and plugged in his laptop, then stood back and waited for the class to enter.

This was going to be less of an 'occasion' than the first session, and normally this would have made Alan relax; but not now. In fact, it seemed to have a slightly different effect. He felt low. Lifeless.

A side door opened, and the Education Officer, who he now knew quite well after many phone calls, entered.

'They'll be here shortly, Alan.'

He stood beside Alan. They said nothing.

They stood there for what seemed like a quarter of an hour, but was probably nearer five minutes. Eventually the man beside him spoke in a low whisper.

'Sorry about this…'

'That's all right.'

What else could he say?

'It's been odd. The place has been weird all day. There's been a security flap. Something to do with illicit mobile phones. Education is based in Bedford, so we've only heard rumours, but when I set out this morning word had it that everyone here is brassed off.'

'Seems odd,' Alan replied under his breath, 'surely phones and prisoners don't mix, do they? Or are the officers taking a cut of the business?'

'There may be some of that, although I'd be surprised if it were the officers. More likely part-time staff. Cleaners, kitchen assistants, that sort of person. No, the problem seems to have been the way they've handled it.'

'What, the Governor?'

'Yes, him – and the Administration. It's common knowledge he's not very popular with the staff. A bit heavy-handed. They say he talks down to them. La-di-da. You know how it is.'

Alan was about to reply when he was cut short by the flashing red light. He counted the prisoners into the room. There were nine of them. So he hadn't even started and three students had already dropped out. He tried not to take it personally, but his pride was wounded. He knew it was ridiculous, after all three less students meant more individual interview time. More time with Ali.

He spotted Ali immediately. He had anticipated that the younger man might try to avoid his gaze, but he didn't. Their eyes met and Ali's stare was intense and unsmiling. It was neither defiant nor threatening. If anything it was worse: it told him absolutely nothing. Deadpan.

But that stare had done the trick.

Alan straightened and almost shuddered; he'd been hit by a massive shot of adrenalin.

As the students settled down, the Education Officer handed Alan a full list of their names, plus a few notes they'd prepared themselves, about their outside interests. Nothing was said about the inmates' crimes, or sentences.

The Education Department had agreed that each session would begin with an hour's talk on a particular subject, followed by an hour and a half 'contact time', when the students would do practical work with artefacts which Alan would provide. During this time too, Alan would have one-to-one interviews with each man, when they'd discuss the previous month's essay, and any other problems to do with the course.

As this was the initial A-level session, there were no essays, so Alan had intended to use the interviews to learn why each student had decided to enrol. Or at least that's what he'd told the powers that be.

The Education Department stipulated that a table and two chairs should be set to one side of the classroom. They'd be positioned close by a panic button, so there'd be no need for closer supervision, as there would be at least one officer in the room. That was the theory. The practice was different.

Alan gave his set piece lecture: starting with a rapid historical introduction to archaeology, which lasted for about half his allotted time. Then he drilled down to detail. He wanted his class to realise what the modern subject could achieve and he used the notes Harriet had given him on DNA, and the analysis of burial rites to estimate the extent and rate of possible Saxon incursions. It was heard in respectful silence and he couldn't judge how well, or how badly, it had gone down. Then, precisely one hour after he had begun speaking, he finished.

At that point an additional officer entered the room and helped the two others arrange the furniture. It wasn't at all what Alan had imagined: instead of a cosy table and two chairs they dragged the lecturer's desk-cum-table to one side and placed chairs at either end, a generous two, maybe two and a half metres apart. An officer was standing at the centre of the long table that separated the two chairs. He looked like an ex-military man. He stood stock still, legs slightly apart, hands behind his back, staring into the middle distance. All he lacked was a sentry box.

When the arrangements had been completed, an officer announced to the Education Officer in a very loud voice:

'Interview arrangements now in place, SIR!'

Visibly deafened by this, the Education Officer flinched and, turning to Alan, muttered under his breath:

'Christ, this is going to be hard work. It's all part of the security row. You must see the Governor before you go home. *Please*. We can't do a damn thing like this.'

In a much louder voice he announced to the class:

'As this is to be a full A-level course, our specialist teacher Mr Alan Cadbury has asked to have some ten minutes for individual interviews with each student.'

He was cut off by one of the officers who whispered something in his ear. The room went silent. Then he resumed.

'I have been reminded that due to current operational difficulties, all unaccompanied one-to-one contacts will have to cease. So supervision will be in place and the interviews will be reduced to just two minutes.'

When he had finished, the officer nodded his approval.

Alan's adrenalin was now surging, red hot and furious. How the hell was he going to get anything out of Ali in this situation? He took a deep breath. Stay cool, he told himself. Take your time and choose your words wisely.

* * *

At the final planning session Alan and the Education Officer had decided to break with tradition and not order the individual sessions alphabetically – an atttempt, pathetic in the current circumstances, to make the process 'less mechanistic'. So there were two other inmates before Ali. The first was a university student who was completely at sea in prison. He had long given up trying to relate to others and his replies were terse, his eyes to the ground. Alan made a note of his name for future sessions. The next man was confident, but very poorly educated; Alan couldn't decide if he'd been let down by the education system; again he made a note of his name, with the simple query: 'Thick?'

Ali Kabul was next. And it didn't help that Alan was now very frustrated. Ali detected Alan's mood, instantly. Slowly he smiled. Alan got the impression that Ali was enjoying seeing him so fed up.

Sitting at opposite ends of the table, Alan could clearly read Ali's body language: he was very confident. Alan deliberately adjusted his posture. He sat up, leant forward and placed both his hands on the table: a gesture of control, he hoped.

He looked down at the sheet before him.

'Tell me, Mr Kabul, why did you join this course?'

'You know why.'

The officer standing between them cleared his throat, then continued to stare straight ahead. His presence had the effect of a reinforced concrete wall between them.

Ali paused briefly before Alan replied.

'I'd like to hear it from you, directly.'

'I like old things.'

'Is there any specific aspect of archaeology that you'd like to focus on?'

'Oh, you know, dead bodies.'

Alan felt like he'd just been punched in the gut. Ali was actually taunting him. The officer was right there, right next to them, and he just didn't care.

He was goading Alan on, daring him to mention Sofia.

OK, thought Alan, if he really wants to play it like that…

Alan leant forward, and spoke to Ali in a softer, more informal tone.

Almost as if he was confiding in him.

'I'm sorry the lecture was a bit disappointing.'

Ali shrugged.

'It was all right.'

'I had limited resources. My house burnt down a few days ago. I lost half my books.'

'You're fucking joking?'

'Language, Mr Kabul,' warned the officer.

Alan willed him not to intervene.

Ali was leaning forward in his chair now. He looked shocked. He seemed genuinely concerned.

'What happened?'

'The police suspect arson.'

Not strictly true, thought Alan. Or at least not yet. But he wanted to ramp up the pressure.

Ali was shaking his head, part angry, part incredulous.

'You got out OK?'

'Luckily, I wasn't there when it happened.'

'Right, so whoever did it just wanted to scare you, not kill you. That's something, I guess.'

The prison officer was staring straight ahead still, but there was an intensity to his gaze that suggested to Alan that he was listening with every fibre in his body. Alan was aware that they were skating on very thin ice indeed.

'Anyway, back to the course. Is there any period that you are particularly interested in?'

But Ali wasn't listening.

'I can't believe you lost your books, man. That really sucks.'

He looked genuinely upset. In that moment, for the first time since they'd re-met, Alan saw the Ali that he used to know was now gazing straight at him.

The officer coughed and looked at his watch.

'Your time's up, Kabul.' He glanced down at the list on his clipboard, 'Tell Evans he's next. Jump to it, lad!'

* * *

At the end of the individual sessions, as the students were filing out of the room, the Education Officer came up and told Alan that the governor was keen to see him, if he could spare the time. This was what Alan wanted, even though he was now desperate to be out of the place and back at Harriet's.

He was feeling as low as he could remember. He'd come hoping for clarity of some sort, but now he felt more confused and muddled than ever. He stared vacantly at the wall and waited, while one of the officers was detailed to escort him to Grant's office. Then they set off.

After five minutes of walking along identical corridors, all brightly lit by overhead strip lights, they passed through a double-locked door into the Administration Block. Alan was aware of a sudden relaxation in the atmosphere. His escorting officer could read it in his face:

'It gets you every time, doesn't it?'

'What, d'you feel the change too?' Alan replied, surprised at this.

'Yes, I do. Every time. But it's worse for the secretaries and people on this side. Some of them refuse point-blank to come over to our side. They won't budge from out of here.'

And with that he closed and locked the heavy door behind him.

The wheels of Blackfen Prison, like so many British civil institutions, were lubricated not so much by harsh discipline, as by endless cups of tea, the latest of which was placed before Alan and the Governor by his Personal Assistant, who then returned to her desk in the anteroom.

'So I see here,' the Governor glanced down at the sheets of paper before him, 'that you've got nine students. That's good.

Very good. You must have made your introduction last month highly enticing. I certainly enjoyed it.'

Alan looked suitably modest.

'I did my best. But having got nine, can I expect to keep them all?'

'As a rule, yes, you can – unless of course they don't come up to scratch and you decide to drop one, or more, of them. That happens quite often. And if somebody isn't coping, it's better to shed them. You can do it quite gently, but if they're obviously struggling, it just adds to the other stresses of prison life. You'd be doing them no favours if you kept them on.'

There was a quiet knock on the door, and Grant's PA came in to remove their tea things. The Governor was thumbing through his files.

'Right,' Grant began, 'those lists. Who do we have here?' He ran his finger down the page. 'None of them have been assessed as dangerous, but of course they wouldn't be here in the first place, if they were little angels. Have a look for yourself.'

He handed Alan three sheets of print-out. Alan went through the motions of reading them through.

'I'm slightly interested in this chap, Ali Kabul.'

He held up the notes and pointed to Ali's name. The governor looked down at the files.

'Ah yes. He arrived last year…'

Alan decided it was time to come clean. Or at least partially.

'I could swear,' he broke in, 'I've seen him before.'

'Oh really?' The Governor was obviously interested. Alan guessed it wasn't often that teaching staff were acquainted with inmates. Again he referred to his notes.

'It says here, he was convicted at Leicester Crown Court for murder.'

'I was on a dig at a place called Flax Hole, in Leicester, back in February 2002 at the time of the murder and this young man…'

'Are you sure it was him? Young…'

Alan suspected he was going to say 'young Asians', but thought better of it. 'Youngsters can look very similar, especially if they're wearing those hoodie things.'

Alan sympathised with Grant's brief moment of discomfort, again those cultural prejudices, lurking just beneath the surface. No-one was immune, not even the most well-meaning prison Governor.

'He never wore a hoodie, but I got to talk to him on several occasions. He was a pleasant young man. Very intelligent and yes, I'm certain the man I saw this afternoon was him.'

'Quite certain?'

'Absolutely. He visited the site several times. He also showed a real interest and ability. I'd have employed him, if I could, but he was already running a small delivery business.'

Alan paused briefly then continued, 'I also met the victim, his sister Sofia, too.'

Norman Grant got up from behind his desk and went over to a filing cabinet from which he withdrew yet another folder. He rapidly scanned it.

'Ah yes,' he said as he resumed his seat, 'I remember this one well. Interesting case, Mr Ali Kabul. A bright lad. He joined us early last February and was sent here direct from Leicester Crown Court. It was one of the first of those unpleasant "honour" killing cases, but Kabul wasn't caught and convicted until almost seven years after the killing.'

'Why on earth did it take so long to arrest him?'

Alan knew the answer of course, but he was keen to see if Grant's version of events tallied with Lane's. Or if there was more to it; if Lane had been selective with his disclosure of information.

'The usual thing. The entire family clammed up. Everyone had ridiculously over-watertight alibis. It was the murdered girl's fiancé…'

He consulted the notes again and continued, 'That shopped them. A young Sikh lawyer named Indajit Singh. He was convinced that his bride-to-be, Sofia, had been murdered.'

'Presumably because he was a Sikh and their union would bring shame on the family.'

'Precisely.'

'They never found the body, did they?'

'I'm afraid I'm not party to that level of detail.'

Alan doubted that very much. From Grant's defensive body language he could tell that this was a sensitive area. And no wonder – a murder conviction based solely on a confession, without any forensic evidence, had to be a contentious issue.

Time to try a different line of questioning.

'So how long did young Ali get?' Alan asked.

Again, he knew the answer, but was keen to hear Grant's interpretation of events.

'Not as long as I'd have thought, to be frank. If he's a good boy, I wouldn't be surprised if the Parole Board don't let him out in nine years, maybe even less.'

'And is he a "good boy"?'

'So far.'

The Governor paused. Then continued, 'How can I put it? He's an operator to his fingertips. And we have some grounds to believe he's involved with illicit mobile phones. He certainly uses them. But then, sadly, so do most inmates.'

'On what grounds? Have you been monitoring their calls?'

Grant smiled.

'If we could do that we'd be able to cut the crime rate in the outside world by a record percentage. No. We just know that the smuggled phones originated from Leicester, which puts Kabul in the frame.'

'You've traced their SIM cards?'

'Oh no, nothing as simple as that. They never have personalised SIMs. To be honest I don't know all the details, but it's something the police have told us. And it's been confirmed by independent security consultants.'

'I must admit I wouldn't be surprised to learn that Ali was involved in the phone scam. Doing business seems to be in his blood.'

'I'm not sure I understand.'

'I offered Ali help to get a place at university but he turned it down in favour of setting up his own van delivery service.'

'That confirms my impression of the man,' Grant replied, pencilling a note in his files, 'he's someone who can organise people and things.'

'He's also clever. Very clever. So what I don't understand is, if there was no concrete evidence against him, why would he confess and condemn himself?'

'According to these notes,' the Governor replied, 'when he did confess he expressed great remorse for what he'd done. Apparently that affected the jury. According to friends and family he regularly attended the Mosque and would pray for forgiveness. They said he was even planning a pilgrimage to Mecca…'

'How much of that do we believe – any of it?'

'You tell me,' the Governor replied. 'I've no idea. But it would seem the jury bought it – or at least some of it. And then of course there was the question of his age – and that can't be disputed, as he still possesses his Turkish birth certificate.'

'So how old was he when he committed the crime?'

Grant referred to his notes.

'One month the wrong side of eighteen. If he'd been a month younger, things wouldn't have gone so hard for him.'

The Governor took the file over to his desk, where he sat down. Then the older man voiced what they were both thinking.

'Honour killing. It's so hard to believe in this day and age, isn't it?'

'It certainly is.'

'But what are the chances,' Grant said, focusing on Alan, 'of you being there at that precise place and time? And then turning up here so soon after his arrival?'

This didn't sound like an accusation, but Alan knew he couldn't be too careful. He tried to sound casual in his reply.

'To be honest, I'd have been surprised if I hadn't been. Nearly all sites for redevelopment near the city centre are crawling with archaeology. And at the time we were being run off our feet.'

'And the sites: I guess most are Roman, aren't they? Like ours here?'

Alan welcomed the opportunity of deflecting attention away from himself and back onto Grant's interest in archaeology. *Ratae Corieltaurum*, Roman Leicester, was a major centre.

'Yes,' Alan replied, 'but the Roman City had large extramural suburbs too. And there's also plenty of Saxon and medieval stuff around, not to mention post-medieval and industrial sites. I began as a Site Supervisor with the City Archaeological Unit. I had a two year contract. I supervised dozens of projects, large and small. Then I set up with another man and we did Flax Hole together.'

'So not for the City Unit?'

'No. We did it ourselves.'

The Governor was interested. He obviously had a huge appetite for archaeology of any period:

'What sort of dig was it?'

'Not exactly drawn-out. Three weeks, as I recall, but a good one. Can't say we found any bodies so we barely made it into the local papers. It was an industrial site. Shallow, clay-lined pits filled with lots and lots of evil-smelling organic mud. Foul stuff. You simply couldn't wash the stink off your hands.'

'It sounds to me like the name of the place was a bit of a clue. Presumably those stagnant pits had something to do with rotting of flax – don't they call it retting?'

'Spot on. Normally flax-processing happens in the wetter parts of Britain, like around Manchester or in Belfast, so to find it that far east was important.'

The Governor referred to the file for a final time, before taking it back to the cabinet. 'That's odd...' he muttered, half to himself, then louder, to Alan: 'There's no mention anywhere here of the dig. When precisely did it happen?'

'It was the first winter I worked with my own small team – and that was 2002. I'd guess it was late winter, because I spent most of January with the City Unit on a far more interesting Roman site near the Jewry Wall.'

'So you were almost certainly working there when the murder happened?'

Alan's attempts to fudge the issue proved useless. He should have guessed that Grant would be a stickler for the facts.

'Well, it's starting to look that way. Must admit, it rather gives me the creeps... not a very nice feeling at all.'

Alan paused for a moment, as if reflecting on the past.

'Yes, of course,' Grant said gently. 'You're not hardened to these situations like the rest of us. I apologise.'

'It's hardly your fault. It's just a bit of a shock, that's all.'

'Just let me know if you need anything. More support. More student supervision. We'd hate to lose you over this.'

Alan saw his chance and he leapt on it.

'Actually, it's not really a matter of more supervision.'

Alan paused and then held out his hands in a gesture of appeal.

'I'm having a great deal of trouble making one-to-one contact with the students.'

'Due to the security crack-down?'

'Yes, I think so.'

'Oh dear,' Grant replied, sighing deeply, 'some of the staff think I'm accusing them. But I'm not.' He paused, then continued, 'But rules are rules and when I'm warned by outside authorities that something's happening in my prison I have to follow a set of strict Home Office guidelines. I've had to raise our Security Level by two points and that has all sorts of unwanted consequences. For everyone, I'm afraid.'

'It's just that it makes things very difficult – almost impossible – if you're trying to get through to students.'

'Yes, I'm so sorry.'

Alan adopted the pose of an over-anxious teacher, desperately keen to 'connect' with his students.

'These aren't ordinary students. They're at a huge disadvantage before we even start on the course work. So somehow I have to get through to them. Establish motivation: the will to succeed, if you know what I mean. The thing is, it's impossible to talk at all freely if there's an officer standing directly beside you. Would it be feasible to arrange something slightly less obtrusively secure?'

Grant stood silently, frowning. Then he replied, 'I'm sure you'll realise that presents us with very real problems. One-to-one interviews with prisoners of this category aren't easy to arrange under any circumstances. Let alone during a security alert...'

'What,' Alan broke in, 'even if there are panic buttons, cameras and everything else?'

'Yes, even then. We're worried about a hostage situation.'

'What about a partition?' Alan suggested, 'or a grill? Like in the main visitors meeting area.'

Grant pondered for a moment.

'Yes, that would probably be our best bet. Under those circumstances the officers could remain outside.'

'D'you think you could fix that up? For next month?'

The Governor smiled. He clearly wasn't going to let Alan push him.

'I'll do what I can.'

Fourteen

Alan was glad to leave the prison car park behind him. That place gave him the creeps. The lights, the corridors, the endless locks and that bloody great wall. He could think of nothing more lonely that being banged up with thousands of strangers. But Ali seemed to be coping. More than coping, actually: he was thriving. Alan could see from the way the other prisoners respected Ali that he'd fitted in. He was part of their community. Not only that, he'd started to climb the ladder. One day he'd be in charge. And what would he be like then, Alan wondered, a malevolent tyrant, or a kindly leader? Alan still couldn't believe that the young man he'd known at Flax Hole was remotely capable of murdering his own sister. But what about the new, and harder, Ali? What about him?

As he drove across the huge, dark open expanse of Dawyck Fen, the blowing snow was starting to accumulate in deep folds in the dykes on either side of the road. But his mind was still on Ali. He suddenly realised, there was another option. Ali had seemed genuinely shocked to hear about the arson attack. What if he'd simply mentioned to a member of his family that Alan had visited the prison? The bungalow could have been torched by the Kabuls without Ali knowing. If one of them had been Sofia's murderer, they certainly wouldn't want Alan snooping around Ali.

Suddenly his back wheels lost traction and Brutus began to slew across the narrow road towards the dyke. Instinctively he lifted his foot to stop it touching the brake and steered towards the side, eventually regaining traction when the knobbly tyres hit some potholes along the edge of the tarmac. Alan sighed heavily. A near squeak. Must concentrate when there's ice below the snow. He stopped and eased the small gear lever into four-wheel drive, low ratio. Grinding forward; peering into the night, but all he could see was a dead straight road. And darkness.

He was on his own.

* * *

By the time Alan arrived at Mavis Startby the snow was blowing in thick from off the Wolds foothills behind the house. That was why the village had a terrible reputation locally for snowdrifts. Most winters, it seemed to find itself cut-off for several days. Now the snow had stopped and the clear night sky was bitterly cold. Harriet's cottage looked wonderfully picturesque in the moonlight, as he parked outside the front garden. But he had no eyes for the scene. He had to speak to Richard Lane, and urgently.

He was fumbling in his pockets for the spare front door key, when Harriet opened it. She proffered him a glass of white wine, which he took and carried into the house.

'It's fish,' she said, 'bought it in Boston market...'

'Won't be a second,' he replied over his shoulder, as she followed him into the kitchen. 'Must quickly phone someone.'

Alan went up to his room, closed the door and dialled Lane's number.

It rang several times. Then Lane answered.

'Alan, how did you get on with Ali?'

'I'll tell you in a sec. But there's something else you need to know. As a matter of urgency.'

A brief pause. Lane was surprised. Quickly he recovered.

'OK, go ahead.'

'I can't remember if I told you, but the first time I met Ali was at that recruiting session after my first talk.'

'That's right…'

'Well, for some reason I mentioned I was living next to the pub in Tubney.'

'Why on earth did you do that?'

Lane almost sounded angry with him. And he had every right to be, it was an amateurish mistake.

'I don't know. Something to say. Put him at ease, maybe.'

'You mentioned the pub's name?'

'Yes, I did. And then the fire happened. One hell of a coincidence. Or was it? And that what makes me worried now. In fact, Richard, I thought I might take you up on your offer to have me stay.'

'Yes,' There was a pause. Alan could sense that Lane had had second thoughts. 'Come to think of it, Alan, I'm not sure that was such a good idea. At the time it made sense: you were an old friend in dire straits, but I've been thinking it through.'

'And?'

'And if something fishy was indeed going on, it would immediately give the game away if you stayed with us.'

'Which would imply that I'm being watched?'

'Possibly, yes. It's always best to suspect the worst, and if the Kabuls thought we were working together, Ali would quit your course immediately and go to ground.'

'Yes,' Alan said quietly, 'You're right, of course.'

'That said, if you wanted to pull out of the whole thing, I wouldn't blame you in the slightest.'

'I can't do that, Richard. I just can't.'

'I rather thought you might say that.'

There was a moment of silence between them. Then Lane was back in business mode:

'So, what's the latest with young Ali?'

'I had an interview with him this afternoon.'

'So it went ahead, despite the security alert?'

'Sort-of. They wouldn't allow me proper one-to-one interviews with any of my class. There had to be a screw standing between us.'

'And?'

'And Ali managed to remain in control. That's the only way I can put it. And when I asked him what area of archaeology he was interested in, you won't believe what he said.'

'Go on.'

'He said he was interested in dead bodies.'

Alan heard a sharp intake of breath from Lane.

'With the officer standing there, hearing every word?'

'Exactly.'

'You're right. It's all about control. But perhaps not directed at you. Maybe his words were meant for the listening officer?'

'Maybe. But why? No, it felt... personal.'

There was a muffled rattling noise, as the phone was placed on something hard. Alan could hear papers rustle, then Lane's voice returned:

'Sorry about the noises-off. I've taken the phone to my desk.'

There was another pause, then he resumed. 'I think we'd be stupid to ignore it out of hand.'

'I'm glad you say that, Richard.'

Alan was more than glad. But he had underestimated his friend. There was more to come.

'Look Alan, everything you've told me so far has been a bit vague, but I'm beginning to think you might be onto something. So I've been doing a little ferreting around in the case files, at our end. Now most of what I've found you already know about, but not necessarily in such detail.'

'Well, give it to me anyhow.'

Again Alan could hear the sound of papers. Lane was muttering as he rapidly read through the notes under his breath. Then he slowed down and raised his voice.

'Oh yes, this was good: "during his confession from the witness box, Ali Kabul stated, while weeping, that he felt much regret at what he had done. It had been a mad impulse. Despite this admission, he then went on to claim that his sister's death was the only way the shame of her forthcoming union could be removed from his family".'

'Presumably that's what they all say, isn't it?'

'Yes, but a pencil note in the margin says "*Rubbed eyes?*"...'

Lane paused.

'Presumably his eyes were red?' Alan added helpfully.

'Yes,' Lane replied, 'but it's an old trick. Turn your back, rub them hard as you can, and it looks like you've been crying.'

There were more sounds of shuffling papers, then Lane spoke again.

'Now, I'm telling you this in strictest confidence, you understand.'

'Of course.'

'It's to do with the body…'

Alan stiffened. This could be crucial.

'Ali said, and I quote, "I took her dead body to the Humber at high tide and threw it into the sea."'

'Despite what the family had said about her going abroad?'

'Yes,' Lane continued, 'at the trial they admitted they'd lied. They said they were "trying to maintain hope". They didn't want to "further upset the younger members of the family".'

Alan remembered, suddenly, how occasionally Little Mehmet would accompany Ali to the site. He would stomp through the mud, determined to keep up with his older brother. And Ali was so patient and kind with him, explaining the layout of the trenches, telling him stories about the people who worked there, past and present. And he didn't tell him fanciful tales. No embroidered kiddies' stories. Just the simple truth; and the little boy seemed to sense it: wide-eyed, he hung on Ali's every word. How bloody awful for them both, thought Alan, to have that close bond ripped apart.

Lane's brisk voice cut through his thoughts.

'What's your gut feeling, Alan?'

'Doesn't sit right with me.'

'I know what you mean. But to be fair, if I was in their position I wouldn't want to inflict any of this on my kids either, until I absolutely had to. Certainly the court accepted it.'

'I suppose so…' Alan was far from convinced.

'What d'you make of the Humber business?' Lane asked.

'I think he's lying. Driving all that way, with his sister's corpse in the back of the van? I just don't think he had it in him.'

'Well, the CID bought it. They went up there and visited the spot.'

'Which was?'

'An old quay on the south shore of the Humber, used in the '50s and '60s for loading grain into coasters.'

'I suppose it's visible from the approach road up onto the Bridge?'

'Yes it is. Why?'

'Surely it's obvious,' Alan replied. 'Ali passed his driving test a week after his eighteenth birthday. I remember him being very proud of that fact. In subsequent years he drove vans for a living. He must have crossed the Humber Bridge hundreds of times. You know what it's like when you drive the same route again and again: you build up a mental picture of the landscape that's so clear you could walk down its lanes in your mind's eye, even though you've never left the main road. And of course Ali's no fool...'

'No, I think we've clearly established that.'

Alan pressed on. He was eager for every last detail.

'Did they find anything?'

'Where?'

'At that old quay.'

'No. But that's no surprise, is it – seven years later? If it had been a crime scene it had long gone cold. Even the van had probably been scrapped. No tyre marks would survive.'

'And I don't suppose,' Alan added, 'the investigating officers were in a hurry to undermine their own case, were they? So they accepted it.'

Lane could hear the scepticism in Alan's voice.

'So you're not convinced he ditched the body at all, are you?'

'No, I'm not.'

'The thing is, Alan, what's he got to gain by lying? The prosecution produced a marine coastal expert, who claimed the currents along the southern Humber estuary could be very strong, and that a body could soon be carried beyond Grimsby and out into the North Sea on a strong ebb tide. I must say I still think Ali Kabul's story makes good sense.'

While Lane was talking, Alan recalled the young Ali sitting beside him in a trench, his eyes bright with excitement as he showed him how to disentangle the various layers of the section before them. He simply couldn't accept that this intelligent young man was capable of sitting alone in a van, with his dead sister in the back, for the two-hour drive to the Humber. And he certainly couldn't imagine him dragging her body out and rolling it over the quayside into the water – having first cold-bloodedly checked the tide tables. But he was also aware that he mustn't sound too incredulous, or Lane might take offence. And at this stage he needed the information that only the police could provide.

'Of course I could be wrong, I admit that, but I'm increasingly certain something's not quite right about this case, and the evidence the court was given.'

'So you want me to help prove my own Force wrong?'

'It sounds bad if you put it like that,' Alan said, trying to placate his friend. 'I'm sure the police *almost* got it right. But I'm beginning to suspect they may also have been deliberately misled. Perhaps they missed something. Maybe something much larger...'

'Like what?'

Alan guessed Lane was now listening keenly.

'If I knew that, Richard, I'd tell you. But I bet it's got something to do with that family. If I can sort out what happened at Flax Hole before Sofia was killed, I suspect the other pieces of the puzzle would drop into place.'

'Just like that?'

Alan ignored the slight sarcasm in Lane's voice, and continued.

'All I'm trying to say is, I don't think the police will be made to look stupid, if I – if we – can sort this business out. I really don't. You must trust me.'

'You're asking a lot, Alan…' The phone went silent. Then he resumed, 'And yes, I can see: you might possibly have a case. But only possibly. There's still a hell of a long way to go.'

'Does that mean you're in?'

Alan winced at the eagerness in his own voice.

'It means that I'm concerned enough to investigate further.'

Alan realised he was holding his breath. Lane was still speaking.

'But my main concern is your safety, Alan. You said you were staying with a colleague?'

'That's right.'

'And is he aware of your suspicions about the fire?'

'She. No. You said this should stay strictly between us.'

'And so it should, at least for now.'

'But I am worried, Richard. She's a very pleasant person and a damn good archaeologist and I'd never forgive myself if she came to any harm. You don't think she's in any danger, do you?'

There was a brief pause, before Lane replied,

'Not at this early stage, and besides, there's no point in alarming her when we don't have all the facts. However, I'll see to it that the local officers are aware of the situation. We'll keep an eye out for anything suspicious. What's your exact location?'

Alan reeled off Harriet's name and address. Lane repeated it back to him verbatim.

'Thanks, Richard, I really appreciate it.'

'Just doing my job. We'll speak again soon.'

Alan put the phone down and breathed a huge sigh of relief. Maybe the Kabuls – if they were indeed involved in the arson attack – had, in a strange way, done him a favour. Lane was finally taking his concerns seriously. And now that the local police force would be informed he could relax about Harriet's safety. He also knew that part of his relief was due to Lane's insistence on confidentiality. From now on he wouldn't be deliberately telling her half-truths, he'd be simply following instructions.

Alan ventured downstairs in time to hear the back door slam shut. There was a blast of freezing cold air and a few snowflakes. Alan wandered through to the sitting room: it was empty. He peered into the kitchen. Nobody there. The Aga's lids were down. But there was a beautifully set table, complete with candles. The bottle of wine was half-drunk. He went back out into the corridor. Then the back door opened wide and Harriet stood framed: furious, the large pan in her hand, dripping herb butter onto patches of snow on the doormat.

'So much for your "quick chat"! That Dover sole cost me eighteen quid. If you want a meal of rubber fish, it's waiting for you out there in the bin. I'm off to bed.'

And with that she stormed upstairs.

Fifteen

Four days later, and the start of another week. The snow had gone, but as so often happens in England, clean, crisp white was replaced by grubby brown. Even the overcast sky seemed brown; passing lorries, piled high with beet or potatoes fresh out of the clamps, covered both lanes with a mist of fine slurry. Alan was driving Brutus across Dawyck Fen. He needed to get to site on time. So he kept his foot down. Like most fen minor roads this one was a mass of humps and bumps, as pockets of deeply buried peat dried out and shrunk. Locals knew that patching the surface was pointless, because it would be just as bad next year. But the Council did it all the same: if not, mouthy Southey incomers would complain – and they had the votes.

He pulled into the small car park at St Guthlic's and walked across to the churchyard, which now looked more like an excavation, than a place of worship.

Late on Thursday afternoon, when he had been away talking to The Lifers' Club, the County Building Control people had phoned the Parish Council and told them they would have to install a different type of septic tank. It would require a larger hole, which in turn would mean the archaeological trench would have to be extended. It was only a small job – an hour or two at the outside – so Alan suggested they hire a self-drive mini-digger and do it then and there, on Friday afternoon.

But Paul would have none of it. No, he insisted, PFC had a long-term contract with their usual firm, AK Plant, and they must stick to it. And the earliest AK could provide a digger and driver was Monday morning. Alan was furious, as deadlines were now starting to look tight. But Paul was absolutely adamant.

He strode into the churchyard. The JCB driver, a young Asian man from Leicester, had just finished the morning lubrication and was replacing the grease-gun and some oily rags in the digger's tool box. He looked up and greeted Alan with a cheery:

'Ready to go when you are, boss!'

He had a large open smile and spoke with that distinctive light Leicester–Asian voice.

Alan took him over to the trench and showed what had to be done. As they walked across he had also checked the back acter bucket to make sure it had a good, straight cutting-edge and all the teeth had been removed. The driver saw what he was doing and said,

'I've done this sort of work before, mate.'

'Oh yes, where?'

'On another church job, over Melton way. For your boss, it was.'

'Paul Flynn?'

'Yea, that's the bloke. Tall. Doesn't smile a lot.'

Then it came back to him. He could have had the same conversation with a closely similar digger driver, but years ago, at Flax Hole. He almost smacked his forehead: AK Plant. K as in Kabul! Christ, how could he have been so thick? Meanwhile the driver was waiting for a reply.

'Yes, he's quite serious, but that goes with the job, when you're excavating churchyards...'

The young man thought this was partly aimed at him.

'Oh, don't worry boss, I'll show respect.'

Alan looked him in the eyes. He meant it.

'Thanks.'

Alan was amazed at how many church jobs PFC had done. They were becoming one of their major earners, encouraged by Lottery grants that had paid for toilets and mini-kitchens, in churches and parish halls throughout the country.

The septic tank was to be sited over by the sexton's shed, just outside the churchyard wall. Alan headed over there, while behind him he could hear the digger start up with a throaty roar. A few minutes later they had set up and begun work.

Soon they came down on the layer of brick rubble that had sealed the two babies' skeletons. The broad bucket simply couldn't cut through it. Alan had hoped they'd be able to find the edge of the rubble spread, and then they could work inwards from the outside. That way they wouldn't have to fit teeth, which always made a mess and often cut into the archaeology below. But it was not to be. So they stopped, changed to a smaller, toothed, bucket and began again. But this time very gently; the engine revs dropped.

Alan was watching closely as the digger driver carefully inserted the bucket's teeth below the base of the rubble. Alan signalled him to stop, got into the trench and dropped down on his hands and knees behind the bucket to have a good close look. This part was crucial. If there were any bones visible now, he'd have to stop the digger and clear the rest of the rubble by hand. And that would cause delay, which wouldn't please Paul, or indeed the clients.

He scraped around the lowest of the broken bricks and crushed mortar with his trowel, then stood back with a sigh of relief. There was nothing. He gave the digger driver a thumbs-up. Slowly the bucket was eased back, while curling up. As soon as the digger arm was out of the trench, Alan jumped back in and scraped down vigorously with his trowel. Again there was nothing. So he gave another thumbs-up, stepped out of the trench and poured himself a much-needed coffee from his flask.

The coffee was warm and comforting. For a moment he took his eye off the digger as he watched the PFC minibus drawing up in the small grass car park, which was already beginning to look muddy, from all the coming and going of the dig. Behind was Harriet's car with her young assistant, Amy, sitting in the front passenger's seat. She gave him a little wave and he doffed his hard hat in return.

Harriet had been a little frosty at home after the Dover sole incident – or Fishgate as Alan had come to think of it – but to give her credit, she was every bit the professional and clearly wasn't going to bring any personal feelings to site. But he still felt guilty about the whole thing. He had tried to explain, told her he was helping out a friend in need but it was obvious she hadn't believed a word of it. In fact, she'd told him that his private life was his own business and who he called and why was hardly at the top of her priority list at the moment. So he was making it up to her the only way he knew. He'd spent the last four evenings up in his room, fine-tuning his work on the landscape contexts of the early Saxon burial sites, in her book. He'd present it to her along with a good bottle of red and he hoped that should do the trick.

Alan forced himself to refocus on the moment; on the job in hand.

When he looked down again he almost leapt out of his skin.

'Bloody hell,' he cried out loud, 'where the fuck's that come from?... STOP! STOP!'

He shouted to the digger driver as he waved both hands and made the throat-cutting gesture. Seeing that, the driver immediately killed the engine.

He beckoned the driver to come out of his cab and asked him to show precisely where he'd dumped the last bucket of rubble. Then together they carefully sifted through the loose earth and bricks with their bare hands. They found half a dozen tiny bone fragments, just like the ones they'd revealed two weeks ago.

Satisfied that they'd recovered everything from the spoil heap, Alan returned to the trench, where Harriet was already kneeling and gently probing with her trowel. Everyone had heard his shouting.

'I'm so sorry, Harry,' he said defensively, 'I'd checked the first few buckets carefully and was having a mug of coffee. Then I looked down and...'

'Don't worry. It's easily done and you did manage to stop in time.'

He gave her a grateful smile and again silently admired her professionalism. Plenty of other people – Paul for example – would have used this as an opportunity to publicly humiliate him and pull rank.

Harriet looked up anxiously.

'Alan, have a close look at this. Tell me what you think.'

She stood up to let him in the trench.

'I don't see anything…' His voice tailed off as he carefully scraped the soil directly above the bones with the point of his penknife. Then he leant back, this time with more assurance.

'Yes,' he said, 'I see what you mean. Those bricks lie directly on top of the bones…' gently he scraped away some more loose earth. 'So that must mean they're both contemporary, they were buried when the wall was built. So the rubble was dumped directly on top of the bodies, maybe to mark or conceal them. Otherwise the grave fill would lie just an inch or two below the topsoil.'

His voice tailed off as he thought the implications through. Then he continued, more confidently, 'Or else, of course, the builders of the sexton's shed had dug down into the ground and disturbed the bones, sometime later.'

Harriet was now kneeling close to him. He could feel the warmth of her thigh against his. She was completely absorbed in what lay before them.

'If that was what happened,' she replied, 'the babies' skeletons could have been disturbed by digging foundations for the hard core of the new sexton's yard. But surely, that's what you'd expect, isn't it?'

Alan shook his head.

'No. On a dry site, perhaps. But not here. Any hole in the ground is likely to fill with water – especially in winter. No, I'd have used any rubble I could find to *raise* the surface. Not lower it.'

Harriet hesitated before responding.

'Surely that must mean those bodies have been concealed – hidden by the rubble, doesn't it?'

Alan sighed. It seemed so improbable.

'On the face of it, yes. But I'd have expected more fragmentation, wouldn't you?'

Harriet was frowning.

'Not necessarily, neonate bones are very flexible. They have to be, if you think about it… '

Alan stood up.

'We won't be able to understand this through a keyhole. We've got to extend the trench anyhow, so I suggest that's what we do.'

Then Harriet broke in.

'But you can't leave these bones in place, Alan, not while you're extending the trench. They're far too fragile.'

'No, I wasn't planning to. You and Amy lift and record them, but we'll do no more digging around them until we've enlarged the trench. How does that sound?'

'Fine,' she agreed.

Alan was pleased she'd accepted his plan, they worked well together – made a good team. Even so, he didn't dare confess that in his entire digging life he had never come across such a strange set of bones in such weird contexts. The gut feeling he had when they discovered the first lot was growing stronger by the minute.

* * *

While Harriet and Amy lifted and recorded the baby bones over by the sexton's shed, Alan took the digger into the body of the churchyard to strip the trench for the pipe-run. By midday they had exposed a dozen graves, all of which showed-up as dark rectangular marks in the paler silty subsoil. None had any bones exposed at this level, except for one which had disturbed a much earlier burial, whose bones were mixed-up in the later grave's filling.

Unlike today, sextons in the past didn't worry too much if they cut through older graves and churned up a few bones. They took the view that so long as the bones remained in sanctified ground, it wouldn't matter if a few got muddled. And anyhow, the Church taught that on the Day of Judgement, all bodies would miraculously be made whole again. For a moment, Alan's imagination conjured up a Stanley Spencer image of resurrected bodies pushing out drawers and climbing off the shelves in forensic laboratories and museums around the world. The ultimate curatorial nightmare.

But nothing could be excavated until the graves had been carefully mapped. Alan and one of the digging team worked for the rest of the day on the detailed plans. By the time they knocked off, they had counted a grand total of sixteen whole or partial graves. In addition, the machine had revealed another three baby burials close by the wall, immediately alongside the two they'd exposed two weeks ago. They had to be part of the same group – most likely the same family. Alan was putting the finishing touches to the plan of the babies' graves, when he saw Harriet approaching.

'Harry,' he asked, looking up, 'these three neonates look rather like the first two. A bit compressed?'

'Yes,' she replied, 'they were bundled-up in some way.'

'Maybe they were buried furtively. At night, when nobody was around? That sort of thing happened in the Middle Ages.'

'And later, as well…'

For a second, Alan had a flashback to his earlier waking nightmare: Sofia, being buried in the dark earth of Flax

Hole, with that faceless man looming over her. He vigorously scraped some dried mud from off his trowel's cutting-edge to shake the image from his mind.

'I know,' said Harriet. 'Poor woman.'

Alan slipped the trowel into his back pocket and refocused on the bones in the trench in front of him.

'You reckon they were all stillborn?' he asked.

'Yes, no doubt about it. But late. Probably even full-term.'

'Horrible,' Alan replied. 'But not altogether unexpected, when viewed in historical context. There's a memorial in the church to someone in the seventeenth century, who had ten stillbirths. It wasn't that rare…'

'No,' Harriet cut in, 'and to make matters worse, in Victorian times it was quite often the husband who caused it all, by sleeping around with prostitutes as a young man.'

'Yes. Sowing his wild oats. It was almost expected in some upper-class circles. People turned a blind eye to it.'

'Quite. But then the young men-about-town caught a dose of syphilis, gave it to their young wives, who then had endless abortions and stillbirths. Many of them went insane before they died. It was gruesome.'

Alan shivered again. Harriet patted his arm briefly, but sympathetically. He smiled back. He couldn't, of course, tell her the truth about his reaction.

Yes it was a horrific historical detail. And yes the collection of the baby bones were disturbing to look at. But there was more to it than that. People and power structures don't change all that much over time. Sofia, in her own way, was equally a victim of her patriarchal family.

* * *

The dig had to end on Friday, and it was Wednesday morning. Alan was working with mattock and shovel at the base of the churchyard wall, but on the graveyard side. On the other side, Harriet was finishing the excavation of the third baby. As soon as she'd done, Alan, who was also the site photographer, would take a picture; then they'd draw the tiny skeleton, and survey it onto the general site plan. Finally, and with very great care, they'd lift it, bone by minuscule bone.

An hour or so later, Harriet's head popped over the wall.

'Alan,' she asked, 'any chance of another quick record pic?'

They could hear the low sound of thunderstorms rumbling away in the distance and they both knew a sharp, heavy shower would undo all her patient work.

'OK,' he replied, 'with you in a jiff. I'll just finish this.'

He immediately began to clear up the loose earth, ready to abandon his excavation and fetch his camera from the Land Rover. As he scraped up the last few scraps, the tip of his trowel hit something pale. He instantly recognised it as pottery. It was white, glazed and quite a big piece. At first glance it looked fairly recent.

After about five minutes, and at least one gentle reminder about the photo from the other side of the wall, he had exposed half a saucer. He picked it up, turned it over and identified it at once as mass-produced blue-and-white tableware. He guessed it could only be late nineteenth or early twentieth century. It was un-chipped and still had sharp edges. This suggested it had been lost and broken when the wall footings were being dug. It was also at precisely the same level as the baby skeletons.

The storm was now getting much closer. He slipped the saucer into a finds bag, which he rapidly labelled with trench, depth and context number. Then he scurried off to get his cameras.

For the next two days the team worked flat out and managed to lift and record the remaining adult burials. By the end of Thursday afternoon they had finished. Everyone felt tired and run down. Alan told them, and they were all well aware, that they'd done a magnificent job: in just three weeks they'd excavated sixteen whole or partial burials, not including the five babies. Heavy rain, turning to wet snow had been forecast for Friday, so everyone was hugely relieved to have finished with a day still in hand. Alan invited the whole team to the nearest pub, the Green Man, in Scoby, for a few celebration pints, knowing full well that Alistair would buy all their drinks – which indeed he did. Alan was returning from the bar with two pints of Old Slodger and he could see Alistair chatting to two of their younger diggers, with a huge grin – as if they'd been friends for years, not days. Alan arrived with the pints and the diggers set off for the bar for refills for themselves. When they'd gone Alan was going to chat about the digging life and how it seemed to suit Alistair so well, then he changed his mind. He'd never seen him so relaxed.

'Funny how life works out, Alistair, if things had been different, I could be farming and you could still be a banker. We'd never have met…'

'And I wouldn't be part of a digging team.'

'Do you ever regret leaving the City? I mean, you were master of your own destiny then, weren't you?'

Alistair shook his head; he was smiling broadly.

'No, don't believe anything you read in the press. Young City types aren't the freewheeling cowboys they're portrayed. Nowadays they're part of "closely integrated workgroups", or some such management-speak bollocks.'

Alan could see the Old Slodger was doing its stuff. While his friend took a long pull on his pint, Alan asked, 'But now, don't you find local expectations of the great Clan Crutchley a bit hard to live up to?'

Alistair was grinning at the idea of a Clan Crutchley.

'You're right, there are expectations. Old AAC is still held in very high esteem locally and it obviously counts for a lot that I'm his direct descendant. But I don't find that even slightly daunting. It's a huge privilege; in fact it gives me influence I'd never hoped to acquire as a City man.'

'And you don't think these family ties have restricted you in any way?'

'No, far from it, the opposite in fact.'

He burped quite loudly and several people turned towards them, all smiling, Alistair had been a popular member of the team.

'No,' he continued, undaunted, 'it's given me the freedom to shape the estate for the twenty-first century. We're really committed to biodiversity and I'm proud that we now employ more local people than we did in my father's time.' He burped again. 'More ale?'

While Alistair headed rather unsteadily back to the bar, accumulating other glasses for refills as he went, Alan paused to think. Maybe his own ideas about families and restriction were all wrong? Far too simplistic. What if Ali wasn't being held back at all?

* * *

It was Friday, the last official day of the Guthlic's dig. The forecast proved correct, and it was tipping down, when Alan arrived on site to clear up. In the afternoon the contractors would come to collect the Portakabin and the two Portaloos. He loaded his Land Rover and the PFC trailer with the remaining tools and equipment. He then picked up a few scraps of litter and removed the last remaining grid pegs. That done, he took the church key round to the Rectory and headed back to base at Priory Farm.

It was proving a horrible late February day, with a sharp wind off the North Sea, blowing in flurries of sleet and snow. He backed the heavily-loaded trailer across the hangar's concrete apron, but found his way into the Archaeological In Store was blocked by a white Ford Escort van. Cursing under his breath, he tracked down the driver in the canteen. He was a rather striking young man – a youthful Omar Sharif, with black hair, a moustache and heavy dark eyebrows. Clearly another Kabul employee, he could even have been a family member – a cousin or something, Alan thought. He might have resented being called away from his cards and coffee, but he smiled broadly and cheerfully moved his van out of the way.

This recent revelation that most of the practical side of the PFC work was contracted out to a family, who may or may not have made an attempt on Alan's life, made him somewhat uncomfortable to say the least. He wanted to ask Paul for more details – when and how this contractual pattern had been established – but his instinct told him to leave well alone. Alan remembered how Paul took any query about paperwork as a personal attack on his managerial prowess. Alan was still waiting for the opportunity to quiz him about their time together at Flax Hole. And to do that, he would need Paul to feel that Alan was on his side, that they were a team. Or, to be more precise, that Alan had nothing but admiration and respect for his new boss.

Backing a trailer behind a long-wheelbase Land Rover is never simple, and it took Alan a couple of attempts to draw-up opposite the open double doors of the In Store. He turned the engine off, went round to the back and saw to his relief that a block of empty steel shelves had been labelled with the Guthlic's site code. Harriet and Clara, PFC's very able and extraordinarily well-organised finds supervisor, had been busy that morning getting everything ready for his arrival.

Alan had grown to like Clara. She was quite short and very active, always bustling about the place, checking shelves, and updating various registers. Her hair would change colour with the season, and she wore very high heels and lavish eye make-up. She always maintained that she needed the heels to reach up to the higher shelves.

Clara ran the large Finds In Store with remarkable efficiency and was famous for the way she went about her work. She was always singing choruses from Gilbert and Sullivan, or operettas. She was a stalwart member of the Boston Choral Society and belonged to at least two amateur dramatic groups. She also had a fearsome reputation for not suffering fools gladly. All in all, she was a force to be reckoned with.

By late morning the snow had turned to rain, and it was still pouring down, as Alan started unloading boxes and sample bags from the trailer. After about five minutes, Clara came to give him a hand. An hour or so later, they'd finished, and Clara started to enter a list of the new accessions into a database. He called out box and bag numbers, while she sat at the computer, her fingers flying. They finished shortly after noon, by which time Alan had developed a strong need for a pint. It had been a long, cold morning and he knew a busy afternoon and evening lay ahead. He suggested a drink to Clara.

'I'd love to, darling,' she spoke to everyone as if they were one of her thespian friends, 'but I'm too busy.'

Then, as an afterthought, she added,

'Oh yes, nearly forgot to mention, but you might have to get everything out of here in a week's time…'

'What?' Alan was incredulous.

As if on cue, the door from the offices to the In Store swung back and a young man entered. He was in his late twenties, and a shade taller than Alan. He was dressed quite smartly for an archaeologist, with clean shoes and a jacket. Alan had seen him around the place, but had never been introduced.

'Talk of the devil,' Clara exclaimed, 'here's Mr Simon Cox. Simon, meet Alan, Alan Cadbury.'

They nodded at each other, but didn't shake hands as Simon was carrying two large cardboard boxes.

'Where shall I put them, Clara?' he asked, trying to smile.

Clara was looking at him, exasperated.

'I'm tempted to say "where the sun don't shine", but leave them on the floor by the door, for the time being. And don't bring any more till after lunch. This isn't a garden shed. Everything here has to be catalogued and shelved properly. Now buzz off, before I get angry.'

And he did. Clara folded her arms and turned to Alan.

'Simon's had to finish early and the farmer won't let them use his barn. So everything's got to come back here.'

Simon Cox was PFC's youngest Project Manager. Paul thought him wonderfully dynamic, but Alan and most other members of staff thought he had an exaggeratedly high opinion of himself.

'When?'

'As I said: in a week. Next Friday'

'So where will all our stuff go?'

'The samples could go outside. The weather should be getting better soon…'

'And the finds… the bones?'

'You'll just have to spread them between your offices and the Out Store. We can't do anything else. The place is chocka. Full up. Stuffed.'

'That won't please Paul…'

Clara raised her eyes to the ceiling and sighed loudly in exasperation. It was most theatrical.

'I don't care if it doesn't please bloody Paul. He's not in charge of finds. I am. And if he gives you any aggro, send him round to me…'

That was a real threat. Everyone at PFC was aware that Clara was capable of a fine towering rage.

Alan was walking back to his office, when he decided to pop his head around Harriet's door. Sod it, he thought. No harm in asking.

She was staring at her screen, with furrowed brows. Whatever it was, wasn't going well.

'Fancy a pint, Harry?'

She looked up.

'I'd die for one, but sadly this won't wait. I've got to get it done by the weekend.'

'You sure? Can't you put it off?'

'Not a chance. I'll lose the grant. And right now I can't afford to kiss five grand goodbye.'

She resumed typing in a purposeful way.

He quietly shut the door. Alan allowed himself a small smile as he anticipated her delight when he handed over his site landscape notes, for her book. And he knew they were short, pithy and factual – just what she wanted. If he had Harriet's sense of discipline he'd go straight home and get stuck in. But he didn't. He really fancied a pint.

He was putting on his coat, when his mobile rang. He looked at the screen. It was DCI Lane.

'Hello, Alan.' He got straight down to business. 'Thought I'd let you know I've been looking into our mutual friend's family background…'

This was good news. Lane's interest had certainly been aroused.

'And?'

'And you'd better come over to see me. There's a lot we need to talk about.'

'I'm all ears.'

'This isn't a conversation we should have on the phone, Alan.'

Alan felt his heart skip a beat. Lane must have found something. Something big. This was it. The breakthrough he'd been so desperate for.

'Can you give me a hint?'

'Well, let's just say we aren't the only people interested in the Kabuls.'

Sixteen

The next day was Saturday and at last the sun had reappeared from behind the clouds that had made Friday so miserable. Alan was anxious. He was excited about whatever Lane was about to tell him and he knew, too, it was going to be important. But he was a realist and was also aware that as things now stood, that meant added complexity – which he didn't need. More could go wrong, maybe even horribly wrong. And what made it ten times worse, was that now he wasn't just worried about himself.

Harriet had left earlier to do some library research in Cambridge, so he did something he had never done before: he washed the Land Rover. Perhaps he was seeking some sort of anonymity, but he found the task oddly satisfying. Soothing, even. He also hoped he wouldn't get quite so many disapproving stares when he drove along the manicured roads around Richard Lane's house. He set off about two in the afternoon and drove steadily west, arriving at Uppingham Close two hours later. Mary opened the front door to him.

'He's in the lounge, deep in his notes,' she said, quietly. 'I didn't like to disturb him…'

She escorted Alan across the small front hall, to the lounge.

'Tell him I'll be back in a few minutes with tea.'

She withdrew to the kitchen.

Richard Lane was sitting at his desk. He rose to his feet, and shook Alan's hand. Alan wasn't entirely at ease with his friend's quiet formality. Lane walked round to the two comfy chairs, carrying a file of notes. They sat down.

Lane pulled out that picture of the family, all together at Mehmet's café. All smiling at the camera, with Sofia flanked by her brothers.

'So,' said Lane. 'Let's begin at the beginning. What do you know about Ali's parents?'

Alan shrugged. He felt slightly ashamed, the question had never occurred to him. He had simply accepted that Ali and all his siblings were being raised by their grandfather. Of course, the moment Lane mentioned it he realised it was a bit odd.

'Can't help you there, I'm sorry.'

'Well, from what we gathered, the mother died in 1990. Four years after Sofia was born. Breast cancer, it says on the death certificate.'

'And the father?'

'Deserted the family soon after the mother was diagnosed. No known contact with his children since.'

Alan felt a chill creep over his skin. Ali essentially orphaned at, what, six years old? Suddenly an image of his own father came to mind: standing on the tractor's step, with a young teenage Alan, teaching him how to steer the machine precisely along the drill rows, while towing a set of Cambridge rolls.

'That's dreadful,' was all that Alan could say.

'Yes, and it was bound to have a big effect on Ali's character. On all of them.'

Alan nodded in agreement. Lane was right, but only up to a point – it didn't necessarily make Ali a killer.

'So, the children were brought up by their paternal grandfather, Mehmet.'

As if to confirm, Alan pointed to him on the photograph. The kindly-looking older man, smiling proudly, surrounded by his loving family.

For a moment they both looked at the picture.

Then Lane asked, 'What did you learn about him while you were taking his company's money at Flax Hole?'

Was that barbed, or humorous? Alan couldn't decide. His reply was deadpan.

'Can't say I got to know him much, even though he was the client. My business partner Paul Flynn dealt with him exclusively. Paul liked that sort of thing. Bit of a control freak.'

Lane was listening intently. He looked away, frowning, when Alan finished. There was a long pause while Lane read through his notes again.

Then he asked, 'We're interested in the grandfather. Mehmet.'

Alan's ears pricked up at the mention of 'we'. It sounded encouraging: more involved, less hands-off than before. But best not to mention it now.

Instead Alan asked, 'Is he still alive?'

'Very much so.'

'And still importing food and spices from Turkey?'

'So far as we know, yes.'

'So what does he actually *do* for a living, now? I'd sort of assumed he'd retired. He was always rather a shady character…'

'What, shifty?' Lane cut in.

'No, shady, as in shade. A background figure. In the shadows. Enigmatic, but influential, I'd say.'

Lane looked up.

'Yes, that's what interests us.' Again he glanced down at the notes. 'According to our records he's still in the wholesale food trade. Does that make sense?'

'Yes, plenty. Back in 2002 most of his wholesale customers were Turks and Asians. Ran restaurants, food shops, that sort of thing. There was a spice counter in that café he ran. I remember buying huge bulbs of garlic there. Very cheap.'

'That place interests me: what exactly was it like?'

'I remember "Mehmet's" as very pleasant. The old man was nearly always there himself, sitting in a large chair behind a combination table-desk thing. It was where he seemed to do most of his work. Out in full view of the public...' He paused. 'Maybe that's how they do things in Turkey? I don't know.'

'Did you go there often?'

'Yes we did, but mostly at weekends if they were on our shift. I don't think I ever paid for a coffee. Not once. And Sofia worked there, which was something of a draw for the lads.'

Suddenly, Alan was hit by a strong, but short, flash of memory. Sofia, bringing him over a cup of tea: milk and two sugars, then ignoring his attempt to pay. Smiling. Alive.

'Have you been back since?'

'No. You know what it's like. You dig. You move on.'

Alan saw a small flash of frustration pass across Lane's face, but he pressed on.

'Anyhow, why's the café so important all of a sudden?

Lane leant back in his chair and studied Alan, clearly weighing up the situation.

Alan found himself getting impatient. He tried to keep his tone even and controlled.

'Look, Richard. You've asked me to come here and report back to you. How can I do that properly if I don't know what you're looking for?'

Lane held his gaze for a moment longer, then nodded.

'OK, I'll be quite straight with you. I've discovered that the Yard and the Drugs Squad are keeping tabs on Mehmet Kabul – and have been doing so ever since the murder came to light, but so far without success. Not even a sniff. No, it may seem odd, but both he and Abdul…'

'So he's still in the family firm?'

'Oh, yes. Very much so,' Lane replied, consulting his notes, 'And running the plant hire side of their business. But they all appear to be clean. The Drugs boys have even done a couple of undercover raids, but found nothing. Having said that, they certainly haven't closed the case, either. Far from it. Our friend Mehmet will be under close observation for a good few years yet.'

At this point Mary Lane entered the room, with a tray of tea things, which she set down quietly and then returned to the kitchen. Alan could see she had been in similar situations before. Lane then handed Alan a steaming cup and continued.

'So my boss has been in touch with the Met and the Drugs Squad and I'm to liaise directly with them on this case, which is still at the intelligence-gathering stage.'

'So they've actually put a case together?' Alan asked.

Lane had laid the old ones aside and was now referring to a different set of notes.

'Yes,' he gave an involuntary sigh, as he thumbed through the papers. 'They've done a lot of work. I've got loads to read through over the weekend, God help me…'

'So, what's their angle?'

'They're suspicious of Kabul's whole set-up. It's very successful and seems to be making loads of money. Of course we've also known for some time that Turkey is a major route for narcotics from western Asia – mainly Afghanistan – reaching Europe. And the Kabul family firm have been involved in the food import business since just after the last war. We know for a fact that Mehmet's contacts in Turkey are very close.'

'But does that necessarily make him a drug baron?' Alan asked.

The evidence seemed to him too obvious, but also too circumstantial.

'No it doesn't, but until we can work out why he is making so much money, we've got to be suspicious. And you can't deny his cover is superb.'

'If indeed it is cover.' Alan still wasn't at all convinced. 'And presumably, whenever Kabul lorries have been stopped at the border and searched, they've been clean?'

'Yes, that's right.'

'D'you think that could be due to corruption – tip-offs – at the Turkish frontier from their customs, or police?' Alan asked.

'Oh, almost certainly, but having said that, we've also done searches in Leicester and at the British border. But again, nothing.'

'That's odd,' mused Alan. 'Unless of course they're being clever. Having delivery lorries moving in and out of Turkey is almost too obvious, isn't it?'

'Which brings me to the other brother.'

Lane pointed to Abdul's image on the photograph.

'Did you have any contact with him?'

'Not really, that was all Paul's department again. Abdul had started running a small plant hire business about five years previously. And was making a go of it, so far as I could tell. We used his machines for the dig, and his drivers were first-rate. Very steady. I gather PFC has been using them ever since.'

'Really?'

Lane seemed surprised, and almost a bit excited.

'Nothing unusual in that. You find good men, you stick with them. Cowboys can ruin a site in minutes – you know that.'

'And presumably your boss would have done a thorough check on their credentials?'

'Absolutely. That's Paul all over. Thorough. Or at least, that's the polite word for it.'

Lane didn't share his grin. He was absolutely focused on the notes.

'Well that fits with our findings. The Drugs boys reckon he must be using other, less conspicuous – more devious – routes.'

'Such as?'

Alan was finding the entire discussion unnerving. So much speculation seemed to be based on nothing solid – unless, of course, they were keeping things from him.

'So far as we're aware, I don't think we know that…'

This again struck Alan as odd.

'How d'you mean, "so far as we're aware?" You're the police, aren't you?'

'True, but many of these intelligence-led operations have to keep some things private. Even from other officers, like me. Anything to do with the safety of informers or undercover agents, for example. You see, one of the problems we still have is access to the Kabul family and the organisation they control. They're a very tight-knit bunch, and almost impossible to infiltrate – and frankly, that's going to be the only way we'll crack this one.'

Lane was looking at Alan as he said this.

'Ah, I get it. So you – or rather they, the Yard – want me to use my contact with Ali, as a way of getting inside his family. Is that it?'

'Precisely,' Lane replied. 'I've already spoken to the Governor, who tells me he will make practical arrangements for more private meetings.'

'I'd already requested that,' Alan added, rather lamely.

'I know, but now he'll be going to special lengths to oblige you. I think you'll be impressed at your next session there – which is when, incidentally?'

'Three weeks' time.'

'Good. Liaise with me afterwards. I'll be sure to be there.'

'And I hope it's not just to pick up the pieces.'

'I'm sure it won't come to that, Alan.' Alan could tell that Lane was trying to make his reply sound reassuring. 'And besides, Ali's in Blackfen Prison, and his family are here in Leicester. Rest assured, we'll have stepped in, long, long before you come under any sort of threat.'

'But haven't I already? In the small matter of my bungalow being torched?'

'I'm not so sure,' Lane replied. 'I got back to that fireman, Clark's assistant, and he said he'd had a second look and a further discussion with Clark and was now inclined to think that the evidence for the deliberate use of accelerant was actually the result of residual oil from the building's scrap days, combined with high temperatures and air movement in that part of the kitchen. The blocking of an old stove flue through the flat roof had burnt out…'

'That's right, there was a mark in the plaster on the ceiling there,' Alan broke in.

'Well, it was a botch-up. They'd jammed some old plastic bags up the flue and then slapped on some cheap wood filler. It burnt in seconds and then fed the fire below with a strong draught.'

'So it wasn't arson? You can prove that?'

'I can't prove it, no. But even if it had been arson, the timing suggests that whoever did it wanted to scare you, not kill you.'

'That's exactly what Ali said.'

'But it makes sense. Your Land Rover was gone, they would have known you were out. If indeed there was a "they"…'

Alan was unconvinced. And more than a little unsettled. Lane, an experienced police detective, was choosing to disregard an attempted arson attack? It was obvious why. Lane needed him. He needed his contact with Ali. Hadn't Mary told him when they last met that Lane was under political pressure at work? A big 'win' like cracking the Kabul drugs cartel would surely help establish his status. But would Lane really do that: risk Alan's safety to suit his own ends? He sighed deeply: no, that was ridiculous. Or was it? Alan was beginning to doubt whether he really knew what anyone around him was actually capable of doing. Or worse, why.

And then he realised. He'd come to that stage which he'd arrived at before, both in life and in archaeology. It was when you knew deep down what you must do, but only you could do it. You were on your own.

Time to go. He rose to his feet.

'Thanks for the tea, Richard. I must be off.'

Lane was observing him anxiously.

'Are you sure you're OK, Alan?'

Alan looked him in the eye.

'Oh yes,' he said slowly, 'I'm fine. Absolutely fine.'

Seventeen

Brutus bucked wildly, as if the Land Rover was still on active service, in Aden or Cyprus. As a farmer's son, Alan didn't mind open, flat landscapes. They were businesslike. OK, not too friendly to songbirds, but there were compensations, he thought, as two huge marsh harriers circled above him, like stern Fen eagles on dawn patrol.

He had a clear run across Dawyck Fen and arrived at Priory Farm early. It was Monday morning, the start of another week. He went straight to his office, turned on his computer and began to organise the Guthlic's data-set. He always enjoyed this stage of any project, because this was where threads, stories, narratives began to emerge. It was also about sorting out problems. It was what made all the digging worthwhile. Sadly many field archaeologists weren't like him. They preferred the butch Indiana Jones lifestyle, out there swashbuckling in the trenches.

For Alan, archaeology was about people-ing, about making sense of the past. And that required thought. Lots of it. And most of the thinking took place after the dig itself, now – during the writing-up phase, known in the trade as 'post-excavation', 'post-exc.' or just 'P/X'. Post-excavation was when you called in help from a huge range of outside specialists: chemists and botanists, experts on pollen, fleas, medieval shoes or World War II ammunition. And today was the first day of Guthlic's P/X.

But before they could start approaching any experts, Alan and Harriet had first to organise all the information from the churchyard. A year ago the PFC computer system had crashed, when they had attempted to integrate all site records: graphics, notes, records and even publications. Then Paul had spent a fortune on a new server and numerous software improvements. It had cost well over a hundred thousand. As a result, the PFC system was now far better than anything even the County Council possessed. It had been worth every penny. It was truly state of the art, and Alan loved it.

He had been working for an hour when he heard Harriet enter her office, next door. By then he was desperate for a coffee. As if reading his mind, he heard her fill her coffee machine. He pulled out his mobile and set the alarm for five minutes. He knew if he didn't do that, the next time he'd look away from his screen would be lunchtime.

His alarm sounded, and he headed round to Harriet's office. When he entered she was pouring out two mugs of coffee. This was as good a time as any, Alan thought. He produced his sheaf of research papers with a flourish. And also placed a good bottle of red on the table beside her.

Harriet was clearly surprised at the gesture.

'Alan, what's this?'

'You mentioned you were struggling with the landscape contexts of the early burial sites and I had a few notes left over from my PhD, so it didn't take me long to update them. Anyhow, they're yours, for what they're worth. Oh yes, and something to wash them down with.'

'There was no need for that.'

'Yes there was,' he said with some feeling. 'I'm aware I can be a bit insensitive, what with us sharing the house, and I wanted you to know that I really appreciate everything you've done for me.'

Alan detected the hint of a blush creeping over Harriet's skin. She bowed her head and flicked through the research notes.

'Honestly Alan, if you carry on like this it'll be me who'll be buying you the wine.'

Alan grinned. His gut instinct was right. This had been the best way to make things up to Harriet for Fishgate, and now all was clearly forgiven.

They sat down and Alan steered the conversation round to P/X. As co-directors their first job was to draw up a detailed P/X plan whose broad timetable they'd already agreed with Paul, at the start of fieldwork. The P/X plan would be their bible for the next few weeks; so they had to get it right.

Alan began.

'Right, Harry, as I see it, the first phase is the completion of the bones inventory.'

'That's done.'

'Bloody hell,' Alan was astonished, 'that was quick. I'd allowed a week at least.'

'No,' Harriet replied, 'young Amy's a whizz with tablets. She's found an iPad app which she modified before we started digging. Anyhow, we used it in the field – and it worked.'

'So no notes?'

'Yes, a few, but in an old-fashioned notebook and not on loose context sheets. So they won't get lost.'

Alan was impressed.

'Right,' he went on, 'so I can tick off human bones. What else was there?'

Harriet looked across at her screen, which she swivelled to face them.

'Er... not much. A few coffin nails, handles, one eighteenth-century nameplate, not *in situ*, and a few bits and pieces of pottery, including that half saucer you found. Not much to write home about really.'

'And how long to catalogue?'

'Done. We did it on Friday morning, while you were clearing up on site. So now Amy's putting the finishing touches to the Sample Register.'

'Blimey, you two have been efficient. We should work together more often.'

'Possibly,' she said, with a grin.

Alan took this as a good sign and pressed on.

'OK,' he said, 'so now you're both doing the full study...'

'Yes, pathology, osteometrics. Everything.'

'And how long will that take?'

'We'll try to get it done by Easter.'

Alan noted this. Then he looked up.

'OK, it's my turn now. I reckon it'll take a couple of days for me to complete the sections and plans master catalogue. Then I'll start digitising. Is there any chance Amy could give me a hand?'

Harriet shook her head.

'I don't think so, Alan, some of those skellies are going to need a very careful going-over. I can't see her having time for anything else, until at least Easter.'

'Remind me, when's that this year?'

Harriet looked at her diary.

'Good Friday's April 2nd.'

'OK. That's alright. I can do it myself, if I've got that long.'

Secretly Alan quite liked doing routine tasks like digitising plans and sections. In the old days he would trace-out the pencil field drawings, in ink. As he worked, he would think about the different layers his pen was following – and how they had formed in the first place. And the same applied to digitising. You needed to understand what you were looking at before you could draw a hard line. That was why he hated the currently fashionable scanned digital images. They were quick and cheap, but they were automatic: no thought went into them; he knew it was why so many errors appeared in modern reports – not that anyone noticed or cared. He was a perfectionist and such sloppiness annoyed him.

Harriet's voice broke into his thoughts.

'Alright. So we'll all be busy until Easter. What, then, do you suggest?'

'You and Amy will have produced the detailed bone reports, and I'll have come up with a stratigraphic phase plan, plus a few selected sections, such as they are. With luck, I'll also have finished the narrative sequence and a detailed context-by-context inventory.'

'Which will go in the archive and on the web?'

'I'll check with the curator, but I assume so. Nobody puts all that stuff in the client's report these days.'

Harriet now took up the story.

'So if all that's done, Easter could be the deadline for deciding which specialists to call in, and how much other stuff we can afford.'

'What, radiocarbon and stable isotopes, that sort of thing?'

'Yes…' She paused, glancing up at the screen where she'd displayed the P/X management accounts. 'But the finances don't look too good at this stage, do they? I guess we could run to a couple of C-14 dates?'

Alan shook his head.

'We'll need more than that. You've got to have more than two, to be statistically reliable.'

'Yes, Alan,' she sounded peeved, 'I'm well aware of that. But if we don't have the money, we can't.'

'Don't worry about the money right now, let's just work out what's essential for the project. We'll need several C-14 dates and no modern report can do without stable isotopes, either. They'd make all the difference and I guess would help your own research, too.'

'Yes, they certainly would. There's so much stuff being written now that's pure speculation and a site like this can, and should, produce real solid facts. And of course they'd be pure gold for my book – especially if they reveal something unexpected about origins. Maybe migration, that sort of thing, but I don't see how…'

'Leave it to me. I'll speak to Alistair. He wants to help us, and he can afford it. So as soon as the P/X plan is finished, I'll drive over to Scoby Hall and speak to the man himself.'

She was looking at him with undisguised admiration.

'If you can, Alan, that sounds great. Really good. Meanwhile, I'll see if I can squeeze anything else out of Paul.'

Alan gave her a grim smile.

'Well, good luck with that.'

* * *

It was late in the afternoon, and Alan had nearly finished the master catalogue. The way his eyes felt reminded him that one day soon he'd have to buy reading glasses. He was making sure all the files he'd worked on were properly backed-up, when there was a knock on the door, and Harriet came in.

'Hi Harry,' he said with a deep sigh of relief, 'that's all the bloody cataloguing done. Tomorrow I can start on the real work.'

'I bet you're pleased.' She was looking over his shoulder, smiling broadly. Alan got a heady whiff of expensive perfume. 'And we've been doing OK too. We've nearly finished the first skellie.'

'Anything interesting?'

'No, not really. Standard early med.: middle-aged man. Natural causes so far as I can tell. Probably worked on the land.'

'Not surprising for this part of the world.'

'You're right. But a big man. Large muscle scars.'

'Yes,' Alan broke in, 'sounds a bit Viking to me…'

She was suitably non-committal. Viking would be a bit late. She wanted some of the bodies in the churchyard, especially those at the base of the tower, to be early and throw light on Anglo-Saxon origins. That's what would set her book apart from others.

'Maybe,' she said doubtfully, before continuing more brightly, 'anyway, I think we've got more pressing concerns at the moment than my research.'

Alan was worried: what had he missed?

'Really?'

Harriet brandished the bottle of red wine with a grin.

'All work and no play, right? Let's go home.'

* * *

The meal of steak and kidney pie, followed by sherry trifle, was exactly what Alan needed and afterwards he fell fast asleep on the sofa, while Harriet did the washing-up. She woke him with a gentle shake just before nine. Her black Labrador Alaric (named after the King of the Visigoths, c. 370–410) was fast asleep alongside him, and snoring like an old man.

'Wake up, Alan, it's nearly nine and you've been out for an hour. If you doze any longer now you won't sleep tonight.'

She handed him a mug of tea.

'Thanks, Harriet.' He felt like he was crawling out of a thick soup. He shook his head, 'Sorry.... I haven't been very good company this evening.'

The wine and food had been delicious, but Alan had found it hard to stay focused on the conversation. It wasn't Harriet's fault, she had been excited about the work that awaited them and eager to talk it all through. But Alan's mind kept on drifting back to Ali, to the whole Kabul family. To the implications of his conversation with Lane. All he had wanted to do was help an innocent young lad. But the deeper he dug the more complex the case became. And now he was being sent back to Blackfen on Lane's orders, essentially to follow the police line of enquiry. Alan felt that he was losing control of the case. Not that he'd had much control over it to begin with…

He forced himself back to the present moment. Harriet was smiling at him, shaking her head in amusement.

'That's all right. You were tired. Put me in mind of when I was a graduate student, endlessly popping two-grain caffeine pills.'

'Same here,' Alan tailed off.

Harriet sat down beside him, as he sipped his tea. She was the first to break the silence.

'I had a short session with Paul about our budget this afternoon.'

'I said I'd talk to Alistair,' Alan replied, slightly irritated. The last thing he needed – if Paul did indeed think they were ganging up on him – was for Harriet to be putting any pressure on him. Alan knew what Paul was like: he'd just clam up. Then there would be no chance at all of Alan getting Paul's side of the Flax Hole story. Although, if he was perfectly honest with himself, he had no idea at all about how he was going to broach it.

Harriet's voice intruded into his thoughts.

'I know, and I'm grateful for that, Alan,' she said. 'But we can't rely on the charitable donations of rich locals at every dig. It's important that Paul understands the implications of the decisions he's making.'

'Sounds serious.'

'It's about the contractors. AK Plant.'

Suddenly Alan was very focused.

'Yes, I've met a couple of their drivers. One of them, Kadir, seemed a nice chap.'

'Despite the… cultural issues?'

Alan was surprised by this. He wouldn't have thought Harriet would have been prejudiced about the race of anyone so long as they did a good job.

'What do you mean, exactly?'

'The language barrier, it isn't a problem?'

Alan shrugged.

'It depends on the man. I've worked with Englishmen who couldn't dig their way out of a wet paper bag. But Kadir's different. He's a brilliant driver with an incredibly light touch.

I'd much rather have him on site than a monosyllabic local who doesn't know how to follow changes in texture, let alone levels. And believe me, there are plenty of them.'

Harriet nodded, and pressed on.

'Anyway, it wasn't about Kadir specifically. AK Plant overcharge for their services. Not much, but enough. The cost of a good set of radiocarbon tests, anyway.'

'Really? That surprised me, what with Paul's insistence on keeping the budget tight.'

'Exactly. So I did a bit of research and came up with a list of alternative contractors. Cheaper options. Paul wouldn't even consider it. Also, he said that on no account should I discuss this with you, or allow you access to the contracts file. He implied there were wheels within wheels and it wasn't just about prices. He even tried to be charming...'

She gave an involuntary shudder, then continued, 'I know you said he could be a bit paranoid, but that's ridiculous.'

'I agree.'

Alan furrowed his brow. Harriet was right, this was more than Paul's paranoia or need for control.

'Anyway, I ignored him, obviously. Anyhow, what do you make of this?'

Harriet pulled out a piece of paper. It was a summary of the annual accounts, dating back for the past seven years, back to when Paul established PFC, just after Flax Hole.

Alan squinted at the much-reduced page. The tiny cells of the spreadsheet made his head hurt.

'I'm sorry, Harry, I'm useless with this sort of thing. What am I looking at exactly?'

Harriet leant over and traced the run of numbers along the columns.

'So, Paul is overpaying AK Plant, here. But look here, at the end of every quarter, he's been paid a retainer fee by them that more than covers their fee.'

'Hang on, so Paul's paying them... but then they are paying him back with interest as a – charitable donation?'

'More like a bonus. But whatever, it's a scam. And there are also these strange funds.' She pointed down to the *Monthly Itemised Notes* columns, 'Look here... and here... Do you know why PFC should have a "Balance Adjustment Fund" or a "Currency Allowance Scheme"?'

Even Alan could see that they looked suspicious.

'It looks a bit like money laundering, doesn't it?'

'I agree. And look here,' she turned to the second sheet, 'these funds don't stay consistent from month to month. They fluctuate hugely...' she paused, doing a rapid calculation, 'that Currency fund went up fifty thousand in April, then down twenty in May. So what's going on?'

Alan sighed deeply. He had suspected as much.

'I don't know,' he replied. 'But whatever it is, I don't like it.'

The fact that the PFC operating profit was so closely related to the Kabul empire was deeply disturbing, especially in the light of his recent chat with Lane. And worse, if Paul really was funding his company with drugs money, then they were all implicated.

He also realised that Harriet wouldn't let this lie, as she had a strong sense of moral outrage. But the last thing he needed right now was for her to challenge Paul, and attract the Kabuls' attention. Even if the arson attack was just a warning – or not an attack at all – she would be treading a very dangerous path.

His thoughts were interrupted when Harriet grasped his arm.

'Alan,' she said with real urgency, 'we've got to do something. We can't let it go on.'

'No, you're right, it's not good. But let's not rock the boat just yet.'

'What, so we do nothing?'

'Oh no. But we don't just blast away. We've got to choose our targets…'

'But, surely we've got enough here?' She tapped the spreadsheets, making no attempt to hide her growing exasperation. Alan realised he must take the initiative, or lose it for good.

'No, Harry, think about it, for Christ's sake! If we report this now, we'll shut down PFC before we have a chance to process the P/X results. Alistair's money will vanish and all that hard work…'

'You can't let Paul break the law and get away with it, just for the sake of some research statistics.'

Alan was surprised – and pleased – by the vehemence of Harriet's response. The St Guthlic's project could boost her academic reputation considerably. But she was more concerned about doing the right thing.

'No. It's not just that. But if we call in the police or HMRC now, he'll be ready for them. More to the point, so will the Kabul's bent accountants. Can't you see: you've just challenged him? He's alerted. And we both know that Paul's got the business savvy to make all this disappear. He'll explain all those funds. Face it, he's bound to have a fall-back plan. He's an expert and we're just amateurs. We don't stand a chance until we've got better evidence. And believe me, I don't think that'll take very long. Honest, I don't.'

By now Alan was holding both her hands.

'You're right, I suppose.' Harriet was deflated, on the verge of tears. She continued, 'So, we sit tight, we make him think he's got away with it?'

'No, Harry, we don't just wait for things to happen. We build a case.'

Harriet nodded. There was a long pause. Alan could feel the tension in her clasped hands slacken. She might be calmer, but Alan was more alert than ever. This was all getting far too close to home.

* * *

The routine of the Guthlic's P/X. was rudely interrupted the following Wednesday, when two three-ton hire vans unexpectedly arrived at Priory Farm. The people there had been led to believe that the dig run by their young Project Manager, Simon Cox, had been scheduled to end on Friday, but a second minor disagreement with the farmer had flared up into another row. A big one this time: hence the need to hire two vans, mid-week. It would seem that what Paul had once described as Simon's superb 'interpersonal skills', had been overrated.

That was certainly what Clara, Harriet and her student Amy thought, as they ferried boxes of Guthlic finds and bones, from the In Store, to their various offices. To make space, they moved others temporarily to the Out Store – as there was nowhere else to put them. Alan blundered into this scene of frantic activity and was given a succinct summary of the situation by a red-faced Clara, clutching two long-bone boxes under one arm and a skull box under the other. She was not happy.

'Yesterday that arrogant little prick Simon lost his rag with the farmer, who told him to fuck off. The next thing I knew he was on his mobile, and bleating at me to hire him two vans to move everything down here today...'

Alan stood listening, his mouth open.

'So be a lamb, put your teacup down. Go to the In Store and move all the Guthlic soil samples out into the car park. But put them on a couple of pallets, or the mice will get to them. And get a move on, those vans are due off hire by noon.'

Alan jumped to it. The bulk samples had been stored in plastic lidded buckets, some of which were quite old and had become brittle after years of daylight. He picked one up, the handle snapped out of its socket and the bucket hit the tarmac, spilling its contents of wet, slimy mud. He leant down and the stagnant smell hit him full in the face. In a flash he was back at Flax Hole and that waking nightmare.

Only this time he knew what it meant.

Eighteen

A few tatty daffodils with short, misshapen stalks had somehow avoided being crushed into the mud. Alongside them were the narrow paths, where hundreds of people had taken short cuts from their cars. Above the network of unofficial paths, a large board proclaimed that Blackfen Prison Car Park was sponsored by a notorious firm of 'no win no fee' solicitors.

I bet that poncy sign cost more than the landscaping of the entire car park, Alan thought, as he walked rapidly through the freezing drizzle towards the Visitors' Entrance. Still, the daffs were a sign of hope. It was the second week in March: the winter had to be ending soon.

Once through the main entrance, Alan waited for his escorting officer to arrive. This time it was a woman. She was dressed in the regulation white blouse and dark trousers. It was hard to tell her age, but forty-something, Alan reckoned. And very fit. Not the lean and athletic type. But fit nonetheless; she had bounce and energy when she walked. They set off and Alan had to lengthen his stride to keep up.

Once out of the main Assembly area, they turned right. Normally they headed straight across towards the Security Wing.

'That's odd,' Alan asked, 'don't we usually go straight over here?'

'Not for the next sessions. The Governor's arranged new facilities for you in the Education Block. It'll be nicer there…'

'Yes,' Alan replied, 'That windowless room was a bit gloomy. And now spring's around the corner it'll be good to see out.'

'Yes, it talks of a cool, dry spring.'

He could tell from her voice she was a local girl.

They went on to talk about the weather as only Fen people can. It's something everyone shares, maybe because you can see it coming, watch it going and be grateful when the storms miss you. As they chatted away, Alan noted the change in atmosphere, after just four weeks. Things got even more relaxed as they entered the Education Wing. Suddenly corridors became wider, and somehow less airless. Inmates were walking around on their own, often carrying books, or mugs of tea.

'So has that security alert ended?' Alan asked

'What, that mobile phone business?'

'Yes.'

'The phones were handed in, but without the SIM cards. Let's just say we've reached an uneasy truce.'

Alan smiled despite himself. That was a clever manoeuvre. Handing over the 'evidence' but keeping the possibility of future communication open. Just the kind of thing Ali would think of.

'Yes, but they've asked us to be "extra vigilant".'

The way she said this lacked enthusiasm.

'Aren't you always?'

'Always what?'

'Vigilant.'

'In that case, I'd better watch my step.'

At this, she gave him an old-fashioned look. Alan made a mental note: never assume prison staff don't have a sense of humour.

A few paces further on, they stopped and she unlocked a door on the left. They had arrived at a small classroom, where she handed him over to a member of the education staff and left.

Another officer, this time from Security, showed him around a small side-office, where Alan was to hold his one-to-one 'contact time' tutorials. Yes, he thought, this should be more private. Having said that, he noted that the security within it had been greatly enhanced. There was a central partition, which resembled a beefed-up Post Office counter. He was also given a personal alarm, which he hung round his neck; two panic buttons had been fitted beneath his desk; a further five were concealed elsewhere in the room. The officer informed him the outside response time to the buttons would be less than half a minute. Finally, two cameras were concealed in the ceiling, and these also recorded sound.

He fingered the alarm hanging from his neck and realised that his hands were sweating. This was more than a show of strength from the powers that be. Nobody brought in security measures like these, unless they were expecting trouble. For a moment he had doubts: did they – did the Drugs Squad – know something he didn't?

Alan was told he should expect officers to enter the interview room without warning, and for non-emergencies he was shown a bell, which could summon a prisoner's escort at any time. Each interview was to last ten minutes, and no longer. Although these new arrangements hardly encouraged intimacy, they had to be a big improvement on the previous session.

* * *

This time there was no flashing red light as the students came in. But Alan did notice they were led in and followed by officers, which suggested they had not been free to walk in the corridors on their own. Being Lifers, they had to travel in a 'crocodile', like primary school kids. Alan counted them in: there were nine students. And there, at the centre of the pack was Ali: back straight, head held high. Did Alan imagine it, or was there a slight look of triumph on his face? After all, such strong security measures were proof that whoever was behind the mobile phone trafficking had got the attention of the authorities. He could well imagine that, in the hierarchy of prison life, such attention would inspire respect amongst the inmates.

Alan began the talk he'd prepared for the first half of the class, on 'Darwin, Evolution and the Birth of Modern Archaeology'. He'd had doubts beforehand, fearing it might be a bit academic, but it got off to a good start. The room was silent as he showed pictures of some of the earliest discoveries, such as the Red 'Lady' of Paviland Cave in south Wales. He explained how the red-painted scarlet 'woman' was in fact a Stone Age man, buried about 26,000 years ago. The group loved this story, and bombarded him with questions. Alan could see he had got through to them. But he still had to see how Ali responded to changing ideas about the biblical story of the Creation. So he laid it on a bit thick, describing how as late as 1654 Archbishop Ussher had decided that the world had been created in just seven days, starting on October 23rd, 4004 BC. This got a good laugh from all but one of the students, including Ali. The exception, a young man in his mid-twenties, suddenly lost his temper and called Alan among other things, the Great Anti-Christ. He was escorted from the room and after the class Alan learned that five years previously he had killed his father, who was having an extramarital affair with a gay man.

Ali was the first to come through for the one-to-one tutorials, in the second half of the session. He entered the small room with his escort, and was shown to the desk in front of the partition by an officer, who then withdrew.

Even though it was their third meeting, Alan couldn't get used to Ali's new image. That almost shaven head and cropped dark beard. So different from the fresh-faced, tousle-headed youth at Flax Hole.

The new Ali was much harder-looking. The gentle young man seemed to have gone for good. But had he? It was extraordinary, Alan thought, how something as superficial as appearance can actually alter one's appreciation. The young man before him sat, stared and said nothing. He was neither hostile, nor friendly. He was just there. Inscrutable. Waiting.

Alan was aware that the clock had started ticking, but last week's farcical 'interview' aside, this was his first chance to view Ali close-up. Of course, he reminded himself, he hadn't seen him for over seven years, but most young men in their mid-twenties, if anything, look better than they did in their late teens. They gain muscle mass and physically 'fill-up'; they haven't yet started to age – that begins to happen in their later thirties. Ali was still only twenty-six. To judge by the set of his arms and shoulders, Alan suspected he was taking regular exercise in the gym.

They began by discussing Darwin and the development of archaeology. Alan kept on pushing at the science versus religion debate. As Mary Lane had been so keen to point out when all this started, an honour killing suggests fundamentalism. But Ali was pragmatic. 'If that's what the radiocarbon dates say, then that's OK by me,' seemed to be his attitude. He was far more interested in the nuts and bolts workings of radiocarbon dating: the way, for example, solar radiation bombarded the earth's outer atmosphere. It didn't seem to worry him that the scientific dates conflicted with religious texts. For a moment Alan wondered whether he had just not made the connection. Then he looked into those intelligent eyes again and no, there was no doubt: it just didn't matter to him.

His mind was now racing. Fundamentalism was one motivation. But only one. What about the family pressure? He only had ten minutes: he'd have to push him. Hard. But first he must re-establish trust.

'I can only imagine what you're going through, Ali. Being locked up, being watched all the time. I just want you to know that you can talk to me, about anything. Everything you say in this classroom will remain strictly between us.'

Alan winced at the hypocrisy of this. Still, ends justified means. In the end, this would be for Ali's benefit.

'Ah, but walls have ears. Never forget that.'

'In this case, Ali, they don't,' he replied, 'I wasn't prepared to do personal supervisions and have every word recorded. That's why we have this horrible screen between us. It was what the prison authorities insisted on as the price of privacy. Security was far too in-your-face last time. I couldn't think straight with that man standing over us.'

Ali shrugged his shoulders. 'Doesn't bother me. You learn to cope once you're inside. You have to. Have a bath, and a screw can come in. The bent ones love it. So you learn to take it. If you don't, it's game over.'

'But you don't seem too downhearted. You coping OK?'

'What do you think?'

Alan detected a minuscule change: a squaring of shoulders; head held a fraction higher.

'Yes, you look OK to me.'

Ali leant forward.

'I'm making the most of it.'

Alan had no idea how to respond to this. If Ali noticed his discomfort he clearly didn't care: he had a point to make.

'It's like my granddad always says, where your average bloke sees a problem, a businessman sees an opportunity. There's competition and scams all around. Some blokes are making fortunes. It's like the world outside, but you also get fed. And a bed at night. Could be worse, if you don't weaken.'

Ali's stare was penetrating, but Alan didn't flinch. He knew he would have to give as good as he got to regain his respect.

'You were always the entrepreneur, Ali. I am sure your grandfather would be proud of you.'

Ali dropped his gaze and looked away, suddenly awkward.

'Yeah, so proud he won't even set foot in this place.'

'That surprises me, he always seemed to be… very much a family man.'

'That's what I mean. They say I've brought shame on the whole family… everyone in it.'

How interesting, thought Alan. Exactly the opposite of what Lane had reported: that the confession had led to Mehmet acquiring status within his community.

But that could wait. He had to keep Ali focused.

'And what about Abdul?'

At the mention of his brother's name, Ali flinched slightly. Just a minute adjustment, but Alan had no doubt now. None at all.

'Does he visit?'

'Once. He couldn't stay long. But we stay in touch.'

The mobile phones, obviously. But that wasn't Alan's concern.

'I suppose he's kept busy with the plant hire business. Paul, my old colleague at Flax Hole, still has dealings with him.'

'You still in touch with that wanker?'

Ali looked genuinely agitated. In fact, the most agitated Alan had seen him. What on earth was his issue with Paul? Alan decided to provoke him further.

'As it happens, he's my boss now. He's not that bad once you get to know him.'

Ali shrugged his shoulders.

'If you say so. It's your funeral.'

Now he was smiling at Alan again. That cold smile, neither hostile nor friendly. Alan felt, yet again, that he was losing control of the conversation. That Ali was now trying to provoke him. Time was running out.

'The thing is, Ali, we're not as different as you might think, you and I.'

At this, Ali looked genuinely amused. Alan pushed on before Ali could derail him with any kind of comeback.

'I've lost both my parents. My older brother, Grahame, took over the family business. He means well but at times he can be quite a bully. Telling me what to do, where to go, even though there's only a couple of years between us.'

Ali leant forward, as close to Alan as the partition would allow.

'You don't know what you're talking about.'

'I was just trying to…'

'Don't give me that.' He lowered his voice. 'You know damn well. I'm here to learn archaeology, right? So stop messing with things that don't concern you.'

The last sentence was said, almost hissed, very softly indeed, lips barely moving.

As Ali finished speaking, the door behind him opened and the escorting officer arrived with the next student. Interview over.

* * *

Outside the prison walls, Alan reached into his pocket for his phone. He rang DCI Lane's number.

'Richard, just checking we're still on.'

'I'll be with you in half an hour.'

And that was it. Lane rang off.

Alan knew that he was just being cautious, not wanting to discuss anything over the phone. But after his conversation with Ali, this curt exchange made him feel even more isolated.

He hadn't wanted to meet Lane at the prison after the interview. It just felt wrong. There were too many eyes in that place, and if Ali managed to detect even the slightest hint that he was seeing the Law, then the whole project would be dead in the water. So he suggested The Slodger's Arms.

Traditionally, 'slodgers' were fenmen of the south Fens; 'yellowbellies' were their Lincolnshire equivalents. This pub was a small independent house with close links to a micro-brewery in Chatteris. Alan knew the beer was always good, the food plentiful and fresh, although a bit robust for London tastes, and the company relaxed. He liked it.

He walked into the bar. A couple of the locals said hello, but then they left him alone. That was another thing he liked about the Slodger: Fen people never crowd you. He ordered a beer and a round of sandwiches, then sat down, taking a copy of the local paper from a rack by the fire. He was starting to warm up and relax. After a quarter of an hour, half a pint and a doorstep sandwich, Lane entered.

A brief handshake and then it was down to business.

'I've done a bit more homework with the local force and Ali was known to be a man on the up.'

'Straight or bent?'

'Straight, so far as I could tell. No, he was running a successful small business. I wouldn't be surprised if he hadn't done a few shady deals along the way. He would have to raise cash somehow,' he paused, 'but no, my sources reckon he was OK.'

Alan nodded in agreement. Ali was asserting his control, for sure but that didn't mean he was a criminal. It just meant that he was protecting his interests – or someone else's.

'For what it's worth, I think you're right. I don't think it's Ali that you need to worry about.'

Lane gestured to Alan to continue.

'I tried to ask him a few questions about the family.'

'And?'

'He shut me down. Told me I didn't know what I was talking about.'

'Well, that's understandable, I suppose. If I were in Ali's position in prison, the only thing that would keep me sane would be my own personal life. My family. I don't think I'd like an outsider meddling in it, either.'

Lane was frowning.

'I don't suppose you mentioned drugs?'

Alan almost choked on his beer.

'Christ no!'

'I realise you have to go carefully, but I just thought…'

'You don't understand what it's like talking through grills with cameras around. It's not like being in a nice cosy pub. It's harder to talk and everything you say seems significant. And I suppose it is. It's not an atmosphere – an *ambiance* they'd call it down south – that invites intimacy.'

He finished his beer, then feeling sorry for his friend, who was now looking crestfallen, he added, 'So to answer your question: no, I didn't get even the slightest hint about drugs or anything of that sort. Nothing.'

'That doesn't surprise me. He's not going to chat about such things openly, is he? So did he say anything, anything at all that we can even start to build on?'

'No, it wasn't what he said so much as…'

Alan faltered, how the hell was he going to explain himself?

'Richard, I think I'm going to need another pint.'

Lane returned from the bar with a pint for Alan and a lemonade for himself. Alan took a large gulp of ale and braced himself.

'The thing is, I've remembered something. About Flax Hole.'

'Remembered? Just like that?'

Alan could hear the scepticism in Lane's voice. It was important, now more than ever, that he kept him on side.

'It came to me the other day at work. I don't know, maybe I'd suppressed it, subconsciously. It was pretty traumatic. And I've also been having these weird dreams…'

Alan stopped himself. Don't overdo it: stick to the facts.

'I haven't been keeping things back from you, Richard, I promise. I want to get to the bottom of this as much as you do.'

'Go on.'

Lane reached into his pocket and took out a note book and pencil.

'It's about his brother. Abdul.'

Lane leant forward in his chair, focused on every word.

'What about him?'

Alan took another long drink and began…

'He visited the site, just the once. I'd been giving Sofia a tour. We'd nearly finished. We were by the wet sieves. She was behaving a bit like a kid who'd bunked-off school. A bit overexcited. Three or four of our people were working at the wet sieves. It was getting late and they were messing around, ready to knock off. You know what it's like: lots of clattering, buckets and mud everywhere, plus squirting water and a bit of horseplay. People were keeping their spirits up after doing a cold, muddy job on a freezing day in February. Anyhow, the din seemed to draw her over to see them. I decided to return to my trench where I was meant to be drawing yet another section of retting pit, but for some reason I still kept half an eye on the girl at the sieves.'

'Was that just because she was a pretty young teenager?'

'Funnily enough, I don't think so, although I won't rule it out. No,' Alan continued, 'to be frank I think I was interested in seeing how the crew at the wet sieves would react to her.

But I needn't have worried: they were great. They showed her what they were doing and some of the finds drying in a tray.'

He paused for a moment. He was aware he needed to get the next bit right.

'But she was quite a short girl... I'd guess five foot one or two. Something like that. But the point is, she couldn't quite see into the sieve, even when standing on the breeze blocks they'd put there. So one of the blokes, a great mountain of a man we all called Wraith, picked her up in a huge bear hug. I must admit alarm bells rang inside my head, but everyone was laughing...'

'Even the girl?'

'Mostly the girl. She was loving it. Having a whale of a time. And then...'

Alan paused and took another swig of ale. Lane looked up from his note-taking.

'Yes?'

'There was a shout from the site entrance. Abdul had come to collect her, but nobody had seen him arrive. He shouted and shook his fists as he ran over to the wet sieves. Of course Wraith put her down, but instead of having a go at him, as most normal...'

'I think you mean Western,' Lane added quietly

'As most normal Western blokes would have done, he ignored Wraith and the rest of the sieve crew. It was as if they weren't there. They didn't exist. And then he shouted a load of angry stuff at her in Turkish and led her off, back to the offices.'

'Did he hit her? Was he physical in any way?'

'No.' Alan shook his head. 'None of that.'

Alan paused. There was no going back now.

'Anyhow, about four or five minutes later there was a loud scream from high in the office building. We could hear two men's voices, shouting. Then silence. Everyone on site had stopped work and all were staring up at the building.'

'How long did the shouting go on for?'

'Not long. Not long at all. Maybe thirty seconds – on and off. A couple of minutes later we resumed work, but it was weird. No, creepy... the site was absolutely silent. We'd all been shaken.'

'And then what did you do.'

Alan looked down at the table. He was deeply ashamed. But it was important, now, that he finished the story.

'I remember the drive back to the Unit was grim. Some people wanted to phone the police then and there. Others, more politically correct, thought they shouldn't interfere.'

'So what happened when you got back to the Unit?'

'Somebody mentioned it to Paul...'

'Your co-director at Flax Hole?'

'And now my boss. He's the PF in PFC.'

Lane nodded. Alan continued.

'Anyhow, he agreed we'd done the right thing.'

'What, by saying nothing?'

'Yes,' Alan continued, 'I don't think he wanted to upset the Kabuls. They were the clients, after all.'

'And that was the last time you saw her alive?'

'Yes, it was.'

Lane was entirely focused now, scribbling down notes in his pad.

'And it didn't occur to you, after a few days, to ask where she was?'

'Like I said, Paul was adamant that we shouldn't interfere. Besides, shortly afterwards my shift patterns changed and Paul and I hardly saw each other, so I didn't really have the chance to discuss it further.'

Alan was aware how pathetic that sounded. To his credit, Lane didn't remark on it.

'Changed how, exactly?'

'Paul suggested that we formalise things. He took charge of all admin and I ran the fieldwork. And that was that.'

Lane leant back in his chair, and stared at Alan thoughtfully, sympathetically even.

'You said you'd been having nightmares?'

'About Sofia, yes.'

'This memory loss thing, it's more common than you think.'

Alan felt a huge wave of relief. Lane was onside.

'We encounter it a lot. You obviously found the whole situation deeply upsetting, so you blanked it out. Then, that newspaper article was the trigger...'

'That makes sense. I remembered the whole thing the other day, when I was moving bulk soil samples at PFC. Strangely, I think it was the smell of mud.'

'Yes,' Lane broke in, 'we now recognise that smells can be deeply evocative.'

'Really? But it was weird, like watching a film clip with me in it.'

'That sounds about right. We come across it all the time. I gather it's a variant of post-traumatic stress disorder.'

Alan buried his head in his hands.

'That scream, that was her being murdered, wasn't it?'

'Let's not jump to conclusions.'

Lane paused, consulted his notes again.

'You said, you heard two male voices, could you recognise either of them?'

Alan shook his head.

'OK, Alan, leave it with me. At the very least, we've got a witness to the event, within the family.'

Alan couldn't help himself, he laughed.

'And you think they'll come forward?'

Now it was Alan's turn to lean across the table, insistent.

'Don't you get it, Richard? Whatever happened, however it happened, they arrested the wrong brother.'

Nineteen

Alan slept fitfully that night. He wasn't plagued by nightmares, at least not dreamt ones. But he couldn't stop thinking about Sofia, being dragged away by Abdul. He couldn't shake the sound of that scream from his mind.

And behind the horror of the relived moment, there was a strong feeling of guilt. What he hadn't told Lane, simply because he couldn't bring himself to admit to it, was that he'd played a big part in persuading people not to make an official fuss. The excavation was just starting to slip behind schedule and their contract had big penalty clauses if there were delays. So at the time he told himself that it had made sense to keep quiet and keep digging. That way, he could criticise Paul all he liked for being self-interested and money-minded but really, when it came down to it was he, Alan, any different? What if he had spoken up? For God's sake, what if the minute he had heard the screams he had run round to the Kabuls' office and broken the bloody door down, would Ali be in prison now? Would Sofia still be alive?

These questions plagued him as he drove to work. Right now PFC was the last place he wanted to be. But he owed it to the project, and to Harriet, to finish the job. Time to be professional.

The four walls of Harriet's office were fitted with white-topped benches. This was where her graduate student assistant, Amy, had laid out all the Guthlic's bones, in neat little labelled groups, separated by strips of masking tape. On the shelves above the benches, again neatly stacked, were the boxes which had held them. Amy was finishing the final box, over by the window, when Alan knocked on the door. Harriet, who was nearest, opened it with a cheery:

'Morning, Alan!'

She walked over to her coffee machine and poured three cups. Amy took hers at the bench. Harriet and Alan sat down.

'OK,' Alan began, 'it's Easter next weekend. We said we'd get the first phase finished by then. Are we going to make it?'

'I think so.' Harriet looked across to Amy. 'We'll have the final check done by Friday, won't we?'

'Oh easily,' Amy replied. 'Maybe Wednesday, if nothing goes wrong. That'll give me a full day to repack and take the all boxes through to the Out Store.'

'Thanks, Amy.' Harriet then turned to Alan. 'So we're on target. What about you?'

'Same here. One or two glitches with digitising sections. Had to scan a few in the end, but otherwise I'm on schedule…'

'Right,' Harriet said, 'so this morning we must select a few to sub-sample for Judd at Saltaire.'

Dr Judd ran the world-renowned Saltaire Palaeopathology Laboratory. Alan had maintained contact ever since he'd met him on the Forensic course, in the mid-nineties.

Harriet turned to Amy.

'You said you wanted to learn about stable isotopes. Now's your chance. Come and join us.'

As Amy came over, Harriet looked across to Alan.

'Amy's background is anatomy. She's got a lot to discover on the archaeological side.'

Amy gave him a shy smile.

'So don't use too many long words, please, Alan.'

She sat down between them, pencil and notepad in hand.

'OK, stable isotope analysis...'

Alan paused for a moment, collecting his thoughts. He hadn't anticipated this, but it was no bad thing. Helped to clarify his mind.

'It's a technique which shows where a person or a skeleton grew up. It's based on the fact that tooth enamel is laid down in childhood and then never alters. In most children, adult teeth start to take shape about three months after birth, and finish developing at around twelve...'

'So it won't work on milk teeth?' Amy asked, looking up from her notepad.

That was a good question.

'I imagine it would, but I think they'd have big problems taking sub-samples. I don't know. But nearly all archaeological samples are from adults.'

'And all the Guthlic's bodies we're interested in are mature,' Harriet added.

Alan continued his explanation.

'As the hard enamel forms, it absorbs the chemicals in the child's environment, especially those in the water he or she drinks. Some of these chemicals are characteristic of particular parts of the world. Levels of lead and strontium, for example, vary a great deal from one region to another.

Oxygen is rather more complex: two of its isotopes, $_{16}O$ and $_{18}O$ vary as a response, not just to different geography, but to changing climate as well.'

'I couldn't have put it better myself,' said Harriet. She rose to her feet and took his mug. 'More coffee?'

While she recharged the coffee machine, Alan continued, this time to Amy:

'So stable isotope analysis can be used to pin down with remarkable precision where a person spent their childhood. That's because the water we all drink as kids directly affects the composition of our teeth. In England, for example, the counties east or west of the Pennines have separate sources of water with very different mineral composition. And it will show up in the analyses. It's as simple as that.'

'But is it?' Amy asked. 'Sounds complicated to me. Especially the analysis. I mean the quantities involved are minute, aren't they?'

'Oh yes.' It was Harriet's turn now, as she returned to her chair, 'the labs are incredibly hi-tec. Spotlessly clean. Judd's place is amazing.'

'Yes,' Alan said, 'you wouldn't be let in wearing a pair of muddy wellies.' Amy managed a smile at this. Alan continued: 'But seriously, that's why we have to be so careful when storing and selecting our material. It's an expensive process, and nobody can afford to waste time and money by sending in dodgy samples. We'll have to get it right.'

'And we will, don't you worry about that,' said Harriet, flashing Alan a smile.

Alan smiled back. He felt better already. There was something very reassuring about working side by side with Harriet. In the cocoon of her office, where facts were facts, where evidence was collected and things could be proved definitely. A welcome contrast with the rest of his life at the moment.

Looking slightly daunted, Amy took her coffee back to the bench and Harriet produced a file of context sheets. Although there were sixteen bodies in all, some were missing skulls, probably due to later disturbance, and others could not be fully excavated. After carefully checking through the collection, they decided on a short list of about a dozen. It had not been a difficult decision. The group of babies were far too immature for tests of their teeth, which hadn't yet fully formed.

It was time for the serious discussion. Harriet began with the obvious question.

'How many samples do you think Alistair will be prepared to pay for?'

'I honestly don't think he's too worried. But I wouldn't want to include any that weren't strictly necessary.' He paused. 'And besides, we might need to touch him for more money when the results come through.'

Alan knew that like himself, Harriet was very enthusiastic about the potential of stable isotope analysis. Even now, she couldn't hide her excitement. If some of the graves contained earlier Saxon remains then stable isotopes might reveal their origins and that would directly affect her own research into the earliest English population.

'What's the betting that tight group of burials around the tower includes at least one or two people from the Continent?'

Alan was less enthusiastic. He still believed that although the analyses might be very precise, their interpretation was still very prone to error. There were factors they still didn't fully understand.

'Quite possibly, but I still have my doubts.'

'Surely it's so straightforward?'

'Is it? Isn't that what everyone said when Libby invented radiocarbon dating, in 1949? It was going to transform everything. Ten years later, they realised sunspots were affecting the upper atmosphere and that some dates could be out by centuries. That little cock-up took thirty years to sort out. I'm just concerned, that's all: it seems too perfect, too fast.'

'Yes, Alan, but this isn't dependent on solar radiation or anything as complex and variable as that. This is down to water and water has always been the same.'

Alan was far from convinced, but he decided not to prolong the discussion. They had work to finish.

'So what,' Alan asked, 'are the main questions you want to resolve with these tests?'

'I'm interested in two basic problems. First, I want to look at the composition of the Middle and Late Saxon population. Were they still maintaining contact with the Continental mainland? Were the children of the elite being brought up abroad, for example? We just don't know. And second, I'm interested in the Middle Ages. It's generally accepted that the non-urban population was stable and essentially feudal around here. People lived out their lives in one parish. And this corner of rural Lincolnshire would be an ideal place to test this model…'

'Yes,' Alan replied, 'wouldn't it be a laugh if half the people buried at Guthlic's came from Wales?'

'Don't be silly, Alan.'

Obviously Harriet didn't altogether approve of his flippancy.

But she smiled as she continued, 'But I agree, we must be prepared for the unexpected.'

After another hour they had selected just ten samples for stable isotope analysis at Saltaire. These were taken to the Out Store for safe keeping. Clara had reserved them part of a shelf – all the space she could spare, as by now the place was cluttered up with a mass of material displaced by the sudden appearance of Simon Cox's entire site archive. They put the samples on their allotted shelf and then reported back to Clara. Clara was still spitting blood. She hated having her well-oiled system disrupted, especially, she fumed, 'By a little prick like the aptly-named Cox.'

Harriet and Alan retreated to the canteen.

The stable isotope samples were too precious to entrust to a delivery service, so they'd arranged that Alan would collect them on the Tuesday after Easter and ferry them to Judd's lab in Saltaire, just outside Bradford. Alan smiled at the coincidence. It almost felt fated. A sign, if he believed in that kind of thing – which he didn't. He was returning to the place where he and Lane first met.

* * *

After lunch they returned to Harriet's office, where Amy had finished laying out all the material for radiocarbon dating. Alan had selected a couple of animal bone samples, but after a brief discussion they rejected them as possibly residual and potentially misleading. So the dating of the site would entirely depend on samples taken from human bone.

'Right,' Alan began, 'I think we're both agreed that all four burials in that tight group at the foot of the tower are worth doing.'

'Absolutely,' Harriet agreed. 'They're so close to the tower they must be our best bets for an early date.'

'So what else…' Alan was thumbing through the various context sheets.

Harriet was doing the same, on-screen.

'How about those few by the south transept?'

'Yes, why not? They're almost certainly post-Conquest.'

'But pre-Reformation,' Alan broke in, 'because most of the Early Modern graves are to the south-west, over by the sexton's shed.'

'Yes, that should give us a good idea of the spread. I mean, what if the stable isotopes throw up something interesting? Won't we then want a better idea of the date range?'

'Yes, I agree. Let's do five,' Alan suggested.

'No, six.'

'Alright, six it is. Glad I'm not paying.'

They paused, as clearly neither of them wanted to raise the difficult problem of the babies. Alan went first.

'What about those neonates? What the hell do we do about them?'

'I don't think we can justify doing all five, do you?'

'No, certainly not at this stage.'

Harriet looked up.

'What do you mean?'

Alan hadn't intended to be so specific. He had a gut feeling about those babies, but he didn't want to share it. At least not today. He'd had enough difficult, emotionally draining conversations for the time being. This one could keep, at least until they had a few more facts.

'Not at this precise stage in the process. It may eventually turn out that we need to do all five, but I do think we ought to ask Alistair first. After all, he's paying for them.'

'Oh that's fine then. Yes, I agree, let's do three. I'm sure it'll be enough.'

For the final two hours of the afternoon they packed the nine radiocarbon samples. They worked as a team: Harriet selected suitable bones from the groups on the bench and weighed them, then Alan sealed them into polythene bags, while Amy recorded details on her laptop. It was important that nothing got muddled. So they worked slowly and methodically. In silence.

When they had finished, they carried the boxes out to the Land Rover. Alan would deliver them from home the following morning. The radiocarbon lab, the Cambridge Radiocarbon Facility, was in the Fisher Science Park just south of the A14 Newmarket Road. He was looking forward to the trip. A day away from PFC was just what he needed at the moment.

* * *

Towards the end of the week after Easter, Alan drove down to Blackfen Prison for his fourth Lifers' Club session.

He had toyed with the idea of working back from the present, as if his lectures were an excavator, digging down to the earliest levels. But then he abandoned the idea and decided to be more conventional and start at the beginning. The first two A-level sessions had set the scene, but now it was time to get down to business, which of course meant the Stone Age. After the lecture, and while the other students were looking through a collection of flint tools, Ali was the first to be taken to the interview room for his individual session. After their previous meeting Alan realised that he needed to be much more careful, more subtle in his conversation – at least make some effort to seem like he was here for the archaeology. So he opened up a discussion on the skill and precision of flint technology.

Ali was enthusiastic and articulate. As they talked, Alan realised that he was a practical person too. He was plainly good with his hands and had no difficulty appreciating the methodology of pressure-flaking. He'd known undergraduates who never grasped it.

As Ali talked, his body language relaxed. Once again, Alan caught a glimpse of the boy he had once been. Alan realised, that was the way to play it. Don't try to compete with the macho posturing of the prisoner. Appeal to the Ali that he still believed was in there, somewhere…

Towards the end of their discussion Alan tried to bring the conversation round to more general thoughts.

'You know what, Ali, you've a great grasp of the subject. I've known third-year students struggle with it. You're a natural, and if you do well on this course, we could register you for a part-time degree.'

'And what's the point of that?'

The defensiveness was suddenly back.

'You've got a real talent. It would be a shame to waste it.'

'So you think I should become an archaeologist and earn, what, eight grand a year?'

Alan wasn't going to rise to this.

'There's lots of avenues you could explore. Take Paul Flynn for example, he's done very well for himself.'

'Yeah, I know all about that.'

There was a tone of pure hatred in Ali's voice. Alan could feel himself holding his breath. Was this it? Was Ali about to spill the beans about the arrangement his family had with PFC? The drug money, perhaps?

Alan tried to keep his voice calm as he replied.

'Of course. Your brother's firm does a lot of work for him. Paul says they're good, and reliable.'

'*Cheap* and reliable, you mean.' Ali was grinning. 'My goodness gracious me sir, we can do it even cheaper for you Sahib...'

Ali's cod Indian accent had a slightly chilling edge.

'Ali, I don't deal with the business side of things at PFC.'

'No. But you do know Flynn. And you go back a long time together, don't you?'

'Yes, but like I said, he's my boss now.'

'Well,' Ali dropped his voice, 'you must tell your old friend Dr Paul Flynn, that my family won't be pushed around. We don't like greedy men. You understand?'

Alan was shocked. He hadn't expected this.

'Er... yes, I think I do. I'll do my best to have a word with him.'

Ali leant forward. His eyes were narrow. He dropped his voice even more.

'No, my friend. You don't understand. Your best isn't good enough. Tell him my brother Abdul is angry. Very angry indeed. You *must* tell him. Right?'

'Right. I'll tell him.'

'And you want some advice?'

Alan nodded slowly, carefully.

'If I were you, I'd find myself another job.'

* * *

DCI Lane was sitting at a corner table in the back bar of the Slodger. Alan joined him and Lane produced a small computer from a padded skin, brightly printed with the logo of a large bulldozer manufacturer. Alan looked at the netbook admiringly.

'You see I'm a plant hire rep and you're a customer.'

'Oh I get it. But could you bluff your way out, if anyone challenged?'

'Of course, don't forget, my old man was in the trade for nearly fifty years, when we lived in Melton. I used to help him quite often, when money was short.'

He put on a spivvy salesman's voice.

'And what can I interest you in sir: have you tried our new 80hp 360, with extra-wide bog-crawler tracks and twenty per cent greater fuel economy at max revs. It's had rave reviews from the biggest contractors in the land.'

He opened the computer.

'Let me take your order, sir… Excellent: A two week hire. And will that be self-drive or our operator?'

Alan was smiling broadly.

'You're almost convincing, Richard. Almost.'

Alan took a long pull from his pint. He needed that.

As he put his glass down, Lane asked,

'So how did it go?'

'He's as confident as ever. Quite extraordinary.'

'Do you think he'll finish your course?'

Something told Alan that Lane's concern had little to do with Ali's intellectual career.

'Why, are you worried my contacts with him might end?'

'Well, it's natural I'd be concerned. There's a lot riding on this, you know.'

'I'm sorry, Richard. I'm well aware of that.'

Alan took another pull from his beer. 'Are they… Are the Yard getting at you – nagging you for results?'

'I wouldn't put it as strongly as that. But they're certainly quite keen.'

'What's the rush? I would have thought that getting a good – correct – result would be the most important thing.'

Lane sat back in his chair. He suddenly looked very tired.

'I think the high-ups are trying to meet a government narcotics target. It's part of a new annual national drug-usage assessment. They're looking for easy pickings. Nice statistics. A *Daily Mail* headline.'

Politics, again, thought Alan. He tried hard not to show his irritation.

'But why pick on you – on us?'

'I don't think they are,' Lane replied, 'So far as I can make out it's countrywide. But I'm trying to find out more.'

'What's the assessment's deadline?'

'Mid-May. Then they write the report over the summer, ready for the next session of Parliament in the autumn.'

'So that means they'll need results fast.'

'More to the point,' Lane suggested, 'it means they're likely to mount a raid, if they think the time's right. And they don't need to give us any prior warning.'

'Oh, shit. That would screw everything.'

'It certainly would. So we've got to give them enough to persuade them that we're establishing a case, but we mustn't suggest that it would be worth going in mob-handed tomorrow.'

'I'd be prepared to bet that Ali or one of his family firms is involved in the mobile phone business.'

'Yes, our people in Leicester have traced a cousin of theirs who runs a mobile phone warehouse. He's in it in a big way.'

'Legit?'

'Hard to say. But not openly bent. Cut priced and bit shady.'

'Not exactly hard-line drugs trafficking though, is it?'

'No,' said Lane. 'And that's the problem.'

'What about Abdul? Did you get anything on him?'

Lane consulted his computer, genuinely this time.

'He's part of the empire all right. He runs AK Plant. But he doesn't own it. He's an employee.'

'Of Old Mehmet?'

'That's right.'

'And is that normal? Within this kind of community?'

Alan winced as he said it, but Lane clearly knew what he meant.

'I've been talking to some of our own specialists in community relations and they tell me that even today, after sometimes three or four generations in the UK we still see,' he referred to his netbook, ' "a pattern of top-down patriarchy within Turkish families". But then, think about your white aristocracy, the landed gentry – it's not so different with them, either, is it?'

Alan had a momentary flashback to the AAC portrait staring down at him from the wall in Alistair's house. He had to agree.

'Yes, those who make the money, always have to control it.'

'Or use it to control others.'

Alan nodded. Lane was absolutely right.

'So, all we've got is two men present at the moment of the murder,' mused Alan. 'They could be any combination of Old Mehmet, Ali and Abdul.'

When Lane spoke next his tone was soft, sympathetic even.

'We haven't even got that. There's no conclusive proof that what you heard was actually the… event itself.'

This offered no comfort to Alan whatsoever. Lane hadn't heard that scream. Alan had. He still did. He was in no doubt at all about what it signified. But in Lane's world, that was all conjecture.

'OK, Richard, so what do we do now?'

'As they say in the movies, we follow the money. So, I want to run a few names past you. See if they ring any bells.'

'Fire away.'

Alan leant back. Lane focused again on his computer.

'The first is something called the Anatolian Foundation…'

Alan sat up abruptly.

'Bloody hell,' he said, thinking hard, 'That does ring bells. Harriet mentioned them.'

'Harriet your… housemate?'

Alan thought he could detect a slight tone of incredulity in Lane's voice. He chose to ignore it.

'My co-director at Guthlic's. She works for PFC.'

'Sorry, go on, Alan.'

'Harriet's working on this massive international dig in Turkey: the Çatol Huyut project.'

'Yes, I've read about it in the Sunday papers.'

'That's the one. Well, I'm pretty certain she mentioned the Anatolian Foundation as one of the principal funding bodies – along with the English Research Council, the English

Academy, the Archaeological Research Fund and various other major bodies.'

'That's very interesting...'

'Yes, it is,' Alan continued, 'because I don't think such top-flight organisations would get into bed with a flaky outfit. There'd be too much at stake. They must have run independent checks on them.'

'I agree,' Lane replied, 'which only goes to show they must be squeaky clean.'

'So what else have you found out?'

'For a start, they're based here in Leicester.'

'Yes, come to think of it, she did have to drive here, about a month ago – with a new proposal for the next season. Apparently they're extremely generous. All she has to do is give an annual lecture to a big Turkish dining club somewhere in the city centre. No official report.'

Lane was now rapidly scanning his computer screen.

'It seems they disburse about two hundred thousand pounds a year. That suggests they must have capital in the region of... maybe ten million. Something of that order?'

'Blimey.' Alan was impressed. Something stirred in the back of his mind. He shut his eyes and thought hard. Then it came to him.

'As I recall, Harriet was put onto them by Paul.'

'That's interesting...'

Alan could see that Lane was very focused now. Perhaps too focused.

'They work together. To be honest, it would be odd if they didn't share funding information.'

Alan was doing his best to sound casual. He wasn't at all sure it was working. He pushed on, regardless, 'Anyhow, from what

Harriet told me, Paul put her in touch with the Foundation about five years ago, when PFC was still quite small. He'd had money from them when his company did the reference collections for the new British School at Izmir…'

He thought for a few moments, then continued: 'That's right, it was one of Paul's other enterprises, *Reference Collections Ltd.'s*, very first projects. I think he still maintains some form of contact with them.'

'Them?'

Lane was getting muddled.

'Them: the Anatolian Foundation – although I'm not sure *how* he manages to keep in touch.'

As Alan said this, he was becoming uncomfortably aware that if Lane continued down this route he'd soon discover the PFC and AK Plant double-accounting system. And that would be it. The St Guthlic's Post/X would be shut down. The whole company would be engulfed by the scandal. He didn't care that much about what happened to Paul, or to himself for that matter; but Harriet… She'd lose valuable research material, it would probably also compromise her book deal. It could ruin the academic reputation that she'd fought so hard to achieve. After all, there were plenty of people out there – the same jealous academic types that spread rumours about her difficult reputation – who would positively delight in such a spectacular fall from grace, of the illustrious Dr Harriet Webb.

Alan realised he'd have to contain the situation the best he could, at least for now. He needed time to think. He focused on Lane's next question.

Lane was still interested in the Foundation.

'I assume they have a properly set-up and established grant-giving side. We do know from Companies House that they're a limited company without share capital and with charitable status.'

'Yes,' Alan cut in, 'that's more or less universal in the heritage/archaeology sector. Usually there's just one nominal share worth a pound. The point is, that such companies don't have to use the word "Limited" in their title, but they do have to conform to Companies House rules and regulations. Like any company they have detailed Mem. and Arts.'

'What?'

Alan was hoping that this smokescreen of jargon and technicalities was doing the trick. He pressed on.

'Memorandas and Articles of Association, and of course they must follow strict accounting rules to retain the tax advantages of a charity. I'm involved with the Walbeach Historical Trust and I can tell you the bureaucracy can be a right pain...'

'Well, anyhow,' Lane continued, 'I also persuaded my friendly forensic accountant to take a look at their published records. It seems that once again, they're entirely above board.'

'And I assume Mehmet is a big donor?'

'No,' Lane replied, 'he's *the* donor.'

'So the tax advantages of maintaining the Foundation's charitable status must be important to him?'

'Oh, certainly. But I think there's more to it than that. I gather the Foundation is held in very high esteem by the British Turkish community and Kabul is seen as the grandfather.'

'Shouldn't that be godfather?'

Alan couldn't resist it. But Lane seemed to have taken it seriously.

'Honestly, I don't know.' Lane paused. 'I'll be frank with you, Alan. I'm also not entirely convinced about the whole drugs business. The more we look into Mehmet, the cleaner he seems.'

'But what about Abdul?'

'Ah, well. He's another matter. We know he's very sharp and has done some distinctly shady things in the past.'

'Does he have form?' Alan asked

'So far not. He's too shrewd for that. Anyhow, he's now running Ali's van business very efficiently too.'

'What,' Alan broke in, 'better than Ali did?'

'My sources say that he's at least as good. Possibly better. It's still too early to know for certain. But the interesting thing is, he's running it as a separate entity to the rest of Old Mehmet's empire. This is Abdul's baby, so's to speak.'

'And you – or rather the Yard – reckon drugs could be behind it all?'

'Yes. I gather they suspect Abdul in particular.'

'But again no proof?

Lane shook his head. But Alan couldn't let it rest there.

'But surely these Middle Eastern families are known to be very close. You've said so yourself. You can't expect me to believe that if Abdul's up to no good, then the man who brought him up – who raised him – his own grandfather, wouldn't be aware of it?'

'I agree. That's what worries me.'

'But don't the high-ups at Scotland Yard share your worries?'

'I don't know.'

Alan was astonished.

'What do you mean, you don't know?'

Lane was getting visibly frustrated.

'What I said. I don't know. They haven't asked me, so I haven't mentioned my views. As far as they're concerned, the opinions of a mere provincial copper aren't very important.'

This was a complicating factor Alan hadn't anticipated.

'Why on earth not?'

'Look, Alan, I have to work in the real world. And I won't get far if I'm constantly bickering with those higher up the tree, in London. And besides, like them, I need evidence to support any allegations.'

It seemed like they were back at square one.

'I know,' Alan broke in. 'We need hard evidence. Of murder. Or drugs. Or both.'

'Exactly,' said Lane grimly. 'And we need it soon.'

* * *

The night sky out in the Slodger's car park was superb. There was a slight amber glow to the north over Walbeach and a larger one far away where Peterborough lit up the western horizon. But the rest of the sky was infinitely black and mysterious. The stars seemed to be hanging there, in three dimensions, as if tethered. Lane was staring upwards, transported for the moment.

'Isn't it amazing, the night sky out here? So clear. I suppose you take it for granted, but in Leicester we never see it.'

But Alan's mind was firmly down on earth. As they'd walked across to their vehicles, it had come to him that Ali wasn't the only route to penetrate the Kabul family. Somebody else had done it, seven years ago.

'There's one other thing, Richard. You told me when I came to see you that first time in Leicester that the main prosecution evidence came from Sofia's fiancé?'

'That's right, Indajit Singh Gupta.'

'At the time we spoke, he was in India. Is he back now?'

'Oh yes. In fact I'll be seeing him shortly, about a new case. D'you want me to put you in touch?'

'That would be great, Richard, it really would. Tell him I'd like to see him over the weekend. Text me his phone number.'

'No problem. I'll mention you're interested in the Flax Hole business. I know he still feels strongly about it.'

By now Lane had got into his car and started the engine.

Alan, standing alongside him, asked:

'Still, after all this time?'

'Yes,' Lane replied, frowning now, his face lit by the dashboard lights, 'so please go carefully, Alan…' He paused, then continued: 'The thing is, I like the man, I really do. And I'd hate to see him more distressed.'

'It's as bad as that, is it?'

'No, not on the surface. But deep down something about Flax Hole still worries him. I sometimes wonder whether it's been the reason he never married. Anyhow, see what you can discover, but please, please tread carefully…'

And with that he drove off into the night.

Alan watched as the tail lights of Lane's car disappeared into the darkness.

He was grappling with his conscience. Lane was being open and honest with him and he was doing the very thing that he had promised he wouldn't: withholding information. Should he have told Lane about Ali's threat to Paul? Probably. Almost certainly. But then it led to the same dilemma as the dodgy accounting: there was simply too much to lose by drawing attention to PFC, at least at the moment.

He told himself he'd take it step by careful step. He could see that he was too close to the case, too emotionally involved.

Ali was certainly not the innocent young man he'd first assumed him to be when he read that news clipping all those months ago. But beyond that, he had no idea what to think.

He needed a different perspective. A lawyer's perspective. He'd listen without prejudice to Indajit Singh's case. Only then could he decide on his next move.

Twenty

Alan was sitting in the waiting room of a smart legal practice in central Leicester, thumbing through a copy of *Country Life*. Mr Singh, the receptionist had told him, would be with him shortly. Lane had warned Singh in advance that Alan would be in touch with him, but even so, Alan didn't find their short phone conversation the previous night particularly pleasant. The lawyer sounded preoccupied and made it quite clear that he didn't need yet another appointment in an already over-stacked diary. But Alan insisted, and at last he relented.

Indajit Singh had been a junior graduate lawyer, then serving in a practice in Nottingham at the time of the killing. He had been twenty-five, then; now Alan reckoned, he must be about thirty-three.

A list of names displayed on a list on the wall had already informed Alan that the confident young man who walked into reception was now a partner in the firm. He was dressed in a sober dark suit and brightly polished black Oxford shoes. His complexion was urban, un-tanned and he wore his hair short. Like many non-religious Sikhs he did not have a beard or a turban. He said a few words to the receptionist, an astonishingly beautiful young Asian woman, and walked across to Alan.

They shook hands.

'I could see you were an archaeologist from the other side of the room. It's your beard, you know. We Sikhs wear them too, but not as often as you archaeologists.'

'I'm sorry to be so predictable, Mr Singh…'

He cut him off as if he were in court:

'I'd rather everyone were predictable,' he said lightly, 'It would make lawyers' lives so much simpler. Now how can I help you?'

He was putting on a light overcoat; he was on his way out to lunch. Alan knew he would have to grab his attention fast if he had any hopes of detaining him for long.

'As I mentioned on the phone last night, I was an archaeologist working at the Flax Hole Depot in 2002.'

The young lawyer's expression had grown somewhat severe.

'Yes, I remember. But how does that affect *me*?'

Alan was surprised at this change in Mr Singh's attitude. He tried to make his reply non-confrontational.

'I know you put together the case against Ali Kabul. I'd like to talk to you about it. To get the full picture.'

Singh brushed this aside, rather irritably.

'He was convicted in court and is now in jail. What more is there to say?'

Indajit Singh had turned on his heels, shaking his head and walked straight out of the office. Despite Lane's recommendation, he plainly thought Alan was another sad – or worse, sick – crank. Through the front window Alan could see the lawyer turn right outside the office main door, probably heading towards the smarter restaurants nearer the centre of town. Alan looked across to the receptionist, who smiled awkwardly and gave a barely perceptible shrug of her shoulders.

Alan went to a local pub and ate something fried. Or microwaved. It didn't matter – either way he knew he'd get heartburn shortly.

A bare quarter of an hour later, he crossed to the other side of the main road opposite Mr Singh's offices. There he waited, partly concealed behind pedestrian traffic lights. After some twenty-five minutes he spotted him. That overcoat was a give-away. He was alone and walking briskly. This time more drastic action was needed. Unnoticed, Alan re-crossed the road, and came up behind him. It was a crowded street.

Just as he was pausing to pull on his office's front door, Alan intercepted him again. This time he took a more personal approach.

'The thing is, I knew Sofia. She visited the dig a couple of times. In fact, I think I might have actually been on site when the murder happened. It's been haunting me ever since I realised. I just need some answers.'

That stopped the lawyer dead. He turned to confront Alan, who fully expected him to summon the community policewoman they could both see standing just two doors away. But he didn't.

'You knew her?'

'Not very well... but she was a lovely girl. And I have to say, I think there's more to this case than meets the eye.'

Indajit stood there silent for a moment, obviously weighing up the situation. Then he briskly nodded his head.

'OK, I'll give you ten minutes, but no more. I've an important client to see,' he glanced down at his watch, 'at two-fifteen.'

They went into the foyer and sat down on two of the low leather armchairs reserved for visitors.

* * *

Indajit Singh sat back pressing the tips of his fingers together, rather like a Buddhist at prayer, Alan thought. But he was also well aware that this non-Buddhist was no mystic. He needed facts. Clear, unambiguous facts.

Alan started by describing his talks to The Lifers' Club and how he was beginning to understand Ali, who certainly wasn't a fundamentalist. He described Sofia's visit to the excavations and overhearing her screams afterwards. He didn't mention Abdul, it was important that he kept the lawyer focused on Alan's own personal relationship with Sofia. That was the most important thing. Throughout Alan's account, Indajit's face remained expressionless. Alan had no idea how he was reacting. So his initial question came as a surprise.

'First, tell me something about the excavation. What did you find – a Roman fortress? A temple? A plague pit? – and why didn't I get to hear about it at the time?'

'It was a routine job. Part of the planning process. There was no publicity. Most commercial clients prefer it that way. The site was an eighteenth-century flax-processing mill. Pits full of rotting fibres. Workshop floors. No bodies. No gold. Lots of mud, but no glamour. Our job was to get in, dig it, and get out. We had to ensure that the builders weren't unnecessarily delayed. Simple as that.'

'And was there a report?'

'Of course. I'll get them to print you one off.'

'Thank you.'

Alan pulled out his diary and jotted a memo to himself.

Then Indajit got to the point.

'So what is it, exactly, that you want to know?'

'It's quite simple really,' said Alan. 'In your professional opinion, what do you think drove Ali Kabul to kill his sister and dump her body in the Humber?'

Alan didn't like using confrontational shock tactics, but he knew he had very little time to get the lawyer's full attention.

There was a long pause while Indajit considered what Alan had said. He closed his eyes, clearly deep in thought. After a minute or so he replied.

'To be honest, Mr Cadbury, I never believed Sofia was in either the Humber or Turkey. I knew she was dead, quite simply because if she were alive, she would have contacted me. We were, after all, engaged. But I must also confess that for some time I, too, have been troubled by aspects of the case. I know we got a good conviction at the trial. Many said we couldn't do it, without the forensic evidence. Even now, I have to say, I find that lack of definitive, physical proof a little unsettling.'

'Well,' said Alan quietly, 'that's where I think I can help. We, the digging team, were there all the time. In fact I wouldn't be at all surprised if there were clues to this mystery still lying out there in, or on, the ground.'

'Oh come, you can't be serious?'

'Look, Mr Singh, modern crime – indeed modern archaeology – isn't about finding blood-soaked daggers. We've come a long way since those days. Some years ago I did an MA course in Forensic Archaeology.'

'With my friend Richard Lane?'

'That's the one. Anyhow, we learned a great deal about the importance of circumstantial evidence. Crime is about far more than the criminal alone. It's all about motivation, opportunity and circumstance. And these are things we understand in archaeology. We're very good at reconstructing past situations: everything from groundwater drainage to vegetation, climate, even diet and passing traffic.'

'OK...'

What he implied was: OK, you're not a nutter.

Indajit, who was clearly concentrating deeply now, continued.

'So what do you propose to do about it?'

Alan knew he must state his case succinctly.

'First I must find out more from Ali. I'm certain he has a great deal to tell me, once, that is, I've regained his trust more fully. Then I plan to discover Sofia's remains.'

Alan knew that this was a bold statement, but it was important that Indajit understood how serious he was about all of this.

Indajit sat back in his chair and smiled indulgently at Alan.

'So you think Ali will just tell you, personally? After he's consistently lied to the court.'

'No,' Alan paused so that his next comment had its full effect.

'Because I'm not sure that he knows where the body is. I'm not entirely convinced that he did it. That's why I've come to hear your side of the story.'

This is it, thought Alan. This is the moment when he physically throws me out of the office. But Indajit just sat there, staring at the floor, deep in thought. When he finally spoke, there was a slight quiver to his voice.

'I have doubted the veracity of the confession for a while now,' he said softly. 'In truth I'm beginning to doubt almost everything, except the fact of Sofia's death…'

Alan was shocked, this was not what he expected at all. Lane had told him that the young man was still struggling to come to terms with the events, which of course explained his initial defensiveness. Alan chose his next words very carefully indeed.

'I still believe she was deliberately killed. I'm sure you were right about that.'

'May I be quite frank with you?'

Alan murmured his assent.

'I honestly do not know. Maybe I can't come to terms with somebody killing their closest relative, simply because she wanted to marry me. You see, I've always had a nagging feeling of guilt…'

'Because she fell in love with you? You must realise that's absurd.'

'Of course. I'm aware of that. But sometimes humans – and even lawyers are human, you know – can feel irrational emotions. I see it every day in my work. Maybe that's why I'm in no rush to get betrothed for a second time. Once bitten, twice shy.'

Alan was surprised by the young lawyer's sudden frankness. He wasn't sure whether he would have been prepared to shed his own reserve before a complete stranger quite so rapidly.

'But enough about me,' Indajit continued, 'tell me, what, in the current slang, "do you bring to the party?" Can you add anything to what was said at the trial?'

'Yes, a certain amount,' Alan replied. 'First, it does seem that our excavation did take place at the same time as the murder, yet nobody from the Crown Court or the police had approached us at the time of the trial. I don't suppose they even knew about the dig – and why should they?'

'You tell me.'

'For a start, it all happened seven years earlier. And that's a long time. The murder is said to have taken place in a building that we weren't concerned with, or working in. It was built, I think, in the earlier nineteenth century and was of no particular architectural or archaeological interest. Second, our dig was a perfectly routine part of the planning process. I don't suppose the police would have interviewed the architects, the consulting engineers, or the builders, either. The Kabul family wanted to enlarge and rebuild the depot and the dig was just a minor step along that process. The next stage was the digging of foundations and the pouring of concrete. So why should anyone have noticed our dig, any more than anything else?'

'That makes sense. So what are you saying?'

'That a potentially important body of evidence was ignored by the police, the prosecution and the defence – and probably for understandable reasons. But it was ignored nonetheless. That's point one.'

Indajit nodded in agreement.

'And point two?'

'As Richard Lane may have told you, I knew young Ali Kabul quite well on the dig. He was a bright, intelligent lad and very westernised. As I said, I've also begun to get to know Ali Kabul for a second time, in the A-level classes I mentioned on the phone...'

'The Dickensian-sounding Lifers' Club?'

'That's right, and he's not at all what I'd expected. He's far more complex than you might suppose. He's rational, articulate, reasonably well educated, and bright. Not what you would expect of a fundamentalist. He's more a freewheeling businessman, or an entrepreneur.'

Alan was aware that he was putting Ali's case very strongly, but he knew too he had to convince the lawyer that he had something new to 'bring to the party'.

'So if Ali is innocent who do you think *did* do it?' Indajit asked.

'I don't know. But I'm reliably informed that in such cases it's nearly always the head of the household…'

'Who in this instance was – is – old man Mehmet. I assume he's still alive?'

'Yes,' Alan replied. 'Alive and kicking. Making loads of money.'

'And what about Ali's older brother, Abdul?'

Alan paused. How to phrase this? He could sense that Indajit, like Lane, would have little time for conjecture.

'I only met him once, but I didn't like him. He seemed a bit of a bully.'

'I agree. I was very surprised when Ali suddenly confessed. Surprised and frankly, delighted.'

'And I don't blame you for one minute. After all, it brought you closure.'

'Of a sort. And for a time, yes.'

After a short pause, Alan continued.

'Do you think, hypothetically, that if either Mehmet or Abdul killed Sofia then they might have forced Ali into a false confession? Knowing the fact that he was so young when the crime was committed, meant he was bound to get a shorter sentence, especially if he expressed remorse?'

'It's certainly an interesting theory.'

Alan sat quietly and gave Indajit time to think it through.

'And if there's any truth in it,' Indajit said softly, 'then Ali is just as much a victim of his family's brutality as Sofia is.'

Alan couldn't have put it better himself. He also noted the lawyer's instinctive use of the present tense.

'The problem is,' continued Indajit, 'I don't think we'd ever be able to overturn the verdict; not unless we come up with some dramatic new evidence.'

Alan was pleased to hear Indajit was now talking in terms of 'we'.

'Why's that?'

'Confessions, especially such a full and frank one as Ali Kabul's, still carry far too much weight in English law. It's one of the things I'd like to see changed, if I could.'

How right he was, Alan thought. A confession says nothing about the most important aspect of any crime, which has to be the motive behind it. It seemed to him that if you took away the religious element, then Ali lacked any real motive. Indeed, any motive at all.

'So what can we do?' asked Alan.

'We go back to the start,' replied Indajit firmly. 'The fact that you heard something at Flax Hole, combined with the fact that the archaeological site was never investigated might – and I stress the word *might* – be enough to reopen the case.'

'I agree completely.' Alan tried to contain his enthusiasm: this was much more than he had hoped to achieve from their meeting.

'So, the first thing I'll do is apply for a permit to re-examine the Flax Hole site. I trust you will be happy to assist the investigation.'

'Absolutely. Anything you need.'

At that point the girl at the desk called across to Indajit:

'Mr Singh, your next client is waiting upstairs in your office.'

As he left, Alan smiled broadly at the receptionist. He'd felt like asking her out for a glass of champagne. But he didn't. Instead, as soon as he was back in the street, he turned left, counted thirty paces, then clapped his hands together in triumph. At last, things were starting to happen.

Twenty-one

Monday morning. Alan was in Paul's office, the largest at Priory Farm. At first he thought the room's size was just about status, but then he realised he was wrong. Paul was an animal bones specialist and he needed lots of space to work. There were bones boxes everywhere, and more on temporary racking outside, in the hall. Alan looked at the boxes, the racks, the microscope, two floodlit magnifyers, and further along the main bench two, no, three computers and a tablet. Was he, was all this equipment, making a statement? Was he proclaiming his expertise for all to see? Alan frowned, maybe he was being unfair; but he couldn't help comparing his own rather cramped office with this opulent set-up. What he did know was that Paul was fiercely protective of his academic reputation. He was currently studying material from a site just outside Lincoln, and every available surface was spread with hundreds of sheep and cattle bones, not to mention the tools of his trade: callipers of all shapes and sizes, plus scales and tape measures.

Paul was intently looking down a microscope, when Alan entered. After a few seconds he looked up, reached over to his desk and handed Alan a letter.

'This arrived earlier. Have a quick read.'

Then he returned to the microscope.

Alan scanned it rapidly. It was from a large firm of architects in Leicester and was headed 'Impingham House'. It was about a brand new development they were undertaking for clients in Leicester: Anatolian Enterprises Ltd. Alan was gripped by dread just looking at the name. Old Mehmet, again, extending his influence over PFC. Pouring his drugs money, or whatever it was, directly into Paul's coffers. But despite this feeling of disgust, he also realised that here was an opportunity, finally, to raise the subject of Flax Hole.

The letter went on to outline a development just east of the city, which included the conversion of a much run-down late Georgian country house, officially Listed at Grade II. It was a large project, which would leave the shell of the building intact, plus one or two important internal features, such as a fine oak staircase. Otherwise the plans involved a complete rebuild.

There was also to be a capacious new landscaped car park and the large, Italianate mid-Victorian buildings of the Home Farm (recently also Listed at Grade II) were to become a conference centre, to be known as The Kabul Centre. Alan could scarcely believe what he was reading: the scale was huge. The Kabul Centre alone included a substantial gym, swimming pool, a bar and restaurant, not to mention thirty bedrooms in a brand new building concealed behind one of the two existing barns.

It wasn't too much of a stretch for Alan to add a tone of incredulity to his voice.

'Kabul, isn't that the family who employed us at Flax Hole all those years ago?'

'That's right.'

'Quite a coincidence, don't you think?'

'Not at all. As you may recall, I've always said it pays to remain loyal to old contacts. That's why we have always used his grandson's plant hire firm. I had long suspected that the old man might have bigger plans in the future.'

'And you were right, Paul.'

For once the flattery seemed to have been wasted; Paul ignored it.

'But read on. Your bit's on the next page.'

Alan returned to the letter. The land around Impingham House had been made into a park in the mid-eighteenth century. During this process, as quite often happened, they had depopulated a small medieval village which survived to this day as a series of humps and bumps in grazed grassland, surrounded by the trees of the park. This deserted medieval village, or DMV in the jargon, was legally protected by being Scheduled, but had never been surveyed in detail, nor dated adequately. And that, Paul told him, was to be Alan's next task.

'It's a fairly tight timetable, so I want fieldwork to begin in exactly a fortnight's time, in the first week of May.'

'Does this mean you've just given me the job?' Alan asked with genuine surprise.

'Of course. And I also suggest you should increase your invoices by ten per cent.'

Normally Alan would have been delighted. But in this case taking an extra ten per cent of Old Mehmet's money left a rather sour taste in his mouth.

Paul continued regardless. 'And as for the DMV survey, you could do it blindfold. It's right up your street.'

'And budgets?'

'Don't worry about them. The developers have already phoned to tell me their only concern is delay – and that usually means they'll pay to avoid any.'

'And how long have we… have I got?'

'That depends on the County's attitude to the DMV. They'll determine what needs to be done, not us. So I've arranged a meeting with them on site tomorrow. I suggest we both assemble here at eight sharp, then drive over.'

Paul returned to his microscope. The interview was over. But Alan remained standing. He cleared his throat. Paul looked up.

'Yes?'

'There's one other thing I have to mention, Paul.'

'Go on…'

Alan gathered his courage. It was now or never.

'I'm afraid I have to declare a conflict of interest here.'

Paul immediately looked irritated. Alan realised that this was a foolish thing to have done, to present the subject as a problem. Paul didn't like problems. Too late now.

'You know I'm running an A-level course at Blackfen?'

'Yes. But you're under a paid contract at PFC. Your work for us should take priority.'

'Of course. It's not that.'

Paul gestured to Alan to continue.

'One of my students is Ali Kabul. Old Mehmet's grandson. You might remember him from Flax Hole? He visited the site several times.'

'I'm afraid not. Mind you, I was somewhat preoccupied with making sure we remained within our budget. Didn't have much time for the trench work.'

Alan was taken aback. Paul was lying. Blatantly. The split of responsibilities between them didn't happen until halfway through the dig. In fact, Alan had a clear memory of Paul discovering Ali and himself in the finds store and warning the young lad about not messing up the artefacts. All right, if Paul was lying, it was time to push him harder.

'He murdered his own sister.'

At this, Paul stopped what he was doing and looked up.

'That's terrible.'

Alan might have been imagining it, but Paul's response sounded almost too sincere, too calm. It certainly wasn't the tone of voice of someone who was hearing such shocking news for the first time. And there were no questions: why? How? When? Alan pressed on.

'I know, it was in all the papers, apparently.'

'You know how it is when you're in the middle of a big project, Alan, the everyday stuff can pass you by.'

'Hardly everyday, though is it? And don't you remember, when we were at Flax Hole that incident…'

Paul cut in, impatient.

'I appreciate your concern, Alan. I see there's a potential issue with PFC being associated with Ali's family. However, as far as I see it, justice has been done and there's no need for the sins of the grandson to be visited upon Mehmet Kabul. In fact, I'd go as far as saying that it would be unethical to do so.'

Alan felt his blood boil. The arrogance of it all astounded him. Here Paul was, using the Kabuls' money to prop up his own empire and he had the gall to quote ethics at Alan. Time to hit him with the hard facts.

'If only it were that simple, Paul. The thing is, on my last visit to Blackfen, Ali told me to pass on what sounds like a threat.'

'What, to me?'

Paul looked puzzled. Amused even. It wasn't the response Alan had anticipated.

'Yes. To Dr Paul Flynn. I'm afraid he was very specific.'

Paul continued to look sceptical.

'What did he say?'

'His precise words were: "Tell him my brother Abdul is angry. Very angry indeed."'

'How very strange, given this letter. I suspect he was bluffing, trying to assert some kind of control. After all, there he is, stuck in prison, disowned by his family.'

Gotcha, thought Alan. How could Paul possibly know about the family estrangement if he was ignorant of Ali's crime? But he decided not to push it. Better to play along with Paul's lies, at least for now.

'No, there's nothing to worry about on that front, Alan. As you know, we've used AK Plant for some years and we're currently negotiating a new long-term contract.'

'So you're not upset?'

'Good heavens, no. I saw Abdul quite recently and he was his usual charming self. Don't forget these people have a long tradition of hard-nosed bargaining. It's part of life in the soukhs and backstreets of places like Istanbul and Baghdad. You mustn't believe everything they say. When the bargaining's over, they'll hug you like a long-lost brother.'

'Well, that's a relief. I was quite worried.'

'Again, I appreciate your concern. However…'

Paul was using his most patronising voice.

'I think you need to focus your attention on your obligations to PFC, don't you?'

Alan was really struggling to contain his rage now.

'Are you saying that I should terminate my work at Blackfen? Abandon my students?'

'Good grief, no.' Paul was smiling now. 'However, with the increased workload of the next few weeks I do hope that you will be able to prioritise accordingly, that's all.'

Alan nodded, then turned on his heel and marched out, before he said something he knew he'd regret.

* * *

That evening Alan was battling with his conscience, yet again. If it was just his and Paul's reputation on the line, he'd have no hesitation in sharing his discoveries with Lane. But Harriet certainly didn't deserve to be dragged down with them. With a heavy heart he decided that the only option was selective disclosure. That and keeping a very close eye on Paul and the Kabul clan.

He shut himself away in his room, and dialled Lane's number. When Lane answered, he got straight to the point.

'Hi Richard. Just a quickie. Did you know that one of our friend Mehmet's companies, Anatolian Developments, was planning to re-develop Impingham House? It's on your patch, isn't it?'

'Yes, I know the place well. Fine old trees. In fact I drive past it regularly and I'd noticed the farm buildings were starting to decay. Windows smashed. Tiles missing. You can just glimpse them through the trees in winter. But the development... no, I didn't know about that.'

'They haven't yet applied for official Planning Approval.'

'That's a relief. If they had, I'd have words with our local team.'

'No,' Alan continued, 'not yet. That's the next stage. But I do know their architects have had informal talks with the Planning people.'

'Bloody hell, why didn't our blokes find out? They're meant to be keeping an eye on the Kabuls.'

'Well,' Alan continued, 'I do think it might be relevant to our investigations.'

'Why's that?'

'For all the world it looks to me like a massive, all-singing-and-all-dancing version of "Mehmet's". The plans I've seen make it look like "Mehmet's" with gold-plated bath taps.'

'Good heavens...'

'I know, it's gross. But it does seem very well thought-out, with acres of car park, bars and meetings rooms everywhere. The architects have done a thorough job. Judging by the plans, it all seems to be about networking and conferences. That sort of thing.'

The phone went silent for a moment.

'Well,' Lane replied, 'that might explain something... This morning I drove past Mehmet's, as I have done, ever since you alerted me to the place, and I could have sworn there were Planning Permission notices in some of the windows. I was going to contact our people about it in the morning.'

'Well, that makes sense then, doesn't it?'

'You mean, close down the old place...'

'And convert it to stores, or offices. After all, it's just across the road from the main Flax Hole Depot. Couldn't be better.'

'Better for what?' Lane asked.

He sounded reflective. Alan needed to know Lane's current thoughts; so he made his reply as oblique, as obscure, as possible.

'Surely it's all about communication and distribution, isn't it?'

'You're saying that the new place will be a junkie's paradise?'

'No, far from it,' Alan replied. 'I very much doubt if you'd find so much as a whiff of illegal substances there. It's too obvious. No, that'll be where the deals are done, the networks established. I suspect it really will be a new "Mehmet's", but one that will be far more acceptable to the wider, non-Turkish community. To my mind it marks a step change in the scale and scope of their operations…'

'But surely,' Lane replied, 'the sheer lavishness of the operation suggests huge sums of money?'

'Which takes us back to drugs, doesn't it?'

'Yes, that would be the most obvious conclusion.'

'But the one thing that I've learnt from my job, Richard, is that the obvious conclusion can get in the way of proper, thorough analysis of the evidence.'

Bloody hell, that sounded pompous, Alan thought, but he didn't want Lane to close his mind to other possibilities.

'I am fully aware of that, thank you, Alan.'

Lane sounded irritated now. The last thing that Alan wanted at this stage was for a repeat of their past misunderstanding.

'Of course you are, I didn't mean to…'

But Lane talked over him, brisk and businesslike.

'You might be interested to know that I have recently discovered that MI5 are also investigating Mehmet's activities. Specifically the Anatolian Foundation.'

'Of course,' Alan said, 'they suppose it's a respectable cover for money laundering, don't they?'

'Well, don't you? I'd have thought it was blindingly obvious. And what you're now saying about this development at Impingham House backs it all up, doesn't it? The Kabuls are swimming in money. Dirty money that needs cleaning.'

'I have to say, Richard, this is all getting very uncomfortably close to home.'

'I can see that, and you have my sympathy. But I need you to hang on in there a little bit longer. Your contact with Ali might just prove vital in getting to the bottom of all this. And rest assured, the local force are being kept up to speed. It may not seem like it but you are being protected. You and Harriet.'

Alan thought it wiser to say nothing more. He rang off.

He sat down and closed his eyes. He needed to think things through.

It seemed so straightforward to Lane. But was it? The more Alan thought, the more convinced he became, that something else was going on. He doubted very much whether old man Mehmet had established the charity as a cover organisation of any sort. For a start, the Board of Trustees – who had to include some people from outside – would eventually smell a rat. And besides, why on earth go to all that trouble simply to provide an umbrella organisation for a gang of drug pushers? It didn't make sense. No, that remarkably respectable organisation had been carefully and skilfully built up, but for some other reason entirely. Then it came to him: Lane had almost got it right when he'd said that Mehmet was at its heart.

Alan was now convinced that the answer was staring them all in the face. It was the simple, existential fact that Mehmet *was* the heart of the Foundation. He wasn't just at the heart. He had given it life, and he was its life. His blood ran in its veins. And Paul, with his love of money and status, was clearly under Mehmet's spell… and possibly his control.

* * *

If Paul had a weakness, it was cars. His were always brand new, polished and expensive; and despite living in a converted farmhouse miles from anywhere, he tried to keep them clean. So when Alan pulled up at Priory Farm, and it was raining hard, he knew they'd be driving over to Impingham in his Land Rover. He was right. Eventually they arrived there, with stiff backs and ears singing, after being jolted by the rock-hard suspension for almost two hours. On the plus side, the overpowering roar of the engine meant that there was little opportunity for conversation – which was something of a relief. At this precise moment Alan had absolutely no idea what to say to him.

They pulled into a temporary car park, signed 'Developers' Car Park' in the Home Farm complex. There was a young Asian man standing by the gate, waving them in. For a second, Alan's gut lurched. He was tall, slender, with a shock of dark hair and an engaging smile. He was the spitting image of Ali as he remembered him from the Flax Hole days. As Alan got out of the Land Rover the young man came bounding up and enthusiastically shook Alan's hand.

'You remember me, I'm Mehmet.'

'Oh really, was that at… er… Flax Hole?'

'Of course. You Muddy Boys called me Little Mehmet. I was twelve then.'

Alan smiled. Gosh, he had changed from that boy staring towards the camera in the family group that Lane had showed him. And yes, it had indeed been a very muddy site. Ali called him Muddy Man, and the name stuck. Local kids would shout 'Hello, Muddy Boys' at them, every afternoon when the schools chucked out.

'That's right, the Muddy Boys…'

And slowly Alan remembered him not as an image in a photo, but as an enthusiastic, bright child who was a great fan of *History Hunters*. Very different from the smartly dressed young man before him. One rainy day he'd even slipped over while the wet sieves were being used and got coated from head to toe in liquid slurry. It took a full kitchen roll from the Finds Shed to clean him up. As Alan looked at him he could see the resemblance to Abdul, his elder brother. And there was even a hint of Sofia in those dark eyes.

Not-so-Little Mehmet then introduced them to two people from the architects' office and his site foreman, a burly, smiling man, named Kevin.

'Kevin's a close colleague of my brother Abdul, Mr Cadbury,' he announced. Then he turned to the group and added, 'Here, his job will be to ensure the project runs to time.'

Kevin muttered a few words of welcome in a broad Norfolk accent, then shook Alan's hand. Alan knew they'd have to work closely with over the next few weeks. So he made a point of being friendly, which wasn't difficult, given Kevin's mile-wide smile.

While they were chatting, Paul and not-so-Little Mehmet had started an animated discussion about details of the plans as they walked over to the new site office, a Portakabin in the farmyard.

After a few minutes Kevin agreed to show Alan the contents of his tool store, just for future reference, but spotted Brutus immediately he stepped out into the car park. He stopped dead in his tracks.

'Is she yours, boy?' he asked Paul, his accent as broad as his grin.

'Yes, I've had her over ten years...'

'Drove one of these for nearly twenty years,' Kevin broke in, his enthusiasm defeating his instinctive good manners. 'Wonderful machines. Go anywhere. Still got the old electrics?'

He patted the spare wheel on the bonnet, as if it were the nose of a faithful plough horse.

'Sadly not,' Alan replied, 'had to replace them. Otherwise she's pretty authentic.'

'LPG conversion?' Kevin was looking at the tank behind the front seats. 'I'm thinking of converting mine. Any chance of a quick look?'

'Be my guest...' Alan opened the driver's door and Kevin climbed in. He sat admiring the interior.

'Mind if I turn her on?'

'No, go ahead,' Alan replied. 'Take her for a spin if you like.'

It was too good an offer to resist.

'Climb aboard, then.'

Kevin leant across and opened the passenger's door. It felt odd. Alan had never been a passenger in Brutus before.

They drove across to the Home Farm buildings, where two other men, perhaps a few years younger than Kevin, were making timber supports for a building about to collapse in the yard.

'Meet Stu and Darren, my two old boys on this job.'

They nodded towards Alan, and were about to continue working, when Alan introduced himself. It wasn't entirely goodwill: these people could come in very useful when work began in earnest on the DMV.

'Hi. I'm Alan. You'll be seeing a lot of me in the next few weeks. My team will be working out in the park.'

'He'll be doing the archaeology,' Kevin explained.

'What,' Darren asked, 'like *History Hunters*?'

'Sort of,' Alan replied, 'but we'll take a bit longer. We won't be finished in two days, like on TV. More like two months…'

Alan had no time for a longer explanation, as Kevin had climbed back into Brutus and was about to head back towards the car park. As they drove, Alan's spirits rose. He looked across to Kevin, who was sitting behind the wheel, plainly on cloud nine. What a relief, Alan thought: once or twice he'd been on jobs where the workmen were hostile to archaeologists, and it made day-to-day life on site so much harder.

But this was all too short-lived. As they passed the Portakabin, Alan saw Paul step out of the office, followed by not-so-Little Mehmet and another man. He recognised him instantly: Old Mehmet. As Alan watched, the older man embraced Paul, kissed him on both cheeks and held him in a tight hug.

Talk about body language.

Twenty-two

A week had passed since his first visit to Impingham. Since then, Alan had barely seen Paul, which suited him fine. However, that image of his boss locked in the embrace of Old Mehmet still lingered. He fell back on the way he usually coped: he threw himself into his work.

Alan was making arrangements for the main survey and dig, sitting at his desk at Priory Farm, working on emails, when one arrived from Dr Judd's Laboratory at Saltaire. It had been copied to Paul Flynn. The subject was 'CONFIDENTIAL: Preliminary Results from St Guthlic's'. It included a short discussion, with an attached spreadsheet of results. For a few seconds Alan froze, his eyes scanning the screen. Then he sat back. He couldn't believe what he'd just read. He had to speak to Harriet immediately, before Paul got to her. He thumped the partition wall three times and heard her door open. She came in and walked straight over to his screen.

She had read it in a couple of seconds.

'Good heavens, Alan: that's fantastic! Absolutely incredible.'

'Yes,' Alan replied, 'I couldn't have put it better myself.'

She detected his cynicism.

'Oh for God's sake, Alan, they make plenty of sense. And they're internally consistent, too. We've got five "foreign" results: one from central Europe, two from Anatolia, one from Ireland and one northern India... It's great!'

Harriet was absolutely delighted. But Alan still had his doubts. He pointed at the screen.

'Judd reckons the Punjab for that one, doesn't he?'

'Yes, or Himalayan foothills. Very distinctive water there, the note says.'

Across the hall they heard Paul's office door open. Then footsteps. Paul entered, without knocking, leaving the door open behind him.

'Aren't they superb?' He held a printout in his hand, 'Not at all what I'd expected. Far better. That should make the news and keep the folk at Guthlic's happy. I bet that chap in the big house there...'

'Alistair?' Alan suggested.

'Yes, him. I bet he's glad he paid us all that money. These results are sensational. I can't believe there were such long-distance contacts at such an early date. And there of all places! It's *so* remote. Extraordinary, isn't it?'

'Yes,' Harriet replied, 'the two bodies from Anatolia came from the small group at the foot of the tower.'

'And their date?'

Alan answered, 'Possibly as early as Middle Saxon.'

As he answered he thought back to when he had collected the original samples. The two Anatolian bodies were stored next to each other, long-bone boxes below skull boxes.

'What about the one from India, surely that's not so early? That really would be sensational.'

'No, Paul,' Alan again replied, 'my best guess is fifteenth, maybe fourteenth century. But certainly later medieval. The grave was further away from the church.'

'Yes,' Harriet broke in, 'out in the main body of the churchyard.'

Paul was plainly delighted. He couldn't conceal it. Alan had no idea he was so interested in the early history of the English church.

'Well, well… that's superb. Absolutely superb. And how does it all fit in with your theories, Harriet? Are you going to have to modify that great book we're all waiting for so eagerly?'

She was smiling broadly. Paul wasn't often this enthusiastic.

'To be honest, Paul, it confirms everything I'd always suspected. For some time now we've set aside the idea that the post-Roman world was frozen in the grip of a Dark Age…'

'Yes,' Paul replied, 'that had even filtered down to people like me. So communities really were moving around more. Trade links with the Continent were a fact, even in this remote part of rural Lincolnshire?'

'Indeed,' Harriet replied, 'that's how it seems. And what's more, those links seem to have continued – expanded even – into the later Middle Ages…'

'What,' Paul broke in, 'that body from the Punjab?'

'Precisely,' Harriet continued. 'Although I think Alan here has reservations…'

Alan was trying to signal with his gaze that she shouldn't bring him in. But she hadn't picked it up.

'Do you, Alan?' Suddenly Paul looked very serious.

'No, not really, Paul,' Alan was improvising freely, 'I've got some doubts about the sensitivity of the method, that's all. It was those results for Anglian graves in Yorkshire, published last week…'

Paul looked mystified:

'Oh really, I hadn't seen them.'

'No,' Alan continued, 'they were published in the MPSG e-newsletter…'

'MPSG?' Paul asked.

'Migration Period Study Group,' Alan explained, 'but the results are still *very* provisional…'

'And what did *they* show? Paul asked, with just a hint of scepticism.

'Just that part of the local East Riding population came from Lancashire, that's all…'

Harriet, then Paul, laughed.

'Yes…' she said, 'I can see that must have gone down well in Yorkshire.'

'It did. But anyhow,' Alan continued, 'movement across the Pennines is one thing, but these results are far more definite. I'm in absolutely no doubt whatsoever…' he was choosing his words carefully: 'they're certainly significant.'

'What,' Paul asked, now much more relaxed, 'so you accept them. They're bona fide?'

'Good heavens, yes,' Alan replied, more confident now, 'of course they're bona fide. Judd's lab is the best there is. I don't think anyone doubts that. Oh no, those results are kosher. Absolutely kosher. And very exciting.'

'Do you think a press release is called for?' Paul asked.

Harriet was the first to respond:

'That's a wonderful idea, Paul.'

Alan urged caution:

'Personally, I'd wait, Paul. Wait till we get the radiocarbon dates. We'd look like complete idiots if those bodies near the tower turned out to be post-medieval, wouldn't we?'

Always cautious himself, Paul agreed. Then he turned to leave.

'Well done everyone. I'm so glad it's all turned out so satisfactorily. Do keep me in the loop as things progress. Now I must get back to my office. Something big's afoot...'

'Really?' Alan asked.

'Yes. Very big. But not for a few weeks. Meanwhile, it's Impingham. One step at a time. And don't worry: after this, I'll keep you both closely informed if there are any significant developments.'

And with that he left.

* * *

As soon as the door had shut, Alan leaned back and sighed heavily.

'What the hell was that all about, Alan?' asked Harriet.

Alan tried his best to look innocent. It didn't work.

'You made it very clear before Paul came in, that you didn't think them kosher?'

Alan didn't want to sow any doubts in her mind until he'd thought it all over, but the coincidence of having two samples, from next-door boxes, that appeared to have originated in Anatolia, modern Turkey, was surely more than just coincidence. The more he thought about it, the more certain he became.

'I don't. At least I've got reservations. Big reservations.'

'So why the charade?'

Alan knew he owed her an explanation.

'I'm sorry, Harry. Leave it with me for a few hours. I need to think. I also need to get to grips with the historical context better.'

'OK,' Harriet replied. She got up and headed for the door. 'I'll leave you in peace, but I'll call in later to see how things are going.'

Alan looked up and smiled. She closed the door behind her, she too was clearly deep in thought.

Alan picked up the office phone, then suddenly thought better of it.

He grabbed his mobile and walked out of the office, through the yard and the outbuildings, until he was sure he was out of sight of Paul's office. Then he dialled.

Lane picked up on the second ring.

'Everything all right, Alan?'

There was no trace of the awkwardness of their previous conversation.

'To be honest, Richard, I don't know. I need to ask a favour.'

'Fire away.'

'Can you look into the Kabuls' background for me? Specifically, I'm interested in precisely where the family originated.'

'Funny you should ask that, but I made a few enquiries last week. The old man's easy enough, as there's stuff on him with the Charity Commission.'

'I imagine he was born and bred in Turkey?'

'Yes, and came here in the 1950s.'

'So his daughter returned to Turkey?'

'In the mid-seventies, where she married a Turk, and had four children in quick succession.'

Alan recalled their previous conversation.

'Then she died soon after the birth of Little Mehmet, of course. Then his namesake – Old Mehmet stepped into the breach and took the kids?'

'Then a year after she had had the youngest, she died. Of breast cancer.'

'Yes. We don't know precisely when he left England, but we do know he had a long struggle with Immigration. Eventually it was all sorted out and he was able to return to Turkey and collect his four grandchildren.'

Presumably, thought Alan, he was stepping into his disgraced son's shoes on behalf of the family – and its reputation.

'When was that?'

'As I said, he had prolonged problems with Immigration…' There was a short pause while Lane consulted some notes, 'That's right,' he resumed, 'the Heathrow Immigration people have a record of him returning with four children, three males and a female, in November 1998.'

Alan did a quick calculation.

'So Sofia would have been about twelve when she came to the UK?'

'Yes, I suppose so. But why? I don't see how that's relevant.'

'It may not be. But please, Richard, you've got to trust me on this one.'

Lane rang off. Alan pocketed his mobile and slowly, reluctantly, walked back towards PFC.

* * *

Just before the end of the day, Harriet put her head into Alan's office. He was immersed in the early history of St Guthlic's, looking for clues that might help explain those foreign burials. He didn't hold out high hopes, but he felt he ought to at least make an effort. He looked up.

'The more I think about it,' she said softly, 'the more I'm coming round to your way of thinking.'

Alan was surprised, but very pleased at this.

'That's good. But I don't think we should discuss it here. It'll take too long and it's not strictly about the project, is it?'

She looked puzzled at this.

'I suppose not…'

'So let's not chew it over during office hours. We can always have a quiet chat later.' Alan sounded very businesslike, and just a little wooden. Almost dismissive. He had never been a good actor. 'I've got far too much on my plate trying to sort out historical context. It's proving a bit of a nightmare. Very complex. There's almost too much to go on…'

'How about something nice for supper?'

'That's very kind. I'll get some wine.'

'Say eight?'

'Splendid. That'll give me a couple of extra hours, which should be all I need; at least at this stage.'

'OK. See you then.'

Briefly he wondered what had made her change her mind. Then without much enthusiasm, he re-immersed himself in the early ecclesiastical history of South Elloe and the Danelaw. It was heavy going.

* * *

The 'quiet chat' began almost as soon as Alan walked into the kitchen. He'd bought a couple of bottles of red wine on his drive over, and he handed her a glass, while she chopped garlic and shallots to go with the Lincoln Red steak. He began.

'I've been going over the early history of the church and I can't find any reasons why there should be foreign bodies in the graveyard, unless of course they were Anglo-Saxon raiders or colonists.'

'But they're too late, and besides, they come from too far afield for that.'

'I agree. I was hoping to find links with somewhere like Boston, Lincoln or York – some centre of power and prestige that might account for such exotic travellers. But there weren't any. Guthlic's is, and was, a small church in an obscure village deep in the Fens. It's very ordinary. There's no getting away from it. To be honest, if we'd found bodies of people who'd grown up in Leicestershire I'd have been surprised. Let alone India, central Europe or Turkey.'

Harriet looked up from the Aga.

'Reluctantly I've come to the same conclusion. It's almost too good to be true. And the worst part is, that at face value, those results support all my pet theories about post-Carolingian trade. They couldn't be better – and my publishers would be sick if they could hear what I'm saying.'

'Still, I'm so glad you've changed your mind. I really am.'

'And do you know what finally won me round to your way of thinking?' she asked.

He assumed she had spotted the same thing as him.

'The two samples from Turkey?'

'No, the Irish and the central European samples. I can just possibly concede that the medieval Punjabi could have arrived as part of the spice trade – although that's also a very long shot – but not the other two, as well. And at different dates, too, in tiny, remote Scoby? I mean think about it: in the Middle Ages Scoby would have been the best part of a day's ride from Boston, across quaking fens? No, the idea's barmy. Absurd.'

'So where does that leave us?' Alan asked.

In actual fact, this was a rhetorical question. All afternoon, while ostensibly reading up about St Guthlic's he'd also been thinking about other, more practical aspects of the problem.

'I'm not sure…' she replied hesitantly.

Alan was more decisive.

'As I see it,' he said, thinking aloud, 'there are two alternatives. Either the lab muddled our samples with somebody else's, or there's something odd about the burial conditions at Guthlic's. I don't know, maybe the groundwater's rich in some mineral or trace element, which has somehow found its way into the tooth enamel?'

She paused for a moment, considering the options.

'That's highly unlikely,' she said, choosing her words with care. 'The whole point of enamel is its density, stability and lack of porosity. It doesn't – it can't – just absorb things.' She paused, thinking; then asked: 'You know Hugh Judd, don't you?'

'Yes, from the Saltaire course. But I haven't met him since he's been in charge of the lab. I spoke to him on the phone when I was arranging the analyses, and he seemed very pleasant. Why?'

'Well, I think one of us needs to talk to him about the possibility of a mix-up at his end, or of contamination in the ground. And it'll need to be handled with some tact, as I've got sixteen more bodies from Çatol Huyut I'd like him to test – and he won't co-operate if we upset him.'

'You obviously know him better than me,' Alan suggested. 'So why don't you do it?'

She looked relieved.

'OK, I'll ring him tomorrow.'

Alan was pleased she'd agreed to this so readily. She got up and removed their plates. He could hear her preparing the next course in the larder.

He raised his voice. 'I think this is very important. Crucial, in fact.'

'Oh I agree,' she called back, 'but I don't hold out many hopes of an easy solution. Look, I know we were scrupulously careful. I double-checked everything. So did Clara. And Judd's lab has a reputation second-to-none. Honestly, I'd be astounded if the error was at his end.'

'Well,' Alan replied, 'we must still go through the motions. We've got to check everything, and thoroughly.'

'Don't worry, I'll do that tomorrow.'

By this point Harriet had returned. She set a plate of cheese and biscuits on the table and sat down.

'You see,' Alan went on, helping himself to some ripe Camembert, 'I'm now convinced those results were no accident. I think they arose through a process of some sort. Something that had been going on at Priory Farm, probably for quite some time, went wrong in this instance.'

'Something to do with finds- and sample-processing, do you think?'

'No. I've been observing things closely and I'm certain that Clara and her Finds team are beyond reproach.'

'So what are you suggesting?'

'At this stage nothing specific. But I can say one thing.'

'Which is?'

'That whatever is, and was, happening is not being organised from the archaeological side. I'm quite convinced of that.'

'So what do you think?'

'I don't know. But I'm increasingly worried about Paul. Or rather his behaviour. Didn't you think he was a bit *too* keen to believe everything was genuine? That those results were one hundred per cent kosher?'

'I agree, that was odd,' she replied, 'especially for someone of his experience – or lack of it.'

'Quite. So do you think he might, for reasons known only to him, have suspected that a cock-up might have happened, and that it could have been revealed to other people…'

'What,' she broke in, 'by Judd's results?'

'Precisely.'

'No, I hadn't thought of that.'

It was Alan's turn to interrupt.

'But it wasn't. By luck nothing was actually revealed: the results *seemed* fine.'

'Hence his relief. That was why he was so pleased I thought the results were genuine?' She paused. 'I'm sorry I nearly gave you away.'

'But don't worry, Harry. You didn't. That's what matters,' he was smiling broadly. 'The main thing is, he's none the wiser.' Then he added: 'But we are.'

They sat in silence for a few moments, thinking things over. Harriet was the first to speak:

'No, you're quite right. It does suggest Paul suspected something might have gone wrong, doesn't it?'

'I was fascinated,' Alan resumed, 'by the way he welcomed my change of mind after you'd suggested I was sceptical about the results. He almost kissed me on both cheeks, didn't he?'

'Yes. He did seem very pleased. Very pleased indeed. In fact he left in high old spirits.'

Alan paused. He knew he was treading a fine line here. He needed to give Harriet enough information to protect herself. If his worst fears were correct then the last thing he wanted was for her to behave in any way that would attract Paul's attention. But he didn't want to give her too much information either, otherwise she would feel duty bound to take a moral stance, he was sure about that. He knew Harriet well enough by now to know that she had a very clear sense of right and wrong, regardless of her own self-interest. It was one of the many qualities he admired about her.

He pressed on, cautiously.

'So, once you combine Paul's odd behaviour and the bones results with the issue of the dubious accounting system...'

'You think this is all connected to the AK Plant family?'

'The Kabuls, yes. You know they are also behind the Impingham House Project?'

'Yes, of course. I'd forgotten that connection. So, you think that the Kabuls and Paul are running some kind of scam together?'

'Everything seems to point in that direction, yes.'

Alan took a deep breath. It was important that he seemed calm and coherent; that his story added up under Harriet's rigorous academic scrutiny.

'PFC is one of the major players in commercial archaeology. The Kabul family is their exclusive contractor. Paul has built his reputation on doing a thorough job in half the time...'

'So you think he's cutting corners? Not processing his finds and results properly?'

'It makes sense, doesn't it?'

'But surely, the potential damage to his academic reputation? To all of ours...'

Harriet looked genuinely shocked. And more than a little angry.

'I'm sorry to say, I think that's a secondary concern for Paul and probably has been for a long time.'

'The little shit.'

Harriet was on her feet now, pacing the room.

'Right, Alan. This is what we're going to do. First thing tomorrow, we resign and we report him to the IFA.'

'I'm not sure that's such a good idea.'

'I can't risk everything I've worked so hard for…'

'Which is why we've got to build a watertight case against him and them. And we're not there yet. Not even slightly.'

Harriet slumped back on the sofa, still angry but resigned.

'You're right, of course.'

'We do have one thing going for us though, Harry,' Alan said gently.

'And what's that?'

'Neither Paul nor anyone in the Kabul clan know we suspect anything. So all right, we still lack definite proof, but I'm sure it won't be long before something comes along. What we mustn't do at this stage is get found out. If we're stupid enough to give ourselves away, God knows what'll happen. So from now on, we must watch our backs and think about the consequences of everything we do at Priory Farm. And I mean that: *everything.*'

She was nodding.

'OK, Alan.'

The message had got home.

Twenty-three

Later that morning Harriet met Alan on the concrete apron outside the Out Store. He looked up as she approached.

'Any news from Judd?'

'Yes,' she replied quietly, 'just checked my emails. No possibility of cross-contamination. All the other material the lab's working on, is Inuit stuff from Alaska, Canada and Greenland. It's a big US–Canadian project into historical migration patterns in the High Arctic.'

'So no chance of contamination from Ireland or Turkey then?'

'None.' She was looking anxious now: 'So where does that leave us?'

'We either have to accept the results...'

'Don't worry,' she cut in, 'I haven't changed my mind again. If anything I'm even more convinced... but I've been thinking and there is one other possible explanation.'

He was perplexed.

'Do you think,' she continued, 'it could have been something to do with the chaos when Simon dumped two vanloads of stuff on Clara and we all had to move boxes, bags and plans to our own offices and the Out Store?'

'Yes, that's what I was thinking about, when I mentioned the Finds Store last night. Normally Clara has everything under control. But not then. Nobody could have controlled everything then. It was panic stations.'

'I know Clara couldn't cope.' Harriet said, 'At least not to her complete satisfaction. And she told me as much, a couple of days ago.'

'But even so,' Alan replied, 'it's hard to get whole boxes confused. For a start all the bone boxes are clearly labelled in your and Amy's handwriting. Hers is very distinctive...'

'And not very legible?'

'Yes, that's true. But it couldn't be anyone else's. That's the point.'

'And you're quite sure the boxes you opened on that Tuesday morning after Easter were in my and Amy's writing?'

'Yes.'

'And the right site code?'

'Yes, of course. I'm absolutely certain,' Alan replied. 'At the time, I remember being aware there'd been that panic a few days earlier, so I took extra care.'

Alan distinctly recalled double-checking everything very carefully.

'You're right,' she replied. 'If there had been mix-ups they'd have been with entire boxes, not the contents of boxes.'

She was looking troubled. Frowning. He continued.

'I can say, hand on heart, that I took the Saltaire samples from the correct numbered and labelled boxes and that the boxes all carried the Guthlic's Site Code. I'm absolutely one hundred per cent certain of that.'

They moved behind the store building and leaned against a stack of pallets. There was a short silence, while Alan allowed the implications of what they'd just said to sink in. He knew the following discussion would need to be handled sensitively. He was the first to speak:

'It seems to me we've done all we can by way of indirect investigation. We've ruled out contamination on site, muddle at Saltaire and here at Priory Farm...'

'At least when the boxes were in our offices under our direct control,' she cut in. 'But there's no knowing what might have been going on in the Out Store, is there?'

'Surely you're not suggesting that Clara tampered with them, are you?'

Alan was surprised at this.

'Of course, I'm not. All I'm saying is that the Out Store is the only place where any possible contamination might have happened. I'm just talking theoretical possibilities here. I'm not pointing the finger.'

'OK. No, that's fair. But it seems to me we can't go much further along that route, other, that is, than ask Clara directly if she noticed anything odd when she returned to work after Easter – that's the obvious next step.'

Her reply surprised him:

'I've already done that. First thing, over coffee this morning...'

'And?'

Harriet shrugged.

'She just looked at me blankly. It was worth a thousand excuses.'

Alan felt a sharp pang of admiration for Harriet. No messing about, she'd got straight to the point. He was unsure whether he'd have the courage to challenge Clara quite so openly.

Harriet continued, focused on the problem.

'It seems to me that the only sources of new information which we still control are the bones themselves...'

'Exactly.' He paused. 'Maybe you can help me, as my memory's a bit rusty, but when I did the Forensics Course we learned about tests to see if bones are ancient or modern. I can't remember much about them, except that one was based around fats, wasn't it?'

'Yes. A simple lipids test.'

'Well, why don't we run some of them?'

'That's an excellent idea,' she replied. 'Can't think why I didn't suggest it myself.'

'We can always ask Alistair over at Scoby Hall to fund them. They can't be very expensive.'

'Oh no, they're not.' She paused, smiling now, then continued: 'In fact I can get them done for nothing. I've got an old and very loyal friend who'll run them and remain absolutely confidential. I can guarantee that.'

'And do you think he'd have the time?'

'Oh I'm sure he would. He'd do anything for me...'

Alan had a small stab of jealousy, which surprised him somewhat. Then he dismissed it as ridiculous. Harriet's private life was none of his business. He tried to sound as breezy and cheerful as possible.

'If the tests work out we'll owe him a few beers.'

'There'll be no need for that.' She paused. 'I tell you what, I'll be seeing him at home on Friday evening...'

'Do you want me to move out of the spare room, give you some space?'

'No need for that, either. But it'll be a good excuse for a nice supper.'

Alan got the slight impression that she was rather enjoying this exchange.

'I'll bring a bottle or two then.'

But Harriet's mood had changed suddenly, she was frowning in concentration.

'One practical thing, Alan.'

'What's that?'

'We'll need precisely the same material to work on. After the mix-up, we can't afford to use different bones. They have to be precisely the same jaws that Judd had.'

'Yes, I know. The trouble is they're all at Saltaire.'

'Well, somehow, we've got to get them back.'

'Leave that with me,' Alan replied, 'if Judd's like any of our other specialists he'll be desperate to get rid of them. Storage space is always short.' He glanced down at his phone. 'It's Wednesday today. I'll see if I can collect them on Friday and bring them over that evening.'

Alan rang Judd's laboratory and explained that he needed two of the samples back urgently, to run additional radiocarbon dates. It was a white lie, but he also knew that he must give some sort of explanation for giving such little notice. The girl at the other end explained that they were in the middle of returning a huge batch of samples to the Royal Ontario Museum, in Toronto, so would he mind waiting a couple of weeks? Again, Alan lied: he'd only managed to extract a short-term grant and had to pay the lab within a few days...

He was put on hold. The tinny music echoed down the phone to him, and then was suddenly interrupted by a chuckling voice.

'Causing more bloody problems for our dedicated staff are you, Cadbury?'

It was Judd. In jovial mood.

'I'm sorry, but I need two of those samples back urgently. Would a nice malt help your decision?'

'Done. Give me the sample numbers.'

Alan had them memorised.

'You're a star,' Alan replied. 'I'll see you bright and early Friday.'

* * *

Things began well the following morning. The Land Rover started on just the third attempt and Alan arrived at Priory Farm fifteen minutes before nine. In the lobby, he met Paul who greeted him with an unexpectedly cheery wave. OK, thought Alan, that's good. Whatever's going on, Paul obviously thinks he's got away with it. Best to play along.

'Alan,' he called across the entrance hall, 'I've got some splendid news.'

Alan looked suitably astonished.

'What, even better than Impingham?'

'Oh yes. Very much better. And better for you too.'

'I'll be right with you.'

Alan dumped his laptop and rucksack on his desk, and then gave himself a little pep talk. Whatever he says or does, stay calm. Think of the bigger picture.

He walked across the hall to Paul's office.

When he entered, Paul was standing by the window, looking intently at the ground outside. As Alan came in, Paul turned round and strode purposefully across to his work station.

'I've just had Sir Christopher Hamble, Chairman of Eborcom Developments on the phone.'

Alan had never heard of the man.

'That's wonderful news, Paul. What's the project?'

'It's the big new city centre development at York. It'll be huge. Mega. Bigger even, than the original Viking Dig of the 1970s.'

'Blimey. That *is* big.' Alan was genuinely impressed.

'But they've learned from the past. This time the archaeologists won't be under such extreme pressure. And it won't all happen so fast, either. Instead it's going to be about Integrated Phased Expansion.'

'Oh, IPE, that's good,' Alan said, on the off-chance that such an acronym existed.

'Precisely,' Paul seemed impressed at Alan's know-how. 'And we've landed the contract for IPE Phase 1. It's the St Cuthbert's cemetery.

Paul took a sip from his coffee, put down the cup and said:

'And I want you, Alan, to direct it. What do you say?'

Every part of Alan wanted to turn the offer down. Right now the thought of taking any more money from PFC made him feel physically sick. But he knew he had to stay in close contact. He also knew they had to establish a sound working relationship. In fact, everything would depend on it.

'Good heavens. That's a very tempting offer. Are you sure I could do it?'

'Of course, man. Wouldn't have asked you otherwise.'

'Very well, Paul, I will. And thank you. It's a much larger project than I'm used to. That's why I hesitated.'

'No, I quite understand. But don't forget, you'll have me and Harriet to back you up. You know that, don't you? And we've made such a good team at Guthlic's, haven't we?'

Alan wasn't aware that Paul had done anything much for Guthlic's, other than land the job in the first place.

'Yes, Guthlic's has been a wonderful experience,' he said, trying to sound convincing.

Paul continued, relentlessly, 'The main project will start in October, but first we've got to enlarge our facilities here. We'd never cope otherwise. So I've had a small team prepare drawings, and we're going to get hold of some sophisticated site laboratories – the sort of things they use after natural disasters: earthquakes, that sort of thing. We won't need them forever, and being officially classed as temporary, the Planning Permission is simpler. Anyhow, I'd like you to supervise the groundworks for them, not that they need a great deal – just a water supply and sewage outlet.'

'Where are you planning to put them?'

'Out there,' he pointed towards the large window.

'Won't that come down on some of the Priory outbuildings?' Alan asked.

'Possibly, but only possibly. We're a long way outside the Scheduled Area and I've cleared it with the County Council. They don't seem at all worried. Seem more concerned about rural employment around here. They were all in favour. They said they're more than happy for you to keep an eye on things. Then send them one of our usual clients' reports.'

'What, a watching-brief?'

'Yes – probably no need for a dig. And they want some geophys in advance. Nothing too elaborate.'

'What, mag?'

Magnetometry was much cheaper than radar.

'Yes, probably. Anyhow they'll send you a spec in a few days.'

The interview was over.

Instead of returning directly to his office, Alan decided to take a short stroll, pretending to look at the area planned for the new building. He needed to show Paul that he was on top of the job. Keen to 'progress it'. Out of the corner of his eye, he could see Paul, in his office, had noted his presence outside.

There was a sharp tap on glass. Alan looked round. The window opened and Paul asked,

'What d'you think?'

'Looks pretty disturbed...' Alan replied, kicking the ground with the side of his foot. 'Should be straightforward enough, if you ask me.'

'Glad to hear it, Alan.'

'Paul, you don't mind me asking, but there's a great deal riding on this new project, isn't there?'

'Yes, the growth and survival of PFC as a going concern. The thing is, we can't survive for ever on little projects like Guthlic's? We need something much bigger and long-lasting if we're to weather the recession. So if we get this right, we're made. I'm depending on you, Alan. I know you won't let me down.'

Alan privately thought that money was the least of Paul's problems right now. But instead he just smiled and nodded.

'Don't worry, Paul,' he said. 'You can rely on me. And Harriet too.'

* * *

On Friday morning Alan drove over to Saltaire in the small PFC van, and collected the two Guthlic's bone samples from the lab. Judd was pleased to see him, but was a little puzzled why

Harriet had phoned through earlier to query the results. Alan explained there'd been a cock-up at their end. He himself had muddled up a couple of long context numbers, which made Harriet think there'd been duplication. But it was all sorted out. As they stood outside the old clothing mill that had been converted by the university twenty years ago, he slipped Judd the promised bottle of old malt whisky. The older man was delighted. Harriet could relax: things would be fine with Judd in the future.

It was getting dark as he came over the steep escarpment into the Dawyck Fen basin. The van window was open, and as he drove down the slope he could feel the air outside grow cooler. He wound the window up and turned on the headlights. It had been a very still evening. At this time of year the ground was colder than the air and the deeper drains soon filled with misty vapour. They look very beautiful, but can cause sudden impenetrable banks of fog, which can be deadly for motorists. His thoughts were entirely focused on the evening ahead. Harriet assured him that her bones expert would be able to give a definitive analysis. He was so close… but he had no sense of academic excitement. Just a horrible feeling that the truth was going to be harder to find than a few results. And what did they mean? Increasingly he was finding it harder to differentiate between the remote past and the present: between Anatolia and Turkey, he thought grimly. Then suddenly his thoughts were broken when he drove slap bang into an impenetrable wall of fog, just outside Harriet's village. He nearly fetched up in the dyke, but somehow managed to stop. He drove the remaining few yards at twenty mph.

He gave a perfunctory knock and walked through into her kitchen. She greeted him with a kiss on the cheek and glass of white wine.

'Gosh Alan, you look pale.'

'It's getting nippy outside.'

He handed her two bottles of red.

'Oo,' she muttered, looking at the French labels, 'that's generous.'

'Yes, nearly fetched up in the dyke, just outside the village…'

'What that patch of mist? It's always there this time of year. Sorry, I should have warned you.'

Somehow he had expected a little more sympathy. But her mind was clearly on other things.

'Do you have the bone samples?'

'Yes, they're in the van.'

'Well,' she laughed, 'don't stand there like an idiot. Get them!'

Alan jumped to it. He was amazed. He could only assume that Harriet's visiting expert was somewhere else, maybe upstairs in the bathroom. Before he closed the front door he looked around for a car. But there wasn't one. Just Harriet's. Presumably, he thought, he's come by train. He lifted the two boxes out of the PFC van and took them inside.

'Right,' she said, taking both the boxes off the kitchen table and placing them on the carpet. 'Which one do you want to do first?'

Alan was at a loss. Where was the expert?

'I don't mind. I suspect they're both the same.'

'OK.' She paused. 'I tell you what. Let's test the method properly.'

Alan looked puzzled.

'These,' she said, mimicking a *Blue Peter* presenter, 'are some samples I prepared earlier.'

She reached into her rucksack and pulled out three small clear plastic bags.

Then she looked up.

'Alaric!' she called.

Her black Labrador, obedient to what he thought would be the call to dinner, came trotting in.

'Stand there, Alan.'

She gestured him back, while keeping a firm grip on the dog's collar.

'I don't want him put off. And he's getting rather hungry. He should have been fed an hour ago.

She picked up a human lower jaw, rather like a stage conjuror. By now Alan knew what was coming. He felt a bit foolish; should have guessed earlier.

'I borrowed these mandibles from my office. They all come from Simon Cox's site and are guaranteed genuine fifteenth century.'

She laid them on the floor and gently drew Alaric's attention to them. He wasn't even slightly interested. Alan watched, fascinated.

'And this…' she paused and opened the box beside her. 'Is what you brought back from Saltaire and is supposedly Saxon…'

She pushed the opened box towards the dog. Alaric's nose shot towards it, twitching wildly. Then he licked the bone with his large and very pink tongue. Quickly she placed her hand over the box and removed it. Alan grabbed the dog's collar.

'OK, I'm convinced,' he said, 'but let's just do the other one.'

'OK.'

She only had to open the lid for Alaric's nose to start vigourously twitching. He gave a small squeak of frustration. He was getting bored by this game and wanted to be fed.

'Point made,' Alan said. 'I think you'd better feed him.'

'There's a good boy,' she cooed, 'there's a good boy! Time for din-dins!'

She reached up to the worktop beside the Aga and took down a dish of dog food, which Alaric pounced on, as if starving.

'That was impressive. But also a bit creepy,' Alan said.

She refilled his wine, which he took and sipped, almost without thinking. Alaric's display had unnerved him badly. It was now getting far, far too close to home.

'I know,' she said sympathetically, 'it's usually the bones of other animals, not us, isn't it? It seems like a sort of cannibalism.'

Alan had got over his surprise and was back on the case.

'What about those babies? Do you think he'd lick them?' he asked.

'I've already thought of that, but I don't want to try it again, as they're so fragile and Alaric's famished.'

'And what happened?'

'Nothing.'

'What d'you mean nothing: he wasn't interested?'

'No. Not even slightly.'

'But we're pretty certain they're late Victorian or early twentieth century. I'd be surprised if they were much more than a century old. And all the fat had already leached out…' He paused. 'So that proves those so-called Saxon and Medieval mandibles have to be *very* recent, doesn't it?'

'Yes,' she replied, 'ten, twenty years will dissolve fats in some soils. And of course neonate bones are so thin, there's not much for the lipids to lock onto.'

'So, what do you reckon: are they five years old?'

'At the most, I'd say. But I'm no expert.'

'No,' he said thinking aloud, 'we're getting into forensics territory here.'

And if there are teeth, mandibles and jaws, Alan mused, then there'll be the rest of the skeleton too. But where? Already smuggled out of PFC in other Out Store boxes?

Eventually Harriet broke the silence:

'I think we'd better tell the police, don't you?'

Alan was thinking hard. Tactically this was a crucial decision.

'Yes, you're right. But I don't think a 999 call would work. Much better go in at the right level.'

'What do you mean?'

Alan gave Harriet a brief résumé of his relationship with Lane. He also told her that it was Lane who had suggested that he got involved with The Lifers' Club. It was a lie but, in the grand scheme of things, a lie so small that he didn't even consider it.

'A detective with archaeological training, sounds perfect.'

She handed him the phone handset.

'I'll get you a brandy – and I think I need one myself.'

'To be honest, Harry, I think I'd better take this in my room, Richard's a stickler for the whole confidentiality thing.'

* * *

When Lane answered he got straight to the point.

'Good heavens, Alan, are you psychic? I've been trying to get you on your mobile. But it's turned off.'

Alan pulled it out of his pocket. He was right, it was dead.

'I'm sorry, Richard, the bloody batteries are flat. I'll have to get a new one soon…'

Lane had no time for excuses, he pressed on – insistent.

'I'm afraid it's serious. The Drugs people are giving me loads of problems. But we're not alone. I've spoken to people from other county forces: they're all moaning like hell.'

'Why?'

'You probably can't remember, but just before the last election the government pushed through a law, which promoted cannabis from Class C to Class B.'

'Yes, I remember it well. They ignored the scientific advice and the chairman of the advisory committee, Professor Something-or-Other, resigned. And I think most of the academic world was behind him. Bloody outrageous political interference.'

'Well,' Lane continued, cutting short Alan's outburst, 'that's had a big knock-on effect. The civil servants in their wisdom failed adequately to adjust the Class B targets for the next NiB Review.'

'NiB?'

'"Narcotics in Britain" Review.'

'So what?'

'I'd have thought it was obvious.'

There was a pause.

'Oh,' Alan replied, 'I get it. With cannabis up a grade, the Drugs Squads are beating their Class B targets.'

'And by a mile. To be honest they've gone on a feeding frenzy. My mate in the Yard says some are even talking about big bonuses for the best squads.'

'So don't tell me. They reckon that if indeed the Kabuls are running a major scam...'

'Then it's big bonuses for the lads. In reality, it's all about jockeying for power in a police force that's about to face major cuts. Anyone who's up now is likely to be riding even higher when the spending axe falls.'

'Pre-emptive strikes?'

'Precisely. There's a huge amount riding on all this, so I very much doubt whether I can do anything to stop them raiding the Kabuls before very long.'

'What, weeks?'

'No, days. If we're lucky. Don't forget, the NiB deadline is mid-May…'

'Bloody hell, just two weeks.' Alan paused. 'And do they know about the grandiose plans to build the Kabul Centre at Impingham?'

'No, I haven't told them about it. But I bet somebody here will leak the news soon. Everyone's trying to grease-up to the Drugs boys.'

Alan had heard enough. Time to cut to the chase.

'To be honest, Richard, I think that's the least of our worries.'

'Have you been listening to a word I said?'

'Of course, but…'

Alan took a large gulp of brandy and braced himself.

'You remember we talked about the Kabuls' family background?'

'That's right.'

'And you know that Sofia spent her childhood in Turkey?'

'Yes, yes,' Lane was growing impatient, 'Get to the point.'

'Then I think we've got something to stop the Drugs lads in their tracks.'

'And what's that?'

'I think we've found Sofia's body. Or at least some of it.'

Alan went back through recent events: the dual accounting, Ali's threat to Paul. As he did, he tried his best to pre-empt Lane's protests.

'The thing is, Richard, I didn't want to put you in a compromising situation. I knew the minute I told you about the money...'

Lane didn't even let him finish.

'The Drugs boys would be all over PFC and you'd be out of a job?'

'No. It's not that. I just needed time.'

'For what, exactly?'

Alan explained briefly about the anomaly in the skeleton results and how Sofia's profile fitted the unknown body.

'Wait a minute, Alan, you're suggesting that Sofia's body has been kept at PFC for seven years and is being disposed of, piece by piece? Are you aware how absurd that sounds?'

'I agree it does, in abstract, but once you start looking at the forensic evidence...'

'If you are now, finally, choosing to tell me the whole truth, then as far as the police are concerned this new evidence clearly shifts suspicion onto Dr Paul Flynn.'

He drew a deep breath, then continued, 'It's a shame you didn't choose to let me into your confidence earlier, Alan, because to a dispassionate outside observer, you and Harriet are also in the frame.'

'Surely you don't believe that?'

'No, I don't. But you must admit you both work for PFC. You both deal with human bone material and its storage, so you'd have had plenty of opportunities...'

'But for Christ's sake, Richard, we've got no motive whatsoever.'

'*I* know that, but my colleagues won't. All they'll see are opportunities to make an arrest. Look, for reasons best known to yourself you've become obsessed with this killing. In fact, when you first contacted me about it, your precise words were "I know he didn't do it. He couldn't have." And now here you are, handing me Sofia's bones on a plate, so to speak. In doing so, you are deflecting attention from yourself and placing Paul Flynn clearly in the frame.'

'Richard. Stop. I know you're angry with me for withholding information, and rightly so. But just hear me out, please.'

Alan took Lane's lack of response as a good sign and he pressed on.

'Paul uses Kabul's firm, AK Plant, exclusively. They also run a delivery service and their vans are in and out of Priory Farm all the time. They could have swapped the bones very easily, piece by piece.'

Lane couldn't conceal his exasperation.

'There are times I think I should close the whole bloody place down and haul the lot of you in for questioning.'

He was beginning to calm down. Alan managed a weak smile and said,

'I wouldn't advise that. We still need to do tests on DNA samples from Ali and from the bones we think are Sofia's. The problem is, if you make a move before then, the Kabuls will know that you're onto them. The rest of the body...'

It was a grim thought. Lane broke the silence.

'Could be redistributed elsewhere?'

'Exactly. So we need to find a way of obtaining Ali's DNA without his knowledge.'

'Which is a fundamental breach of his human rights and highly illegal,' replied Lane.

'I thought you'd say that,' said Alan. 'But you can't be held responsible if you don't know how I'm going to do it, can you?'

There was a long pause. When Lane spoke again he sounded like he'd made a decision. He sounded professional.

'Send me an email. Make it appear very forensic. Use all the jargon you can, as it's *got* to sound authoritative. I'll take it directly to the Chief Constable.'

'Shall I send it to your office?'

'No, best not. Send it here and I'll print it out. I don't want it floating around the office system, not as things are now.'

'Do you reckon it'll work?'

'Yes, I do.'

'Why?'

'Simple: murder always trumps drugs.'

'But we still don't know that it *is* murder, do we?'

'No we don't, but bodies of any sort also trump drugs. More to the point, if the media ever got to learn that we did an abortive drugs bust and in the process screwed up a major murder investigation…'

'Are you suggesting I'd tell the press?' Alan feigned surprise.

'To the Chief Constable, and in private, I'll suggest anything I bloody want.'

'Thanks Richard, I really do appreciate it.'

'Don't think for a second that I'm doing this as a personal favour to you, Alan. I'm just doing my job. However if you withhold any further information from me, anything at all, then I won't hesitate to throw the book at you.'

And with that, the line went dead.

Alan was left staring at the phone in his hand. He had no doubt at all that Lane meant every word.

* * *

Alan took a few minutes to compose himself and then returned to the sofa in the sitting room. Harriet came across and sat beside him. Her grey-green eyes looked frightened. She took a sip from her brandy. Her hand was shaking. Alan put a consoling arm around her shoulder.

'Well,' he said, 'I've done it.'

'And they're taking it seriously?'

'Yes, very. It's corporate fraud on a grand scale, potentially millions. They're taking it very seriously indeed.'

Alan was aware that he was getting almost too good at the spontaneous lies now. 'So what does that mean for us?' Harriet's nervous question broke into Alan's thoughts. This was important, he had to make her feel safe.

'Lane knows we're not involved. In fact, he's alerted the local force to our situation. So if anything happens, we're protected.'

This time, it wasn't so much a lie as a strategic half-truth. Still, Alan hated himself for it.

They sat in silence for some time. Alan fully expected her to buckle; to breakdown and sob into his consoling embrace. But she didn't. Far from it.

'OK,' she said, looking up at him, 'so what's going to happen next?'

'Don't be scared, Harry.'

'Richard's on the case now. So please try not to worry. We'll need to keep clear heads for the next few weeks.'

'And you think that possible?'

Alan smiled. He hadn't expected her to be so strong.

'Of course I do.' He tried to sound convincing.

'So they're prepared to protect us for weeks?'

'For as long as it takes. But we must work together. We're a team now, Harry, whether we like it or not.'

'I like it...' she whispered, leaning towards him.

She put her arms around his neck and kissed him. Then she took both his hands, and slowly led him upstairs.

A Sense of Place III

Priory Farm

Twenty-four

The following Monday morning, Alan drove to Priory Farm to meet his new site assistant for the up-coming Impingham job. He'd worked with Steve Allen on many other projects and they were old mates. Steve's specialist skill was surveying and site graphics, and he also brought with him his own GPS satellite kit, which they loaded into the Land Rover. This was the first morning of the new project, so they didn't take a full crew with them, just a young student who wanted to learn surveying.

Steve was showing the student how to level the equipment, while Alan fired-up his small portable camping gas cooker-ring to make a pot of tea. Breaking all rules of safety, he did this on the Land Rover's tailboard, regardless of the LPG tank a few feet away. A few minutes later Steve's voice came from behind.

'It's great to be back, Alan. I've missed your pots of tea…'

'What, soggy bags in cold mugs?'

'Yes.' Their eyes met: they'd been through some tough assignments together. 'And it's nice to dice with death too. Like old times.'

Steve glanced at the LPG tank and they both smiled broadly.

First days on rural sites can be chaotic. Unplanned things happen as soon as fences are shifted and rusted gates are prized open. Alan was standing rather mournfully by some old posts and stock-wire that the sheep had trodden down overnight. He could see why: the grazing on the DMV was much greener, having been fenced-off for a couple of weeks. But he knew what to do. He cut the wire to make a gap and walked round to the back of the sheep and started to drive them forward, but they stubbornly refused to see the way out. Alan cursed under his breath; they didn't want to leave.

Then he heard the sound of voices, and turned round to see Kevin, Stu and Darren, who happened to be passing by. They were happy to help, and soon the sheep had been driven out.

'Should we call in every morning?' Darren said with a broad grin.

'Probably no bad thing, but next time, bring coffee and cakes.'

'A few beers, more like…' added Stu.

Alan regarded him with mock solemnity.

'Tut tut, my good man.'

Alan was feeling much more relaxed. He knew he could work with these people. By then, Steve and the student had assembled his GPS kit, which was top of the range and very sophisticated. Kevin inspected it with undisguised envy: he was trying to get his boss, Little Mehmet, to upgrade their instrument, but was having trouble persuading him. More to the point, Steve knew how to work it and was able to pass on some useful short cuts.

Alan could hear the two of them chatting together as he, Stu, Darren and the student tied up the last of the damaged fencing. Later, on the drive back to Priory Farm, he learned that Kevin had given Steve a weekend job, re-surveying the old Home Farm buildings, which weren't accurately positioned on existing estate maps. This would require a lot of kit, so whenever he needed it, Alan agreed to lend him the Land Rover in exchange for the PFC van.

All in all, at the end of the afternoon both Alan and Steve knew they'd done well. The new project had got off to a good start. More importantly, they'd established a good working relationship with the contractor's men on site.

The next day Steve took the Land Rover and a couple of experienced surveyors to Impingham to lay out the grid and do a contour survey; while Alan remained at Priory Farm, to finish editing the first draft of the Guthlic's report.

Once Steve had left, Alan returned to his office. Part of him wanted to be out and about at Impingham, but at the same time Ali and Guthlic's were worrying him. Why was life never simple? Something you really want to do happens, while something else stops you enjoying it. So with some foreboding he turned on his computer, only to find an email with the preliminary radiocarbon dates from Cambridge. Suddenly his doubts vanished. This was important. It had been sent to Paul and copied to Harriet, who was round in his office a few minutes later, with the printout in her hand,

'Well that's interesting,' she began reading from the list, 'the three from that Saxon group near the tower are all kosher. And a bit earlier than I'd expected.'

'Yes…' Alan replied, still slightly preoccupied, as he absorbed the new information, 'Mid-eighth to early ninth centuries…Yes, that *is* on the early side.'

'And the Indian,' Harriet added, 'he's slightly earlier than we expected too, but not quite so much.'

'No, I'd have said early to mid-fifteenth is about right. It's what I'd have guessed.'

'But those three babies are interesting, aren't they?' she asked, half to herself, 'And so very similar. The whole group's got to be contemporary, don't you reckon?'

'Yes, without a doubt.' Alan was choosing his words carefully. 'Late nineteenth or just possibly early twentieth century. That's remarkably late for such things.' He paused for a few moments. Then asked brightly: 'Fancy an early cup of coffee?'

By now she knew this was code for: 'we need to discuss this somewhere private.'

Once outside, they headed round to the hangar apron, instinctively taking the route that avoided Paul's office window. Alan began:

'That large piece of pottery…'

She shook her head; she obviously couldn't recall it. 'D'you remember, the half saucer I found sealed in the churchyard wall foundation trench?'

Suddenly she smiled.

'Yes, right, I remember. A modern glazed one…'

'Well, that made me think they were probably late nineteenth century. No earlier. And the new carbon dates confirm it. If anything they're more Edwardian than Victorian.'

'It's getting very recent, isn't it?'

Alan nodded pensively. But not half as recent as those bones Alaric sniffed, he thought. Better stall for time. Things are bound to get clearer soon. Very soon. Meanwhile he didn't want Harry jumping in – that would complicate an already tricky situation.

'Yes it is. In fact we're probably going to have legal problems with those babies.'

'The fact they're so recent?'

'Of course. And you don't have to massage the figures, either. If you take the upper range of the standard deviations it puts them at the start of the First World War. I've no choice: I'll have to report them to the coroner before too long, or I'll lose my Home Office licence, but it's going to need careful handling.'

'Is it? I thought it was fairly straightforward, not as cumbersome as...'

She'd missed the point.

'No, not the coroner, Harry,' Alan broke in impatiently, '*Alistair*. He's going to need very careful handling. So not a word: certainly not to Paul, and probably not to Amy either. OK?'

Harriet was looking serious.

'OK.'

'I don't think it can wait,' Alan continued, 'I'd better go and see him this morning.'

'I'm sorry, have I missed something?'

'Those dates make the babies more or less contemporary with the new sexton's shed. That was also the time when the churchyard wall was diverted. And who carried out that work?'

'Presumably a member of Alistair's family. Didn't it have the Crutchley coat of arms on its gable end?'

'Yes, his great-great-grandfather built it. More to the point, I'd be willing to bet good money those babies are – or were – Alistair's direct relatives.'

'Oh my God...' This clearly hadn't occurred to her. 'How horrible. Poor man. Yes, I agree, you'd better go and see him.'

They paused for a few minutes while Alan read through the technical information from the Cambridge laboratory; it was about calibration curves and standard deviations. Routine stuff, but all seemed in order.

'Right,' he said, folding the printout and stuffing it into his pocket, 'I'm off to Scoby Hall…'

'Wait a sec, Alan,' she said, laying a restraining hand on his arm. 'What am I going to say, if Paul phones through?'

'He won't. He's in York all day, isn't he?'

'Yes, but he's just got an iPhone, which he loves very dearly. I think it's his new little friend. Anyhow, he's bound to check his emails with it. Probably already has.'

'Just tell him they confirm your original views – which they do. Say there's no conflict with the stable isotopes. He mustn't suspect anything.'

She lowered her voice, as if even outside walls had ears.

'You don't think those results change the things we were worried about, do you?'

'No. Not a bit. Don't forget, I selected the samples myself before Easter when there was all that chaos in the Stores. I'm certain the contamination happened after I took them out of their boxes, and before they went back to the Out Store. The C-14 dates have got to be kosher.'

'So the mix-up must have happened over Easter weekend?'

'Yes. And the dates themselves prove it.'

'So there's no doubt about it,' said Harriet sadly. 'At best, Paul's stretched himself so thin that he's become incompetent and at worst he just doesn't care.'

'Let's just take it one step at a time,' said Alan.

Harriet nodded, and squeezed his hand.

Alan watched as Harriet slowly made her way back towards the office.

The more time that passed, the more Alan hated lying to her. He wondered for a second whether this is how it had happened for Paul: a series of small scams and fiddles at first, easy to justify when he worked so hard, had sacrificed so much for his job. And then, step by step the thing had snowballed…

A part of Alan still had a trace of sympathy for the bloke. After all, he had survived on his wits in a competitive world. And now Lane suspected him of murder. Poor bastard. But whatever he had or hadn't done, Paul was up to his neck in it. There could be absolutely no doubt now: the money and the modern Anatolian bones were both inextricably linked to PFC.

* * *

A chilly breeze was blowing off the North Sea, as Alan drove Brutus up the tree-lined avenue to Scoby Hall. He rang the bell and Alistair came to the door.

He was on his own. A few minutes later sitting comfortably in the warm kitchen, over mugs of hot tea and biscuits, Alistair was keen to discover the latest Guthlic's PX news. Alan was warming to him: not only had he been a good excavator, but he also cared about what had been found – and it was unusual to find someone from outside the profession who treated it as more than a good healthy hobby. Alan was also painfully aware that his friend's amateur interest was about to become closer – and very personal. He just hoped against hope that he had the moral strength to follow the trail to its very end. Alistair began.

'Now tell me, what have you been learning from all those tests?'

Alan began by telling him about the radiocarbon results from the graveyard. Then he moved on to the stable isotopes and how the results might fit with Harriet's theories about migrations and folk movements in Saxon England. He thought it wisest not to discuss his and Harriet's doubts about those results at this stage, and not just because that might cause Alistair to withhold future funding. He was also becoming aware that there were now a number of disturbing parallels between the Kabuls and Alistair's family, the Crutchleys, which were better left unstated at this stage.

Alistair listened closely, while Alan spoke. Normally his natural shyness made him look people in the eye in short bursts, often when enthusiasm or affection made him bolder. But while he was speaking Alan was acutely aware that Alistair was staring deep into his eyes, the whole time. It was as if he were trying to bore into his brain to recover every last grain, every atom of information. When Alan had finished, Alistair sat back and sighed deeply.

'Well,' he began, 'wasn't that fantastic. I don't think I've ever spent money better.' He paused. 'No, never.' As he rose to collect the teapot from the edge of the Aga, he turned to Alan and asked, 'But what about those babies you found over by the sexton's shed?'

First the good news, now for the bad news. Alan was not looking forward to this. Harriet had made him promise that he would never tell Alistair about Alaric's 'lipids test'. To his discredit Alan had argued the point with her. But now he had to agree: human bones, especially those human bones, should never be offered to dogs.

'Yes, I was coming to them,' Alan began, gathering his thoughts, 'the radiocarbon results suggested quite strongly that they were all put in the ground at the same time.'

Alistair was leaning forward, his eyes wide open. He couldn't contain himself.

'And the dates? How old are they?'

'As you know, it's not unusual to find young children and babies buried near churchyard wall in the Middle Ages, but these were far more recent…'

Again, Alistair cut in. 'What, Victorian?'

'Possibly, but more probably Edwardian, or early twentieth century.'

'And there can be no doubt?' This was asked in a far quieter voice. By now he was sitting back, his stare towards the ground.

'I have to say, Alistair,' Alan continued as gently as he could, 'I was very struck by the fact that the babies were found so close to the sexton's shed. It made me think there might be a family connection?'

'Yes, it sounds to me like they were buried at about the time AAC built it.'

'Doubtless the person or people concerned wanted to take advantage of the building works. Disturbed ground, that sort of thing. It happens today, all the time.'

'So you don't think there has to be a family connection?'

Alan didn't want to hit him with the whole truth in one sitting. Much better give the process time. It would be easier to accept.

'Good heavens, no. As I said, building sites disturb the ground and offer opportunities. Think of those concrete bridges in east London where gangsters disposed of their victims.'

'Could we analyse their teeth, like the other bodies?'

'No, that won't work, I'm afraid. They were too young; their teeth weren't properly developed.'

'Is there anything else?'

'Well actually yes, there is,' Alan replied. 'DNA tests would soon be able to determine if they were related in any way to the Crutchleys.'

'Fine, fine,' Alistair said assertively. 'Let's do that. And I don't care what it costs.'

Alan then explained that he didn't want to involve the police at this stage and he could get the DNA work done through friends at Biomedia, a small company in Cambridge set up by two postgraduate students in the Genetics Department. They'd done some very low-cost samples for him, back in 2005. Alistair agreed to this with a nod. Words had become superfluous.

* * *

Two days later, Alan was back in the secure classroom at Blackfen. He'd told himself that it would be unfair on the other students if he pitched the lesson to suit his investigation of Ali, but he was also painfully aware that somehow he must raise the pressure. So he moved the session on Death, Burial and the Afterlife, that he was going to give the following month forward. To today.

He began the talk by pointing out that people in the remote past were no different to ourselves. All they lacked was our science-based view of the world, and just like us, they were struck by grief when a close member of their family died. One of their ways of coping was to focus on the afterlife through special 'ritual' objects that were placed in and around the grave, at the funeral. He had half suspected that his audience, most of whom were convicted killers, or multi-murderers, would have smiled, or worse, sneered at what he was saying. But as he looked around, he could see his words had made quite a profound impression. As the lights went up at the end of his talk, at least two men were wiping their eyes with their sleeves.

At the start of their one-to-one session Alan noticed that Ali had lost much of his former energy. He also seemed more like the Ali he knew back in 2002. More natural, if not more relaxed. Alan decided to stick to archaeology at first and then see how things developed. He reached below the desk and took out three boxes. The first contained a roll of plastic gloves, which they both put on. The second contained a head torch and large magnifying lens, which he passed through the little hatch below the grill.

'Blimey,' Ali said quietly. 'Quite a build-up. What's coming next?'

Alan was concentrating on the third box before him, but he could hear the suppressed enthusiasm in Ali's voice.

'It's rather special, Ali, in fact I excavated it myself, so I don't want it damaged. Hence the gloves…'

Alan lifted the lid and removed something that looked like the blade of a huge paper knife, but it was dark greenish brown and the cutting edge was rough and uneven.

'What's that?' Ali asked as Alan carefully passed it through to him. As Alan expected, Ali's gloved hands handled it with great delicacy.

'It's a broken sword blade…'

'And how old?' Ali cut in. He couldn't contain his excitement.

'Late Bronze Age. About 900 BC.'

'I've never held something that old before…' Ali murmured, more to himself than Alan.

'Now put on your head torch and look at the edge of the blade under the lens.'

Ali did as he was told.

'Looks like someone's bashed it against a brick or something with a hard edge.'

'You're absolutely right, Ali. That's exactly what happened.'

'But why do that?'

'We'll never know for certain, of course, but it was probably their way of removing it from our world – from the world of the living – and transferring it to the afterlife.'

Ali looked puzzled.

'It was probably done shortly after the man who owned it died and it would have been done as part of his funeral service.'

Ali adjusted his head torch to a slightly different angle and peered at it even more closely.

'And it seems to have been broken clean across the blade. That seems odd?'

'Well spotted. I've had students miss that.'

'But why the break?'

'The sword was miscast and had broken across a flaw, a fault, in the metal. Hence the clean snap.'

Ali shook his head in amazement. He was completely wrapped-up in the magic of the three-thousand-year-old object in his hands.

Time to move things on. He motioned to Ali to return the blade, which he did even more carefully than before.

'You know Ali, it would be such a waste if you didn't pursue your interest in all of this.'

Ali shrugged.

'Like I said, there's no money in it.'

'So what do you plan to do when you get out of here?'

Ali replied without hesitation:

'Run my van business.'

'Of course, your white escorts. I've seen them at Priory Farm.'

It was a long shot, but it worked. Suddenly Ali's mood darkened.

'How long has that been happening?'

Alan thought fast. He knew when Ali had been sent to Blackfen.

'I'd guess about a year and a half. Maybe slightly more…'

This wasn't what Ali wanted to hear.

'What sort of work are they doing? Do they drop off stuff at other places nearby, too?'

Alan knew there weren't any places nearby. But this wasn't relevant.

'No. No, they don't,' Alan replied. 'They seem to come specifically to the hangar at Priory Farm. They never go to our building, where the archaeologists work…'

'So your friend Paul runs the hangar, does he?'

'That's right. He's got two main businesses that operate there. They do museum supplies, that sort of thing.'

Ali frowned. There was a short pause, then Alan asked,

'Why, what's the problem?'

Ali sat silently, staring down at the floor.

'Abdul… he broke our agreement.'

'And what agreement was that, Ali?'

The minute Alan said it he knew he'd made a mistake. He'd pushed too hard. In a gesture of defiance Ali roughly pulled off his head torch and shoved it through the hatch. Then he leant back in his chair and folded his arms. His body looked rigid. Resolved and silent.

Alan glanced at the clock. Time was short.

'Ali, whatever's going on here, I know it's something to do with Paul and your family and it's connected to the past.'

Ali remained stony-faced, giving nothing away.

Sod it, thought Alan.

'To Flax Hole, Ali. And I want you to know that I can help. I can protect you.'

At this, Ali let out a snort of laughter.

'I'm all right, so long as I'm in here. I'm not the one who needs protecting. Look out for yourself. Get out. Go somewhere else. Go anywhere, man.' He paused. Their eyes met. 'And I *mean* it…'

Before Alan had a chance to react, the door opened and the escorting officer appeared. He took Ali by the arm and led him out.

Alan looked down at the head torch before him. It had worked: the extra strip of Velcro he had glued to the back of the strap had accumulated several dark hairs. Then his gloved hands put it carefully back in its box…

Twenty-five

A week later Alan received two calls on his mobile. The first was from Lane, who wanted to speak to him about 'something important'. By now, work at Impingham was flat out, so they arranged to meet the following Saturday, in Leicester. The second call was from Indajit Singh, who needed 'to put a proposition to him'. Neither caller would say any more, but both made it quite clear they wanted to see him urgently.

Normally Alan enjoyed driving to Leicester. The countryside around was so distinctive. Its neat hedged fields, small woods and grass fields were such a contrast with the huge, bleak grain plains of the Fens. This was the most prestigious fox hunting landscape of Victorian Britain, and some of the wealth it attracted could still be seen in the centre of its pleasant market towns. But even the sight of thousands of young lambs frolicking in the morning dew failed to raise his spirits.

The unexpected warning Ali had given him in the last moments of their Lifers' Club interview had unnerved him. In hindsight Ali's earlier threat to Paul had felt like posturing, but this was real. Very real. Ali was genuinely concerned.

Alan was also worried about Harriet. He still couldn't believe his luck, at the way their relationship had developed. She was smart, beautiful, generous, and for reasons he couldn't understand, she genuinely wanted to be with him. Alan had always struggled with the idea of being part of a 'couple'. So lovey-dovey. But this time he felt no sense of pressure. He wasn't trapped – liberated, if anything. 'Hm,' he thought, 'Apart from the lies, of course.' He was also aware that he, that they, were being watched. In truth, they probably were – hadn't Lane promised to keep them protected? Or were there others, too?

To add to his problems, the Impingham project was proving far more difficult than he had anticipated and he was seriously worried about meeting their Site Assessment deadlines.

Lane was waiting for him in a Starbucks near the station. After their difficult phone conversation Alan was a little worried. But the minute he saw Lane that feeling disappeared. There was that firm handshake and even the hint of a smile. Lane, like Alan, was not a man to bear a grudge. He had said his piece. Now it was back to business.

'Alan,' he began, 'you look very tired – and you could use a haircut.'

'I know. Things haven't been running too smoothly of late.'

'Good grief, Alan, you're so bloody English. If nuclear war broke out you'd probably grumble about the drains.'

Alan was finding the small talk hard work. He wanted to cut to the chase.

'Any luck with the Chief Constable?'

'Yes, that's what I wanted to speak to you about…'

'And that Narcotics Review business?'

'No, it seems the Narcotics Review isn't the main driver here. I'm told there's more to it than just targets.'

Alan was listening closely. Leaning forward, he asked, 'What, something new? Hard evidence?'

'Not of actual drugs, no. But a pattern is starting to develop. After your revelation about PFC and the Kabul's dodgy accounting our officers managed to take soil samples from beneath the wheel arches of several of Ali's vans.'

'Where, at Priory Farm?' Alan asked with some concern. If their undercover operation had managed to do that without him detecting them, it must be pretty good.

'No, here in Leicester.' Lane replied impatiently. 'Anyhow, all the ones they tested had traces of those distinctive Lincolnshire silts. Our forensic geologist was in no doubt. No doubt at all.'

'I'm sure he was, but even so, that's hardly conclusive, is it? Surely delivery vans go all over the place. And the Lincolnshire silt Fens are huge.'

'Fair point, but it was the patterning that was so distinctive. Lots and lots of Leicestershire and Rutland clays and then once in a while a thin lens of those fen silts. The lab report said that at least one van went out there regularly – probably weekly. That sort of thing. Apart from those single, episodic trips out east, all their other deliveries were closer to home.'

Alan was looking more thoughtful.

'I agree,' he replied. 'That does sound odd. Very odd.'

'So, tell me more about the *Reference Collections* side of the Priory Farm operation.'

'To be honest, neither Harry nor I have much to do with it. It's very much Paul's baby. Always has been.'

'We understand that the firm's vans, and I assume they were Escorts, usually delivered to them.'

'That doesn't surprise me. In fact I've seen white Escort vans there myself. By and large archaeological units do most of their fetching and carrying themselves. You don't trust artefacts to commercial firms. And I'd imagine the less precious reference material was constantly being taken away for delivery to customers.'

'And with all that fetching and carrying, it would be quite easy to redistribute...'

Lane didn't need to finish the sentence. Alan nodded.

'If that's what they've done with Sofia then that means they must have buried her privately and then disinterred...'

Alan shuddered at the thought of it.

'I know it sounds extreme, but believe me, I've seen a lot worse in my time.'

Alan held up his hand. A clear signal that the last thing he wanted was for Lane to elaborate.

Lane paused. When he spoke again, his voice was gentler, less the authoritative policeman, more the concerned friend.

'I know it's tough, Alan, but we're nearly there. Once we can prove that the bones are Sofia's.'

'I'm working on it.'

Lane nodded at him.

'I told you, didn't I, that you would make an excellent detective?'

Alan smiled grimly.

'What is it, Alan? What else is bothering you?'

'I'm meeting Indajit this afternoon. I tried to put him off but...'

'He was having none of it? Doesn't surprise me.'

'What the hell am I going to tell him, Richard?'

'Nothing. Not yet. You can't.'

'I rather thought you'd say that.'

'If we have found Sofia, once we've got definitive proof then a trained counsellor will...'

'Don't you think it would be better coming from a friend, Richard? From you?'

Lane studied Alan for a moment, giving nothing away.

'Step by step, Alan,' he said softly. 'Step by step.'

* * *

When Alan arrived at the office Indajit greeted him with a warm handshake and then suggested that they went for a stroll along New Walk. It was a peaceful place made for reflection. They strolled side by side in silence for a while. Then Indajit, like a true lawyer, cut straight to the point.

'I've been thinking about Sofia's body.'

Alan was sure the shock was written all over his face. Indajit pushed on, regardless.

'I think my gut feeling was right. What better place to dispose of her, than an excavation?'

'Possibly, but...'

'The fact is, we've been denied our right of investigative access.'

'I'm sorry, what's that in English?'

Indajit remained stony-faced. He was right, this wasn't a time for crass jokes.

'We can't go into Flax Hole and dig the whole place up.'

Alan was somewhat relieved. The last thing he wanted was another site to manage. He would also have felt very bad if he found himself leading Indajit on a wild goose chase, raising his hopes of finding Sofia's remains laid gently to rest when... He shook the thought from his mind. He was aware that the young lawyer had stopped walking now and was waiting for some kind of response.

'Right. So our case wasn't strong enough?'

'Not exactly. You see, because the land belongs to the Kabul family they need to grant permission for a general inspection.'

'The family, you mean. Not the authorities?'

Indajit nodded.

Alan felt his heart skip a beat. He was an idiot not to have thought about it earlier. If the Kabuls knew that they were sniffing around Flax Hole…

'Rest assured, Alan, they had no idea that the request came from my office or indeed that it was about a search for human remains. I called in a favour from a friend in a different firm. He dressed it up as a search for historic contraband from 30 years ago. Even offered a site fee as an incentive, but they refused it.'

'Which suggests that they have something to hide.'

Then another thought hit Alan.

'When did you lodge the request?'

'The day after we met.'

'So, about a month ago?'

'That's right, yes. They took their time to reply.'

I bet they did, thought Alan. Too busy disinterring and dismantling the evidence and distributing it through PFC. So, they must have started the process the minute that he made contact with Ali. Carefully, piece by piece. Still, he thought grimly, you might be able to remove bones, but you can never, ever, conceal a grave.

Again, Alan was aware that Indajit was awaiting a response. He tried to keep his voice calm and even.

'OK, so what are our options?'

'It all comes back to Ali again, I'm afraid. You said you were working on gaining his trust?'

Alan nodded.

'If – and I do concede that it's a big if – he knows where the body is…'

'He's hardly going to tell me.'

'He might, by default, if he thinks that you already know.'

'You mean double bluff him?'

Alan was acutely aware of the irony of this conversation, as Indajit pushed on.

'You're an archaeologist. Tell me honestly, where would you conceal a body on an excavation, if you wanted to get rid of it without anyone knowing? A well? A pit?'

Alan considered this carefully for a few moments.

'No. Almost certainly not. On most urban sites deep features like that are often backfilled with rubble. Then the contractors supplying the foundation stone like to see that they're tipping onto cleanly exposed natural geology. So all archaeological deposits are removed. It's all about load-bearing factors. Nobody wants to bury mud or rubbish beneath their buildings in case they cause the foundations to crack or collapse.'

'Ah,' Indajit was listening intently, 'I hadn't thought about that.'

'I also wouldn't put it in one of the dig spoil heaps, even if they were to be trucked off site. The chances of somebody spotting it would be far too great. The soil in those heaps can often be spread on fields or gardens, sometimes in the same development.'

'So what does that leave you?'

'Not a lot. But each site would be very different. You'd have to find somewhere that was going to be landscaped, but would never have buildings on it. You'd also have to find a feature of some sort that would be deep enough not to be disturbed by any of the landscape designer's groundworks…'

'What, shaping banks, scooping out ponds – that sort of thing?'

'Yes. In my experience most ponds near office blocks are usually quite shallow…'

'Presumably for health and safety reasons?' Indajit asked.

'Yes. And very often too, they're lined with something like butyl rubber. So again, they don't need to be deep.'

'Well, can you think of somewhere like that at Flax Hole?'

'There was a well. Quite a deep one. Late eighteenth century, as I recall. It was certainly filled with rubble and then consolidated. I very much doubt if a body could have been slipped into that.'

'Why not?'

'Because I was supervising the work and I remember shining a flashlight down it just before the rubble went in. I was worried in case we buried an expensive electric pump.'

'Anywhere else?'

'Yes, loads of mucky retting pits. But at the end of the dig, all the pits we hadn't excavated by hand were then dug-out by the contractor's machines. With one of us watching all the time. Often it was me.'

'Presumably the pits' filling wasn't very load-bearing…'

'Load bearing?' Alan laughed, 'far from it. Those pits were filled with something resembling wet chocolate blancmange, with load-bearing capacity little better than water. No, to be quite honest I can't think of anywhere suitable.'

'But then of course you would say that, wouldn't you? If you had disposed of Sofia's body you wouldn't tell me where you put her?'

Alan suddenly went cold.

'Indajit, you don't seriously think…'

'No.' Indajit shook his head. 'Forgive me. I was using the hypothetical you, not the personal.'

Alan took a deep breath and refocused, trying to sound as casual as possible.

'The problem is, why would anyone apart from the Kabul family have any motive at all?'

'I agree. But if the site was continually manned, there could have been witnesses. Accomplices even. From what you've just said, it seems like it would require specialist knowledge to know where to place a corpse so that it remains hidden.'

Alan admired Indajit's ability to depersonalise the issue, to turn it into an intellectual problem. He tried to follow suit.

'Not necessarily. Not if you were visiting the site regularly, or even simply overlooking it from the depot.'

Indajit thought for a moment then continued.

'So how exactly did you organise the work on site?'

'How do you mean?'

'Well, who would have been present when you weren't there?'

'We worked a six-day shift system, so I had no idea what actually happened on the days when Paul and his team were on site. But having said that, we worked an overlap day and many of the specialists people – our planner and surveyor – would work when they were needed, regardless of whose shift it was.'

'So you don't think anything major could have been hushed up? Like a killing... dressed-up to look like an accident?'

'Not even then.' Alan was in no doubt. 'It's quite inconceivable. Frankly, it's ludicrous.'

Indajit laid a hand on Alan's arm.

'Look, I share your frustration, my friend, but we have got to think along such lines. In my experience crimes do get committed in the most public of places, yet nobody perceives what's going on. They see; they pass by; but they don't comprehend. And that's what I think may have happened here.'

'Perhaps, but...'

'We must somehow find Sofia's remains. It's the only sure way to prove anything. And if they are indeed at Flax Hole then you're the only person who can do this. The only one.'

Alan could hear the desperation in the young man's voice. Alan owed it to him to at least look like he was taking his concerns seriously. And besides, if Indajit's attention was focused on Flax Hole, it would divert him from looking too closely at the Kabuls' business arrangments and making the connection with PFC. It would give Alan and Lane the time they needed to put together the final pieces of the puzzle, with no risk of being interrupted.

It was yet another lie of course, but a fairly justifiable one. He was, after all, entirely focused on finding Sofia's remains – just not where Indajit had instructed him to.

'OK,' Alan replied at last, 'we must decide precisely where to look.'

'A simple enough archaeological conundrum, surely?'

Indajit said this with a hint of mischief.

'Oh yes,' Alan replied, his mind already racing, despite himself.

'Let me at it.'

Twenty-six

Back in his office, Alan contemplated the problem further. Indajit was a stickler for detail. He'd be keeping an eye on Alan, if not actually directly checking up on him. He'd need to find the time to revisit the Flax Hole records. And he'd need to do this without Paul finding out. Alan was utterly convinced now that Paul and the Kabuls' business interests were so tightly interwoven that if Paul thought Alan was doing anything that placed their combined empire in jeopardy then he wouldn't hesitate to hand him over to Old Mehmet.

And behind that thought lurked another one. Paul's insistence on the split shifts. The anxiety that Harriet spotted when Alan first casually mentioned Flax Hole. Paul's clumsy lies: the fact that he denied any knowledge of Ali's sentencing; his absurd assertion that he hadn't done any trench work at Flax Hole. The way that he had shut down the conversation so completely before Alan even had a chance to mention the episode at the wet sieves and the subsequent scream.

Obviously, the thought of Paul murdering Sofia was as absurd as the idea that Alan himself could have done it. But what if he'd seen something? A man, with a body, wading through the mud of Flax Hole? What if Paul's silence had been bought? And what if this had been the basis of the Kabul and PFC business deal?

Alan shook his head. This was conjecture upon conjecture and it wasn't helping at all. He needed facts.

So early on Monday morning he phoned Steve and told him to drive to Impingham in the PFC van, and take an experienced person along with him. Originally they'd planned to spend the day on their own, doing a rapid and very unofficial survey of the land in the park well outside the deserted medieval village.

Alan arrived at Impingham after a slow drive across the Fens. It was a cold, windy day, not at all typical of mid-May and several times he had almost been blown off the road. He drove into the Developers' Car Park, and waited for Steve and his assistant to arrive. He turned off the engine and reached for yesterday's newspaper which lay on the passenger's seat beside him.

There was a tap on the window. It was Kevin, the developers' site foreman, who again looked at Brutus with undisguised envy.

'I'm struggling with my electrics web,' Kevin said.

'You've started converting?'

'Yes. Couldn't put it off. Nearly had a fire a couple of weeks ago. The wife insisted.'

'Oh yes, don't tell me,' Alan replied with feeling. 'Been there myself. You'd better start soldering fast!'

They'd started to discuss practical problems of rewiring Land Rovers, when the PFC van arrived with Steve and his young assistant. Alan barely had time to murmur 'Good morning', when across the car park the Portakabin door was flung wide open. Little Mehmet stood there. He was very excited. He shouted over to them:

'I've just got the final drawings. Come and have a look. They're fantastic!'

His enthusiasm was infectious and the three archaeologists hurried over. Kevin didn't move; his head was deep inside Alan's Haynes Land Rover handbook. They left him there.

In the Portakabin Alan was completely taken aback by the drawings spread across the desk. The whole thing seemed far more ambitious than the plans that followed the original architect's letter, which Paul had shown him at Priory Farm. Then he looked more closely. It didn't appear that the actual ground plan – the footprint – had grown much. Instead all, and not just some, of the farm buildings were now being converted, and the new Kabul wing seemed to have doubled in size and acquired an additional storey. The architects had done their job well. Alan muttered in amazement under his breath. It was going to be one hell of a complex.

'Good grief, Mehmet this really is going to be incredible...' Alan said, while staring, open-mouthed, at the drawings.

'Look out NEC, look out Earls Court, here comes Impingham House!' laughed Steve.

'Will these new plans affect the archaeology?' Mehmet asked.

'Maybe around the western end of the car park,' Alan replied, looking carefully at the main ground plan, 'but otherwise, no. The footprint seems much the same.'

'Any chance of seeing those plans?' Steve asked.

Mehmet made tea while his assistant rummaged through the files in the next office. Once again, Alan was strongly reminded of young Ali. His eagerness just to get on with whatever project he was engaged with. For a moment he felt a strong pang of sympathy for Little Mehmet. The Impingham House management was probably some kind of rite of passage for him. A chance to prove himself to his grandfather, to take his place in the family business. He was an innocent. What was going to happen to him when the whole empire came crashing down?

Five minutes later they were staring down at the fully detailed plans.

'That's quite an extension,' Alan said, 'but it's at the other end – away from the DMV. So I guess it'll be OK. But I'd better check.'

'Why not phone now?' Little Mehmet was clearly keen to get on. He handed Alan a handset.

By the time he'd finished on the phone to County Hall his tea was getting cold. He had one final question for Little Mehmet, just to be sure:

'And the rest of the planning's sorted out?'

'Yes, came through last Thursday. So it's all systems go. We've got to get cracking.'

This was a clear hint.

'Thanks for that, Mehmet. Glad everything's sorted out. We'd better get going.'

And with that they headed towards the door, and went back into the car park. They were about to go their separate ways when they felt a few drops of rain. They looked up at the sky: an even grey ceiling. The clouds didn't look particularly stormy, or threatening, so if it did rain it was likely to be light, but persistent. And anyone who has ever worked on parkland knows that light persistent rain soon reduces a pleasant green sward to a slippery nightmare, where road tyres spin ineffectively. Both Alan and Steve knew they'd be needing four-wheel drive to get around on the wet grass.

So they decided to swap vehicles. Steve and his assistant loaded the GPS and various range-poles, scales, staffs, tapes and plans from the van into the Land Rover, while Alan checked through the cameras, which he also loaded into the Land Rover.

'Right,' Alan announced when they'd finished, 'that's everything, I think. I'd better be off to Leicester. Love you and leave you.'

He got into the PFC van and wound down the window.

Steve, who was standing by the Land Rover, looked up at the sky and asked:

'I didn't see the forecast first thing. Slept through the alarm. Is it going to get worse?'

'Possibly,' Alan replied. 'It all depends on storms over Kent, apparently. They probably won't get much beyond London, but if they do…'

'Point taken. Better get the trousers.'

He reached into the van and pulled out two pairs of rolled-up waterproofs, which he threw across to his assistant.

'Right,' he said, 'that's it. See you back here… when?'

'Just before six, I'd guess,' Alan replied. 'The museum store closes at five and then I've got to escape Leicester in the rush hour.'

'Have fun!'

And with that Steve and his assistant climbed into Brutus and headed out into the park.

* * *

Alan arrived at the Museum's Reserve Collections Store which was housed on an industrial estate not far from the city centre. The Store's Curator was Brenda Hughes, who'd been Finds Assistant at Flax Hole. They'd only met once since, so they greeted each other warmly. After a cup of tea in her office, they set off to the Archive Stacks.

Her job brought her in contact with innumerable boxes and files, but sometimes she craved human company. Alan was well aware that she had always been rather a nosey person, who loved a good gossip, after work.

'Why are you suddenly interested in Flax Hole after all this time?' she asked.

'Well, it's a–' He was about to explain it was a long story in the hope that he could play for time, but she cut in.

'I never got to see the published report, so it was printed, wasn't it?'

'Oh, yes.' This suited Alan far better. 'It was going to go in the county journal, but at the last minute Paul managed to persuade the editor of the *Proceedings of the Early Industrial Society* to take it.'

'No, I don't take that.'

'Nor do I. It's too expensive, and it's in the issue for 2004. But don't worry, I've got an offprint I could send you.'

'That would be nice, Alan. Thanks. And tell me about Paul? Is he very high and mighty, now that PFC's such a big success?'

'Yes,' Alan replied, 'very. If anything he's even less approachable than at Flax Hole…'

'Blimey,' she cut in, 'that's saying something.'

Alan raised his eyes to heaven, as he asked:

'But I imagine he's brought quite a lot of business your way?'

'You bet, they must have paid us thousands over the past few years. But that doesn't tell me why you've returned – and I'm curious.'

Then Alan had a thought.

'It was Paul's idea. He liked the way we organised the archive. Since then, PFC have changed their system and it doesn't work too well, so he wants to return to the old system for a big job we've got lined up in York.' It was all pure fiction, but it did the trick.

'So it's not the site, as such, that you're interested in?'

'No. Just the paperwork, worst luck.'

Alan grimaced and Brenda nodded her agreement. She too had once been a full-time fieldworker and hadn't adjusted well to the life of a paper-pusher.

They headed along a brightly lit corridor, which put Alan in mind of Blackfen Prison – apart from the fact that there were no doors to be unlocked and locked behind them. Eventually they arrived at the area of roller-racking for site archives of 1995–2005. Together they pushed the heavy racks apart, to reveal the shelves for 2002. The Flax Hole archive was near the top, so Brenda found him a set of folding steps. She also showed him to a table for his laptop and notepad. Then she left.

Alan stood before the huge stack of shelving. Modern roller-racking always amazed him. Those shelves, stacked with papers, samples and finds weighed several tons, yet they could be pushed by one man, with no effort. Flax Hole occupied just two shelves and all around were other sites that Alan had worked on in 2001 and 2002. Their names brought back memories: Corporation Road, Benchley Drift, and that amazing Bronze Age barrow just outside the park at

Bengrave Hall. They should have made more of that barrow, Alan thought as he glanced through the files, but the clients weren't too happy about publicity. Strangely, they didn't think first-time buyers would want to live in houses built on the site of a Bronze Age cremation pyre.

Then he climbed the ladder and took down the first box of Flax Hole papers. After a couple of hours, his eyes and head were aching. After all that research, he'd seen nothing even remotely suited to the disposal of a body. Instead, he was amazed at the size of the sample lists. There were hundreds of them. He had no idea they had processed so much material. The wet sieve lists were even bigger.

Then his imagination returned back to the dig. There were times when it had been bloody unpleasant, especially working the wet sieves. There was ice, mud and water everywhere; a soakaway which didn't work, because it soon got saturated. But here were the finds' lists. There was list after list of thousands of artefacts, ranging from buttons to wood-chips. He sighed. It was dispiriting. All that work in the freezing cold and now this: a box of grubby lists in a museum archive. Had it all been worth the effort and discomfort? His spirits fell; he was feeling daunted by the task that faced him.

By the end of the day he had written several pages of notes, but hadn't had a single bright idea. No breakthroughs. Everything was as he remembered it. The previous evening he had gone through his old diary for 2002 and had marked the days when he had been off-duty at Flax Hole. Carefully he went through the same dates in the site Day Books, but again he could find nothing, other than the Site Supervisor's account of the weather, names of staff on site, and then neat lists of features excavated and finds boxes removed from site.

It was routine and boring – just like a well-run excavation should be. And just as he'd expected. Still, at least he'd gone through the motions. Indajit would appreciate that.

At four o'clock he had finished. It took a few minutes to put various files and boxes back in their correct places, then he slid the roller-racking shut and locked it. As he climbed the stairs out of the basement, to return the key to Brenda's office, he looked out of the window. It was raining heavily. Those poor sods out at Impingham, he thought, it's horrible having to survey in the wet, even with modern digital equipment. Every time you bend down to pick up a find, or take a spot level, water trickles down your neck. Fingers get numb and press the wrong buttons on the GPS. Everything takes twice as long. He knew he'd have to buy them both a pint as soon as they'd all left site. Alan was a good site director, who cared about his staff. The survey hadn't been going too well, and morale wasn't that good. He couldn't afford to let it slip any further.

As he drove the PFC van out of the Museum Store car park and into the afternoon rush hour traffic, the sky grew darker and the rain heavier. There was lightning on the horizon and the radio crackled loudly whenever there was a flash.

* * *

Even in the heavy traffic it took less than half an hour to reach Impingham. He turned into the drive and drove up to the Developers' Car Park. Steve and his assistant were sitting in the Land Rover. He paused for a moment before getting out, then reached over for his waterproof jacket. As he struggled into it, still sitting behind the wheel, he became aware that the sound of rain on the roof had grown quieter. He rolled down the misty window and looked out. There were breaks in the clouds to the south. To the north all was black and thundery.

Summer storms can come and go quickly, and a few minutes later, Alan got out of the van and walked over to the Land Rover. The windows were misted over and the radio was playing loud rock music. They hadn't noticed his arrival. He tapped on the driver's window, which slid back.

'Bloody hell,' Steve looked startled, 'you gave me a fright. When did you get here?'

'About five minutes ago.'

Alan could see they were both writing up their notes. He didn't want to interrupt them.

'How long will you be?'

'We're nearly done. Give us a couple of minutes.'

He shut the window.

Alan took out his mobile and phoned Harriet. He explained that they'd just finished, but would be having a pint on the way home, as spirits were a bit low after all the rain. Then he returned to the van and listened to the news on the radio. After ten minutes he could see they'd finished. He walked across to them:

'Do I have time to move your stuff back to the van?'

'No,' Steve replied, 'it's all carefully packed away. While we were out surveying, Kevin found me some old sacks to cushion the Trimble. He's fitted them into a wooden frame. Made a neat job of it, too.'

Alan smiled. After his girlfriend, Steve's Trimble GPS kit was the other love of his life. Then Alan asked:

'Is anyone in the Portakabin?'

'No, we waved goodbye to Mr Kabul and Kevin, who headed home around five. By then it was starting to tip down.'

'When did you two come in?'

'About fifteen minutes later. We decided to tough it out, finish the survey, then write up our notes in here.'

'Well done, and thanks for doing that. It'll make a big difference. You can also have your comfy van back.' Steve gave a huge yawn and stretched his arms. Alan continued: 'You two need a pint. Out you hop. I'll lead the way.'

They both clambered stiffly out of the Land Rover, and Alan climbed in. Poor sods, he could see they were soaked to the skin.

'And don't worry: the dig will pay for the beers. You've earned them, both of you.'

About five miles east of Impingham, they arrived at The King's Head. Steve spotted a small space at the front of the pub, while Alan took the less manoeuvrable Brutus round to the back, where he drew up beneath some big old chestnut trees. The Land Rover's roof was beginning to leak, and the trees' broadly spreading branches would provide a bit of shelter when the next downpour hit them. Alan strode briskly across the large car park, which was almost empty.

They met up in the bar, and Alan ordered three beers and six baskets of chips. Instinctively they headed over to the open fireplace and sat down at a table by the fire, which the landlord had lit earlier in the afternoon, when the first of the storms had arrived. The logs in the grate began to smoke in a downdraught, as the wind outside got up. Alan could sense another thunderstorm was approaching.

After they'd all taken long drinks from their pints, Steve put his glass down and asked Alan how it had gone in Leicester.

'Bloody waste of time,' he replied, 'couldn't find what I was looking for.' His frustration was unfeigned, even if the explanation behind it was fiction. 'I could have sworn there was a Saxon level there. Cut through by the later pits. But all the unglazed pottery I could see was Iron Age. Shell-gritted scored wares. No sandy stuff in sight.'

As ill-luck would have it, Steve's assistant, Paula, was doing an MA in Saxon pottery, at Nottingham.

'You were looking for parallels?' she asked. Alan nodded, already regretting his little fable. Then she continued, 'What, Early, Middle or Late?'

Alan had to improvise.

'Middle, mostly. Ipswich-type. We found a few possible sherds around the graves beneath the tower at Guthlic's…'

Alan paused to think. He should have kept his damn mouth shut. Out to the west he could see lightning. Good, he thought, it'll give me an excuse to change the subject.

But he didn't have time to say a word.

Alan was raising his glass to his lips. Suddenly everyone's ears went deaf as the shockwave hit them. All the windows at the back of the pub blew in. It seemed to happen so slowly, as if a giant in the rear car park had huffed and puffed and blown the house down. Behind them, the curtains in a large bay window were lacerated by shards of flying glass, which scythed into the plaster of the wall. Scraps of fabric floated silently to the floor.

A long-haired white cat, quietly snoozing on a settle below the window, rose gracefully into the air, like a leaping dolphin, its back arched and already suffused with blood. There was an echoing, almost distant scream from the nearby kitchen and one of the chefs appeared to waltz through the swing door into the bar, his face covered with blood. As Alan watched, his graceful dance folded into collapse, as the poor man fell painfully to the floor, now at normal speed. He lay there, screaming in agony, blood welling out from between the fingers that were pressed tightly over the place where his eyes had once been.

Twenty-seven

After what seemed like several minutes, but was probably less than a second, their hearing returned. But now the sound was turned up loud. The blast of the explosion had left ears singing and senses numbed.

They sat frozen in time and space.

As if coming out of a trance, Alan rose to his feet. He had to stop that terrible screaming. His companions were still transfixed to their seats, as he stumbled behind the bar to fetch water and a clean dishcloth. The man's lacerated face resembled more a plate of raw meat than a living being. As Alan bent down to him, the injured chef passed out. Alan made no attempt to revive him. He was better out of it. From of the corner of his eye he detected Steve's figure, running towards the kitchen, his mobile phone held to his ear.

Alan dabbed the young chef's face and was tempted to pull several shards of window glass from his forehead and cheeks but stopped when he found this started further bleeding. Best leave that to the experts, he thought. The manager, a trained first-aider, had somehow escaped the blast. He ran up to the felled chef and took over, thanking Alan for his efforts.

By now the eye of the storm hit them, head-on. The rain didn't so much fall as flow out of the sky, accompanied by a swirling, eddying gale from the south and south-west. Alan stood in the doorway through which he had entered the pub less than half an hour ago, and looked back towards the chestnut trees. They were still there. But the Land Rover had gone. In its place was a twisted heap of smoking metal and two rear wheels. It looked like it had driven over a landmine. Alan remembered thinking that at least it had died a military death.

Two of the cars nearby had their bodywork bent and windows blown in. Steve was standing next to the shattered remains of the Land Rover. There were tears in his eyes. Alan had a sudden, wild thought: what about that nice girl, his assistant. Don't say, she hadn't got out? Maybe she'd stayed behind to text her boyfriend? Then he took hold of his racing brain and clearly recalled her sitting at their table the moment the explosion happened. All Steve could do was sob, 'My Trimble, my Trimble.' He was in deep shock, mourning his GPS total station. If it wasn't so tragic, it would be funny, Alan thought. It's strange how differently we all cope with extreme stress.

He ran back to the bar and found Paula sitting at the table, surrounded by shattered beer glasses. She was leaning forward, her face expressionless, but her arms were reaching around her, as if tidying up after an afternoon tea party. He watched as she gathered up crisps from the floor and the window seat, which were now splattered with drops of the white cat's blood. She got up and picked a bloody crisp off the seat and to Alan's astonishment ate it, her mouth open and lips parted. She ate another. Then another. The cat's still warm blood stained her mouth and teeth. It was as if she hadn't seen it. Alan felt his gorge rise, but he managed to retain his self-control and gently placed a hand on her shoulder. He looked into her eyes.

'Anyone at home?'

There was no response. Gently, he shook her shoulders.

'Paula, are you hurt?' The mention of her name seemed to have an effect. She looked him in the face.

'What... what...' she was staring at him now, her eyes wide open and terrified. She gripped his arm with both hands. So hard it hurt. 'What happened? WHAT HAPPENED?' This was shouted, then screamed.

Alan was about to slap her face, but stopped when she fell forward in a dead faint. He rolled her limp body over into the recovery position and draped her with curtains instead of blankets. After a few minutes she started to come round. This time she knew where she was.

'So what happened?' she whispered in a tiny, tremulous voice.

Alan could only guess.

'The Land Rover was struck by lightning and the gas tank exploded.'

'And Steve, how's Steve?'

As if in answer to her question, Steve re-entered the bar. Alan looked up at him anxiously, but the mask of shocked disbelief and grief had gone. He just looked tired. Shattered. Across the room a framed wall mirror had miraculously survived, protected behind a pillar. Alan glanced at it. His own face looked like Steve's – as if they had both aged twenty years in as many seconds.

Paula was looking at blood on the back of her hand. She had just wiped her mouth and had gone pale. It was a young woman's worst nightmare.

'My face... my face... is it cut? Please tell me, Steve, is it cut?'

He put two arms around her and held her in a warm bear hug. No, you're fine, your face is fine. You haven't been scratched.'

'Honest,' she whispered, 'not even scratched?'

'No, not even scratched.'

'Nowhere?'

'Nowhere.'

'But the blood?'

'That was on the seat.'

'But it's in my mouth. I can taste it...' She was looking aghast, her memory working overtime. 'There was a cat there. Is that its blood? Is it? IS IT?'

Steve didn't have time to reply before she lurched sideways, towards the fire, vomiting violently. In the process her knee came down on a thick, sharp shard of bottle glass and sliced through her jeans like a razor. It must have cut an artery. Soon her blood was pumping across the fireplace. Alan pulled her back and together with Steve they fashioned a tourniquet from a length of curtain. After a few seconds the flow stopped. It had worked. Thank God for that.

* * *

Although it felt more like two hours, it was in fact about twelve minutes after Steve's 999 call, when they first heard the sound of sirens. An ambulance, escorted by a police car, was roaring towards them down the Melton Road. Alan ran out and guided the two paramedics round to the bar, where the injured young chef was starting to come round. Alan felt inside his white coat and found a slim wallet. He emptied its contents, looking for allergy warnings. There was nothing. Immediately they gave him an intravenous pain-killing injection.

The manager then came through. He could find no other serious casualties. So the young chef and Paula, her knee now properly bandaged, were carried out to the ambulance, which accelerated out of the car park, sirens and lights blazing.

It must have been about twenty minutes after the explosion, that Alan realised he hadn't told anyone himself. He glanced down at his mobile. She should be home about now, he thought. He called Harriet.

'You won't believe it, Harry,' he began, 'but we've had the most amazing storm.'

The weather was not the way he would normally have started such a conversation, but his mind wasn't yet working too well.

'Yes, it must have been the one we've got now. It's directly over Scoby. Very spectacular.' She paused, while the storm raged overhead. 'Actually it's quite scary. Wish you were here, darling…'

Alan missed her last remark when the signal started to break up. His reply was meant to sound calm and factual, but it almost sent her into orbit:

'I've never seen such lightning. The Land Rover got struck. The LPG tank blew-up. Took poor Steve's GPS kit with it. There's nothing left: just bits of chassis and four wheels…'

'WHAT?' Then immediately: 'Alan, are you hurt?'

'No. I'm OK. A bit shaken, but don't worry, I'll be fine.'

'What about Steve? Is he OK?'

'Yes, he's fine. A bit shocked, too. So's poor Paula. She also cut her knee badly on some glass and has been taken to A&E in Leicester. I think she'll need stitches.'

'What are you doing? Are you stranded?'

'Yes, although we've got the PFC van. But the police won't let us drive. They say we're in shock. They'll have it towed to Boston later, where we can collect it. Any chance of a lift home? Somehow I don't fancy a ride in a police car.'

'I'll be with you in an hour.'

He knew that when she had to, Harriet could drive like a rocket.

Sixty minutes to kill. For a moment he thought about ordering a pint, but dropped the idea. So he wandered across to where Brutus's remains were being inspected by two scene-of-crime officers wearing hooded white coveralls. Alan could see their van was parked nearby. One of them was taking measurements with a long tape beneath the chestnut trees. He jotted the distances down in a notebook. The grass between the tree and the Land Rover had been singed by the heat of the fire and all the leaves above the explosion were in tatters, hanging limply in the still air. It was the calm before the next onslaught.

Alan found he didn't care anymore. Sod everything. The analgesics the paramedic had given him had made him drowsy. Light-headed. He started to drift off. Far away on the southern horizon, he could see the distinctive hammerhead cloud of another storm developing. As he watched the cumulus grow and develop, he began to realise he was feeling anxious. He glanced at his watch. Fifteen minutes to go. Now he was fervently hoping that Harriet would reach them before it did. He couldn't face having to live through a rerun. More lightning. More rain. Nothing would drive him back into that pub again. Nothing. He focused his gaze on his hands. They were shaking like a man with Parkinson's. As he watched them twitch, he was almost convinced they belonged to someone else.

When Harriet drove into the car park, Alan was slipping deeper into shock. His teeth were chattering uncontrollably. He was sitting alongside a police paramedic with a silver casualty blanket draped around his shoulders. Later he recalled that, despite shaking limbs, his mind had remained strangely clear and detached. He remembered pulling his gaze away from his hands. He was looking on, while the paramedic and Harriet helped him into the car. Somebody pulled his seat belt across. He heard the snick as it fastened; then the door was shut and locked. It felt cool and close inside. Claustrophobic. He pushed the button and the window wound down. That was better. Much better.

For a few moments he looked at people moving around in the car park. Then he shifted his gaze. Away from the pub and the chestnut trees, far away to the northern horizon, where the ominous dark clouds of the previous storm slowly took on human shape. Alan watched, transfixed. A face began to form. There was the nose. And the lips. The ears. And the eyes. Yes, the eyes, those eyes: they were unmistakable. It was Little Mehmet's side-kick, Kevin. But this time his stare was direct and cold. So cold. Alan could feel its chill. He jabbed at the button and the window began its ascent.

Then the painkillers kicked in again and the first large raindrops of the next storm smacked against the windscreen. His last words before falling deeply asleep:

'Let's get going.'

Twenty-eight

Harriet wanted Alan to take the next day off, but he stubbornly refused. He needed to immerse himself in his work. Otherwise he'd just sit around and brood on what had happened and what might have been. Alan simply couldn't accept that a lightning strike had taken out his Land Rover. The explosion happened several minutes before the eye of the storm had passed over them. Yes, there was much thunder and lightning close by, but he remembered very shortly before the explosion, counting the gap between a flash and the thunder that followed, and it was still about five seconds. As a Fenman, where the flat landscape makes lightning strike a very real possibility, he was well aware that five seconds – say five miles – was still too distant for a direct hit.

Of course he had no proof at all, because the very blast would have removed the evidence. But he trusted his subconcious. That surreal moment of vision meant something. Logically, Kevin had had access to his Land Rover, when he left it in the Developers' Car Park at Impingham. He was also known to have worked on, or rather in it, on the afternoon of the explosion, when he had made Steve the padded wooden case for his Trimble.

Steve and Kevin had worked together for several days, and Alan learned that Kevin had been very friendly. From Steve he discovered that Kevin, Stu and Darren had all served in the Royal Engineers together, Kevin as a Sergeant, the other two as Sappers. As with Paul, Alan didn't want to arouse Kevin's suspicions. But that wouldn't be easy. Maybe it was already too late. Either way, Alan was determined not to be scared off. If the person who had done this thought that he could be frightened away from PFC, then they were very much mistaken. If nothing else, the bungalow fire had also strengthened his resolve. Alan, he told himself with a certain grim satisfaction: you're becoming quite pig-headed.

Despite Harriet's protests, Alan was heading out of the door when the phone rang. It was the local police, from Boston. Would it be all right if an officer came round to take a full statement? A routine call, they said. Alan agreed.

When the WPC arrived, Alan was only able to show her his licence and a copy of the insurance papers. The MOT certificate had been destroyed in the explosion. She left fifteen minutes later, at eleven. At five past, the phone rang, again. This time it was the loss adjuster from the insurance company, with a string of questions. Obviously, two claims in such close succession had aroused the company's suspicions somewhat. Alan could imagine him ticking an endless succession of boxes. Why must everything be done by rote these days? Why not ask a few direct questions to discover what actually happened? But no, he thought, his mood getting blacker, that would require a functioning brain.

After he had put the phone down, his ear felt sore. He was now getting desperate to get away. Back to work or back to the Kabuls. He didn't care which. He felt restless: unable to relax, or sit still. And he knew the men at Impingham weren't sitting at home, twiddling their thumbs. As soon as they found out he'd survived, they'd be after him again. They had made the first move. Now it was his turn. Suddenly he felt better. He was going to do something – anything, rather than sit at Harriet's and fret. But first he'd better phone Lane. No need to exaggerate, but he'd soon find out and then he'd be angry and accuse Alan of concealing things from him. And he didn't want to go through that again.

He was reaching out for the handset, when it rang. Made him jump out of his skin.

Talk of the devil, it was Lane.

'Glad to see your Land Rover's insurance was up to date, Alan...'

Alan didn't let him get any further.

'Look, Richard, I was about to phone you, honest I was, but I haven't had a chance. It's been a succession of jobsworths asking me idiot questions. And I don't suppose the bloody bungalow fire helped, either. My insurers must think I'm jinxed.'

'And maybe they'd be right, Alan. Or maybe not.' He paused to let this sink in. 'But what do you think?'

'To be honest, Richard, I think it was deliberate. The Land Rover exploded about five minutes before the real lightning started, but having said that, there was plenty of rain and thunder. So I could be wrong. It's like the bungalow fire. I suspect that might have been deliberate, too. But again, where's the hard evidence? I wish to God I could find something definite to go on. I hate all this suspicion and uncertainty. In some ways I'd rather they *were* trying to get me...' He paused. 'At least that way I'd bloody know.'

'Look Alan, there's nothing to be gained by fretting. Soon things will be clearer. Something's bound to turn up when scenes-of-crime search the wreck. Meanwhile, don't do anything unexpected. Stay at home or at work and try not to worry too much, we're keeping a very close eye on you both.'

'Thanks, Richard.' Even to Alan's ears this reply sounded lame.

'Don't thank me, Alan, thank Chief Inspector Hissop.'

'Who?' The name meant nothing to Alan.

'That supposed WPC who just visited you. She's a full CI, has several firearm certificates and is a black belt in Taekwon-do. And for what it's worth, she thought you patronised her.'

* * *

Shortly before two o'clock, there was a hesitant knock on Alan's office door. He was standing close by it, poring over old mud-spattered working plans of Flax Hole from PFC's own archive. He opened the door and was surprised to see his old friend, Dr Isobel Chancy, who now managed Biomedia Ltd, the Cambridge firm who were running the DNA tests on the five babies. He'd completely forgotten that they had arranged to meet today. Thank goodness he had defied Harriet's orders and come in to work.

They'd worked closely on a large project fifteen years ago and had got on well ever since. She was about ten years older than Alan and had put on a few pounds since they'd last met, but she wasn't the sort of person who cared much about such things. She was very good at her work and still rather missed moving out of archaeology. But as she said when she got the job, the salaries paid in the Fisher Science Park were hard to resist.

'Izzy!' They hugged each other warmly. Alan whispered in her ear,

'I can't talk here. Let's go outside.'

Quickly Alan phoned Harriet. In a couple of minutes she had joined them on the concrete apron.

They headed over to a couple of benches near the trees and hawthorn scrub that fringed the south side of the hangar. This was where smokers from the Portakabins in the hangar used to spend their breaks. There were fag ends everywhere. Three tin ashtrays needed emptying and were half-full of water. Izzy and Harriet sat down and were chatting away about mutual friends. Alan didn't interrupt. While they gossiped, he stood, staring across the apron towards the dark bulk of the hangar.

The scene before him was very evocative. With the hangar closed up, it could have been part of a movie. It felt like a Lancaster might be towed onto the apron at any minute. As he watched, one of the great doors rolled back, and a forklift truck, carrying a stack of pallets, drove out. The interior of the hangar was a complete contrast with the sunlit space of the apron. It was dark and filled with stacked Portakabins along the walls. Behind them were the old wartime service areas, where aircraft engines had once been stripped down and repaired. It was a maze, back there, often poorly lit and impossible to navigate, unless of course one had detailed inside information. Alan had some of that knowledge, but his brother Grahame had even more. He was aware that it was something he would very soon have to improve and build upon. For a few moments he stood in silence contemplating this next task.

He was smiling as he turned towards the two women.

'I'm sorry about the cloak-and-dagger stuff, Izzy, but for reasons that might soon become apparent we don't want to be overheard. If anyone approaches, especially, our boss Paul Flynn, you were one of our local volunteer diggers out at Guthlic's. Is that OK?'

Izzy smiled. She was rather enjoying this.

'OK. That's fine.'

'That's why,' Alan continued, 'I'm keeping quiet that I sent those bones to you. The costs will be paid directly to you by the client.'

This was unusual. She had to ask,

'So what's the problem?'

Alan improvised.

'If Paul learns I'm getting so much cash from the client, he'll cut our budget. He's said as much. He can be very hard-nosed when he wants to be.'

'Hmm.' She paused. 'Then I think I might have something of interest for you…'

She produced a tiny computer from within her bag. Harriet was leaning forward, her eyes shining with anticipation.

Izzy began, pointing at five DNA bar charts on the screen, 'It's quite simple really. Your neonatal bones are all siblings.'

There was a short silence while they digested this. Harriet was the first to react:

'I think that's what Alan and I more or less expected, wasn't it?'

She looked across to him.

'Yes,' Alan added. 'Are they all full siblings? We're not talking about different mothers, are we?'

'No. The same mother. You said they were quite recent?'

'Yes, radiocarbon dates are consistent, too: late nineteenth, early twentieth. Late Victorian/Edwardian. That sort of thing.'

'Any suspects?'

Now Harriet was also looking at him with interest.

'Sadly, yes,' he replied, 'and I think I know where to get hair samples that might sort it out. I'll bring them down to you this evening, Izzy, as soon as I've collected them.'

* * *

Later that afternoon Alan negotiated the short-term loan of an old PFC van, until he could find a replacement for Brutus. Then he drove it over to Scoby Hall. Alistair invited him in for a coffee and Alan told him about the DNA test results.

'I was just wondering whether there was an outside chance they might somehow be related…'

Alistair broke in, sparing him the difficult bit:

'To my family?'

'Well, yes,' Alan continued, 'it's hard to ignore the fact that they're buried so close to that sexton's shed with the Crutchley coat of arms.'

He knew this was not going to be easy.

'What, some long-dead bastard relative. That sort of thing?'

'It had crossed my mind, yes.'

'Not much chance of that, I'm afraid. AAC, my great-great-grandfather bought the place, you know.'

'But I remember you showed me a picture of that young woman…'

'Who, Tiny?'

'Yes her. The thing is, those strands of hair behind the picture could give us what we need.'

There was a long pause. Eventually Alistair got up, walked across to the picture which he took off the wall and handed to Alan. He turned it over. Carefully he removed one of the two small bunches of hair from behind the frame. He thought it best not to remove samples at this stage, in case of contamination. The lab could do that themselves, later. Alan put it in a small sample bag, labelled and sealed it. Then Alistair added, seemingly as an afterthought:

'You might as well take AAC's as well. It would be good to sort this business out for once and for all...'

By now Alistair was frowning. Alan couldn't help wondering – does he know more than he's letting on?

As he walked back to his car, that last thought wouldn't leave him. He was surprised at how readily Alistair had let him take the samples. It was almost as if he, too, had suspected something about that long-dead relationship.

As soon as Alan had driven down the tree-lined avenue and turned back onto the Spalding road, he pulled over and texted Izzy who would be waiting at Biomedia to receive the hair samples. Then he set out for Cambridge.

He arrived on the back of the rush hour and was able to find parking close by. He rang the bell and Izzy came to the door. She'd already made mugs of tea, which they took through to her office.

'Right, what've you got for me, Alan?

'You remember those sibling baby bones you analysed earlier, well, I rather suspect they may well be closely related to these two individuals.'

'OK, that seems fairly straightforward.' She held the two bags up to the light. 'And yes, the samples are big enough.'

'Again, Izzy, this is all very confidential, but I can tell you the police have been fully informed.' Alan was aware that this was only a semi-truth. 'And they're happy for me to be consulting you.'

At this point he pulled another two bags from his small rucksack.

'This bone sample is supposedly from one of the bodies that we excavated at the foot of the tower of St Guthlic's.'

'Supposedly?'

'I think there might have been a bit of a mix-up somewhere...'

'OK, well, that's potentially awkward.'

'To say the least. So I want to be very sure that we know what we're dealing with before I start risking anyone's career or reputation.'

'Understood. So what's the issue?'

'Stable isotope analyses of the teeth by Judd's Lab. at Saltaire suggest the body came from Anatolia.'

'And how old?'

'Supposedly Middle Saxon, or thereabouts, but lipid tests suggest that some elements of the skeleton might be more recent.'

'Ah.' Alan couldn't help but smile. That was Izzy through and through. Pragmatic and understated. He knew he could trust her.

'And the last sample?' she asked, softly.

'That's hair, taken from someone I personally believe was a brother of the person represented by the bone sample.'

'So not Saxon?'

'No. Very modern. Alive, in fact.'

Izzy promised Alan results in about ten days' time. As they made their way down the corridor to the front door, she mentioned that the following week she was going to visit her mother up in Yorkshire and could call in with the results on her way back south on Monday. Rather than rendezvous at Priory Farm, they agreed to meet in the garden of the local pub, at lunchtime.

Alan waved her off, with a great sense of relief. Ten days, and then this would all be over.

* * *

On the day when the Land Rover had exploded, most of the team had remained at Priory Farm. This meant that although Steve's equipment and the GPS total station had been destroyed, the main survey data-sets had been downloaded before the weekend, and had survived. But all their plans and notes of that day's survey in the outer park had gone – which was why Alan and Steve were about to repeat the entire process, just two days after the explosion, but now using Steve's old theodolite.

It was a cool, misty morning, but the forecast didn't look too bad. Steve was setting up the theodolite, when Alan strolled over.

'Any good, Steve?' Alan asked, in theory enquiring about the equipment, but as soon as he answered they both realised they were talking about themselves.

'She's an old friend, used her for ten years, before the whole world went digital. But as we've set out the basic grid with the

GPS she'll do the job fine. I've also got a couple of dumpy levels for when the dig starts. So don't worry, we'll be OK.'

'So you reckon she'll last the project, or d'you want to hire a GPS?'

Steve patted the battered polished wooden case affectionately.

'No, she's as tough as they come.'

'And what about our friends Kevin, Darren and Stu? Seen any sign of them?'

'Yes, I saw Kevin drive into the car park. He seemed fine.'

As they spoke, the developer's Gator six-wheel drive buggy drove by carrying a load of survey pegs and hazard tape. Darren was driving and he too gave them both a cheery wave. Alan couldn't bring himself to respond and pretended to be texting on his phone. Steve returned his wave energetically.

'It's good to get back to normal,' he said, still waving, 'A few days' work and we'll both be right as rain.'

Alan thought it best to continue texting.

Alan and Steve were now well into the park at Impingham and were about to enter a small round copse north of the main drive, when Alan's mobile rang. He was half-expecting another interminable call from the loss adjusters. But it was Paul. This was another call Alan had been waiting for. Earlier, Paul had said he'd ask his insurers whether they could claim for the extra work they were now having to redo, as the Impingham budget was getting very tight.

'Hi, Paul,' Alan answered. 'Any news from the insurers?'

'I'm sorry. Forgot all about it,' came the unexpected reply.

Despite all his resolutions, this annoyed Alan; it was so bloody typical of the man. *He* didn't have to work within such ludicrously tight budgets. Such things were for his underlings. Then he pulled himself together.

'Oh well,' he heard himself saying calmly, 'fingers crossed, we'll manage somehow. Must keep pressing on. So what's your problem, Paul?'

'It's the new building here. I've just been sent the service trench plan by the architects…'

'I hope it's not too elaborate. Simpler the better, as far as I'm concerned.'

'I agree. No, all they've shown is a single water main, a cable feed and a branching foul drain, which can T onto the existing pipe into the septic tank.'

'And archaeology? What's it going to hit?'

'Again, not much. Maybe a wall associated with an extension to the monastery barn and a possible garden building off the guest range. No point doing geophys over there by the crew yard. That's all messed up with Victorian drains, etc. The County seem happy for us to go ahead, but they insist on doing geophys first. So could you come back and mark-out the area we should survey?'

Alan had thought of a practical problem.

'I can foresee two potential snags.' He didn't want to sound uncooperative, but still, the facts couldn't be avoided: 'First, we really can't afford to lose another day's surveying out here. We're behind as it is, and we're using Steve's old theodolite now that the GPS has gone.'

'So you want to keep the theodolite and the levels out there?'

'Yes, for the day. We're lost without them.' Then he added reluctantly, 'I suppose Steve and I could do it for you when we get back to base, this evening.'

'Oh no, that's far too much to ask. Wouldn't dream of it.'

Alan was astonished. It was not what he'd expected Paul to say.

'Oh, that's very kind.'

'Don't worry,' Paul continued, 'Clara or Harriet could help me measure the area with tapes. It won't take long. We'll mark it with pegs and red spray. We've got more than enough fixed points with the building so close. No, don't worry, we can manage.'

'Thanks a lot, Paul. In times like these you get to discover who your real friends are.'

Alan wondered whether this was too emollient – even for Paul. He needn't have worried.

'Always keen to help a loyal colleague. We'll mark it very clearly with loads and loads of spray-paint. You won't be able to miss it.'

That won't please Clara and Harriet, Alan thought, both of whom were already overstretched.

'Thanks, Paul. That'll be great.'

Alan was about to ring off, but Paul had resumed:

'Frankly I think a full geophys survey is over-the-top. So I tried to dissuade the County, but they wouldn't have it. I told them there's nothing there. All we're going to find is a few robbed-out walls. If we're lucky. But they're in charge, worse luck.'

Again, Alan felt his anger rise. In theory Paul was an archaeologist, so why the hell was he trying to dissuade the County curators from making a perfectly reasonable request? Paul up to his old tricks again, cutting costs, the bastard. But he remained calm.

'Fine. When d'you want the geophys done?' Alan asked, as if eager to oblige.

'As soon as you can. The builders are booked for next week.'

'Hmm.' Alan's response was unusually muted. His immediate reaction would have been very much stronger. He heard his own voice continuing, as if nothing had happened. 'That doesn't give us very long, does it? What if we find anything?'

'We'll worry about that when, and if, it happens.'

'Very good,' Alan replied.

And with that Paul hung up. Alan sighed deeply.

'Problems?' Steve asked.

'Yes, they want us to geophys for the services to the new building at Priory...'

'And they'll survey it?'

'Yes.'

'When do the builders turn up?'

'Sometime next week.'

'Bloody hell, that's a bit tight.' Steve paused. 'Still, it's work – and I could use the money.'

Alan glanced down at his phone. Bloody batteries going flat again. He was about to ask Steve where he could get a new one, when the Gator drew up at the deer park bank that marked the edge of the copse where they were surveying. Kevin was driving a man in a dark suit who got out of the passenger seat. They exchanged a few words, then Kevin took the Gator back towards the site offices. The man, who was wearing green wellies into which his trousers had been neatly tucked, walked towards them. Alan immediately recognised him.

'Alan,' he said with a broad smile while still several paces away, 'I couldn't be visiting Impingham without finding out how you are, after that terrible accident.'

He fixed Alan with his gaze. Abdul may have been smiling, but his eyes were cold. Expressionless.

Alan was at a loss for words.

'Oh, I'm fine. A bit shaken but…'

'And the young woman, I heard she had been hurt quite badly?'

'No, she's much better. She cut herself after the explosion… so it wasn't quite as bad.'

He was aware that sounded a bit lame.

'And you must be Steve?'

They shook hands.

'Pleased to meet you.'

'I'm Abdul Kabul. I'm the overall Project Manager at Impingham and I've just decided to set up a new office here. The Leicester traffic is so heavy and this is such a big project, you understand; so I'd rather be on the spot.'

At that point his phone rang. He turned round, walked away a few paces. Steve and Alan had time to exchange glances. But Abdul was already back with them.

'So sorry. They need me back at base. Nice to have met you both. And don't hesitate to contact me if there are any problems that Mehmet can't deal with.'

And with that he walked away. Then his phone rang again as he skirted round the humps and bumps of the DMV earthworks. Alan couldn't quite believe what had just happened. The arrogance of the man. The manipulation. And that cold straight stare. He suddenly realised: he'd seen that look before, on his first visit to Blackfen Prison, from the handcuffed man at the back of the class. Why hadn't he seen it earlier?

Abdul Kabul was a psychopath.

* * *

That evening, in an attempt to keep his mind occupied, Alan read up on the Carthusians, the order who'd built the original priory, which gave Priory Farm its name. The monastery had been dissolved in 1539, along with most others in Britain, but it had been far from typical. Not being a medievalist, he wasn't too familiar with this particular band of monastic brothers. And the more he read, the odder they seemed. Their lives were spent in individual cells, which at first sounded rather strict. Then he realised that each cell was in fact a small self-contained, two-storey house, where meals were delivered from the priory kitchens, through a special hatch in the wall downstairs by the front door. There was also a small private walled garden for each cell.

So, Alan thought, as monastic cells went, these were more like modern well-to-do retirement homes, than a hermit's lonely dwelling. He knew that Mount Grace Priory in Yorkshire was the finest of these monasteries, which were known at the time as Charterhouses. Mount Grace was also special because a hundred years ago the owner had restored one of the cells and its garden to their former glory.

Normally Alan would have loved this sort of thing. He enjoyed stepping outside his own field of expertise and glimpsing other worlds. And monasticism had always fascinated him. He wouldn't have admitted it for a moment, but there was an ascetic side to him that sympathised with what those medieval monks were trying to achieve. But even so, his eyes kept wandering from the page. He was struggling to remain focused. If he was right and Kevin – presumably acting on Abdul or Old Mehmet's instructions – was indeed responsible for the attack on the Land Rover, then really, honestly, how protected were he and Harriet? Lane might be able to watch over them at home. But behind the closed doors of PFC? That was another matter entirely. He smiled. He found himself envying the Carthusians and their safe, self-contained world. Then suddenly it struck him.

Alan shoved his books to one side and went downstairs. Harriet was at the kitchen table surrounded by a sea of paper.

'How are you getting on?' he asked, placing an arm round her shoulders and staring down at pages of tabulated osteometrics

'Just as well Amy and I did all the measurements early on, before the muddle in the Finds Store,' replied Harriet grimly. 'God knows what we'd be measuring if we went back there now…' Her voice tailed off, as she totted up a column of figures. Alan stood behind her chair while she finished adding up.

'I've been thinking,' he said quietly, placing both hands on her shoulders, 'with everything that's been going on recently, you and I haven't had much time together, just the two of us.'

'You're right, I'm sorry…'

Alan cut in before she could continue.

'Not your fault. I blame Paul.'

'Me too.'

They shared a conspiratorial grin.

'So, why don't we take a long weekend away? I was thinking Whitby…' He paused for effect, then continued, 'and Mount Grace.'

Harriet immediately perked up.

'You know I've never been. I'd love to. It's a brilliant idea, Alan.'

'Good. That's settled, then. I'll book us a remote hotel somewhere. We'll go out for a stupidly expensive dinner and have smokehouse kippers for breakfast in bed.'

'You old romantic. Sounds perfect.'

Then she leant back and kissed him.

Twenty-nine

The next day a tight-lipped Paul informed Alan that the County Planning authorities now required a full geophysical survey – both magnetometry and resistivity – for the new building at Priory Farm. So Alan, and two people from the Impingham team, rapidly surveyed a grid within the area marked out by Paul, Clara and Harriet in red spray-paint the previous day. Then they did the two surveys. Even before the data had been processed it was clear to Alan that neither had revealed very much: just a couple of robbed-out walls and a high mag anomaly towards the barn – most probably a dump of old horseshoes or nails. Rather disappointing, Alan thought, after all that effort.

It took just six hours to process the data and produced the usual plans, plus a few pages of text, which they emailed to the County Planning people. They phoned back the next day to say that a watching-brief with full recording would be sufficient. Alan was relieved that they didn't need an excavation. It would be yet another thing to write up, and now his backlog was growing fast. Paul had arranged for the JCB to arrive the following Thursday morning, at eight. Alan reckoned the job would take about two or three days, certainly no more. Meanwhile, they all went back to Impingham where, largely thanks to the unexpected delays caused by the additional work at Priory Farm, the main survey of the deserted medieval village was now almost four days behind schedule. Normally this would have bothered Alan but since his decision to escape to Whitby with Harriet he felt as if a weight had been lifted. Izzy would have delivered the results by then. With luck he'd be able to give Lane all the information he needed. Then they'd both get the hell out of there, while Lane and his boys did the necessary.

* * *

The day before the JCB was due to arrive at Priory Farm, Alan and Izzy Chancy from Biomedia met, as arranged, in the garden of a local village pub. Izzy greeted Alan with a perfunctory kiss on both cheeks, and then a frown.

'Harriet not with you?'

'She's up against it with her book.'

Not a lie this time, but still Alan winced slightly. Harriet had been so grateful for Alan's offer to meet Izzy and then report back – it gave her two hours to get on with her work. She was now so behind. This also suited Alan, who reckoned that the less Harriet knew, the safer she'd be.

Izzy opened her laptop on the table before them. She also gave Alan a set of hard copies to keep. Izzy took a deep breath.

'OK,' she began, 'Let's start with the difficult stuff.'

'The neonates?'

Izzy nodded.

'Right,' she was frowning as she spoke. 'I don't know how you'll react to this, but I have to say I was shocked. I've seen all sorts of horrors in my line of work, but this really did give me a turn.'

'We're talking incest, are we?'

'Yes, got it first time. And very much so, I'm afraid.'

'If it's any consolation, I'm not surprised. But can you be more specific?'

'How good are you on the biochemistry behind genetics?'

'I'm reasonably up to speed. Have to be with all the mitochondrial DNA work being done on Saxon sites.'

'OK…'

Izzy looked down at her screen for a few moments, then took a deep breath.

'Just to recap, we've got three neonatal boys and two girls. We decided to examine the boys only, as it's quite an expensive test, and nothing useful would be gained by checking the girls as well. The mitochondrial haplotype of the three boys matched their mother who was, as you've probably guessed by now, the young woman known as Tiny.'

'So who was the father?'

'Again, there can be no doubt about that. The Y-STRs matched.'

'Sorry, remind me…'

'For our purposes it doesn't matter precisely what they are, but male genes have hyper variable Y-chromosomal short tandem repeats, or Y-STRs, which match those of the father: in our three samples that man is the person whose hair you had labelled AAC.'

Indeed, Alan had suspected as much. But to have it confirmed in this way was still shocking.

'So Alistair's great-great-grandfather was inseminating – was knocking off – his own, disabled, daughter?'

'Yes,' Izzy said quietly, 'but after first infecting her – presumably as a young girl – with VD. Syphilis, I'd guess. That seems by far the most likely reason for all five siblings to die at, or just before, birth. It's horrible, isn't it?'

Despite himself, Alan was getting angry.

'So this pillar of Victorian society actually built a swanky new sexton's shed, emblazoned with his own bloody coat of arms, to conceal the bodies of his dead children! The sheer hypocrisy is breathtaking! Then the final little touch. The gilding on the sanctimonious lily. We mustn't forget, he moved the churchyard wall to make sure they were all buried in hallowed ground. Wasn't that thoughtful of him?'

'Presumably,' Izzy replied, 'he didn't want them to join him in hell.'

'What a shame,' Alan murmured, 'that it doesn't exist.'

'Yes,' Izzy added, 'if anyone deserved to fry for all eternity, it's him.'

There was an angry, gloomy pause, before Alan broke the mood. He didn't relish the task that now lay before him.

'And somehow I must now tell poor Alistair what a poisonous piece of work he's directly descended from...'

Izzy looked at him with real sympathy.

'That's one way of looking at it.'

'What, you think there's a bright side?'

'Well, from what you say about Alistair, he's kind, clever and compassionate. He's broken the family mould. That's something, isn't it?'

Alan shrugged. Perhaps she was right but he really wasn't in the mood for a nature vs nurture debate.

'The other samples, you said that they were highly sensitive? Possibly controversial?'

Alan nodded. This was it. Ali's hair sample and Sofia's bone. He had to focus. Lane would expect him to repeat everything back verbatim.

'Well, I've got some good news. It's a false alarm.'

'I'm sorry?'

'There's nothing for you to worry about. There's absolutely no way that they can be related.'

Alan sat in silence as Izzy moved on to the bone sample, which they once thought came from the base of the church tower, but which Alaric had shown was entirely modern. Rather to his surprise it turned out to belong to a woman from a genetic group centred on Eastern Europe and the Caucasus. Not that that mattered much. His theory about the disposal of Sofia's bones had just gone up in smoke. And yes, the science was solid. No doubt about that.

Nobody likes to see a pet theory go tits up, but Alan knew he didn't have time to allow himself the luxury of regret. It was the implications of the new results that were starting to worry him now. So if the bones weren't Sofia's, then whose were they? How did they arrive at PFC? And behind that, lurked another, darker thought: was Indajit right? Could Sofia still be out there at Flax Hole somewhere? Otherwise, why would the Kabuls obstruct an investigation? He had come here with high hopes, that the final pieces of the puzzle would fall into place, that he would be free of all of this. Instead, there were just more questions within questions and more confusion.

'You all right, Alan?' Izzy touched him on the arm. He hadn't even noticed that she had stopped talking.

'Fine, thanks Izzy,' he said, 'you're a star. Send me the bill and I'll see it gets paid. Now it's time I was heading off to Scoby Hall.'

In truth, he had to escape.

* * *

Alan texted Lane. Two simple words: RESULTS IN. By the time he drove into Lane's cul-de-sac, the detective was there waiting for him.

Lane ushered Alan into his office.

Alan placed the bags with the bone fragment and the hair on the table between him. He handed over Izzy's report. Lane studied it, and gave out a low whistle.

'So that's it,' said Alan glumly. 'We're screwed. Right back to square one.'

'Hardly,' said Lane quietly, passing his hand slowly across his face.

Alan could tell he was thinking, weighing up his words before he spoke. He bit back the many questions forming in his mind and waited for Lane to continue.

'It's not Sofia, but it's still some poor Eastern European girl who died.'

'That reminds me, Richard, I also got them to run lipids tests, which suggested the bone was no more than five years old.'

A slight white lie. But so what. Lane nodded.

'So the question now is, who was she and how the hell did she get to PFC?'

Of course, Lane had a point. Alan had just been too wrapped up in his own quest to see it. Best come clean.

'The original tests suggested that other bodies, supposedly buried at Guthlic's, had origins outside the area, in Ireland, central Europe and even one from India.'

'Good grief! And you thought they were all ancient?'

Alan now realised just how over-focused he had been.

'Well, they were explicable, after a fashion. Spice trade, that sort of thing. In fact, Paul was certainly happy with them.'

'And you, and Harriet?'

'At first yes, we accepted them. But the more we thought about it, the more we wondered.' He paused, 'Anyhow, that's why we ran the lipids tests.'

Alan could see that Lane realised there was nothing to be gained by raking over old coals. But even so, he was shocked.

'I'm astonished, Alan, I really am.'

'So even though it's not Sofia, there's still enough to keep the drugs boys off our backs?'

Lane sighed heavily.

'Absolutely. And to ramp up the security around you and Harriet.'

'I'm not sure I follow.'

'Your house fire might have been an accident but the attack on poor old Brutus certainly wasn't. I had a look at the report, there was clear evidence of tampering with the earth wires from the LPG tank and the petrol feed to the carburettor had two pin-pricks which sprayed fuel onto the exhaust manifold. You were lucky it didn't blow up on the way to the pub.'

'I thought as much. Funnily enough, it doesn't make me feel any better.'

'Well, no, but in terms of our investigation… Think about it, Alan. To attempt to kill you they must suspect that you know something that's a huge threat to the Kabul empire. Maybe it's not even about Sofia. Or maybe she was just the start of it.'

'What are you saying, Richard? That we're dealing with a serial killer?'

'Perhaps this time, yes.'

Lane smiled wryly, a subtle nod to the Whittlesey case, all those years ago.

'So, let's work backwards. Who had access to your Land Rover?'

'A number of people. But my gut feeling? There's this guy, Kevin. I saw him and Abdul together, shortly after it happened. Abdul was all smiles and sincere concern. Gave me the willies, if you must know.'

'OK, well, that's interesting but it's...'

'Circumstantial, I know.'

Alan found he was staring at the sample bags on the table between them. This was getting out of control. All he had wanted to do was help a young man whom he had believed was innocent. Now he was stuck in the middle of a multiple murder enquiry.

'We need more facts, Alan. I'll assemble as much as I can about missing persons that fit these profiles. I'll also see what else I can find out about Paul Flynn and Abdul Kabul. You never know, something might turn up. We'll also do a closer check on vehicle movements on routes near Priory Farm.'

'So, Richard, what do I do?'

'You're off to Whitby when?'

'Next weekend.'

'Good. Carry on as normal at work. Don't do or say anything that might arouse suspicion. Then go on holiday with Harriet and don't come back until I call you.'

'What, abandon the P/X? Harriet would never accept that.'

'Persuade her. If it seems like you have taken the attack on Brutus seriously, the killer might just leave you alone.'

'Might? Well that's reassuring.'

'I've got your back covered, Alan. But you still have to help yourself. No more visits to Blackfen until we know what we're dealing with. And don't even think about setting foot near Flax Hole. OK?'

Alan sat in silence. Lane repeated:

'OK?'

Alan nodded, then added,

'So you've spoken to Indajit then?'

'I have, and I do agree, the Kabuls' official refusal of access is highly suspicious, and we could take it to a higher level, but I don't think that's the way forward. We've got to tread very carefully. Better to investigate the site once we've made an arrest.'

'Which will be when, exactly?'

'Soon. I'm sure of that. The bombing of the Land Rover was the act of a desperate man. Whatever this is, and whoever's behind it, they're getting nervous. Jumpy. And that's when people start making mistakes. My job is to see you're not around when it happens.'

He paused,

'Understood?'

Alan nodded.

But he was miles away. And he had to smile at the irony. Policeman and prisoner giving him the same advice: get out and stay out. He'd been determined to ignore Ali's warning, now he was doubly resolved. Nothing would make him step aside. And he knew where he had to go. All roads were leading back to The Lifers' Club.

* * *

Alan called Harriet from the van. He explained the neonate results. She, like him, was saddened but not surprised. She offered to come with him to break the news to Alistair but he reassured her there was no need. Much better for him to do it man to man, he said. He needed time to himself, to digest all the information. He was also deeply frustrated. He'd made a basic error, an undergraduate mistake. He'd got too closely involved. Missed the wood for the trees. And why? Because she was so pretty, or because he'd not made a fuss when the screams happened? Probably a bit of each, but either way, he'd lost sight of the general picture. And in archaeology that's a hanging offence. He was furious with himself: he'd been so convinced that the bones had to be Sofia's that he'd squeezed the evidence to fit his blinkered beliefs. He'd seen it so many times with colleagues who had obsessions. Sometimes it was about trade, recently it had been about social organisation and the appearance of the first hierarchies – the emergence of chiefdoms. So they manipulated the evidence to fit with their pet – and usually fashionable – theories. And to hell with reality. He'd just done precisely the same thing. What an idiot he had been. He sighed, and turned on the ignition. He'd learnt his lesson.

Time to reassess. Time for an alternative explanation. But time, too, was running out.

He wouldn't have admitted it to himself, but Alan was getting to like the PFC van. For a start it was warm and the heater could be turned higher and lower, not just on and off. It had a soundproofed cab and was quiet. He could hear the radio and even play CDs. The seat was adjustable and supported his back. All in all, it was a huge improvement on Brutus. One unexpected benefit was the fact that now he could think about more than just the road, while driving. He wasn't being deafened. And he didn't have to worry constantly about switching between fuel tanks, running short of gas – or smoking electrics.

He was heading north and east. He could just discern the Lincolnshire Wolds as a thin blue band at the horizon, far to his left. On his right was the tower of the Boston Stump across five miles of open flat Fen, transected by dead straight water-filled dykes. His mind turned towards the people who had drained this Fen and how landowners in the past needed to have knowledge about what they possessed. In previous centuries it wasn't like it is today, when ownership of land or real estate is merely about acquiring yet another 'asset', to sell at the drop of a hat.

In many ways, he thought, AAC was the first of this modern species of landowner. He didn't need to de-water his estate, as that had been done four or five generations previously. He didn't even have to worry about maintaining his dykes and ditches, as that was done by somebody else too – usually one of the small, newly established Internal Drainage Boards. No, he just had to make his new possession look good, and in the process he would glorify himself and his family. Hence those ludicrous terracotta coats of arms.

Then Alan got to thinking about the other landowner in his life. In some respects Mehmet was more old-fashioned than AAC, who had made money somewhere else and then bought his estate, pre-prepared and fully operational. Mehmet was more like those Jacobean and Georgian landowners, who actually did new and creative things with their properties – things that made them money. That was how they glorified themselves and their families. They didn't need to buy fancy coats of arms. These thoughts led naturally to the Kabul centre, with the large statue in the foyer. How did he explain the motives behind all that?

Then it came to him. The parallel for the statue in the foyer was the full-length portrait of AAC in the drawing room at Scoby

Hall. Both were of the men after they had consolidated their big achievements. They weren't about art at all. What they did was proclaim to everyone who saw them, one simple message: I have arrived. And you'd better accept it. Or else... And in both instances, the 'or else' was no mere physical or financial threat. No, far worse than that, the sanctions were social. Cross swords with these men, and you would be cast out of polite society. You'd be adrift and alone. And that meant, of course, that you would lose your identity, your friends, your relations – and all self-respect.

Ultimately, Alan mused, the painting and the statue were symbols of power and respectability. No young person could have commissioned them. They'd have been ridiculed; but it was perfectly acceptable to do such things, at a later stage in life. As he drove further east, leaving the black peat fen and coming onto the paler silty fields, closer to the Wash, Alan realised there was another, darker side to such things, too.

The question that arose from these thoughts was simple: was Mehmet doing the same thing? Was this new development at Impingham, complete with that ludicrous statue – was that all about raising him *so* far above the common herd that he'd be beyond question, and suspicion?

And if so, what was he hiding? Alan thought back to the psychopath who had attended that first lecture at Blackfen. That stare, devoid of emotion. Wasn't there some ancient tribe somewhere that believed if you murdered a man your victim took your soul with him, leaving you devoid of thought or feeling – just an empty husk? So, if you had killed once, were future murders simply a matter of automated action? Just as once you'd got over causing one incestuous stillbirth, the rest were easier to live with. But these were black thoughts and if archaeology had taught him anything, it was hope. There was always hope, so long as you could find it. And as far as Alistair was concerned, that would be his next task.

Alan thought back to Alistair's ancestor, AAC. He had successfully distanced himself so far above the rest of rural Lincolnshire society, that he could safely indulge his sexual perversion, without anyone daring to challenge him. Similarly, the vast, lavish Kabul Centre would effectively move Mehmet higher up the social scale, to realms inhabited by council leaders, high sheriffs, members of parliament, chief constables and the like. If that were the case, Alan reasoned, it would be far harder to crack the mystery once the centre had been built and officially opened. Once the Establishment had taken Mehmet under its gilded wing, doors that were now open, or at least ajar, would suddenly be banged shut.

* * *

Alan drove the van up the avenue to Scoby Hall. Alistair was standing at the front door and greeted him warmly. His wife, Claire, was in London again, and he was on his own. The place was absolutely empty; it was even the housekeeper's day off.

In the kitchen, Alistair made them both a pot of tea and they sat at the table, enjoying the Aga's warmth. Outside it was overcast and a cold east wind had go up; early summer had briefly reverted to winter, as it can sometimes, even in May, close to the North Sea coast.

Alan did his best to break the news about AAC and the DNA gently, but as he spoke he could see it was not going down well. Still, he was determined not to leave anything out, right down to the venereal disease. When the truth hurts so severely, it's generally better to take the pain in one sharp dose. But at the same time, Alan had grown to like Alistair and he wasn't enjoying what he was telling him.

Then he finished, and for two or three full minutes Alistair sat still, staring at the wall, and saying nothing. He was on the verge of tears, deeply shocked; there was so much to come to terms with. Eventually he spoke.

'Oh dear, dear, dear… Poor little Tiny. How heartbreaking.'

Characteristically, his thoughts were for the victim first.

'Had you ever suspected anything of the sort?' Alan asked, as gently as he could.

'No – well, not as bad as this. AAC had the reputation in the family for being very arrogant, but that was how Victorian heads of households used to behave, wasn't it?' He paused. 'But not this…'

'Look, Alistair,' Alan said quietly, 'I don't think there'll be any need to report this to the police. So far as I'm concerned it's all over and done with. Nothing can be gained by raking over such old coals.'

'You're right… and thank you…'

He paused for some time, his brow furrowed. Alan let him be. Then he looked up:

'But again…' he continued, at first slowly, but with gathering pace, 'it does explain, or it might help to explain some other things.'

'To do with AAC?' Alan prompted.

'Yes. Or rather no… it's about other people as well, but it might explain what happened.'

He took a sip from his tea, which was now tepid. He pulled a face and took the warm teapot off the Aga. Alan gratefully accepted a top-up. Then he sat down again, looking puzzled.

'Three or four years ago, when I was still in the City, I thought I'd use some of my money to assemble a book about the family. I'd write most of it with help from various relatives, and I'd edit it together. Two of my young cousins down in Suffolk are brilliant on the internet and they've done a lot of useful research, which they were happy for me to use.'

'It sounds interesting. Did it get published?' Alan asked, not sure where all this was leading.

'Those two cousins wanted to publish it on the web, and not as a book. I wasn't too keen, myself. Too many people would know too much about the family. There's a big difference between an expensive illustrated book and a website.'

'Yes, and I suppose the revelations about AAC have proved you right.'

'Oh, yes. I must admit my initial researches into AAC didn't endear him to me. He was generous, yes, but capricious too. He also had favourites, and now I'm beginning to realise why.'

'Who were these people – members of the local county set?'

'No, they weren't. His diaries were very self-important and verbose, Trollope with knobs on. They read more like a series of sermons than accounts of daily life; but they make it clear that Tiny was looked after by the housekeeper, Mrs Jope, whose husband was the head gardener.'

'That's interesting.'

'Well exactly. It seems to me that Mr and Mrs Jope could easily have disposed of the babies' bodies and it might also explain why they, unlike any of the other servants, were given freehold possession of the house and garden they rented during AAC's lifetime.'

'This was all in AAC's will, I presume?'

'Yes it was. It's in a deed box in the Muniments Room here. According to those papers, the will was contested by my great-great-uncle Hubert, but without success. It was absolutely watertight, because it wasn't drawn up by the family solicitor in Boston, but by an expensive firm in London. At the time it struck me as odd. AAC was normally very consistent and this wasn't the sort of thing Victorian gentlemen did.'

'How do you mean?'

'Well, Victorian gents tended not to be over-generous to their servants. Generally speaking, their concerns were entirely about the well-being of their own descendants. After all, these would be the people who would carry their reputation forward to posterity. Just like modern politicians, they were concerned about their historical legacy.'

'As a matter of interest,' Alan broke in, 'do the Jopes' descendants still own that house?'

'Yes, although the estate has tried to buy them out many, many times.'

'And do they still work for the estate?'

'No,' Alistair replied, 'as soon as AAC died, they set up in business on their own. The family still run a small nursery – I suppose you'd call it a garden centre today – on the outskirts of Boston.'

Presumably, Alan thought, they set up the new business with money they had also inherited from AAC.

'I imagine,' Alan replied, 'having just one privately-owned property in such a large complex of buildings is, to say the very least, administratively inconvenient…'

'Absolutely. And it doesn't do much to enhance the overall value of the Hall and its surrounding buildings, either. To be quite frank it's a pain in the neck.' Alistair paused for a moment. 'But at least now I know why it hurts so much.'

Poor man, Alan thought, as he watched him empty the teapot down the sink, this place – his ancestral home – could never be the same again.

'Look, this may seem odd, Alistair, but I once came across something a bit like this when I was at college. I was doing a vacation job, hop-picking up in Worcestershire, and the farmer was caught abusing his own children.'

'What, incest?

Alistair looked appalled.

'Yes, incest. He was a rich man, a pillar of society, a magistrate – the works. The case caused quite a stir locally, and because I'd just been working for him, I followed what happened with great interest.'

'I bet you did…'Alistair was listening closely.

'Well, it then turned out that this seemingly honest farmer had been involved in all sorts of dodgy scams, ranging from race fixing to pyramid selling. That's how he acquired the capital to buy his farm. Once he'd done that, he became a leading member of the local county set; he was appointed to the Bench and the rest of it.'

'So he was rotten through and through? And you think AAC might be a similar case?'

'Well it's possible, isn't it? Think of it this way: both men were heads of families and highly respected by society at large. What I want to know is this: were their family crimes the only ones they ever committed? Or were they part of a broader pattern of dishonest behaviour, which they had learned how to conceal and control – in the Worcestershire farmer's case unsuccessfully? Put another way, had they mastered the art of being villains, while simultaneously acting the high status big man, who was beyond the reach of mere mortals, and of course the law too?'

'And that's supposed to make me feel better?' Alistair asked with a wry smile.

'I'd be fascinated to know what you could unearth. Otherwise his behaviour seems inexplicable to me. And I *do* think you're owed an explanation, Alistair, I really do, but I can't think of anyone else better qualified to provide one...'

'Why do you say that?' Alistair was curious.

Alan paused. He wasn't too certain how to phrase what he now had to say.

'I know we can never make excuses for certain crimes, and what AAC did was terrible. Absolutely terrible, but I do genuinely believe that even the nastiest crimes become understandable if we can set them in context. A kind of archaeology of the emotions, if you like. That's the only way we can discover what drove people to do what they did. Somehow, AAC seems even more of a monster, if all the other aspects of his life were beyond reproach. It means he abused his daughter Tiny in... in cold blood, purely for pleasure and for his own gratification, doesn't it?'

'Yes, it does...'

Alistair was beginning to sound more convinced.

'But if her abuse was part of a pattern of long-term crime,' Alan continued, 'then somehow it seems less aberrant – and in a horrible way, a bit more human. It's the massive crimes you can't get your head around.'

'Like the gassing of eight million Jews?' Alistair suggested.

'Exactly. Like the Holocaust. Those things will always remain horrors beyond our experience or imagination.

And that's what makes them so utterly loathsome. Somehow they've sunk, to a different dimension – almost beyond human experience. Just to deny them suggests a degree of moral complicity. As I see it, you must try to pull AAC's reputation back from those levels of insane evil.'

Alan paused for a moment; these were difficult concepts.

'For what it's worth,' he finished, 'I do genuinely believe he did love Tiny, despite everything he did to her.'

For a few minutes they both stared out of the window. By now the clouds weren't quite as heavy as they had been earlier in the day. Through an open window he could hear the insistent cries of a nestful of hungry fledglings, calling for food from somewhere deep in the wisteria.

'As I see it now,' Alistair was thinking aloud, 'AAC must have known very well what he was doing, and he was prepared to spend money to deal with the consequences. That's the bit I find almost impossible to forgive. As you say, it's so cold-blooded… only it's far, far more horrible even than that.'

He stared down at the floor, lost for words, then continued, almost to himself:

'But if this was just one aspect of a life in which he saw evil as the only means of achieving his goals, it somehow becomes more explicable.'

At last, Alan thought, Alistair was starting to think about the future.

'That way,' Alan suggested, 'at least we begin to understand the man, and what drove his life.'

'Anything's better than the way things are now.' Alistair took a deep breath. 'Believe me, anything.'

'Yes,' Alan replied, rising slowly to his feet, 'I wonder whether he wasn't more amoral – he didn't acknowledge that morality existed – than immoral. Some people are like that, you know. They have lost, or never knew, the difference between good and evil. Right and wrong.'

He was thinking again of those piercing, expressionless eyes in the back row at that first Lifers' Club talk. Were they AAC's eyes as well? Were they Old Mehmet's?

'Yes,' Alistair said with just a slight hint of hope in his voice. 'It might help explain things. Make him more like a human being.'

They were now standing by the front door. They shook hands warmly, then Alan headed towards the van. As he started the engine Alistair gave him a wave; now his shoulders were back. He seemed more relaxed. With luck, Alan hoped, for him the worst would soon be over.

For him, he thought. For him.

Thirty

The day after his sad afternoon at Scoby Hall, Alan found himself standing on the rough ground outside Paul's office window, waiting for the JCB to turn up. He'd done everything he could to make the job run smoothly. By now, the Impingham trial trenches were starting to be interesting, and he didn't want to be away from them for too long. Of course Lane's advice was still fresh in his mind. But could he really do it? Leave everything behind and stand aside until it was all over? Twice before he'd been faced with similar situations, when managers had told him to return to the office and complete paperwork, and leave the survey to others. And in both cases he had ignored them. The first time it happened he had found a buried late Ice Age island, surrounded by intact Mesolithic settlements. The second, he was sacked. So which was it to be, now? For Alan, it was a no-brainer.

Then it started to rain, and he took shelter in the porch of the Out Store, feeling increasingly fed up. He had booked the digger himself, and the man he spoke to at the AK Plant depot in Leicester, swore blind it would be at Priory Farm sharp at eight this morning.

By half-past ten the JCB still hadn't arrived, and Alan decided to go indoors and get a warm mug of coffee. Normally, he'd have phoned AK Plant and told them what he thought of them, but as things were now, he most certainly didn't want to antagonise Paul. But around eleven, his patience ran out. He was just about to pull the mobile from inside his waterproof, when there was a sharp rap from Paul's office window. Alan looked up. The window opened, and Paul shouted out.

'Alan, I've just had Leicester on the phone. The digger's been delayed on its previous job, and they don't have another one to spare. If he came early on Saturday, could you get everything done before the builders arrive? It shouldn't take more than a couple of days, at the very outside, should it?'

'They still due here Monday morning?' Alan asked, knowing the answer.

'Yes, they've also just rung and confirmed. I know it's tight, but could you get it done? Please say yes.'

Alan sighed. He didn't particularly want to work over the weekend. Normally he would have been furious at this, but now he checked his anger: he had to stay friendly with Paul.

'Well I'll have to, won't I? And I'm sure we can come to some arrangement if there's still a bit to finish on Monday. I've never met builders yet, who started precisely when they said they would. They never do…'

Paul smiled broadly and gave him a thumbs-up.

'Thanks, Alan, I really do appreciate that.'

Then he closed the window.

* * *

The rain had passed over by lunchtime. Alan was driving the PFC van in warm sunshine. He was heading towards Impingham and munching on one of Harriet's haslet salad sandwiches. Their first trial trenches in the park had demonstrated that an area of disturbance outside the deserted village earthworks was certainly medieval, but what it was, and why it was there, was still a mystery.

Once on site, he discussed the various problems with Steve and they laid out a couple of new trenches. Then he drove back to Harriet's. On his way home it hit him. He'd been so furious with Paul that his weekend plans had entirely slipped his mind. He'd have to cancel Whitby. Lane wouldn't be happy. And neither would Harriet.

When he walked into the kitchen he found her deeply immersed on an internet site which detailed the hidden treasures of Mount Grace. Nothing for it but to cut to the chase.

Alan felt terrible. He was starting to explain that the digger had been delayed on another job and he'd have to work over the weekend. Then he stopped. He was getting fed up. Why was it always *him* who had to compromise, when other people changed pre-arranged plans? He vented this frustration on Harriet.

'Oh, bugger Paul,' he said. 'He wants me to watch the digger at Priory Farm on Saturday.'

'I thought it was meant to arrive today?'

'It was. But you know what AK Plant are like. They've put it off until Saturday. But isn't that bloody typical of Paul? He's got the knack of screwing-up other people's lives, but never his own. I don't suppose he thought for one minute he could do the bloody job himself.'

To his surprise Harriet defended the man.

'Well hardly. He's employed you to do it for him, hasn't he?'

'I suppose so.'

That didn't make him feel any better, either.

Then Harriet asked, 'And who are *you* employing in your budget to help *you*? Surely you can ask someone at Impingham. Watching a digger isn't exactly difficult, is it?'

Alan thought for a moment.

'D'you mean Steve? You reckon he'd do it?'

'Well, you won't know till you ask him, will you?'

Steve was already grateful to Alan for giving him work in the first place, and when he received his phone call, he sounded perfectly willing. He hadn't got anything special planned for the weekend and he could always use the overtime. So he agreed.

Problem solved.

* * *

Alan had booked them into the Black Horse and Dragon, at Whitby, for the Friday and Saturday nights. They had originally intended to set out bright and early the following morning. But their plans didn't work out, and they eventually found themselves heading north on the A16, shortly before noon. After a bite of lunch at Louth, and a pleasant afternoon drive through the Lincolnshire Wolds, they crossed the Humber Bridge and found themselves in Yorkshire, in time for a farmhouse cream tea on the edge of the North Yorkshire Moors. The further north they drove, the more Alan should have unwound. But, if anything, he was getting more anxious.

They spent Saturday around the old town, visiting the famous Abbey ruins, and paying homage to the spot where Count Dracula had arrived in England. In the afternoon Harriet took him to the parish church, which is one of the most charming in Britain, with very evocative models of lost ships and a fabulous semi-domestic eighteenth-century interior. It was a unique and magical place. But Alan was having trouble connecting. It was as if he was a third visitor, a CCTV camera, observing himself and Harriet enjoying the sights of Whitby. And he was doing quite well. At times he'd be enthusiastic, but not too much, and he didn't think that Harriet realised it was an act; that his mind, his subconscious, was elsewhere. The more he thought about it, the more he realised that their 'escape' was going to be nothing of the sort. Quite the opposite, in fact.

It was dawn on Sunday morning. The first hints of light were visible through a chink in their curtains. Alan lay staring up at the ceiling, while seagulls called out in the harbour. He rolled over, so as not to wake Harriet, who was sleeping deeply beside him. He should have been feeling relaxed and at ease with life. But no. Instead he was knotted up and sweating from every pore. He had slept fitfully, on and off all night, but never for more than fifteen minutes. He glanced down, for the hundredth time, at his watch. Far too bloody early to wake Harriet.

He'd hoped this break would let him relax, but it hadn't. It'd had the opposite effect. He knew that if he'd stayed in the Fens, at least he could have kept watch on the world. His mind was always working, but so were his eyes and if anything they were just as useful. Up here the views were gorgeous, but he wasn't after views. He was after connections. Links. Something or some things that connected an exploding Land Rover, to

Ali in prison, pieces of modern human bone and people who wanted him out of the way. He was seeking motives too. What was it that drove people to murder, or attempt murder? Money? Fear? Or worst of all, control, because that never stopped.

But he also knew they *had* needed to get away. Apart from anything else, the tension surrounding Paul's dealings at PFC was getting to Harriet. He could see that. And before they came north it had been getting worse, daily. He looked down at her sleeping face. At least, he thought, she'd had a good night's sleep.

He slipped silently out of bed and pulled on his jeans. Down by the harbour, the big three-masted sailing ship was getting ready for another day as a static tourist attraction. The crew were loading supplies and scrubbing the decks. It was good to see, and it took his mind off his own problems, but only for a few minutes.

Half an hour later, he climbed the stairs back to their room. When he arrived, Harriet was sitting up in bed. The kettle had boiled, and the tea was brewing in the pot on her bedside table.

'Where've you been?' she asked.

'Down to the harbour. I fancied some air.'

'You feeling better, now?'

'Why?'

'You were on edge yesterday. You must try to relax, Alan. We're supposed to be on holiday…'

'I'm so sorry, Harry. I'll be better today, I promise. Honest.'

She looked at him, obviously uncertain whether she agreed.

'Well. Whatever happens, we must enjoy Mount Grace. I'm *so* looking forward to it.'

While she was speaking, Alan had given himself a mental kicking. He couldn't go on like this. It simply wasn't fair. Tired or not, he was determined they would both have a good time. And to hell with Paul, to hell with Mehmet and with Kevin, Stu, Darren and the rest of them. He was damned if he'd let them spoil their holiday.

So he ate a huge breakfast: three whole kippers, then bacon and eggs.

* * *

The Carthusian church at Mount Grace is the best preserved in Britain. And the ruins of the monastery buildings around it were basking in the late May afternoon sunshine.

A light, but chill breeze began to blow, after they'd been there an hour or so, and they decided to escape it in the reconstructed monk's cell in the north range of the Great Cloister. Harriet had just returned from the walled garden, where she'd been noting down herbs. They were upstairs, on the first floor, when his phone rang.

Harriet looked at him, as if to ask who's calling. He glanced down at the screen. Despite himself, despite his anxieties, he felt a quick surge of adrenalin. Something must have happened. He did his best to mask his excitement as he spoke to Harriet.

'It's Paul.'

'Oh no. That's all we bloody need…'

'I'll get him to call back later,' he whispered as he pressed the green button.

'Alan,' Paul's voice was urgent, 'there's been a terrible accident. The trench caved in and Steve has been killed.'

Alan leant against the wall, gripped by a deep sense of foreboding.

'How did it happen?'

'They don't know for sure, but apparently the trench collapsed into an old brick-lined cistern. It was full of water. Anyhow, the police are there now, poking around. They phoned me a few minutes ago at the BM…'

'The British Museum?'

What on earth, Alan wondered, was he doing there on a Sunday?

'Yes.' Paul's veneer of concern had slipped. He now sounded irritable: 'Yes, the British Museum. I'm now at Kings Cross, right, waiting for a train. I'll be there in just over a couple of hours, if all goes to plan. Where are you?'

'North Yorkshire. I'll leave at once.'

Suddenly Alan was eighteen again, watching as paramedics carried his father to the helicopter, leaving a thin trail of blood behind them. He could picture the scene at Priory Farm. He'd come across those big old brick cisterns – all the brickwork out-of-sight below ground and often jerry-built. For an instant the two images merged in a moment of massive guilt: he should have been driving that tractor, not his elderly Dad. And what the hell was he doing in Yorkshire when he knew things were coming to a head with Paul and PFC?

Thirty-one

The sunshine of the afternoon had given way to an overcast evening and the light was beginning to fail, as Alan walked across to where it had happened. He had insisted that Harriet stayed at home. This was his fault. His problem. She didn't need to see the full extent of the horror.

He was relieved to see that Steve's body had already been taken away. Its place was taken by a rather crudely executed outline in yellow marker paint – altogether inferior, Alan thought, to the neat white shapes on TV cop shows. Steve's shovel lay where he had dropped it when the disaster struck. Its blade was still pointing upwards – something no experienced archaeologist would ever allow. A shovel blade can cut deeply and anyone accidentally stepping on it gets the full force of the handle in the crotch. Sounds comic, but isn't. Alan realised that whatever had happened, must have been very sudden.

He stood and looked around him. The shattered brickwork of the cistern – the bricks themselves, their bond and the mortar that bound them together – was identical to the farm buildings immediately alongside it, and he could see where rusted downpipes from the roof gutters kept it topped-up with water. The sheds had probably been used in Victorian times to over-winter sheep and cattle, both of which drink huge quantities of water when lactating – hence the size of the underground cistern. Alan paced out the distance between the marks left by the two rear stabiliser feet, which showed exactly where the JCB had last been working, and the furthest extent of the cistern. It was about three and a half metres – which was also the distance to the shovel. If I'd been banksman on that job, he thought, that's exactly where I'd have been, too. So Steve hadn't been standing too close. In a way that came as a relief.

'Something told me you wouldn't follow bloody orders.'

Alan looked up. It was Lane.

'He was my friend. How could I stay away?'

Lane nodded. Alan guessed he would have responded exactly the same.

'We removed the JCB and the body two hours ago.'

Alan was deep in thought, staring down into the huge water-filled hole.

'Why remove the digger?'

'Health and Safety insisted. They said its weight might collapse the brickwork.'

Alan was sceptical. He took a couple of steps sideways and crouched down to look into the cistern. Reluctantly he had to agree: they'd been right; the brickwork was deeply cracked. Recently, too, to judge by the mortar. Something had given it an almighty whack. He stood up.

'Has anyone seen that crack?'

'Yes, the H and S man said it was due to the machine's vibration. Old brickwork gets brittle through time, especially the mortar. That's what did it. He was in no doubt.'

Lane could see Alan was upset. He placed a hand on his shoulder.

'Poor Alan, this must be horribly grim for you?'

'It is. We were good mates. And I'm glad the body has gone. I was dreading seeing that. I've never seen a friend dead.'

They stood looking down into the cistern. After a few moments Alan asked the obvious question:

'Do you think it was an accident?'

'You tell me.' Lane's reply was non-committal. 'On the face of it: yes, it was. A fairly standard accident. Just the sort of thing that happens around old buildings...'

'But?'

'But it happened at Priory Farm.'

Alan knew he should say nothing about Paul's original plan to have him do the banksman's job. Right now, the last thing he wanted was for Lane to force him to go into hiding, which he almost certainly would. Alan had to be completely free to do what would shortly need doing. But he also needed to learn more about the way Steve had died. Or been killed.

'Was he in a bad mess?'

'Yes, he was,' Lane replied. 'Bruises and severe abrasions around the head and shoulders.'

'Is that what you'd expect from such an accident? I'd have thought he would just have fallen in and drowned. End of story.'

'I agree, but our accident team say that rarely happens. Many deaths are actually caused by rescue efforts...'

'Is that what you think happened here?' Alan asked.

'Yes, but the digger driver's gone. He was genuinely very shaken. The paramedics sent him off to hospital.'

'Where?'

'The Pilgrim, Boston. Why, are you thinking of talking to him?'

'It had crossed my mind.' Alan said.

'Well, I wouldn't bother. He barely spoke any English. You'd be wasting your time. But he's been seen by an officer who can speak Turkish. It would seem the driver raised the digger arm to reach out to Mr Allen and by doing so released a mass of unstable brickwork which came crashing down on his head...'

Driver didn't speak much English. Must have been Kadir, Alan throught. And yes, Lane's account sort of rang true. He would have tried to use the digger arm to rescue Steve. A more able-bodied man might have jumped into the cistern, but not poor Kadir – his legs were so short and misshapen.

'And that was that?'

'Yes, sadly. It was.'

DI Lane said this softly. He laid a supporting arm on Alan's shoulder and steered him towards his car. Once safely inside, he poured out a mug of coffee, reached into the glovebox and produced a hip flask. He gave Alan the generously laced steaming mug.

Alan drank deeply for a few moments, clasping the mug in both hands. The warmth flowed through his body. He breathed in deeply.

'Thanks, Richard.' He took a few more sips. 'You know, I sort of expected to see you down here...'

'Sort of?' Lane replied in mock astonishment. 'You know we've got this place under observation. Our bloke was on the scene five minutes before the ambulance.'

'Did he see anything?'

'Sadly, he didn't. He called us when the driver ran over from here, shouting stuff in Turkish, and waving his arms in the air. Our informer raised the alarm. He works as a temporary packer in the hangar.'

'For *Reference Collections*?'

Alan was amazed. Lane had placed an undercover officer right in the heart of PFC and Alan hadn't noticed a thing. But then why would he? There was a stream of temporary staff who came and went through the place when the pressure was on. And if he hadn't noticed he was pretty damn sure Paul wouldn't have done either. For the first time in a long while, he felt reassured.

'Who is he?'

'You know I can't tell you that.'

Alan nodded. Of course. The last thing Lane needed was for Alan to accidentally let that slip.

'Anyway, he informs me that they've a big job on.'

'I know, for somewhere in the Middle East.'

'Oh yes. Your man Paul told us all about it.'

'When he got here from London?'

'Yes. Didn't stay long. Maybe fifteen minutes. Had an appointment somewhere else.'

'Bloody typical.'

'He seemed very proud of it.'

Briefly Alan's mind had wandered off. What was he talking about?

'Sorry, Richard, you've lost me: proud of what?'

'The *Reference Collections* Middle Eastern project. Said it was very high profile and prestigious. To be honest he seemed to be thinking more about that, than the accident. Odd bloke, isn't he?'

'Oh, yes,' Alan replied with feeling.

But was it just odd, he wondered. Was it just Paul being self-centred and oblivious? Or was it something else, more like displacement? Or covering up? He refocused on Lane. He was still talking about their undercover man.

'Anyhow, his department dispatches parcels to museums and galleries all over the world. He's kept a daily log. Just in case.'

Lane paused, taking a sip from his own, un-laced, mug, then continued:

'Today he and another bloke were working overtime in the hangar. They had to dispatch an urgent order to another big customer, this time in the States. It was going air freight. The van was standing by.'

'Presumably one of Abdul's vans?'

'Yes, an old Escort. Our man got the number.'

'What about the driver?'

'There were two of them. They went to the canteen outside the hangar, while they waited for the order to be assembled. Then they helped load up.'

'And has it – have they – gone?'

'Yes, we had to release them,' Lane replied, frowning, 'the material they were dispatching was clean. No drugs. And nothing else, either.'

Again, Alan felt rather relieved that Lane was leaving any mention of the bones unsaid.

'You're certain of that, Richard?'

'Our dogs gave it a good sniff, but we've also alerted Customs at Stanstead who'll give it a thorough going-over. But no, the paperwork was all in order and above board. So we let them go. It was a valuable order and we'd have to justify our actions later.'

Yes, Alan thought, and when friend Mehmet gets even more power and influence, you'll certainly have to justify such moves. They sat in silence for a few minutes. Alan was the first to speak; he couldn't conceal his disbelief.

'So, what, we just sit here and do nothing?'

'Alan, I share your frustration. But we're police, we're servants of the public; we have to act within the Law. Maybe if something new crops up, we'll be able to take action. But not now: not as things stand.'

As he listened, Alan realised that Lane was right, but for another reason. And yes, he too had to forget Steve's death. But only for now. It was just another fact in the case: to be stored away and produced later. Nothing would be gained by making a fuss now. Nothing.

'No, you're right, of course. I'm sorry. It just seemed such a waste. Such a God-awful waste.'

Whatever Richard Lane or the police might think, Alan was certain that Steve had been killed – and in error, for him.

'When did Paul leave?'

Lane glanced at his watch.

'An hour and a half ago.'

'Did he see your blokes snooping around?'

'Oh, no. We made sure of that, don't worry.'

There was a short pause while they both stood still, staring into the gathering dusk. Alan broke the silence.

'So how long d'you think it'll be, before the next raid – assuming, that is, they find nothing today?'

'They'd have to wait two or three weeks – for the dust to settle. Or for a tip-off.'

'What then? D'you think they'll drop it?'

'God knows.'

'I mean, *could* they drop it after today – if they find nothing?'

'No,' Lane replied, 'I think that very unlikely. This "accident" is far too suspicious.'

'You keep saying "accident" in that way.' Alan still wanted to learn more about Lane's own, personal views. 'D'you think he could have been killed deliberately?'

'Well,' Lane replied, 'you must admit, it looks very odd. First it happens at a place we've got under observation. Second, it happens on a weekend when nobody's around and, third, the Kabul family are involved.'

'Through AK Plant?'

'That's right.'

'Surely you don't think Steve was involved in any way, do you?'

'No,' Lane replied, 'so far as we know he's completely in the clear.'

'So who then?'

Alan waited expectantly for the reply. This was a crucial question.

'Well,' Lane seemed to be thinking aloud, 'the dispatch note we found in the digger cab was signed by Paul Flynn, as were all the documents from the County Planning Service.'

'Where did you find them?' Alan cut in.

'In Flynn's office. The window wasn't even fastened, let alone locked…'

'Yes, but they're just the order and delivery notes. They say nothing about who's going to be actually supervising the machine, do they?'

'I don't know. But I don't think that matters. It's the impression that counts, isn't it? I think the people at AK Plant *thought* it was going to be Paul. After all, he does live here and it's the weekend. Not many people about. It all adds up, you must admit.'

'I suppose so.'

Alan was surprised at that. It was completely unexpected. But, on reflection, not unwelcome. It might give him the time he needed to get ready.

'But why kill Paul?'

'I'm still not wholly convinced,' Lane replied, 'that was their intention. My instinct is always to go for the simplest explanation – cock-up, not conspiracy. But that aside, there could be all sorts of reasons they'd want him out of the way: maybe their business arrangement had gone sour? You remember that threat from Ali? Or maybe they've got wind of the fact that you intercepted the modern bones? Or perhaps they just don't trust him. He's not part of the family, is he?'

That last question was the only part of Richard Lane's reply that made any sense to Alan. But now he knew how Lane and the police were thinking. And as far as he was concerned, he didn't mind if they did believe Paul was the target. No, he thought as he walked back to his van in the dark, as horrors went, it could have been a lot worse.

Time to get home. He headed down the drive. The archaeological offices were dark, but a couple of lights were still on upstairs at the farmhouse. They won't find much up there, Alan thought, as he swung the van out into the open fields of Dawyck Fen.

* * *

Alan got back to Harriet's around eleven. They shared a simple spaghetti, which they mostly ate in silence. Harriet was feeling very low, as she'd spent most of the evening on the phone to

Steve's girlfriend Angie, who was then about to drive north to stay with her parents for a few days. Harriet agreed that was the best way to cope. She needed to get away, completely.

Afterwards, they moved into the sitting room, as neither of them felt much like going to bed. She had turned the television on – sound off – for company as much as anything else. They sat on the sofa and Harriet asked:

'Tell me honestly, Alan, was it an accident? Don't you think it's a bit coincidental, happening so soon after the Land Rover explosion?'

Alan knew he must keep Harriet calm for the next few days. He still had much to do.

'I don't think so. The police health and safety people were convinced the collapse happened through the JCB's vibration. And surely nobody's in any doubt about the Land Rover. That *has* to have been a lightning strike.'

But he had misjudged her.

'Does it?' she said, somewhat forcefully.

'Well, what else can you suggest?'

'Look, Alan, you're the clever one with all the ideas. So don't try to hide things from me.'

Alan could see she meant business. Time for a tactical withdrawal. He sat back as she continued:

'When we went around Mount Grace your head was somewhere else entirely. I might as well have been with my Alzheimer's Gran, than with another archaeologist. Honestly, you were miles away. And you were worrying. Constantly. I could see it. Not that you were thinking over a particular problem. When you do that, you come to a conclusion and then return to the real world. At Mount Grace it never ended.'

She paused. Alan was about to say something when she gestured him to be quiet and continued.

'Until, that is, your bloody phone went. And then it was as if you'd been waiting for it, all along. I was expecting you to react with stunned amazement at the news. After all, he is – was – a close colleague. A friend even. But no. It was as if you'd been expecting it to happen. I know this is about more than just the dodgy accounting. So what the hell is going on?'

It was too much. Alan knew Harriet well enough to realise that now she had an intuition, a feeling that something wasn't right, she wouldn't let it go.

So he took a deep breath and he began from the start, right back at Flax Hole. And he didn't stop until he'd told her everything.

When he'd finished, Harriet sat quietly for a moment, staring at the floor. When she looked up at him, her eyes were full of hurt – and anger.

'So let me get this right,' she said. Her voice was even and calm. Too calm. 'When your bungalow burnt down, you suspected you were the victim of an arson attack perpetrated by an unknown member of the Kabul family as a result of your renewed contact with their son. Yet you still came here, to my home…'

'I told you that I spoke the the police, I made very sure…'

'Please, Alan, you've had your say. Let me have mine.'

Alan sat back and gestured to her to carry on.

'Then you continued your investigations, using information about the PFC accounts that I had shown you in confidence. You also used PFC contacts to clarify the origin of modern bones that I identified and that you suspected belonged to the murder victim. Even after you were directly targeted in the bomb attack on your Land Rover you still persisted…'

Alan couldn't take any more. He had to cut in.

'It was important to me, Harry. I couldn't just let it go.'

'And what about me? Was I not important to you too?'

'Of course. That's why I thought the less you knew…'

'Do you have any idea how insulting that is?'

Harriet was up on her feet now, pacing the room.

'I thought we were a good match. Partners. I thought we had a chance. But all this time, you've been treating me like a child, whilst also implicating me in your investigations and putting my life at risk.'

'I'm sorry.'

Alan was acutely aware of how pathetic that sounded.

'So am I, Alan. I really am.'

It was just gone 1 a.m. by the time Alan drove into the courtyard of Crudens Farm. He knocked on the door, and Grahame answered immediately.

'So,' said Alan wearily. 'You were right. It's all blown up in my face.'

Grahame put his arm around his brother's shoulder and guided him inside.

Thirty-two

Alan arrived at PFC the next morning with a sore head and a heavy heart. He'd stayed up late with Grahame, filling him in on the catalogue of disasters that had culminated in his arriving on the doorstep in the middle of the night. Grahame had sat and listened, only interrupting his flow to get another bottle of whisky from the kitchen. The sky had been getting light by the time Alan had stumbled off to bed.

As he walked across the apron, Harriet strode out to meet him. As she approached, Alan could tell that she had also had a restless night. She looked dreadful.

'Harry, I don't know what to say.'

'Then just listen,' she said curtly. 'I had a long chat with your detective friend this morning.'

'Good.' Alan had left Lane a garbled message before he drove out to Grahame's. He was very glad that Lane had acted on it so swiftly.

'He insisted that at least some of this deception was a result of his direct orders.'

'That's the truth,' said Alan. He knew that any kind of emotional conversation was not Lane's speciality, and he was grateful for his friend's attempt to intervene.

'But don't you see, Alan? You still chose to confide in him and leave me completely in the dark.'

From Harriet's determined tone, Alan knew better than to try to offer any further excuses.

'However, Detective Inspector Lane assures me that security measures have been taken to monitor my home and PFC. He also suggested that now we are no longer together the level of threat to me personally has significantly diminished.'

There was a slight tremor to her voice. Alan was desperate to reach out to her, to hold her – but he kept his distance.

'He also made it very apparent that if I speak to anyone else about this situation I risk my own safety and the integrity of the investigation.'

'He knows what he's talking about.'

'I'm sure he does. So I just wanted to inform you that I agreed to his request. But I want nothing more to do with any of this. You're on your own.'

Alan nodded. Never was a truer word said.

'Meanwhile, it won't be easy, but we've still got to maintain a professional relationship. OK?'

Her gaze was intent.

'Of course Harry. Whatever you want…'

But Harriet had already turned her back on him and was walking briskly away.

Steve had died at Priory Farm on the last weekend of May. The month had ended with a spell of warm sunny weather, which followed on from the stormy week, when the Land

Rover had exploded. The minute Alan got into his office he started checking the Met Office website to see what the next two weeks had in store for them at Impingham. Little had been done on site the previous day, as people were too shocked by Steve's death, and even Paul realised it would be inappropriate to force them back to work. But now all that Alan could do was throw himself into his work. It was the only distraction he had. Otherwise, his mind was full of images he'd rather not revisit: the gaping hole in the ground where Steve had drowned. Harriet, trying to hold back the tears as he handed over the spare keys and walked away. So Alan spent his day reworking the excavation schedule and updating the trench-by-trench log, which should have been done the previous week.

But just before it was time to go home, Paul came round to Alan's office and announced in no uncertain terms that he was getting very worried about progress. Alan described the favourable weather forecast for the next few days, but decided not to tell him that most of the delays were in fact caused by the new works here at Priory Farm. Come what may, he had to stay friendly with Paul.

They'd been discussing Impingham for about ten minutes, when Paul walked over to the year planner on Alan's wall. This was where he'd plotted the various stages of the Guthlic's and Impingham projects. Paul was in dynamic manager mode. Perhaps this is his way of coping, thought Alan. Or perhaps he's so far gone that he doesn't give a shit that an innocent man is dead.

'OK, so tomorrow's June 1st, and according to this we've got to have all fieldwork at Impingham finished by the 25th. Is that right?'

'Yes,' Alan replied, 'that's what you – we – provisionally agreed with the architects, but it's not inscribed on tablets of stone.'

'Well actually it is.' Paul sounded resolute. 'The contractors want us off by then. And no later. It's what the clients want. I've been to Leicester and they left me in no doubt whatsoever. We've got to be off by the 25th. Earlier, if possible. And they don't really care if we incur additional costs.'

'I bet they don't,' Alan cut in, 'we'll be the ones who have to pay.'

'Actually you're wrong, Alan.' Paul was sounding pleased with himself. 'The Kabuls are good people to work with. If any on-costs are reasonable, they've agreed they'll cover them. They just want the work finished and us off site. That's all.'

'Well, OK, if…'

'I don't want any bloody "ifs" at this stage, Alan. Just make sure we finish on time. Am I making myself clear?'

Alan appeared suitably cowed.

'Absolutely. You can rely on me, Paul.'

You arsehole, he thought. I'll get even.

* * *

The next day was Tuesday, and Alan was again on the Met Office website, where the forecast had changed dramatically. Overnight the jet stream had veered sharply north, and associated cold fronts were now heading south-west, from off the North Sea. The new map looked distinctly grim, with heavy, thundery rain every day until the weekend, possibly followed by better, if unsettled, conditions the following week.

If anything, the revised forecast proved optimistic, and with the best will in the world, Alan and his team were now making very slow progress on the heavy clay soil at Impingham. Every morning they had to bail out pits and pump ditches for at least an hour before they could even think of doing any work. The site was covered with scaffold planks, or duck-boards, and already two of his diggers had twisted wrists and ankles trying to force heavy wheelbarrows through the mire. It was grim. To make matters worse, thunder and lightning had affected PFC's expensive new GPS system, so recording was slow and hazardous.

Had it not been for Paul's little pep talk at the start of the week, Alan would have called the team in long ago, but he felt he had to press on, more or less regardless. Then, and to everyone's great surprise, on Friday afternoon Paul came out to visit them. His visit coincided with a particularly heavy downpour. At tea break, he made a brief speech in which he paid handsome tribute to Alan and the work they were all doing.

Afterwards, as they stood by his spotlessly clean car in the developers' car park, Paul placed both hands on Alan's shoulders and said in the warmest tones how much he appreciated what he was doing 'for PFC'. He wouldn't forget it. Alan acted the loyal employee. But he was well aware that despite all their efforts, they had made very little real progress. Although he thought it best to say nothing, he now seriously doubted that they'd meet the client's deadline of June 25th, just three short weeks away. But in reality, that was the least of his concerns.

* * *

Saturday morning dawned clear and sunny. Even though it clouded over around midday, and there were odd showers in the afternoon, the barometer in Grahame's hall showed pressure rising. With luck, Alan thought, the unsettled weather will soon give way to something a bit better. Alan was hoping to get out of the house, go for a good long walk and clear his head. But Grahame was having none of it. Since Alan's late night confession on his arrival, the brothers had barely seen each other. Grahame has been up very early to tend to the farm and Alan had been working late at PFC. Now with a full day ahead of them, there was no escape. Grahame brewed a strong pot of coffee and placed it on the table between them.

'Right,' he said. 'Tell me about this Kevin bloke.'

Alan hesitated, reluctant. He'd already put Harriet in an impossible situation. He didn't want to make the same mistake twice.

'Honestly, Grahame, it's not your problem.'

'You're my little brother. Of course it's my bloody problem.'

Alan smiled. He couldn't remember Grahame calling him that for years – not since their dad died.

'OK. I'll be straight with you.'

He found he was relieved to be talking freely, at last.

'I can't prove anything about the Land Rover, but I don't like Kevin and his two mates – and I know for a fact he had plenty of opportunities to rig something up on the Land Rover, during the day. The police showed that the fuel supply had been tampered with, too.'

'Really, and who d'you think did that?'

'Ultimately, we can only guess, but I do know that Kevin was in the Royal Engineers, and although I think he's nasty – a real PK – he's also not stupid. And if he was a Sapper, he must have been trained in demolition, booby traps, that sort of thing. He's also trained to take orders. So if the Kabuls had indeed instructed him to eliminate me, that's what he'd do.'

'So are you also saying that Steve's death was another botched attempt to kill you?'

'I can't be certain, of course, but there's a lot about that "accident" that worries me.'

'Like what?'

'Well, Steve's an experienced banksman. He knows,' he corrected himself, 'he *knew* how to do the job safely. He was wearing Hi-vis and a hard hat.'

'But they're not much use when the ground beneath your feet gives way, are they?'

'Of course not, but I'm also pretty certain he'd have been standing outside the back acter's slewing arc. His shovel was lying well back from the hole. It's basic stuff. You never stand so close that you'd be caught in a collapse.'

'What was Steve like to work with? Did he take idiotic risks like you?'

Alan smiled ruefully, his brother had a point. Then he pressed on.

'That's what worries me. He was red hot on health and safety. It's so unlike Steve to be caught like that. Now I admit they were operating well outside the area we had geophys'd...'

'Why was that? Why hadn't you geophys'd it?'

'Simply because of the Victorian disturbance. All that brick rubble would completely defeat a magnetometer, although with hindsight GPR would...'

'GPR?'

'Ground-penetrating radar. That would certainly have detected the water-filled cistern. It was what they were originally designed to do, in Japan, back in the 1970s. They were used to detect empty voids beneath roads in a sandy district. Saved many lives, apparently.'

Then Alan remembered it was Paul who had vetoed the need to use GPR, as they'd have to hire in the equipment. He said the expense was over the top; that magnetometry and resistivity would be more than enough. Maybe he'd suggested as much to the County?

'But surely,' Grahame asked, 'you don't think that somehow they deliberately set out to find a buried cistern and then smash it, do you? And besides, you said the driver couldn't speak a word of English.'

Alan wasn't quite sure why the driver's language was relevant. But he did have a point.

'I agree. I think the digger and its driver might be incidental. They're part of it, but not instrumental, if you see what I mean.'

'So what – who – *is*, as you put it, "instrumental"?'

'The police think Paul was the intended victim. But he can't be linked in any way with Impingham or the Land Rover, although he can be linked to those anomalous bone samples. I think that's where the pattern – the links – really begin…'

'So not with the Land Rover?'

'Not at this stage. I think that could turn out to be part of something very different. No, in this instance, I'd rather concentrate closer to home.'

'That's good, if it means you're thinking about your own skin for a change.'

Alan ignored this.

'Look, I'm not interested in the threat, or threats to me at this stage. In a sense they're irrelevant. It's what lies behind all this that needs to be sorted out. Otherwise we're just treating symptoms.'

'But if those symptoms are life-threatening and involve collapsing cisterns and exploding Land Rovers, we can't just sit here and do nothing.'

'I'm not doing nothing ...'

'So what are you doing?'

He had to get him to understand.

'Look,' he paused briefly, before continuing. 'We've got to think about the links between the Kabuls and Priory Farm.'

He walked across to the table, picked up an orange and started peeling it, while assembling his thoughts.

'I'm convinced Paul is the way into this problem. He must be the original link with the Kabuls. We know for a fact that their relationship goes right back to Flax Hole, in 2002, right?'

'But that doesn't mean they were up to no good back then, does it?'

'The fact is,' he continued, standing with his back to the unlit fireplace, 'Paul was never told that Steve had replaced me. And don't you think it was a bit odd, the way the digger was delayed till the weekend, when there was nobody around?'

'But was that necessarily Paul? It could equally well have been the Kabuls, couldn't it?'

'Possibly. We'll probably never know for sure.' He paused. 'No, it's that link with the Kabuls again...'

He tailed off, then resumed.

'I didn't want to say anything to Richard Lane, as it would only add fuel to the police drugs theories, which I still think are bonkers, but Paul does seem to have had a very close relationship with the Kabuls. I wouldn't be at all surprised if they hadn't provided – by loan or by grant – some of the capital required to build the new facilities PFC need for the big York job.'

'Do the Kabuls have interests in a bank or mortgage broker?'

'No, not that I know of... But they do have access to loads of money. The new archaeology building may in theory be temporary, but it must be worth hundreds of thousands. Apart from the basic frame, it's purpose-built. And I've no idea how Paul found the capital.'

'So you think Paul and the Kabuls have come to a big financial deal, do you? That the dodgy accounting is just the tip of the iceberg?'

'It's the most likely scenario so far...' He paused. 'And it might also explain that strange business of the threat.'

'Yes, but what's behind it?' Grahame asked.

Alan looked puzzled. He didn't get what he was driving at. 'Behind what?'

'Behind the deal. If it is a deal: what's the collateral? You don't invest large sums of money on a whim, do you?'

'You certainly don't. To be honest I don't know what it's about, except I'd be most surprised if Paul would ever get involved with drugs.'

'Why's that?'

'He's far too intelligent. He'd know one day he'd be found out. Too many well-funded law enforcement agencies – police, customs, Special Branch, even MI5 – are sniffing around the narcotics world. Opium poppies provide most of the cash that funds the Taliban. No, whatever he's up to is more subtle than that. And it's also on a smaller, national, not an international, scale.'

'But he's definitely up to something, isn't he? Whether acting under the Kabuls' orders or not.'

'Definitely. Not least because Paul himself surveyed the area he wanted me to geophys.'

'Maybe he was just trying to help.'

'Paul doesn't really do help – not without his own agenda. He could just as well have asked us to do it when we got back from Impingham in the afternoon. Even without Steve's GPS kit, we'd have finished it in a fraction of the time.'

'And why is that so important?'

'Don't you see, if we had surveyed it, I'd have spotted the manhole covers over the cistern and would have included them in the geophys area, just to be safe.'

Grahame nodded and gestured to Alan to continue.

'It seems to me he didn't want us to recce the bits outside that one little area, he'd so carefully and vividly defined.'

Alan had suddenly realised the word 'vividly' was crucial to this. He remembered thinking, as they arrived to do the actual survey, that it was all a bit over the top, with lots of red spray and bright red pegs. You'd have to be blind to miss it. He remembered saying to Steve that it was almost as if Paul thought they were stupid. And how right he was...

'So you're saying he planned the whole thing?'

'I think so. He knows how an archaeologist's mind works. Mine especially, we've worked together enough. I always focus in on something, as soon as it's given a clear edge. Like those graves within the pipe trench at Guthlic's. I honestly couldn't tell you much about the rest of the graveyard, not without chasing up maps and plans.'

They both thought about the implications of this. Alan was the first to speak.

'As I said, the man's not stupid. He knew how to manage my response. And I think he achieved almost everything he wanted...'

'"Almost" everything?'

'Yes,' Alan continued, 'except, of course, there was one huge problem.'

'And what's that?'

'He got the wrong man.'

'Right,' said Grahame. He got up and rummaged through the kitchen table drawer, until he found a scrap of paper and a pencil. Next he walked over to the shelves where he kept his books on Fenland wartime defences. He paused for a moment, then pulled out a large volume with a picture of a Lancaster in front of a hangar on the cover. Then he sat back down next to Alan.

'I reckon you're all right for a few days. They'll know that the police are keeping an eye on them. Gives us time to make a plan.'

'Really, Grahame, you don't have to…'

Grahame gestured at Alan to shut up. He did so.

'Do you remember that awful accident granddad used to tell us about?'

Alan frowned. Of course he did. His grandfather was a doctor in Bourne. He was an integral part of the community – and the incident had shaken him to the core. He'd received a call from the local brewery. One of the workers, whose job was to skim the dead yeast off the surface of the fermentation vessels, had reached in too far. Carbon dioxide is a by-product of fermentation. It's heavier than air, and it lay in an invisible cloud directly above the liquid. The man had inadvertently breathed some of this in, as he leaned forward with the rake. Normally it wouldn't have been fatal, CO_2 being suffocating rather than toxic, but he was also at full stretch and out of breath. So he pitched in, face-down, and drowned. There was nothing their grandfather could have done to prevent it, but he was plagued by a feeling of guilt for the rest of his life.

'Of course, but I don't see what that's got to do…'

'You will,' Grahame replied. He opened the large book and thumbed through a series of ground plans and elevations.

'Aah,' he muttered to himself, 'Type B1 prefabricated. This is it...'

Alan looked on while his brother picked up his pencil and began to work.

The pictures were clear, detailed and precise. Alan had always wished he could draw as well as his brother, who had a real flair.

'A back up plan, right?' said Grahame.

Alan looked at it for a long time. Then slowly, he nodded in agreement.

* * *

Dawn on Sunday was superb, and even better, the forecast confidently predicted the next five days would remain fine.

Shortly after breakfast, Alan set out for St Guthlic's and the ceremonial opening of the new toilets. The tape was to be cut by the Rural Dean. Three weeks previously, the vicar, in his covering note that accompanied their invitation, had said how much he hoped they could attend this special 'Christening'. It was the last thing he wanted to do but then, on the other hand, Harriet might just be there...

He parked in a field gateway, as the narrow lane to the church was full of cars and four-wheel drives. The small church car park was overflowing, too. As he approached, he could see members of the congregation filing out through the porch. Harriet was amongst them. She gave him a small nod, and then purposefully started engaging in animated conversation with the elderly lady standing beside her. Alan got the message, and he could hardly blame her. The vicar and Rural Dean were standing side-by-side, in full cassock and surplice, each shaking the hand of every member of the congregation. After the unveiling of a small plaque, Alistair invited everyone back to Scoby Hall for 'a bite of lunch and a glass of wine'.

Towards the end of lunch, when Alistair felt he could now escape from his duties as hereditary Squire of Scoby, he approached Alan for a quiet word. Meanwhile Harriet and Alistair's wife Claire had gone out into the garden together.

Alan and Alistair withdrew to the library, which, despite its name, was lined more with hunting prints than shelves of books; but it was a quiet and pleasant room, with a high ceiling and comfortable leather-covered armchairs. And it must be bitterly cold in winter, Alan thought. They sat down and Alistair produced a manila folder from a locked drawer, in one of three large desks, at the centre of the room.

'Well, Alan, I have to say you were dead right. I went to various City archives along with my young cousin Davey.'

'Yes, you mentioned him the last time I was here.'

'That's right. The eldest of the two lads. I say "lads". But Davey's now nineteen and about to go up to Oxford. He's very bright and keen on history. Incidentally, I mentioned your name and he'd heard of your work in the Fens.'

'I'm honoured.'

'Yes, but that shows he's a thorough-going sort of chap. Doesn't skate over the surface. Anyhow, we started researching AAC's activities in the City and soon found some strange goings-on.'

'Like what?' Alan was intrigued.

'Like investing heavily in high-risk commodities, such as rubber and sugar in places like South America, where the political situation was far from stable. But he seemed to have got away with it. So far so good, we thought. Then the record went quiet for about five years and we couldn't work out what he'd been up to. The next time he surfaces, he seems to have involved himself in South African affairs.'

'Hardly a stable part of the world at the time, either?'

'No.' Alistair continued: 'But again he seems to have been remarkably astute. He was well in with the Boers, after their initial victory over the British in 1880 to 1881, and established good contacts in the young independent republics of the Transvaal and the Orange Free State. The next big thing to happen was the discovery of the immense Witwatersrand gold field in 1886. He seems to have done quite well out of the mines, but not content with that, he used his new capital and his existing contacts to sell arms to the Boers, in 1899.'

'Wasn't that the start of the Boer War that made it into history?'

'Yes. Before that it was more undercover.'

'And we went on the offensive, to get the mines and the Transvaal safely back in the Empire?'

'Yes, and of course we were successful.' Alistair resumed his story: 'But so far as I could make out, he seems to have made even more money selling guns, than he did from gold. Anyhow, he used these largely ill-gotten gains to buy the Scoby estate. So although he always told people that he made his money from the City and from banking, in reality he traded arms to a state that was fighting the British army. I don't think you can sink much lower than that...' His voice tailed off.

For a traditional Englishman, this was the sin against the Holy Ghost. They sat for a moment in silence. Through the library's French windows he could see Harriet and Claire turning back towards the house.

'Does Claire know about AAC's various exploits?' Alan asked quickly.

'No. Not yet.'

'Do you plan to tell her?'

'Funny you asked that. I certainly wouldn't have done, if all we knew about was his incest with poor Tiny. But now he seems a more – how can I put it? – a more... a more... *well-rounded* villain, it's somehow a bit different. You were quite right, you know: yes, I now realise he was an out-and-out shit, with eyes only for himself and the main chance, but somehow he's also become more comprehensible.'

'Why's that, do you think?' Alan asked. 'Because he was also a crooked arms dealer?'

'I know. Sounds odd, doesn't it? But yes. As you said the last time we met, somehow he's become more human.'

To an outsider that might have sounded strange, but Alan knew what he was saying.

'So to answer your question, Alan: yes, I've decided I *will* tell her. But not just yet, if you don't mind.'

Alan could see Harriet lean towards Claire and gesture towards the library windows. Claire nodded, squeezed her arm and led her out of his sight.

'You want my advice,' Alan said softly. 'Don't leave it too long. Secrets are like gun dogs: they have a nasty habit of biting you on the arse, when you least expect it.'

Thirty-three

Sunday's forecast proved correct. The fine weather continued the following week, and Alan's team began to make better progress at Impingham. After five days' work, they had almost completely caught up. As soon as conditions started to improve, Alan persuaded the team to stay an extra hour at the end of the day. This hadn't escaped Paul's attention, as his office window looked onto the concrete apron in front of the hangar, where they parked the PFC minibus overnight.

On Thursday morning Paul visited Impingham for a second time, and again showed his gratitude to both Alan and the team. As Alan had told Grahame the previous evening, he didn't feel comfortable with the new, friendly Paul.

'Better friend than foe' was his sensible response. Alan agreed, but in his heart of hearts he knew he must never let his guard slip.

Paul left site shortly before lunch, and Alan headed off for his sixth Lifers' Club session, directly afterwards. By now he had bought himself a more reliable, second-hand, Daihatsu Fourtrak 4x4, which ran on diesel rather than explosive gas. Registered in 1998, it was grey and suitably anonymous.

It wasn't that he had ignored Lane's advice, exactly. It was more a matter of weighing up the pros and cons. Someone, related to the Kabuls, was out to get him. There was no doubt about that. So he had two options: he could either hide away up at the farm and hope that they wouldn't track him down. Or he could tackle the problem head-on. And the only person who could help him choose was Ali.

Alan knew this was to be an important session. It was also a subject close to his heart: the Birth of Modern Archaeology. It was a topic, too, he knew off pat. He was familiar with all the old reports – the Swiss Lake Villages, Cranborne Chase, Glastonbury and Meare – and he'd taken the trouble to prepare some good slides. So he was feeling very confident when he entered the room. But then things began to go wrong.

Like most good lecturers, Alan relied on adrenalin to help him make contact with the audience, but this time something wasn't quite right. Yes, he realised, the adrenalin was there: in fact he was positively pumped up. But it wasn't the right sort. It hadn't been produced by the sight of his audience. It had been there all along, when he entered the room. It was anxiety, not enthusiasm. And as this sunk in, he began to lose the plot. His audience became restive. He was glad when the lights came up and the whole thing was over.

Ali was the first student to be interviewed. As soon as he sat down and looked up, Alan could see the changes he had observed the last time, had not gone away. The confident hard man had vanished.

For a couple of minutes they went through the motions of discussing the monthly essay. Then Ali asked the first question. It went directly to the point.

'Did they try to get you?'

Alan was taken off guard.

'Yes… yes, they did.'

There was a pause.

'I'm glad they failed,' Ali said softly.

Alan could see he meant it. This was his chance. He'd appeal to Ali's compassion. To his humanity.

'Who are they, exactly, Ali? Who's behind all this?'

Ali's face darkened. He shrank back into himself.

He's frightened, Alan realised, with a sudden shock. The poor lad is frightened of his own family.

'It doesn't matter,' Alan said softly, 'you don't have to tell me.'

Ali hunched his shoulders and leant towards the grill that divided them. When he spoke his words were urgent, insistent.

'You've got to get away. I mean it. You must escape. Go abroad.'

'No, Ali. I can't do that. I never run away. And besides, I'd never find any work.'

'Change your job. Do something else. At least you'd be alive.'

Although he now trusted Ali, he also knew it would be rash to tell him what he planned to do next.

'Ali, don't worry about me, I can look after myself.'

Again Ali shook his head, this time in disbelief. Alan continued:

'I'm more worried about you, Ali. You know damn well you shouldn't be here.'

'It's not that simple.'

Alan too leant forward in his chair. This was important. This was the nearest that Ali had come to confiding in him. He mustn't let the opportunity slip through his fingers.

'I understand that, Ali. Families never are. Especially when there's money involved.'

'It's not just the money.'

'For you maybe, but for Abdul?'

Ali's body language shifted again. Alan reckoned he was getting angry. Mustn't overdo it, but more must be said.

'He's taken over your vans, and he's using them for the family business, isn't he? I see them at PFC almost every day. That was never the agreement, was it?'

Ali shook his head and then paused, as if he was weighing up his words.

'I've spoken to my grandfather about it.'

'And do you think he can control Abdul? He is an old man, isn't he?'

'Yes, but he's head of the family.'

The way he said this left Alan in no doubt that Ali believed Mehmet's status was beyond question.

'And you're certain that's enough?'

'Enough for what?'

'Enough to control Abdul.'

Ali was staring at the floor. Alan continued,

'Forget about the family business for a minute, Ali. Think about yourself. You're a young man. You could do anything you want. Why waste ten years of your life locked up in this place?'

Ali shrugged, as if the very question was irrelevant.

'We made a deal. As a family.'

This was getting to the heart of things. Alan was now convinced that his early suspicions were correct: Ali had been pressured to confess to a crime he didn't commit in order to protect Old Mehmet. Alan could imagine how this might have played out: Ali would have had very little choice in the matter.

'And have the terms of that deal been kept? Or are your grandfather and your brother too busy expanding their little empire to even bother to come and see you?'

Alan could see that this had touched a raw nerve. He pressed on.

'All I'm saying, Ali, is that you need to rethink the terms of the deal. If you tell me what you all agreed, I can help you.'

Ali glared at him.

'And what's in it for you?'

'Nothing. Honestly. All I care is that justice has been done. I'm convinced you didn't kill Sofia.'

He paused to let this sink in. 'And what's more I don't think Indajit Singh believes you killed her, either. The trouble is, you confessed, and unless you tell me, or the police, the complete truth, it's going to be very difficult to help you. And you're going to be stuck in here for a very long time.'

'You really don't get it, do you?' said Ali fiercely. 'This isn't just about Sofia. It goes way beyond that.'

Suddenly there was the clatter of the door behind him. Alan glanced up at the clock. Bloody hell! Their time was up.

* * *

That interview gave Alan much to think about. Normally his post-Lifers discussions in the pub helped him organise and sort his thoughts, but he could hardly call Lane up and tell him that he'd gone directly against his advice. At least not until he'd got something concrete to give him. Alan still needed to think things through. So he pulled the Fourtrak off the road and parked in a field gateway. He'd started smoking again, so rolled a cigarette and opened a window to let the smoke escape. About half a mile away he counted thirteen wind turbines. They were becoming a major feature of the Fen landscape. Twenty-first-century weather vanes. They were all facing south-west and revolving very, very slowly. That meant fine weather was set to continue for a while.

Like many archaeologists, Alan was a visual thinker. Put him in front of a section and he could unravel the most complex sequence of layers and recuts. Maybe this was why he liked to jot things down. With his problem summarised and tabulated on a single page, he could see the true strength of an argument. He pulled a dog-eared reporter's notebook from his rucksack and began to write:

1 *Sofia's killing:*

Then he paused, sucking his pencil, before adding:

Ali didn't do it. Maybe, Mehmet wanted to take credit?

Then he crossed the last sentence out and wrote instead:

2 *Mehmet's role. His motivation: be a big man, leader of a powerful family in the Turkish community.*

Again he paused. This was the crux. He went on:

By persuading Ali to confess he showed:

   a   He had absolute control of his family and
   b   He could take a strong moral line when needed, because
   c   Nobody in the T. community would believe Ali had done it. They knew it would have been M. But there was a price he had to pay:

3 *'The deal' with Ali. He had been just 18 when it happened. So his
   sentence light. Mehmet's main concessions:*
   a *Grants him 'freedom' from family after sentence served.*
   b *Even his van business is free from 'family business'. But Abdul
      reneged on the deal. Why?*

Then he crossed out the final question mark and replaced it
with a colon. This was where Abdul came in. Maybe he wasn't
waiting idly in the wings until it was his turn to run things.
Perhaps he was playing a more active part? He picked up his
pencil again and jotted down:

4 *Abdul's role. Whatever the 'family business' that began at Flax
   Hole in 2002 was, Abdul ran it day to day.*

That, Alan suddenly realised, was the crucial thing here: Abdul's
involvement. He underlined the last six words several times.

OK, so there was a lot at stake here. It wasn't just about
money, although that was a powerful motivator. This was a
struggle for family control. For reputation. For honour. And
Alan had inadvertently rattled the collective cage.

He thought about Ali's warnings – and his parting words.
If this wasn't just about Sofia then what the hell was it about?
What warranted such a direct, personal attack on Alan? The
bungalow blaze could possibly have been an accident, but the
Land Rover explosion certainly wasn't. Abdul and/or Mehmet
must have been behind it. But the 'accident' at Priory Farm
was different. He was convinced Paul was involved with this
closely, although with a fair bit of help from Abdul and the
boys at AK Plant. Alan wondered, for instance, whether the
two men in the delivery van hadn't been sipping coffee while

the export order was being prepared, but instead had nipped across to give the digger driver a hand 'dealing' with Steve.

Alan suddenly realised, with considerable frustration that he had been conflating two entirely separate issues. If the bungalow fire was indeed accidental then it *wasn't* his contact with Ali that had got the Kabuls' attention. And indeed, why should they care, when Ali was clearly, even now, under their control? Playing the part that the deal demanded.

So, the only logical conclusion was that it must have been his chance discovery of the financial arrangements between PFC and the Kabuls that had got them so agitated. Time for another list.

* * *

When he had finished it looked like this:

1 *Paul and Kabuls have a financial deal. Who/What benefits?*
   Kabuls gain: sole contracting of AK Plant + Money laundering?
   Source of income? 'Family business'? Drugs or other?
   Paul gains: Exclusive site contracts from Kabuls.
   Additional income from 'charitable donations'.
   Business/ social contacts initiated by the Kabuls?
   BUT Paul risks: reputation of PFC.
   Why? For money? Status?
   Who is in control of the relationship?
   Kabuls risk: NOTHING

2 *Modern bones*
   Mistake? Anomaly? Murder?

Alan frowned at this second heading. Again, he was risking getting caught up in conjecture. Stick to the known facts: they were modern bones. God alone knows how they got there; but it wasn't an accident. He returned to the list, crossing out the three words of the last line. But item three was far more straightforward:

3 *Impingham House development*
The next stage of the Kabuls' plan for social supremacy?
Paul needs Impingham House to expand PFC further.
They both benefit.
Money and status at stake.
Project based on reputation of both parties.

4 *Combination of bones and financial corruption would sink the project.*
Is this the motivation for the attacks?
If so, under whose instruction?
Has to be Paul and/or the Kabuls (working together?) to protect their interests.

1–4 the culmination of an arrangement that began at Flax Hole in 2002.

Alan put the two lists side by side. They had one glaring issue in common: the last one, *'at Flax Hole in 2002'.*

As he watched the wind turbines relentlessly grinding their way round and round he found himself thinking back to those heavy steel wet sieves, rolling forwards and back, forwards and back, covering everyone with freezing wet slurry. And then there were those endless lists of samples and finds; and finds and samples. A thin mist was now creeping across the lower-lying parts of the vast fields of winter wheat, just like the bleak fogs of countless dark February afternoons at Flax Hole. He was almost back there, and felt very dispirited. It wasn't just the work they'd done on the dig all those years ago; but it was also the later and completely fruitless poring over inventories, plans and context sheets. And all to no avail. A complete bloody waste of time.

He was feeling dog-tired and was about to drop off. As he did so, the memories of Flax Hole grew more real. He was standing beside the wet sieve, holding a clipboard on which was one of those interminable lists. He was about to write something down, aware that his fingers were numb with cold. He looked to one side, down to the ground and the mud around the broken pallet he was standing on. It was everywhere, that mud. Everywhere.

Then, just for an instant, two images came into focus. One was the mud. The other was a box of clipboards, lists and grubby notebooks, nailed to the corner of the pallet and covered with a torn and muddy plastic bag. That set him thinking. Was all that research in the Museum actually telling him something? Maybe he'd been looking in the wrong places? Like a good archaeologist his head had been in the trenches. Sometimes he had been examining and re-examining plans and sections; other times it was lists and samples in stuffy basement stores. So far he'd worried about features, plans and samples: in other words, results. But shouldn't he have been more concerned with processes: with how those plans and lists were created?

He was starting to wake up. He'd been obsessed by those lists. But he'd been missing the point. The lists were irrelevant. The trenches, the features, even the archaeology were all irrelevant, too. Everything was irrelevant. Except, that is, for the mud. The ubiquitous sodding mud. The stuff of his nightmares. That's where the answer lay.

'Oh shit,' he mouthed under his breath in exasperation, 'how could I have missed it. It's so bloody obvious!'

He sat back and smiled. Now he realised the truth behind Indajit's words: he had seen but he did not comprehend. He had looked, but had not perceived. But no longer. It was so simple: he was the Muddy Man, they were the Muddy Boys. And they'd all been in it up to their bollocks.

At last he knew where to search.

* * *

He had to tell Grahame. He phoned and learned he was on his own. Liz was away at her mother's. It was coming on to rain when he pushed open the back door. Alan appeared not to notice, but Grahame was standing at the Aga wearing one of his wife's frilly aprons when Alan entered the kitchen. Without any greeting he strode over to the fridge and took out two bottles of beer. Grahame looked on astonished, as he gently pushed the two saucepans off the hotplates and lowered the lids. Alan thrust a beer into his hand and steered him towards the table. Slightly confused, Grahame pulled off the apron and sat down.

'I think I've got it.' he began.

Alan took a long pull from the bottle and a deep breath.

'It came to me a few minutes ago, on the way home, after my last Lifers session.'

'What, something Ali had said?'

He shook his head, the bottle at his lips.

'Surprisingly not. No, this came to me in a field gateway.' He took a pull. 'It was my fault.'

Grahame was astonished.

'Your fault?'

'Yes, my fault. I'd been doing what all archaeologists do. Routine stuff. I'd been poring over those sodding mud-spattered plans and sections, till my brain hurt. But I was only looking in the trenches. It was getting me nowhere.'

'Yes, but where else could you look?'

'The thing is I'd forgotten – lost sight of – the original question: where would you dispose of a body on a dig? Only an archaeologist would think in terms of trenches and features. A normal person would take other things into account as well.'

'What, places like toilet pits?'

'Exactly. Places just like that.'

He got up and helped himself to another beer.

'So where were they?'

'What?'

'The toilet pits?'

'We didn't have any. That was the first year the City Planning people insisted we had to hire in chemical Portaloos.'

'Which are serviced weekly by the hire people.'

'Precisely. So I asked myself, "where else was there?" '

Alan smiled. He enjoyed making revelations.

'And?'

'And it came to me. The wet sieves. They were in constant use and were always flooding. Early on we'd used the digger to sink two large soakaways, but the ground there is such heavy clay that they soon backed-up and never functioned properly. Hence all that bloody mud.'

'You forget, Alan, I wasn't there.'

Alan ignored this.

'We worked two 5mm wet sieves, each on a roller-frame. The sludge was emptied into buckets, which were tipped into the soakaway pits. One was in use, while the other drained dry, which took a day. We nearly had to dig a third, but then the weather improved.'

'And where were the pits and the sieves?'

'On a patch of ground disturbed just after the war. We knew there'd be no archaeology there…' His eyes were closed as he thought back to the scene: 'It was near the edge of what is now the lorry park, on land that was going to be landscaped.'

'But wouldn't the landscaping have disturbed them?' Grahame asked.

'No.' He had opened his eyes now. 'No, they were right on the edge. At the time I reckoned the footings of a nearby wall would also act as a bit of a soakaway – which they did, sort of…'

Grahame had seen the implications of what he'd just said:

'So they're probably still there?'

'I don't see why not. They may be under the low perimeter bank, which I noticed the other day they'd planted with trees, presumably when all the building and landscaping work was finished.' He paused briefly, 'but I'm not certain it…'

'It?' Grahame cut in.

'The bank. I don't think it reached as far as the pits. I'd be able to find them easily enough, though, because I'd placed them as close as I could to that wall, which also helped cut the wind. It was February, remember. Anyhow,' he ended with conviction, 'I bet you anything you like, that the wall or its footings are still there.'

'I don't suppose I need to ask what you're going to do now?'

Grahame's brow was furrowed with concern. Alan smiled, he was, after all, still the sensible, cautious big brother.

'I'm going to reopen the site and we're going to find Sofia.'

Five minutes later Alan phoned Indajit on his home number. It was late and the lawyer sounded drowsy, but he soon woke up when Alan explained what he planned to do.

'Right,' he said when Alan had finished, 'I'll be there. You should always have a lawyer alongside you, especially when you plan anything illegal.'

* * *

Alan was a great admirer of the soldier and archaeologist, Sir Mortimer Wheeler, who used to tell both his military colleagues and the many archaeologists working for him that 'time spent in reconnaissance is never wasted'. How right he was, Alan thought. Now he must make careful preparations himself. The people who wanted him out of the way were ruthless, thorough and violent. They also had imagination. Both the Land Rover explosion and the 'accident' that killed Steve were unusual – and quite inventive. So he'd have to do even better.

As a first step, he phoned Paul and asked him if he could borrow some tools over the weekend. Alan's story was that a group of friends were coming over to help him dig Clara's garden. Paul was in a good mood and agreed readily to this.

Alan was about to ring off, when Paul added, 'Could I ask you a small favour, in return?'

'By all means.'

'D'you think you could return the tools early on Sunday evening?'

'Sure. I could bring them round earlier if you want, we'll be finished well before then.'

'No, no,' Paul was adamant, 'Sunday evening would be fine. The thing is, I'm away all Saturday and I've got to do some work on the farmhouse cesspit with the mini-digger on Sunday afternoon. And I'll need to make good afterwards. Plant a few roses, that sort of thing.'

Alan was far from convinced: Paul's 'garden' at the farmhouse was little more than a weed patch. There was also something not-quite-right about the request; most faulty cesspit soakaways usually stink – it's the smell that shows there's something wrong. But Alan could swear he'd never detected a whiff from Paul's drains. And it wasn't as if he was there long enough to use them much, either. He was always away, somewhere else. And besides, there were loads of tools in the Tool Store he could use.

'OK. What say I give you a hand when I come round?' Alan replied.

'Excellent.' Paul sounded delighted. 'Many thanks, Alan. Drop the other tools back in the Store then bring a couple of spades and a fork over. We'll soon knock the job on the head.'

Yes, thought Alan, we most certainly will.

Thirty-four

Friday had been a good day at Impingham and the team arrived back at Priory Farm in high spirits. Everyone was ready for the weekend. Steve's replacement, Jake Williamson, asked Alan if he'd join them for a quick pint before heading home. Sadly Alan had to decline. He told Jake that he was planning to get away early for the weekend. Jake and the diggers then headed noisily down the road towards the village pub. Alan walked over to the hangar. He tried to appear relaxed and slightly bored, as if doing the final chores of the week. But beneath the surface he was wired and ready to go. Much to do, so little time.

The *Reference Collections* office was the lower of the first two stacked Portakabins along the left-hand side of the hangar. Inside it, the admin staff were getting ready to leave for home. A middle-aged lady, Alan thought her name was Elsie, who was still sitting at her desk, handed him the keys to the Tool Store.

Alan asked about Paul's whereabouts, as he didn't want to bump into him in the next few minutes.

'He's in a meeting with important clients,' Elsie replied, 'it's about the big York job.'

'Odd time for a meeting?'

'Yes, they phoned from Leicester this morning. Poor Paul didn't seem too happy. Still, as I said, if you want to be a high-flyer you sometimes have to burn the candle at both ends.'

'Where are they now?'

'Still in the board room, I think.'

Alan leant across to the window and glanced at the upstairs windows. The board room was in the top layer of the two Portakabins. He could just see the outline of people sitting around a table. Even with one of the hangar's main sliding doors open, it was gloomy inside the vast interior. They already had the lights on.

'When's it ending?' He asked.

'Late, apparently. Then they're going back to Leicester for an architect's meeting first thing tomorrow. It'll probably last all morning.'

'What, on Saturday? Everyone? Even Paul?'

Alan pretended this was news to him.

'Why the surprise?' Elsie replied. 'That's what happened last weekend too. It's the way they do things these days. "Intensive brainstorming" they call it.'

'Blimey,' Alan replied, 'glad I'm not doing it. By Friday night my brain's too whacked to be stormed.'

She smiled.

'Me too. But I wouldn't worry, they're all well paid. Anyhow, one of the chaps from Leicester told me not to hang around after I'd brought them tea. He said they'd all be having something a bit stronger later on, when their spirits started flagging.'

'One of *those* meetings, then?'

'A booze-up, d'you mean? No, they were serious, alright. They all had laptops with them. They meant business. Like you said, glad I'm not up there with them.'

Quietly Alan slipped out of the Portakabin, leaving Elsie busily preparing the tea tray for the meeting in the board room. He headed for the main hangar doors, one of which was rolled back, open. He walked around the edge of the hangar then stood briefly on the dark side of the closed door and looked back at the board room window. The angle was better here and yes, he could clearly see Paul and Abdul's distinctive silhouettes, sitting next to each other,

Relieved to be out of the gloom of the hangar, and back in the warmth of the sunshine, Alan went round to the Tool Store and checked out a selection of spades, mattocks, shovels and forks, which he loaded into the back of his Fourtrak.

But he still had one more essential thing to do.

He returned to the Tool Store and locked the door behind him. But instead of selecting more tools, he walked across to a small door at the back of the store. This opened onto the narrow space between the stacked *Reference Collections* Portakabins and the north wall of the hangar. Very slowly he pushed on the door and looked out, taking care not to be seen. All was clear. High above his head, the lights in the board room provided some welcome illumination. He walked along the inside of the hangar, staying close to the base of the Portakabins, so as not to be seen, should anyone up there look down.

Halfway along the hangar wall was a side door into a place that Paul had named – rather pretentiously Alan thought – the Innovations Space. This was a fairly standard wartime extension to the hangar, used by RAF maintenance crews to strip down and run Merlin engines. It was a large space with insulated, double-thickness walls, plus fitted floor-to-ceiling racks and cupboards along two walls. Originally these had held engine parts and spares; they were heavily built, but were now used to store reference materials and packaging. The purpose of the small team working in the Innovations Space was to devise eye-catching products that would appeal to specialists and collectors alike. They were responsible directly to Paul. Theirs was development, rather than production work, which was done elsewhere.

Once in the Innovations Space, Alan turned on the light, knowing that the thick walls would reveal nothing on the outside. He jammed a short baulk of timber into the grab handles that the RAF had welded to the side door he had just come through. This shut it permanently. Then he took out a piece of paper from his pocket. It was the diagram that Grahame had drawn for him on that Saturday morning as they'd sat together at the kitchen table. He stared at the image on the page for a long time. Then he looked around. There was a large table in the centre of the room and a bench at the far end. To the left was a standard self-contained laboratory emergency shower, and directly opposite it, a fume cupboard. Beside the cupboard were two pressurised cylinders of carbon dioxide.

He took a package out of his pocket: a set of small, decorative birthday cake candles.

He walked past the table, over to the bench and gathered-up as many storage boxes as he could find. Next, he collapsed them, making a three-foot high stack of cardboard at the foot of the workbench, along the back wall. Then he lit two candles and made small puddles of soft wax: one on the table, the other just above the door of the corridor from the Main Office. Into each of these puddles he pressed an unlit candle. Finally, he moved the access stepladder across to the shelves above the workbench, and lashed it securely in place. He climbed the ladder to the top shelf and again lashed it in place. He was taking no chances. From the ladder, he pulled at the shelf firmly. It didn't budge. It was good and strong. He also checked with his hand to make sure there was nothing sharp up there. But it was clean. Just cobwebs and dead flies.

There was one last thing he had to do. He left the Innovations Space and walked down the corridor into the General Office, where he let himself out into the main hangar, having first locked the door and put the key in his pocket. Next he made his way to the hangar's north-east corner, where he knew there was a small door to the outside. On his first visit to Priory Farm, back in 2002, there'd been a toilet there – probably left over from the war, to judge from the crazed glaze of the War Department utility bowl. It was almost completely dark at the back of the hangar, but he could just make out it was still there.

The toilet was enclosed within a plywood cubicle, which he now clambered up. Once on top, he loosened a sheet of plywood with the blade of his pocketknife, and lowered it carefully to the ground. Then he climbed into the space where the cistern was housed. He knew this would have to be accessed by a trapdoor, which he removed and placed to one side. Then he lowered himself into the little compartment below, standing on the bowl. He looked down: it was dry and held two mouse skeletons. He remembered the water supply had been cut-off after a sharp frost in 2003. Strangely, the seat was still up.

A couple of dead, but very thorny bramble stems had penetrated through the external door. He snapped them off and pushed down hard on the handle. The latch was rusty and gave way easily. It didn't take much effort to open it. Once outside, he pushed the door ajar and then made his way through the hawthorn scrub along the hangar's east back wall, round to the concrete apron at the front.

As he climbed into the driver's seat he saw his face in the Fourtrak's mirror. He was thickly covered with dark grey dust and grime. He didn't look like himself at all.

Thirty-five

The next day dawned bright and sunny. Alan checked his watch, yes it was Saturday. He put on his only suit and a borrowed tie from Grahame. He hurried across to the table where he spotted some coffee in the jug and poured it into a mug. Grahame was horrified.

'But it'll be icy cold!'

Alan shook his head.

'No, delicious,' he mumbled as he hastily buttered a Marmite sandwich. 'Must dash.' He slapped Grahame on the shoulder and hurried from the room.

The drive across the Fens to Scoby seemed interminable, with big hold-ups at roadworks in Spalding. Then he noticed he was almost out of diesel. He arrived at Scoby Church dead on eleven, just as the undertaker's black van drew up outside the porch.

He slipped quietly into the porch. Alistair was standing there with Claire, waiting. One glance showed him that Alistair had told her everything: she stood up straight, her arm around his waist, whereas he looked tired and dishevelled. Two dark-suited undertakers reverently placed the five black velvet bags on a mahogany bier. Then Alan and Alistair each took a handle and together the four men carried the precious load into the church, with Claire following, behind. Once in the nave, the vicar sprinkled the babies with holy water and pronounced a blessing. Of course, Alan thought, they probably hadn't been christened, so technically speaking he was breaking the rules. But it was plain that this funeral, like all others, was for the benefit of the living, not the dead. Tears were now running freely down Alistair's cheeks.

They slowly processed through the nave and into the chancel, where they halted next to the carved Victorian stone lid that once covered Tiny's grave. It had been lifted off and now rested on two wooden batons. The vicar said a few words, then nodded to Alistair who placed the bags within it, alongside the bones of their mother. He stood up and lowered his head in prayer. Only then did the tears stop flowing.

Noiselessly the vicar withdrew. He realised Alistair needed peace. Claire was the first to speak.

'We're so glad you could come, Alan.'

Alan was about to mumble something suitable, when Alistair said,

'And you were so right, Alan, it's always best to face up to these things. It's been difficult, but with Claire's help,' Alan could see her arm tighten around her husband's waist, 'I think we might achieve closure. Of some sort.'

It was a calming, sobering moment for all of them. Yes, Alan thought, you've resolved the horrors of the past and put your demons to rest. Maybe I will one day.

* * *

Alan had agreed to meet Indajit at his brother's farm, later that day. Indajit's sat nav found it without any trouble, and in true English style they sat down to tea, before getting ready. The morning had left Alan emotionally drained, but now he found himself on edge, wired. The lawyer, on the other hand, made no effort to conceal his excitement. Alan reckoned he was actually enjoying himself, which was odd, given what they were about to do.

After tea they went out to one of the secure grain store barns, where Grahame had housed Indajit's car. They entered through a side door and Grahame turned on the light. Alan was carrying an old fertiliser sack, which was bulging with something.

Alan pulled out the dark blue overalls that PFC issued to all its staff. The previous night, Alan had razor-bladed off the dayglo yellow PFC logo emblazoned across their backs. It had been one of the many small jobs that had stopped him dwelling on what had to be done today. Then, the whole thing had seemed rather unreal. But now it was very different. As he pulled on the sombre overalls Alan felt that reality was starting to strike home. But there was no turning back.

He knew they faced many hazards. Even at the most trivial level, they could be stopped by depot security staff, or by the police. Either way, they'd have trouble explaining what they were up to, although having someone as plausible as Indajit alongside them, would help. But if, *if,* the Kabuls had guessed Alan's plans, they both knew the consequences would be far worse: instant and final.

Indajit struggled into his overalls awkwardly. They could see it wasn't something he'd done before. Smiling, Grahame showed him how to reach into his trousers, through a slot in the overall's pockets. Indajit was delighted with this. He gave Grahame his phone.

'Please Grahame, you must take a picture. "Top lawyer in workmen's overalls", it could go viral on FaceBook.' Grahame took the picture. And another with Alan beside him. Both men were smiling hugely. Almost too hugely.

They both got into the grey Fourtrak and headed off towards Leicester. By now it was starting to get dark and the sky had clouded over. After an hour's steady drive, they pulled into a side street a couple of blocks away from 'Mehmet's', which they could hear was still doing brisk business, despite its imminent closure. By this stage, Indajit's cheeriness was starting to evaporate. Tension was mounting. They parked in a small side street, waiting for darkness to gather.

Around 11.30 Alan decided it was time to make a quick recce. They pulled away and headed slowly towards the back of Flax Hole Depot, which had now closed for the night. He pulled up in a spot where they could observe the pattern of security patrols. As Indajit had already reported, they were confined to the depot itself, which was brightly floodlit. They waited for two patrols to go by.

'Right,' Alan said in a low voice, 'patrols every half hour. That's what I'd have expected. So the next one's due at 12.30.'

'But we're not floodlit out here. Surely we'd be OK, wouldn't we?' Indajit asked. It was obvious he was keen to get started.

'No,' Alan was confident, 'you'd be surprised how easy it is to spot movement at a distance, especially in low light. All they need is a glint off a shiny mattock blade. That'll do it. So when the patrol's out, whatever we're doing, we'll freeze. OK?'

They unloaded a mattock, a fork and a road-spike, which Alan tossed over the chain-link security fence. They'd spotted on the recce it wasn't very secure at this point. Alan soon discovered why, as his boot crunched on an abandoned syringe. Druggies had been using the shrubs inside the fence, as cover. They clambered through a hole in the wire. Alan walked ahead, looking for the remains of the brick wall that had run beside their long-abandoned wet sieve soakaway pits. He soon found it. By this point, the landscaping had given way to scrub, and the older buildings that bounded the depot to the south, were fringed with hawthorn and elder bushes.

'There it is,' Alan called under his breath, pointing down at a ridge of bricks and mortar which had been bulldozed almost flat during the landscaping. Another cheap and nasty job, he thought, knowing full well that the landscape contractors ought to have removed the wall's footings, not just flattened them. They continued for about thirty metres. Then Alan stopped and looked around him.

By now his eyes had become accustomed to the poor light. It took a couple of minutes to get his bearings. He could just make out the shadow of the Victorian warehouse and the main entranceway into the site. Yes, he thought, that's about right. He tapped Indajit on the shoulder and whispered:

'Pass me the mattock.'

Indajit handed it to him. But instead of swinging it, Alan used it like a pile-driver, vigorously thumping its head on the dry ground. After about a dozen thumps he stopped.

'I think one of them's here. It's certainly sounds hollow and feels a tiny bit softer.'

'Hollow?' Indajit was surprised, 'I didn't expect that. Surely it can't still be an empty hole?'

'No, it'll be full all right,' Alan replied, 'it's just the high water content and softer filling can sometimes give a hollow, booming effect. It doesn't always work, but here the clay's so heavy, I think it will. Anyhow, there's only one way to find out...'

Indajit was about to swing the mattock, but Alan stopped him.

'Too noisy. We'll use a fork. Much quieter.'

He drove down on the fork with his boot. It went in easily.

'That's softer than I thought. Much softer.'

'Is that significant?' Indajit asked.

Alan didn't reply. For a few moments he shone a shaded torch and looked closely at the soil. He turned it off, but continued to finger the soil's texture, lost in thought.

Then to Indajit's evident surprise he put a tiny piece in his mouth. He closed his eyes and concentrated hard. There was smooth, buttery clay there. Next his tongue felt the slight abrasion of silt. Gently his front teeth encountered the grittiness of fine sand; for a bizarre moment it was rather like a wine-taster savouring a fine cabernet sauvignon. Then it was done. He spat it out, wiping his mouth twice on his sleeve. He looked up:

'Yes, Indajit, it is significant. This stuff is a silty clay loam with a high organic component. That's precisely what we were sieving. I checked the records carefully last week. So we could be in one of them.'

Indajit was now staring at him wide-eyed:

'What, in one of the soakaways?'

'Yes.'

'Let's hope it's the right one...' Indajit muttered, as he grimly trod the fork into the ground.

* * *

464

Twenty minutes later they both froze, as the expected security patrol passed in front of the depot building below them, and headed across the lorry park. When it had gone they resumed digging.

It was approaching dawn, and several patrols had been by. It had been slow work in the dark, but they had managed to expose all four sides of the pit and Alan was contemplating moving on to the second one, when his fork went through something soft. He'd felt something similar before, when excavating a Bronze Age field system near Peterborough. In that case, it had been half a soft-fired pottery vessel that lay on the bottom of the ditch. But there was no mistaking that crunchy feeling. A bit like breaking into a huge soft-boiled egg. Alan glanced down. He didn't want poor Indajit to have too much of a shock.

'Indajit, are you ready for this?'

The lawyer nodded grimly.

Alan dropped down to his knees and shone his torch. Thinnish bone, but with pronounced muscle scars. He pulled at it hard and turned it over. As he suspected, a dog skull. Probably someone's pet.

By now they were almost three feet down and the soil was getting much softer. Alan put the fork aside and took hold of the steel road-spike. It was about five feet long, had a curly pig's tail top and a sharpened point. Indajit looked on, fascinated, as Alan very carefully leant on the pig-tail and the spike sank into the soft ground for about a foot. Then he repeated the process a short distance away. On his eighth attempt he distinctly felt a crunch, about six inches below the surface. He produced a trowel from his back pocket and rapidly dug down.

And, yes, this time it was human. A skull. He was sure of that. Few other large mammal crania are so thin.

'I think we've found her.'

'Are you sure?'

'Yes, I've felt inside the orbit. The eye-socket. It's very sharp. Almost certainly female...' He had turned on a small pen torch which he cupped in one hand.

'Ah,' he whispered, 'what's this?' Alan could feel that Indajit wanted to join him, but he gestured to him to stay back.

'Sorry, Indajit, best not to look too closely. Wait till you're ready.'

The lawyer nodded silently.

Alan held up a scrap of fabric up to the emerging light of a new day. 'That's silk alright. At least they didn't strip her. I don't think we need disturb her anymore.'

By now there was a very slight, almost indiscernible smell of putrefaction, which Alan recognised instantly from his time on the farm. Although he said nothing, he was surprised that decay was still so actively under way, after so many years.

As he climbed out of the trench, there was a rustle in the bushes behind them. Immediately Alan made a grab for his mattock. Then they were blinded by four powerful flashlights that cut through the feeble, misty morning light, like so many lasers. The words were chilling, but the voice was familiar.

* * *

'I trust you found what you were looking for?'

Alan tightened his grip on the mattock.

'Relax, Alan, relax. You've nothing to fear. You've all proved your point.'

It was Lane. As he spoke, he pointed his flashlight at his three companions, whose blue and white checked baseball caps revealed they were all police officers. Armed police officers, Alan noted. They were anticipating trouble.

'Don't tell me,' Alan said, slightly exasperated, 'my brother tipped you off, did he?'

'Yes, he did,' Lane replied, 'and quite right too.'

'Shhh…' Indajit hissed sharply, pointing towards the depot. They all looked: a security patrol had started its rounds.

'Kill the lights!' Alan whispered as loud as he dared.

Suddenly it was dark again. He knew that if they were discovered, Mehmet and Abdul would immediately be alerted. After a couple of minutes, the danger had passed.

Then Lane bent forward, shining his shaded torch on the ground. 'So what do we have here?'

'A female,' Alan replied, 'decomposition very advanced, but shreds of silk and probably hair too. If she was buried in 2002 this suggests very acidic soil conditions. In another five to ten years the body would have vanished completely.'

Lane looked at Alan.

'D'you want to excavate her yourselves?'

Indajit turned to Alan. He shook his head.

'No, if you don't mind, Richard. I think we can leave this one to you.'

Then he had a thought.

'Why not fetch in that woman we met at Saltaire?'

Lane's brow furrowed as he tried to think back. Then it came to him.

'Ruth?' He queried.

'Yes,' Alan replied, 'I've heard she's based in Norfolk. This would be right up her street.'

Indajit had stood silently while this was going on. Then he spoke softly.

'May I spend a few moments with Sofia alone? I think I'm ready now.'

They withdrew up the bank and stood amongst the young trees and mown grass. Two officers remained with Indajit, but they faced away. By now it was bright enough to see clearly. Alan noticed they had unslung their weapons. Indajit knelt alone with his fiancée, his shoulders heaving as he wept. The scene had a quiet dignity. All was silence, only broken by the growing sound of the dawn chorus from birds in the young trees and shrubs around them. Then Indajit wiped his eyes. He looked up.

'Thank you all. This has meant much to me.'

'And to me,' Lane said, walking forward. He shook his hand warmly. 'Thank you for all your help.'

It was a warm night, but Indajit had begun to shiver. Lane nodded to one of the officers.

'This gentleman needs a lift home. Make sure he stays warm,' he paused, 'and treat him like a celebrity. Because he is one,' and then as an afterthought, 'we can take a statement from him later in the morning. And I want two officers stationed outside his house until I personally give you the all clear. Understood?'

'Yes, sir!'

They stood and watched while Indajit was escorted back to a car.

Then they laid a police reflective jacket over Sofia's remains and Alan shovelled loose earth onto it. At this stage they still needed to hide what they had been doing from casual prying eyes. An officer stayed behind to guard her, crouching down out of sight. Meanwhile the rest of the group headed out through the security fence, before the next security patrol arrived.

* * *

Alan drove to the Central Police Station to have a short statement taken, while the reinforcements Lane had summoned, continued to arrive. While they were waiting, they discussed what to do next. They were both keen to have Paul picked up, as they were convinced he had to have known about Sofia's burial, even if he didn't organise it himself – which he almost certainly must have done: only an archaeologist who'd worked on that site would have known about those pits.

'But even so,' Lane responded, 'he's still just an accessory after the fact. He's not likely to run away and I don't think he's the brains behind all this. That person is Mehmet, we've got to catch the bastard. And Abdul.'

As he said the last words there was a ruthlessness in his voice that Alan hadn't heard before.

'So what's the plan, Richard? I don't think we've got much time.'

'No, we certainly don't. I've already called in the team I'd reserved for this job.'

'Oh no,' Alan broke in, 'surely not Drugs Squad heavies?'

'Certainly not.' Lane looked a little peeved at this. 'This is Leicestershire and we'll use our own force, *if* you don't mind.'

'I'm sorry…'

But he was relieved, nonetheless. Then he had another thought:

'Richard, shouldn't we be keeping more of an eye on Priory Farm? Your single undercover man wouldn't stand much of a chance if things got nasty there, would he?'

'Don't worry, Alan,' Lane replied, 'I've already thought of that. I sent two men round there an hour ago.'

For a moment Alan thought about the implications. He was certain they'd stay round the front and not venture into the hawthorn thicket at the rear of the hangar. Still, he'd done everything he could. Now it was in the hands of fate.

Thirty-six

DCI Lane's team had all assembled in the station Incident Room by six o'clock on Sunday morning. While they were making plans to raid Mehmet's home, an undercover officer on the team, who was keeping the house under surveillance, radioed in to say that Mehmet had just left. He had been carrying a suitcase when he got into his large Mercedes.

'Tail him!' Lane barked into the radio. 'Don't let him out of your sight. He mustn't escape!'

Alan was listening closely.

Two additional patrol cars were despatched to assist him. Then Alan had a thought. Maybe Mehmet wasn't trying to escape. He wasn't a mind-reader: how could he possibly know what had happened? This was real life, not a drama. And anyhow, a suitcase isn't what a multimillionaire takes with him to the airport.

Richard Lane was on the telephone when Alan came up to him. He hung up.

Alan said quietly, 'Don't pull him in, yet, Richard. Let's see where he's heading. I think this could be interesting.'

Lane looked at him doubtfully.

'Are you sure?'

'Yes, quite sure.'

A short time later a report came in that he'd pulled up outside a large brick building in Albert Road and had gone inside, carrying his case.

'Albert Road?'

'That's down by the canal, isn't it?' Alan suggested.

Lane was looking pensive.

'Yes, I know it. An old leather works converted by the County Council with a Lottery grant. Usual old bollocks: cheap studios for so-called community artists, who couldn't cut it in the real world.'

The radio crackled into life again:

'There's a big sign. Says "Waterside Studios". The subject has gone inside.'

'Report back immediately, if he comes out.'

'He won't do that,' Alan said quietly. Lane shot a glance towards him.

'Why not?'

'He'll be there for at least a couple of hours. Maybe more. Any time before then, and he's ours for the taking.'

'You certain about that?' Lane asked.

'Yes. Quite certain.'

Lane stood up quickly, taking his coat from a row of pegs by the door. In a loud voice he announced to the room.

'We'll do this one mob-handed. Call everyone in.'

In a few minutes fifteen men and two WPCs had assembled; Lane briefed four officers who hurried on ahead. Then he turned to the rest of the room:

'OK, everyone, let's go.'

Then, almost as an afterthought he gestured to Alan.

'You too, Alan.'

'What on earth can I do?'

'I've no idea. But if you think that after last night's excursion, I'm letting you out of my sight until this is all over, then you can think again.'

* * *

Waterside Studios opened to the public every weekend. There were two coffee shops on the ground floor and a gallery on the first. This was a big open-plan space, occupying the entire footprint of the building. Above it were two further storeys, which contained the artists' studios. These could only be visited by appointment. Alan glanced at the list of names: two painters, a sculptor, three photographers, a silversmith, two commercial artists and a 'textile artisan' – whatever that was.

Richard Lane's brow furrowed as he read the list. Alan smiled.

'The vain bastard,' he said, 'I know where he's heading. Follow me.'

Alan headed toward the emergency stairs. Meanwhile Lane had rapidly positioned men at all the downstairs exits. He produced his warrant card and ordered the main admission doors to be locked shut. The two early customers in the coffee shop looked on with open mouths. One held a cup to her lips.

'Drink up, it'll get cold,' a cheeky constable advised as he hurried past their table. Lane gave him a dirty look.

A couple of minutes later, Alan, Lane and three constables gathered silently outside the sculptor's studio. Lane turned the latch, but it was locked. They were meant to use the intercom by the door, but this might alert the people they'd come to see. So two of the constables, built like rugby forwards, hit the double door with their shoulders and burst in.

For a second or two Alan felt as if he had stumbled into a Victorian still life. The room was in semi-darkness, illuminated by a single sepia spotlight. Mehmet was standing on a stout wooden plinth, one arm raised as if delivering a papal benediction. On his head was a laurel wreath, which was meant to look noble, but failed miserably. His portly body was bedecked with the sculptor's attempt at a Roman toga, complete with purple edging. He was bare-footed, presumably because the two sandals that lay on the floor had been too tight a fit for his podgy feet. The sculptor was taking photographs, his head beneath a black cloth.

The sight was too much, even for the hardened police officers as they crashed into the room. They were still laughing when they grabbed Mehmet. By this stage the toga which had only been draped for effect, now lay on the floor and Mehmet was wearing nothing but a capacious pair of boxer shorts. Alan was about to show the sculptor how a toga ought to have been folded, but decided not to.

* * *

Back at the City Centre Police Station the officers in charge of the two parties sent to arrest Abdul, either at his house or at the AK Plant Hire depot, reported back to Lane. Alan was sitting in the corner of the room.

'We arrived at the Plant Hire shop and found it packed. Loads of customers getting stuff for the weekend.'

'Yes, that's why we thought he'd be there,' Lane replied, 'it's a busy time.'

'Well he wasn't. No sign of him anywhere.'

Alan cleared his throat. The three policemen looked towards him.

'I know he had a meeting yesterday evening. I think it was scheduled to go on till late.'

To his relief, nobody asked why he knew so much about Abdul's movements.

'So you found him at home?' Lane asked the second Inspector.

'Yes, as I reported in, sir, we arrived at the house and the suspect's wife opened the door. A WPC asked for immediate admittance.'

'So no problems getting in?'

'None. It was a complete surprise. I had two of the lads standing by to thump the front door, but they weren't needed. We entered and found the suspect standing at the top of the stairs in his pyjamas. He'd been having breakfast in bed.'

'So you read him his rights and arrested him?' Lane asked.

'Yes, sir. He's in the cells now. But not next to the other Mr Kabul, as you requested.'

Lane seemed satisfied at this.

'Very good. They mustn't talk to each other at all. Understood?' They nodded. 'I want them to stew in their own juice. That'll be far more effective than any amount of questioning.'

'The younger man is demanding to see his lawyer, sir.'

'Tell the desk sergeant down there to turn a deaf ear.'

'I already have, sir.'

'Good man.'

Listening to this exchange, Alan found he was growing increasingly irritated. What about Paul? Surely he too had attended the previous evening's meeting? And if so, why wasn't he around? To the police, on the other hand, Paul was a minor figure. For Lane, the Leicester force and probably even the Yard, the real out-and-out villains were still the Kabuls.

But Alan was determined that Paul should be held to account. He had, at best, turned a blind eye to events. And must have played a part in arranging the financial agreement that bound PFC and the Kabuls so tightly together. At worst, Paul had disposed of the body for them. And then what? There was still the question of the modern bones to deal with. A question that seemed to have slipped Lane's mind entirely.

The two officers left the room.

When the door had closed Alan approached Lane.

'Did the people you sent over to Priory Farm find anything?'

'They reported the house was locked up. Deserted.'

'What about the hangar?'

'The main double doors were locked shut; so they cut the padlock, and opened up. The entire place was in darkness. No light at all.'

'Sounds like they were spooked…'

'Yes,' Lane replied, 'I think they were. Anyhow, they had a look around and were convinced it was empty.'

'So what are you planning now?'

'At Priory Farm? Frankly it's slipped down my agenda. Don't forget, if that body is indeed young Sofia…'

'And I'm in no doubt at all that it is.'

'And you're probably correct. If it is her, then the Flax Hole honour killing will have raised its ugly head again…'

'The press will go mad,' Alan added helpfully.

'You don't say. But yes, the shit will hit the fan. The tabloids will go ape. And I'll be the person who has to deal with it all. So if you don't mind, Alan, I'd better start making practical arrangements. I'll need to sort out a press centre, speak to the Chief Constable and God knows what else.'

'So Priory Farm must wait?'

'I've no alternative, at least till Monday morning. But I've had a word with Lincolnshire Police. They've detailed a local patrol to check the place every three hours. That should be enough.'

Alan said nothing, but he didn't share his friend's optimism. The more he thought about it, the more he felt Priory Farm was relentlessly moving up the agenda. For Alan, Flax Hole and the Kabuls was yesterday's news. A sideshow.

* * *

Nobody had said a word to Mehmet or Abdul that the police had found Sofia's remains. Lane reckoned they should be left to stew in solitary, until the Scene-of-Crime Team and the forensic archaeologist from Norfolk had exposed her body fully. Then her identity could be confirmed from dental records. They needed maximum impact. Maximum shock. Somehow they had to smash through the two Kabuls' confident complacency.

Later in the afternoon, Alan returned to Flax Hole and looked down at Ruth. She was a large woman, but she wielded a white plastic spatula with speed and extraordinary dexterity. She was carefully exposing Sofia's leg bones. He hadn't come across her work before, and he was keen to see if she was any good. They both wore masks and disposable white forensic overalls. Alan found it hard to look down at the girl's body without feeling sick. It wasn't that she had been cut up or abused in any way, but no effort had been made to give her any dignity in death. Her body lay twisted and tumbled, as if shoved out of a wheelbarrow.

Any normal person – any family member – would have made some concessions to her humanity: maybe they'd have straightened her legs, or crossed her arms; they wouldn't have left her sprawled out in that fashion. She looked less like a young woman than a rejected doll, tossed into a landfill site. This had to be Paul's work.

Alan felt his anger rising. He'd once been on an excavation of plague victims in the East End of London. Although the dead had been buried in a long mass cemetery, the bodies had been properly laid-out, with arms at their sides; all were carefully aligned east–west, as in a churchyard. Even though doing this might have cost the gravediggers their own lives, they couldn't treat their fellow citizens like garbage.

But Paul hadn't bothered with such refinement. And why? Alan wondered. It was just part of his character. It wasn't deliberate. He wasn't attempting to smear her reputation. No, he was just self-centred and thoughtless. He couldn't empathise in the smallest way with her, or with anyone else who might have the misfortune to stumble across her body. As Harriet had observed: he couldn't connect. For him, the burial of Sofia's body for Mehmet and Abdul was just a process of disposal. A business transaction. Another contract. There was nothing human, or humane, about it.

'Oh,' Alan said softly, as he looked down at Ruth's meticulous handiwork, 'that's horrible. Beautifully excavated, don't get me wrong, but bloody horrible. She's been dumped there, like a piece of meat.'

Then his eye was caught by a patch of damaged bone at the side of her skull. He pointed at it. 'Is that where I caught her with my road-spike last night?'

'Yes,' she replied, looking up at him, 'I've seen worse. At least you didn't hit her a second time. Or with a mattock.'

'It was pitch black and I was working more by feel than anything else. I sensed the bone go crunch and recognised what it was. The trouble is, we couldn't pussyfoot around. I knew we had to get our evidence by the end of the night. But I'm still very sorry about that damage…'

He meant it. He paused and leant forward, looking more closely.

'You've done a fabulous job on her, Ruth. Bloody brilliant. Thanks for that.'

She sat up and straightened her back, shaking her shoulders to relieve the tension.

'Oh yes,' she said, 'there was something I was meaning to ask you, Alan. The pit filling's incredibly corrosive. Were you doing anything unusual with the wet sieves?'

'Back in 2002?'

'Yes.'

For a moment he couldn't think what she meant. Then he remembered.

'That's right. We used hydrogen peroxide to help break down the clay. We knew it wouldn't damage the flax fibres. We bought it in bulk from an industrial chemist just up the road. Horrid stuff, but it seemed to work. You don't see it used much nowadays, do you?'

'No,' she replied, resuming her work. 'Same old story: Health and Safety. But it explains the slow decomposition of the flesh. It acts as a general biocide.'

* * *

At around seven in the evening, Lane called Alan to see him. Ruth had phoned to say that the body and grave were now in a fit state to be viewed. It had been a long and meticulous excavation and she was exhausted. Meanwhile, Mehmet and Abdul were being driven to Flax Hole in separate cars. Lane had been at the mobile incident room all afternoon, fending off questions from the dozens of press and television crews that now surrounded the crime scene. Although he had tried at first, it had soon become impossible to keep the forensic excavation a secret. The simple fact that a police team was back at Flax Hole was more than enough for the local hacks, who had immediately put two and two together. By lunchtime the story had gone national and two large satellite dishes had already been erected on the top level of a multi-storey car park nearby.

Although becoming used to the ways of the media from his work with *History Hunters*, Alan had never witnessed anything on this scale before. It was bedlam. A feeding-frenzy and some journalists would stop at nothing. They were everywhere, like hungry rats. It got even worse when the two Kabuls arrived. The two men were bundled out of their cars, their heads draped in blankets, and were guided behind the tall screens, that now shielded the temporary shelter over Ruth's excavation.

Once past the screens, an officer was about to lift Mehmet's blanket, when Lane intervened.

'Keep the blanket on till I give the order! I want this image to stick in their minds for the rest of their bloody lives.'

The group had gone very quiet. They weren't used to seeing their boss this angry.

'OK,' he continued in a more normal voice, 'take them in and get the lighting set up. But don't lift the blankets till I say so.'

The two Kabuls, grandfather and grandson, were positioned on either side of the grave, each one handcuffed to two police officers. Lane looked across to Ruth.

'Everything ready?'

She nodded.

'Well,' he announced, 'I hope you two feel proud of this. Lift their blankets.'

Abdul passed out cold and was caught by the officers restraining him. Mehmet started as if to bluster, but Sofia's body was so grotesque that he fell to his knees, sobbing.

Ruth handed Lane a finds tray, in which were arranged strands of hair and silk from her blouse and headscarf.

'Do you recognise any of this?' Lane's voice was icy.

Mehmet nodded his head.

'Speak up, sir. I can't hear you. I repeat, do you recognise it?'

Inside the shelter there was complete silence, while outside the background noise was, if anything, louder. Then Mehmet whispered. It sounded like the voice of a young child:

'Yes. It's Sofia… My little Sofia…'

* * *

The press had a field day. Anyone wearing a police uniform in the area was fair game and would be pounced on by reporters. Realising the story was growing bigger by the minute, the Leicestershire police had brought in a frame tent, which they erected in the depot lorry park. This was where they were to launch a major press conference. The press release was short and to the point:

> *For immediate release, dateline Sunday, June 13th. Sofia Kabul's body has been identified by her brother and grandfather at the Flax Hole Depot, Leicester. She is known to have been murdered in a so-called 'honour killing', in February, 2002. Two men have been detained and are currently helping police with their enquiries. The police confidently expect that charges will be laid within 48 hours.*

Mehmet and Abdul had identified Sofia's corpse shortly before eight in the evening, and the press conference was scheduled for an hour later. Walking back to the new incident room with Lane, Alan had hoped to discuss what he planned to do next, but it was impossible. The news media and police PR people had taken Lane over completely. He was on his radio and mobile phone continuously. It would appear that everyone, from the Home Secretary downwards, needed to speak to him urgently.

They were climbing the steps into the incident room. Alan had at last managed to catch Lane's attention and was about to speak to him, when the policeman's phone rang again. It was the Chair of the Community Inter-Action Forum, known to the police as the CIA. She was a notorious political motormouth with a high opinion of herself and views on everyone and everything. Lane closed his eyes in exasperation, as the torrent of jargon began. He gave Alan a resigned look and shrugged his shoulders. Then he sat down heavily on a wooden bench just inside the door and sighed, as the shrill voice jabbered in his ear.

At that, Alan shook his shoulder and signalled goodbye. Lane acknowledged and Alan stood up. No sooner was he down the steps, than he melted silently into the crowd. He knew that staying in Leicester would achieve nothing. And he was needed elsewhere.

Thirty-seven

The police station car park was jammed full. It took Alan nearly fifteen minutes to escape. The streets of Leicester were busy with people travelling towards the city centre for the bars and nightlife, but traffic began to thin out as he drove down the Uppingham Road and reached the suburbs. He was driving east, with the setting midsummer sun now low in his wing mirrors. He breathed a sigh of relief as he left the city behind, and headed out into the low hills of Rutland.

It was starting to grow dark as he crossed the county line into Lincolnshire, and became aware that his mobile phone was beeping. Its batteries were going flat. He hadn't yet had the time to go into town and buy a DC adaptor for his new Fourtrak; so he turned it off. The noise irritated him and he needed peace to think.

About a mile from Priory Farm, he turned the headlights off. It was a lonely road and he knew he was unlikely to meet anyone. He slowly drove along a hedged track that led to a long-abandoned duck decoy pond, which the County Conservation Trust had made into a mini nature reserve. He pulled up in a stand of reeds and willow, and got out. He approached the hangar from the rear, using the cover of the overgrown hedge.

Alan crossed the boundary fence and crept along the hedge on the east side of the hangar, until he came to the corner with the small door. It was almost as he'd left it on Friday afternoon. But slightly wider open. He examined it as closely as he could in the moonlight, but could see nothing. No time to worry. Probably wind, or a fox.

It opened easily. Once inside, he pulled the door closed behind him and stood on the toilet bowl. He pulled himself through the open trapdoor in the ceiling. After lowering himself back to the ground, through the gap left by the plywood panel, he stood stock still, listening. He was now inside the main body of the hangar. It was absolutely pitch dark.

He knew he'd been as quiet as possible, but there is nowhere on earth quite as echoing and soundless, as an empty hangar on a still night. He could see why so many are thought to be haunted by dead bomber crews. If anyone was out there, in that vast space between the two stacks of Portakabins, they'd have heard him come in by now.

He'd have to move fast. He took a pair of thick socks from his pocket and pulled them over his boots to muffle his steps. Then he ran along the north wall, in the space behind the *Reference Collections* Portakabins. He eased himself through a narrow gap between two of them.

He felt his way along the front of the Portakabins up to the door of the General Office. Froze. Listened. Nothing. He pulled the key from his jeans and silently turned it.

He was about to step in, when he heard it: a sound from the other side of the hangar. Maybe it was nothing: just something shifting in the gloom. But it could have been somebody coughing or sneezing into their sleeve. He was up the steps and pulled the door, behind him. Again he froze, listening intently through a crack by the door. Was that it again?

It was.

But it had moved. It was further to the right, this time.

And there was another sound: something metallic. A gun being cocked?

He thought about what he'd heard. There were certainly two, more likely three people. He was pretty sure he knew who they were. As he'd guessed, Paul had tipped them off. Silently he closed the General Office door and locked it.

The Innovations Space was entered by a corridor from the back of the General Office. There was no other way in or out, apart from the side door he'd blocked the previous evening. As he walked along the corridor, he resisted the temptation to run. He had to be methodical. Panic was not an option.

Once inside, he locked the door behind him. First he checked everything was still in place. Then he did it again, just to be sure. He stood for a moment, his eyes closed. He tilted his head forward while breathing deeply. Slowly and methodically he relaxed the muscles in his neck, then his arms, then his back, his thighs and legs. Deep breaths. He could feel his senses sharpen. A few more breaths. It was time for action.

He pulled out his lighter and lit the candles he'd fixed to the central table and above the door. Next he crossed over to the fume cupboard and cut the wires to the extractor fan. He removed the emergency safety goggles from behind their reinforced glass screen and slung them around his neck. Then he released the valve on the carbon dioxide cylinder, opened the fume cupboard doors and carefully tied them back. The gas was hissing as it escaped and he moved a short distance away to avoid it. He paused and checked what he had done. At this stage he knew he couldn't make any mistakes. He took a few more deep breaths, while consciously relaxing his muscles. Again he stood still and checked everything. All seemed in order.

As if in slow motion, and anxious not to stir up clouds of invisible gas, he made his way to the ladder, checking the pile of cardboard was still there. Then he started to climb, listening intently. One step at a time. Slowly and methodically. After what seemed like an age, he reached the top layer of shelves. Carefully he leant across and grabbed an overhead steel joist, swinging his legs up behind him. Now he was lying safely on the shelf. Still listening. Listening, while consciously taking deep silent breaths. He knew he needed to take his body to the verge of hyperventilation.

After two and a half minutes he heard a loud crash outside. The General Office door had been forced. Almost immediately he thought he felt cool air on his face. Or was it imagination? He wasn't sure. Either way, he hadn't heard them closing the outside door. If it was left open that would make his next task much simpler.

His thoughts were sharply broken by a harsh voice from somewhere in the General Office.

'We're coming to fuckin' get you, Alan-smart-arse. This time you won't fuckin' get away. We know where you are, boy.'

Alan recognised the Norfolk accent only too well. It was Kevin, the Kabuls' ex-squaddie hit man from Impingham. He probably thinks it's third time lucky, Alan thought grimly.

Alan was still deep-breathing. He could hear further sounds from the General Office. But they didn't matter. He had to control his mind, not just his body.

Precise timing would be essential. There were three of them, and one of him. And they were armed. He was now completely focused on the sounds from around the General Office. A slight scrape here, a creak there, told him the three men were still in the General Office. He looked at his watch. Although it seemed like hours, they had only been there a minute.

He'd given himself a 50:50 chance he'd pull it off. Everything depended on them doing what he needed them to do. They had to be at certain places at key times. Delay would be disastrous.

The hiss of escaping gas seemed to be getting louder. He breathed deeply some more and the sound quietened. Dammit, Alan thought, it was me, not the gas. More deep breaths. Down below they were ransacking office cupboards. One, two three drawers hit the floor. Then a thud as the wardrobe was pulled to the ground.

He looked down at his watch. Two minutes. Then he heard Stu open the side door into the toilet and small kitchen. This was worrying. Alan found he was holding his breath. Angrily he forced himself to breathe out. The gas was still a long way below him. He was aware that the small kitchen would take them into the neighbouring Portakabin, the Packaging Store, where they'd be surrounded by more files and rack after rack of completed orders, boxes and bubble wrap. Again he glanced at his watch. They'd be delayed there too long: five minutes, maybe more.

As he looked down, the candle on the bench-top suddenly went out. A wisp of smoke. It had been smothered by rising gas. He glanced at his watch: the gas had taken three minutes to reach the top of the bench. By now he reckoned it was above the lower half of the space, where the large work benches were recessed well back into the walls. The volume of air above them was smaller. Alan did a rapid calculation. It would take another three minutes to reach him. Maybe even less.

They must be speeded up. He called out as loud as he could:

'Kevin, won't you be reasonable? I'm sure we can come to a deal.'

He tried to make his voice sound like a supercilious officer-and-gentleman. He needed to provoke them. Get their adrenalin pumping. He was being patronising, and it worked. He heard them come crashing back into the General Office. At that moment the second candle above the door flickered briefly and went out. Again he checked his watch: give them another minute. The gas was rising faster than he'd expected. Only six feet to go.

He was counting. After thirty seconds he called out a second time:

'I say, why don't we talk, Kevin? Do be reasonable, old chap. Stop acting like an angry schoolboy!'

'Fuck you, arsehole!'

They had heard where his voice was coming from. Their footsteps thundered down the corridor. The door handle rattle. Locked. Alan cursed: had that been a mistake? He thought he'd need the extra time. He'd know in a few seconds. He was breathing deep and fast, making no attempt to keep quiet.

There was a short pause, as they drew back and charged. Then with a loud crash, the door smashed open. There was the sound of bodies crashing to the ground, and a sharp wheezing. Alan imagined them thrashing around, grabbing at their throats, gasping for air.

Alan took a final deep breath. He pulled down the goggles and jumped onto the heap of cardboard far below.

He dashed for the door, kicking Darren and Stu's pistols out of reach. As he passed Kevin he stooped down and grabbed his machine pistol, which lay on the ground beside him. Leaving doors open behind him, he gulped down fresh air outside the General Office, then ran back in and shut off the gas. All three men were now fully unconscious, but not, he hoped, dead. He went outside a second time and waited for a couple of minutes while the worst of the gas cleared.

Then he returned. He checked their pulses, which were weak. But still just there. He was relieved. They were alive, if not kicking. Rapidly he dragged Kevin and his two mates out into the Packaging Store and tied their wrists, before securely wrapping them in thick layers of cling film, bubble wrap and parcel tape. Nobody could escape from that.

He was about to turn off the light when he looked back at them, lying on the floor. They lay there absolutely still. These were people who had just tried to kill him. There was something pathetic about them. To his surprise he felt contempt, not anger. Some people might have forgiven him if he had kicked each one of them in the balls, just to make himself feel better. Stretched out unconscious on the floor, his would-be assassins lacked even the dignity of the dead. He flicked the switch and shut the door, turning the key in the lock.

Thirty-eight

Alan stood alone in the middle of the hangar. He bit into a Mars Bar he'd bought from a machine at the police station. Then he started to shiver as the glucose hit his empty stomach. He was about to turn the main arc light on, but then thought better of it. He had no wish to alert the Lincolnshire Police patrol, when next they decided to call in. Briefly he contemplated phoning Lane and his men in Leicester, but immediately thought better of that, too. Their presence would also cramp his style. No, he thought, it's much better I sort everything out myself, here and now.

He returned to the General Office and opened the main key cupboard. He knew the combination of this secure metal box which held keys to all the Portakabin units in the hangar. He removed the keys in threes, then visited each of the places they secured. After forty-five minutes he had found nothing.

As he walked out of the last Portakabin his heart sank: Paul was nowhere to be seen. That meant he could be in only one place – a place Alan would have done anything not to revisit.

Back in the General Office he opened the key cupboard and saw immediately that the hook labelled 'BCA' was empty. Everyone working at Priory Farm knew that this was potentially the most hazardous facility in the entire complex and it was a sacking offence to leave the door unlocked. That empty hook was an ominous sign.

Anxiously, Alan hurried across to the other side of the hangar. From a distance he could see the door to the BCA was unlocked, and the padlock was lying on the floor, just outside it. Realising that this was a potential crime scene, Alan ran back to the General Office and put on a clean pair of lab overalls, plus new white wellies and long rubber gloves. He was taking no chances.

Gingerly he pushed open the door and turned on the light.

Something moved on the floor a few feet to his right. It was a rat – which he had interrupted while feeding. He walked across and looked down. Suddenly he felt violently sick and just made it to one of the many bench sinks around the edge of the room. The bloated-looking rat had been chewing on a human ear.

Wiping his mouth on folds of blue absorbent lab paper, which he took from a large roll on the wall, he walked over to the medium-sized maggot tank. It was the only one with an active population of maggots, as all the others had been cleaned out. Had he not been sick already, what now met his eyes would have made the strongest man vomit.

Lolling half-in, and half-out, of the tank was Paul. His shoes had been removed and lay nearby on the floor, but a slight movement beneath his shirt and trousers gave a ghastly impression of life. Alan could see that this was actually caused by a heaving mass of maggots beneath his clothes.

There were maggots everywhere: around and within his gaping throat and windpipe. Most of the flesh on his face and gums had gone and the teeth in his lipless mouth gleamed bright white in the fluorescent laboratory light. Trying to ignore the horror of the scene before him, Alan attempted to work out what must have happened.

Although he couldn't tell for certain, because so much flesh had been removed, he supposed that Paul had been either drugged or given a knockout blow to the head. His body had then been dumped in the maggot tank – presumably in the belief that all evidence for precisely how he was killed would soon be removed. A case could even be made that he had committed suicide.

But then something truly disgusting must have happened. The blow or the drugs wore off, and he temporarily regained some measure of consciousness – enough to realise where he was and what was happening to him. He was being eaten alive. Somehow he managed to sit upright and in the process short-circuited the wires running around the rim of the tank. This allowed thousands of maggots to escape and the rat to get in and sever his left ear. On the plus side, Alan thought, it also slowed down the process of defleshing, probably by hours.

Many years ago, Alan had been on holiday with his parents on a hill farm in Wales. It had been a hot summer and one day he'd found a lamb with severe fly strike lying in a hedge. The shepherd was nearby and Alan called him over, much upset. The old man took one look and killed the animal with a blow to the head, to put it out of its misery. Alan asked why he didn't take it back to the farm and kill off the maggots? The shepherd then explained that as they ate through the living flesh, maggots secreted toxins that built up and would eventually kill the lamb, whatever else happened. But it would take a long time. So a rapid death was infinitely kinder.

So presumably, Alan thought as he looked down on the corpse, it was the accumulation of toxins that had prevented Paul from getting the strength to climb out of the tank. And eventually of course, they, the toxins, had killed him.

Alan realised it was essential to stop the maggots before they consumed all the forensic evidence. So, steeling himself, he dragged the body over to a large chest freezer and bundled it in, before carefully closing the lid. He turned round and looked behind him. On the floor was a writhing, living rope of maggots that had dropped from the corpse, as Alan had dragged it across to the freezer. Unable to stop himself he trampled his way slowly through the wriggling mass, killing thousands of them, while coating his shoes with their – with Paul's – blood. Somehow that made him feel better. At least he'd done something.

He then returned to the tank. He had no wish to, but he needed to take another look, now that Paul's body had gone. Lying at the bottom, in a few inches of the stinking slimy 'soup', formed by the acids of putrefaction, were the miniature bones and dark brown wool of what appeared to be a Soay lamb. Gently his gloved fingers lifted it out of the way.

Beneath, and lying directly on the bottom of the tank, he could see a group of tarsals and metatarsals, the small and very characteristic bones of the human foot. As if to remove any doubt in his mind, the toenails, still painted a glossy dark pink, lay beside them, in a little pool of yellow jelly, like so many bright fallen petals off a grisly flower.

Thirty-nine

Aware that his mobile battery had gone down, Alan returned to the General Office and picked up the phone. He looked at his watch. It was nearly two, on Monday morning. He was about to phone DCI Lane, when he remembered the three men he'd trussed up in the Packing Store. They were recovering. Kevin had even managed to half sit up. They groaned. All three men had sore heads and running eyes. But they were alive, which was more than they deserved. After he had pulled off his overalls Alan gave each of them a few sips of water, then returned to the office and phoned an ambulance. That done, he redialled Richard Lane.

A very sleepy voice answered, but by the time Alan had outlined the events of the night, he was wide awake and promised to be with him within the hour. He would also alert the local police who'd be there very shortly.

There was just one other thing Alan had to do to satisfy his own curiosity before the police arrived, and he was aware he didn't have much time. He ran across to the main hangar doors, where he noticed the padlock had been cut and lay on the ground. Then he remembered that Lane had told him the police had done it. He rolled one of the massive sliding doors back and turned on the main arc lights. That, he thought, should keep them busy for a few minutes.

As he ran across the apron he could hear sirens approaching from Boston, far out in Dawyck Fen, breaking the stillness of the approaching dawn. They were still a mile away. Maybe more. Quickly he ducked behind a wall and ran round the outside of the archaeological building, to the side entrance. Once inside, he stumbled along unlit corridors, past his own office, across the main hall and into the Coffee Room. The door to the Out Store was locked. Paul liked to keep these keys to himself, but Alan knew Clara kept an illicit set in the top drawer of her desk. They were still there.

Back in the Coffee Room, he fumbled with the cheap duplicate key which wasn't a very good fit. Meanwhile, out on the apron the world had suddenly come alive. Expecting trouble, DCI Lane had alerted the firearms squad, three of whom stood around the perimeter facing outwards. Two others were escorting three officers and four paramedics into the open central area of the hangar. Alan had left the door to the General Office wide open, so he hoped they'd discover the Packaging Store, where Kevin and his mates were lying. But he'd left the door to the BCA, which still held the horrors in the freezer and maggot tanks, securely locked.

At last the catch in the Out Store door moved, and he opened it. He felt around and soon found the light switch. There were no windows to the outside. In the time it took the tubes to flicker on, he had crossed to the shelves marked 'For Christian Reburial'. He saw six boxes, in two sizes. At PFC, as at most museums, larger long-bone boxes, held all the non-cranial bones of the skeleton, whereas the more fragile skull and its mandible were placed on their own, in a smaller, square skull-box.

By and large ancient bones, with all fat and most unstable protein long gone, weigh a fraction of their immediate post-mortem weight. But each of these long-bone boxes felt unusually heavy. Alan lifted their lids, one by one. They were all packed with bones. He was certain that each long-bone box held far more than just a single individual. The skull boxes, however, contained just single heads. Carefully he lifted one out with both hands. It was light. Almost certainly ancient. He replaced it carefully.

He lowered one of the long-bone boxes to the floor and gently tipped out its contents onto a sheet of newspaper. Lying at the bottom, like so many broken pieces of a large, white-chocolate Easter egg, were shattered fragments of skull. Alan knew a certain amount about bone fracture patterns, as these were good indicators of ancient butchery techniques. One glance convinced him that the spiral fracture he could plainly see on at least two mandibles had happened when the bone was still pliable and 'green'. 'Green' bone fractures cannot happen once the bone has lost its fat content and gone brittle. And that takes time.

Alan went to his own office, turning on lights as he did so. It didn't matter if the police came in now. He picked up the phone and dialled Harriet's number.

It was approaching 2.45 a.m., when a very sleepy Harriet answered the phone.

'Harry, it's Alan. I know I'm probably the last person you want to talk to right now.'

Harriet cut through his bluster. She suddenly sounded very awake indeed.

'Oh, thank heavens you've called. I've been worried sick. Where are you?'

'In my office.'

'At Priory Farm?

'What the hell are you doing there?'

Alan's mind was too fixated on the present situation to register her concern.

'Look, it's too long to explain, but Richard Lane will be here soon, and I must have Alaric. I need him to repeat that lipids test. As soon as possible. It's very important.'

'Yes, I'm sure it bloody well is.'

And then she hung up.

Everyone could hear the scream of the siren, when it was a mile away. Then the car came hurtling up the drive and onto the hangar apron. Lane jumped out and ran across to Alan who was now standing by one of the stretchers just outside the open doors of the ambulance. A paramedic was removing the last of the cling film and parcel tape. Kevin lay there resolutely silent.

'So he's our man, is he?'

'Yes,' Alan replied. 'He certainly had a go at me. Him and his two mates over there.' He pointed across at two other stretchers, then being carried across the apron towards them.

'So what happened?'

Alan then gave him a brief account of the attack and the carbon dioxide. Then he remembered the machine pistol, which he'd shoved under the Portakabin steps as he gasped for air. They walked across and retrieved it. Lane, picking it up in a handkerchief, called over to a Scene-of-Crime Officer who hurried across. SOCO pulled a new plastic bag from a roll and put the gun in it.

'You say the man Kevin was carrying this?' Alan asked.

'That's right. His prints should be on it, along, of course with mine.'

'Anything I need to see in there?' Lane nodded towards the General Office.

'No,' Alan replied, 'it can wait. This is far more important.'

He turned round and headed across to the BCA and the maggot tank.

In the background they could see the flashing lights of another ambulance crossing the apron.

'Wait,' Lane restrained him. 'We'll need penguin suits.'

'Just getting them, sir.' SOCO left them and returned a few minutes later with the white paper suits and overshoes, which they carried across to the door labelled Biological Cleansing Area. Outside they all pulled on their suits. Mindful of the way Abdul had passed out the night before, at the sight of Sofia's remains, Alan didn't want Lane and SOCO to do the same. He thought it best to warn them.

'Before we go in, gentlemen, I should warn you that what's inside this room is pretty upsetting. Please be prepared.' He undid the padlock. 'I know you're both used to grim sights, but there are at least two bodies in here and many thousands of maggots. You will need strong stomachs. And I mean it: I've already been sick myself once.'

This short statement had a big effect. The two men looked grim.

They had put on their paper overalls about three paces back from the door. As they approached it, and as if to forewarn them, they caught the stench of putrefaction. It was nearly overpowering, as they stood waiting by the door. Then Alan asked:

'Are we ready?'

His two companions nodded. He opened the door. The severed ear was still lying on the floor. Outside, the first light of dawn was visible behind the trees. Alan suddenly felt very tired. Maybe the adrenalin was wearing off. He hadn't slept a wink for two nights. The rat had probably returned to its run for the day. It wouldn't be back for several hours. Rats didn't like daylight.

While they slowly walked towards the tanks, Alan explained what he had discovered and how he had moved through the room. As he did so, SOCO held out a small sound recorder. They needed an accurate record.

They walked to the maggot tank and looked in. Alan pointed out the foot at the bottom, and as he peered at it more closely he also thought he saw long strands of dark, straight human hair.

By this point both policemen were silent and very pale. Alan then walked over to the freezer and lifted the lid. Paul was not a pretty sight, especially as his half-eaten eyebrows had frozen on contact with the lid and were ripped off when it was opened. SOCO had to turn round rapidly, his hand to his mouth. Lane placed a comforting arm on his shoulder.

'Hang in there, son, we're nearly through. But you must warn the others. And choose the team carefully. Who'll be in charge?'

There was a pause while he recovered.

'I'll be working with Sergeant Thackeray, sir.'

'He's a good man. But make sure he sees me first, before anyone else comes in here. This is not for people with weak stomachs.'

Back in the main hangar the light was steadily improving. They closed the BCA door behind them and walked a few paces more to escape the stench. DCI Lane was the first to speak:

'I'd be grateful if you could bring Sergeant Thackeray to see me here. And thank you for what you've just done. It couldn't have been easy. Well done.'

SOCO headed towards the apron, where a mobile incident room had just parked-up. Lane turned to Alan:

'How many people used those tanks?'

'Paul was the only animal bones specialist working here. He set the tanks up and was the only one to use them, so far as I know. It's actually quite difficult to service them. Specimens have to be kept separate and clearly labelled. And Paul was a perfectionist. He'd never let anything out of the BCA without checking every bone to see that all were present and correct.'

'No,' Lane replied thoughtfully, 'and it would seem that perfection wasn't his only motive.'

* * *

Alan was desperate for a coffee and he sucked the warm sweet liquid down, as if it were a pint of the very best bitter. He was just finishing, when Harriet's car pulled in. She had, as the old phrase went, a brow of thunder as she got out. She released Alaric from the back and put him on a lead. By now, and to Alan's considerable relief, Lane had rejoined them.

'I'm delighted to see you, Harriet,' Lane said with his customary well-mannered charm, 'but I admit the circumstances are somewhat unusual. Do you normally start work this early?'

'No I don't,' Harriet replied tetchily. 'But when you're worried sick because somebody has gone AWOL after unearthing a human corpse and has been too obsessed to think of giving you so much as a single call, then sometimes you do odd things. At least I do...'

She paused:

'But then I'm normal.'

Alan intervened, trying to ease the tension. He gestured towards the dog.

'Richard, this is Alaric. He's here to help us with the investigation.'

'Good heavens, really?' Lane asked Alan.

Harriet turned to Alan, her grip on the lead tightened.

'And are you going to tell me how, exactly, or do I have to guess at that too?'

'I think,' Alan replied quietly, suddenly feeling very tired, 'we may have found the other evidence we were looking for. It's over here, in the Out Store.'

The Out Store was exactly as Alan had left it. The lights were still on and one long-bone box was lying on the floor, its contents partially spread over the sheets of newspaper beside it.

'Right, Richard,' Alan said to Lane as they entered: 'Watch this.'

The others stood back, just inside the door, as Alan took a cranium from a skull box on the shelf and placed it gingerly on the floor in front of the dog. Alaric turned his head away. It was written all over his canine face: they were going to play that strange game again.

Alan pretended to encourage him:

'Go on, lick it boy!'

But he got no response from the dog. He put the skull back in its box.

'Right,' he said to his small audience, 'that skull was medieval. No response from the dog, because all the fats had been leached out. Shall I continue?'

Lane nodded. Alan then turned to the bones in the larger box and selected two broken pieces of skull. As he carried them towards the dog, Harriet spoke sharply.

'That's cranium. What the hell are they doing in a long-bone box?'

'Exactly, Harriet,' Alan said, 'I fear Paul is the only person who knows the answer to that – and he's dead.'

Harriet stared open-mouthed, trying to grasp what he had just said – almost casually. Alan was so tired he'd become oblivious. He continued, as if conducting a well-rehearsed conjuring trick.

'Now let's see the dog's reaction to these two skull bones.'

As he approached with the bones, Alaric strained forward on his lead, his nose quivering with anticipation. There were flecks of spittle around his mouth, and his tongue was hanging out, drooling.

'You've made your point, Alan.' Lane said, 'that dog would eat those bits of skull if you let him. So presumably they're not very old?'

'No. I doubt if they're more than five years old.'

'Or less,' Harriet added, her academic mind overriding her emotions. She was focusing on the facts. 'In acidic soils you can lose fats in half that time.'

'Alan,' Lane said in a firm voice, 'you've made your point very well. So are we right to assume that many of these boxes contain modern bones?'

'Yes. I think Paul was processing modern bodies at an alarming rate. And had been doing so for several years.'

Lane was now looking very serious.

'Right,' he said, still looking down at the floor, 'we'll discuss all that later.' He paused and looked up: 'Right now I'm more concerned that Ms Webb has not been properly informed about Paul Flynn's death. I think you had better leave that to me, Alan. I suggest you go and fetch yourself something to eat from our canteen trailer.'

He summoned a constable on his walkie-talkie. When he arrived, he gave instructions that this storeroom was also a scene-of-crime. It must be taped-off immediately. They would also need to conduct a full forensic survey. Meanwhile it must remain locked, sealed and guarded.

Alan withdrew. He had more sense than to argue with Lane, who seemed to understand and handle people rather better than he did.

In fact, as Lane put a comforting arm around Harriet's shoulder, Alan felt a short stab of envy. And behind that, an uncomfortable, nagging question. He'd got his answers now. He'd found Sofia. He'd exposed the Kabuls' corruption. But Paul was dead and he'd lost Harriet. Had it all really been worth it?

Wearily, Alan turned his back on the scene and slowly walked away.

Forty

Alan slept for a straight twenty-four hours. Somehow Grahame had managed to get him into bed upstairs, washed and undressed. He was like a sleepwalker. When he awoke on Wednesday morning, Grahame was busily preparing breakfast below in the kitchen. Then he could hear the phone, ring and Grahame called up the stairs. It was Norman Grant, Governor of Blackfen Prison. Alan stumbled downstairs, bleary-eyed. He took the phone.

The Governor told him that Richard Lane had contacted him informally, in advance of an official response to the events of the weekend, which would be released by the Home Office very shortly. He thought it likely that Ali would be transferred to an open prison any day now, pending a full reassessment of his case. In view of this, did he want the opportunity for a final interview, as his next Lifers' Club session would not be happening until the second week in July? Alan leapt at the chance and agreed to be in the Governor's office the next day.

* * *

They'd arranged to meet mid-morning, but Alan didn't arrive until closer to noon, as the loss adjuster had telephoned, with yet another interminable query about the Land Rover explosion. This time, on the Governor's instructions, Alan parked in the small car park reserved for visitors to the Administration Block. This was very much more select than the general car park. It was overhung with lime trees, which Alan noted would shortly be covering all cars beneath them with a sticky, sugary mist of sap.

He walked straight into the lobby, where there was a reception desk, like in an estate agents or lawyers. And also like them, it was unmanned. He rang a bell. The woman who answered lacked the glamour of Indajit's Asian lady, but she was warm and friendly. Just what a prison needed, Alan thought. He fully expected her to offer him a hot buttered teacake, as she pointed the way to the Governor's office.

Norman Grant was dictating a letter to his PA in her anteroom, when Alan entered. He rose to his feet and shook Alan's hand warmly. Then he arranged for Ali to be brought to his office.

The young man, with an officer in attendance, arrived some fifteen minutes later. His hair was still short, but he had shaved off his beard. The Governor then asked the officer to wait in Reception. Meanwhile his PA was collecting up various papers and files. That done, they both withdrew into the main office, leaving Ali and Alan, plus two cups of tea and a plate of biscuits, in the anteroom.

Alan began the interview.

'Well, this is a bit different, isn't it?'

'Is it?'

This was said without much enthusiasm.

Alan had expected him to be looking better. After all, he was almost certainly about to be released. But, if anything, he looked worse than at the previous Lifers' Club session. He was tired and listless; on edge.

'You've heard what's been happening?' Alan asked gently.

'Yes, the Governor told me last night. They've got granddad and Abdul.' He went silent, looking down at his hands. Then he raised his head, looking Alan in the eyes: 'And it was you that did it, wasn't it?'

There was more than a hint of menace in the way he asked this question.

It was not the response Alan had anticipated. He knew he shouldn't expect gratitude, but not this. It took him a moment to collect his thoughts.

'How do you mean "did it"? I just drew attention to the fact that you'd been unjustly imprisoned. Most people would have been grateful...'

Alan tailed off. He could see this person most certainly wasn't grateful. Not even slightly.

Anger was now replacing resentment.

'Why didn't you leave me alone? Why did you have to stick your sodding oar in? I didn't ask you to poke about.'

Alan sat back in his chair. Stunned. But Ali hadn't stopped.

'Can't you get it into your thick head that I'm here because I wanted to be here? I'm here because I love my granddad. I love Abdul. I loved Sofia...'

He was stopped by a cascade of sobs. He fell forward, his face in his arms. Slouched over the table, his shoulders shaking.

Maybe it was a way of escaping the young man's distress, but Alan found he had skipped back a hundred years, to Tiny's final scene with AAC, her father and her only 'lover', if that was the right word. Alistair had told him he'd heard a family legend that she had 'wasted away' after ten years of progressive illness, which became much more severe for the final six months. Alan reckoned that her final 'illness' could only have been pregnancy. So how would Tiny have responded to the man, who had brought her into the world, had used her so cruelly, and then had caused her to die a horrible, lingering death? How would she have reacted when that man entered her bedroom for the very last time?

Would it have been hate? Anger? Fear? Loathing? No, he realised as he looked down at Ali's still heaving shoulders: it would have been none of these things. It would have been love. Pure and simple. For better or for worse, family love, will always remain the deepest and least rational emotion of all. Strip everything away, right down to our DNA and it's what makes us, not just human, but animals. Sentient beasts. And we meddle with it at our peril.

Alan focused on the moment. This was his last chance.

'I know you loved Sofia, Ali. And I know you didn't kill her. It's all going to come out in the next few days anyway so…'

'You really want to know?'

'How she died. Yes, I do.'

Ali sat back, wiping his eyes. His reply was calm and measured. Almost resigned. He'd had his moment of catharsis.

'Yes, I'll tell you what happened. Granddad, Abdul and me were standing at the top landing in the old building. Granddad was showing us the latest architect's plans and we were all excited about the next stage. He was telling us where my new offices would be. I hadn't expected it. He was very generous like that. Then a door opened down at the ground floor and Sofia ran in. She ran up the stairs. She was very happy. Smiling. I remember her scarf slipped, but we were family, so it didn't matter.'

He paused to take a long sip from his now tepid cup of tea.

'She reached us and blurted out the news. She said she was going to marry that Sikh bloke.' Alan realised that he still couldn't bring himself to speak Indajit's name. 'Granddad was gobsmacked. She hadn't asked him first. He looked very angry. Then she stopped. She looked at him, scared like, her hands at her face. Worried. Then she stepped back.' He paused, tears welling up in his eyes, '...stepped back, over the edge. And dropped. Screaming. Screaming so loud...'

He paused, took a deep breath and continued:

'There was no rail...' There was a long silence. 'That's all that happened.'

There was another silence. Eventually Alan asked:

'So the family tried to cover it up?'

'What would you have done? Of course we did. And your mate Paul made us pay for it, too. Then, years later, that smart-arse Indian dreamed-up the "honour killing" bollocks. The next we know is that everyone is suspecting granddad. I was young, and would get a shorter sentence, so I said I did it. Nobody would believe it was an accident, would they? Would they?'

'Maybe if you'd explained, all of you, together?'

'We were fucking Muslims. All fanatics. Bloody Jihadis. The *Daily Sun* called granddad "Mental Mehmet", until I confessed.' He allowed himself a rueful smile. 'That shut the buggers up. And that's how the family stayed together...'

He paused for a moment, then looked up with unconcealed malevolence.

'Until you came along.'

* * *

Alan drove round to the back room of The Slodger's Arms. This time he was alone. And he needed a long drink after that interview. Two packets of crisps were his midday meal. He wanted to sort things out in his own mind, before he spoke to Richard Lane. He knew he owed him a few explanations.

So, he thought as he put his pint glass back on the table beside him, the 'crime' that started the whole thing off, was no such thing. They couldn't accuse either Mehmet or Abdul of murder. The drugs business was also rubbish, unless the police's detailed forensic examination of Priory Farm found anything – and that wouldn't be finished for at least another week. He suspected it would reveal nothing – just like all the other searches. By now he was thinking hard. So it all came down to the 'family business' that Ali had mentioned in some of his interviews. That *had* to be the crux of it all.

The second body in the maggot tank beneath Paul's corpse showed that Paul had been in the business of processing human remains. And, Alan guessed, probably on a near-industrial scale. But any industrial process requires input and output. There has to be a source and a market for the product, or else the firm goes bust. And this surely was where the Kabul empire came in.

His thoughts were interrupted by a tap on his shoulder.

'Thought I might find you here,' Lane said, as he sat down beside Alan. 'Norman Grant told me you'd been seeing friend Ali this morning.'

Lane took a drink from his lemonade and lime. Then he asked, 'So did he bid you a fond farewell?'

'No, he didn't. Far from it. But he did tell me how Sofia died.'

Alan didn't want his friend to think the meeting had been completely fruitless. At least he'd managed to salvage something.

'Really? So, who did it, Abdul or Mehmet?'

'Neither,' said Alan quietly. 'It was an accident. Like you said, cock-up, rather than conspiracy.'

Alan registered the shock on Lane's face. He took a moment to let the news sink in.

'Ali said she was in the old depot building. She told her granddad she was going to marry Indajit. He looked angry...'

Alan could visualise the moment so clearly, he could hear those screams echoing through the air. It was a struggle to finish the story.

'Then she stepped back – and fell straight over the edge, down into the stairwell.'

'D'you believe that?'

Lane asked the question as a factual problem. He didn't seem to have views himself.

'Yes, I do. With the rails and banisters gone, that staircase was a deathtrap. Bloody lethal.'

'But a crime was still comitted,' said Lane quietly. 'They didn't report her death, and they unlawfully buried a body. How and why do you think they did that?'

'I don't know the precise date when Sofia died, but it was a cold February, and they could easily have hidden the body somewhere, where nobody would find her. Then, when Paul took over on his shift he either found the body, or more likely, overheard the Kabuls making plans. Maybe they asked him outright? I don't know.'

'We'll never know.'

'But whatever happened,' Alan continued, 'he agreed to get rid of the corpse somewhere in the excavation. Come to think of it, he did go back there after the last day to empty the sheds and arrange for the Portaloos to be collected. That sort of thing. Maybe he stayed overnight, I honestly can't remember. But that was when he would have buried her. The rest of us had finished. And all the wet sieving had been done.'

'Do you think Paul tried to blackmail the Kabuls?'

'No, his mind didn't work like that,' Alan replied, 'he would have seen it as a business opportunity. And it was, a very profitable one.'

'So you think they then paid him a fat cheque and that was the money he used to buy Priory Farm and set up *Reference Collections* and those grisly tanks.'

'Yes. The thing is, they were always there and could be used as and when required. And at short notice, if needs be. It was ideal for a developing "business", if that's what you want to call it.'

'And it was disposing of Sofia's body that gave him the idea,' Lane added.

'Yes, he realised there were easier ways of doing it.'

Lane paused for a moment, obviously thinking about the implications of what Alan had just said.

'That all makes plenty of sense, but I still can't understand why they pretended Sofia had gone abroad. Surely they must have known that eventually they stood a good chance of being found out? And besides, it had been an accident so why not come clean in the first place?'

'That question's the key to it,' Alan replied. 'They couldn't just "come clean". Nobody would have believed them. Put yourself in their shoes: the daughter comes running in, having accepted a proposal from a Sikh. The next thing the world knows is that she falls into a stairwell, having just confronted her father and two brothers. And all of them Muslims. Would any British jury accept that?'

'But surely…'

'OK, if you don't accept that, just look at the way an English jury lapped up Ali's fake confession. They simply accepted he was a fanatic, and because nobody on the defence side offered witnesses to the contrary, that was how matters were allowed to rest. In my view the judge should have intervened. But he didn't, presumably because he also shared the view that a high proportion of Muslims are fanatics, or religious nutters, who treat their women like chattels. So he was convicted. And quite quickly. The trial didn't last very long, did it?'

'Two or three days, as I recall.' Lane replied. 'So what do you think would have happened if the family *had* tried to come clean?'

'That's simple. It's nearly always the head of the family who does these things, so Mehmet would have been accused of her "honour killing".'

'And do you think he'd have been convicted?'

'You tell me, Richard. All I can say is, the jury were quick enough to convict his younger grandson – and without a body, too. A victimless murder and seven years after the event?' He took a pull from his glass, then continued: 'Normally that would be a tall order, but not when "fanatics" and "Muslims" are involved. And that's what makes it all so bloody unjust.'

Lane was now agreeing with Alan's argument, if not with his invective.

'Yes, and if the trial had happened at the time of the supposed crime, I would imagine that local feelings would have been even stronger than they were seven years later. And that's saying quite a lot.'

'I agree. I think the family were in an impossible position. A case of a rock and a hard place, if ever there was one.'

Lane went up to the bar and bought four packets of crisps which he tossed onto the table. Absent-mindedly, Alan opened one. The salt tasted good.

Then Lane asked, 'So what did you think about Ali?'

'I think, in his own way, he really believed he was doing the right thing by his family,' said Alan thoughtfully. 'And who the hell was I to tell him otherwise?'

Lane was thoughtful, too.

'OK. So let's go back to the PFC connection. You think it was disposing of Sofia's body that gave Paul the idea he could do this on a regular basis using techniques designed for the job. Maggot tanks and so on…'

'Yes, that's where a horrible sort of genius comes in. He must have made the connection between defleshing museum specimens and disposing of corpses very early on.'

'So the bloke's a serial killer, a psychopath who made a healthy profit out of satisfying his urges. Then you think that Kevin bloke found out and took a moral stance?'

'I wish. No, I think it was a lot darker than that.'

'Go on.'

Lane was leaning forward listening intently.

'I believe the Kabuls' "family business" that Ali referred to, was nothing less than the routine disposal of unwanted bodies.'

'So, do you think we're back to honour killings again?' said Lane thoughtfully.

'Maybe. Who knows. You're the detective, you tell me, why does anyone kill another human being?'

For a moment, Alan was back in that first Lifers' Club session, delivering his introductory lecture, with those rows and rows of faces staring down at him. Unremarkable, everyday faces. And yet all of them had committed unspeakable acts of violence…

'You OK, Alan? We finish up another time if you'd rather.'

Alan looked up to see Lane frowning at him, his face full of concern.

'I'm fine,' Alan answered curtly, forcing himself to follow his theory to its natural conclusion.

'Sometimes Paul would have been able to sell a nicely cleaned skeleton to a reference collection, somewhere in the world,' Alan continued, 'but those, I suspect, were the exceptions rather than the rule.'

'So how did they get rid of them?' Lane asked, 'they couldn't just stick human bones in the garbage.'

'That,' said Alan, 'is where Paul's archaeological knowledge and experience came in. Even I can remember, in the old days of the digging "circuit" any bodies we dug up were shoved into boxes and stuffed in museum basements. Sometimes, though rarely, they'd be studied by palaeopathologists, physical anthropologists, and the like. But mostly they'd stew in the boxes. Forgotten and unwanted. As good as in a grave.'

Alan paused to take a sup from his pint. Then he went on:

'Then in the nineties, various native groups in places like Canada and Australia objected, quite rightly, that skeletons of their dead relatives shouldn't be treated in this cavalier fashion. They didn't want their ancestors to be seen as mere artefacts, like bits of broken pot, or flint. Many believed too, that their ancestral bones still hosted human spirits and should be allowed to rest somewhere more dignified, than a museum basement.'

'Didn't those Pagans and Druids make a similar fuss about British bones?'

'Yes they did. Then others joined in. So now it's routine that Christian bones from archaeological sites are given Christian reburial in sanctified ground.'

'And those are what's stored in the boxes in the Out Store?'

'Precisely,' Alan replied. 'Paul would personally oversee their storage and transport to the sanctified ground. That is, until the chaos back in April, when a dig was forced to end early. That's how the mix-up happened.'

'How d'you mean?'

'I think Paul used to introduce modern bones into the Out Store boxes at weekends, when the place was usually deserted. He knew nobody would want to examine them, and they'd all shortly be given official Christian Reburial. And that was permanent. He used to arrange these reburials with the Church, himself. And even then, nobody would check them. And why should they? What's the point? After all, it's the very end of the process. And anyhow, how many times did you look inside your granddad's coffin when they buried him?'

'Quite.'

They mulled this over for a few moments.

Lane was the next to speak. 'So what happened on that weekend, over Easter?'

Alan was speaking slowly, trying to recall everything. 'At the end of the previous week I clearly recall extracting all the samples for radiocarbon dating. Then the boxes went back to the Out Store over Easter…'

He paused, then continued, 'Then I took the C-14 samples straight to Cambridge. So all those dates are kosher.'

'So Paul "introduced" the modern bones in the Out Store, but after you'd taken the radiocarbon samples?'

'Exactly. We removed the jaws for Saltaire the Tuesday after Easter Monday. Trouble is, I didn't know it then, but some of the ones I took were modern.'

For a few moments they sipped their drinks in silence. Lane was the first to speak.

'Well,' he said, leaning back in his seat, 'we know it must have been a nice little earner.'

This time it was Alan's turn to ask the questions.

'Who for? Paul, or the Kabuls?'

'Oh, mostly for the Kabuls. Mehmet's bank account is flush. That's what brought the drugs boys running, of course. '

'But surely Paul was taking all the risks, wasn't he?'

'Yes, he was. But it seems that he made the mistake that IBM made, when they handed the most profitable side of their business to Microsoft, who then controlled not just the software, but its supply and marketing. All Paul did was offer a body disposal service. The Kabuls handled the difficult and profitable bits.'

'So was that,' Alan asked, 'why they wanted to bump him off, d'you think?'

'What,' Lane replied, 'get rid of the middleman? No, I don't think so.' He was thinking aloud now. 'No, they wanted both him and you out of the way, as soon as he'd made the mistake of telling them that the CID arrived after the "accident" with the buried cistern that killed your friend Steve.'

'But I thought he'd gone?'

'So did I, at least when you and I were together.'

'So where was he?'

'Back in his flat at Priory Farm. I saw him at an upstairs window when I drove out. He must have seen you and me talking in the yard, getting into my car...'

Shit, Alan thought, I should have realised that. The lights were on upstairs. But what could I have done?

'So he told the Kabuls all about it. Probably thought they'd be pleased with him, poor fool. After that, you were both dead men walking. Kevin and his merry men made sure of that.'

'Do you suppose,' Alan asked, 'that he told them at that meeting on Friday in the hangar Board Room?'

'Seems most likely.' Lane replied. 'It certainly fits with what the pathologist has since found out. Trouble is, she says, it's hard to be certain precisely when he died, because of those maggots and the fact that you stuffed him in the freezer. But sometime in the preceding 24 hours seems the most probable.'

Alan knew he shouldn't, as he was driving. But what the hell. He got up and went to the bar.

* * *

Lane raised his eyes to the ceiling when Alan returned with a pint and a large Scotch, both for himself. But he said nothing. Instead he kept focus on the events of the previous days. Alan could see he wasn't going to be happy until every loose end was thoroughly tied up.

'Tell me, Alan, how on earth did you think up that plan and then entice three professional killers into the hangar? It was a triumph and it's the only bloody reason I'll be driving you home when you've had those drinks – and the next ones, which I'll pay for, if you don't mind.'

Alan was grinning sheepishly.

'That was Grahame's idea. He's always looked out for me.'

'But how did you entice them in, and then stage-manage the entire business? Because they all had to be there and you had to have the time to set things up, didn't you?'

'Well some of it was a bit hit-or-miss, but I knew they'd be there on Sunday evening, for sure.'

'But how?' Lane was still intrigued.

'Oh that was easy. I knew from that threat Ali wanted me to pass on, that Paul had fallen out with the Kabuls. He had to repair the damage somehow. His whole business, even his life, depended on it. So he decided to sacrifice me. I was the interfering idiot who was asking questions and stirring all sorts of shit with Ali.'

The drink was starting to go to his head, but he pressed on.

'All I did was phone Paul and arrange to borrow some tools from the Priory Farm Tool Store. I knew he'd then find some excuse to see me when I returned them. Which is precisely what happened. If I were writing a novel I'd describe it as my Invitation to Death. I was certainly aware of it at the time. I must admit, as soon as he asked me over it was bloody obvious he was spinning me a line…'

'Who, Kevin?'

'No, *Paul*, you idiot. When I phoned, he told me a load of gibberish about repairing a soakaway. It was all bollocks: the drains from his house barely ever get used. I don't think anyone at PFC had ever seen his septic tank being emptied. What little there was, just sort of soaked away, like it does in old houses. And besides, during the week he's in his office, and at weekends he's either sorting bones into boxes, emptying maggot tanks, or away in London or Leicester somewhere.

Either way, he wasn't upstairs in the farmhouse sitting on the toilet.'

Alan pulled himself up short. He didn't like Paul, but he hadn't wanted him to die, either.

'Poor devil,' he went on, 'for all that effort, he hadn't given himself much of a life, had he?'

Forty-one

In the last week of June, Richard Lane phoned Alan's mobile. Could he come over the following week to Indajit Singh's office in Leicester? Of course he said yes.

They assembled mid-morning. Indajit's office was large, but split in two halves: a desk with two chairs and beyond, a lower, more informal area. Here the furniture was more domestic-looking: two easy chairs and a curved sofa around a beautiful carved Indian coffee table, with four elephant legs and delicate ivory inlay. To Alan, the copy of *The Times* lying on it seemed somehow gross and intrusive. The room overlooked a surprisingly large back garden, with a stately plane tree at the centre of a lawn, which was surrounded by beds of roses, now in full flower.

'Indajit,' Alan said, looking out of the double window, 'what a remarkable garden you've got there.'

Alan would have loved to have had such a garden. The roses were in full, magnificent, flower.

'I'm glad you like it,' Indajit replied. 'Apart from the tree, it was weeds and rubbish when we took the building over. It's been my pet project. Between you and me, I did it in memory of Sofia. I collect old roses. Most of those are English: Hybrid Musks – they smell superb, especially in the sunshine.'

Indajit was smiling and relaxed. The discovery of Sofia's body had indeed proved cathartic for him. Alan looked at the young lawyer closely: he might even have put on a little weight around the middle. But he was too polite to mention it.

Lane cleared his throat and began the conversation.

'Thank you so much for having us here, Indajit; it's certainly far more pleasant than my little cell at the police station.'

Alan nodded his agreement with a mouthful of biscuit.

'But there've been some developments I thought you two ought to be told about, before we release details to the press. First, Ali.'

He began, paused, took a sip from his cup of tea, then continued.

'I think we're all convinced he didn't do it. The Home Office now think so too. He's been moved to an Open Prison, and a full pardon should follow on a Judicial Review.'

'That's good,' Alan said, 'Despite what he said to me, I think jail would eventually have destroyed him.'

'We're still looking into Mehmet and Abdul's affairs,' Lane went on. 'It should take another couple of months to prepare a detailed case.'

Then he turned to Indajit.

'I told you what Alan had learned from Ali about the supposed killing, and I'm still inclined to believe it. Whatever the truth, I don't think we could prove a firm case for murder, let alone establish a suspect. Even with that confession.'

'Especially with that confession,' Indajit added. 'In retrospect I'm not at all happy with it, either. As my Scottish colleagues might say: I think it's almost certainly a "Case Not Proven". No, having thought about it at some length, I now honestly don't think Ali was ever guilty of Sofia's death.'

'That's very generous of you,' Lane replied, clearly impressed at his frankness. 'But do you think she was murdered, at all?'

'No, I agree with Alan. Ali's account seems far more plausible.'

Alan needed to be quite clear.

'What, accidentally falling down the stairwell?'

'Yes. That makes real sense. I suggest we go with it.'

Lane nodded in agreement.

'What about Kevin?' Alan asked.

'It's pretty straightforward,' Lane replied. 'When we told him we'd got Abdul, he broke down and admitted everything. He did booby trap your Land Rover – on a timer – and he admitted he was carrying the gun to kill you.'

'And the bungalow?' Alan asked.

Lane shook his head.

'No, he was adamant he knew nothing about it.'

'D'you believe him?'

'Yes. On the whole I do.'

'Oh, well, accidents do happen…' Alan shrugged his shoulders. Then he asked, 'But what about Paul – did he kill him too?'

'Sort of. He confessed he dumped him in the maggot tank…'

'On Abdul's instructions?'

'Yes,' Lane replied. 'Kevin was keen to offload blame in that direction, but he didn't administer the opiates.'

'Opiates?' Indajit asked surprised.

'The lab identified them from his stomach contents – or what was left of them. A hefty dose.'

'But not quite big enough,' Alan added grimly.

'No,' Lane agreed.

'So I was right. The poor bastard did come round in the tank...'

For a moment Alan relived the horror of that discovery.

'Presumably somebody gave him a jab at the board room meeting?'

'Again, yes. Abdul has confessed to that. We also found the syringe chucked into the hedge outside.'

'Well done, I bet that took some finding?' asked Alan.

'It did. But it's got Abdul's fingerprints on it.'

Alan was still dwelling on Paul. He sighed, then said, 'Poor bastard. What a way to go.'

'I wouldn't be too sorry for him, Alan. Thanks to you, we now know just how unpleasant he was.'

Indajit looked puzzled.

'What, that business Alan discovered? The modern bones and the faked-up reburials?'

'Yes,' Lane replied. 'The results of our own tests show that most of the bodies came from Eastern Europe and western Asia with a smaller number from the Indian subcontinent – even a woman from China. Then we went back through the records and disinterred one of the previous Christian reburials.'

'How many were there?' Indajit asked in astonishment.

'What, bodies or burials?' Lane replied.

'Both, I suppose.'

'The records that you put me onto...'

'The ones held by PFC,' Alan added for Indajit's benefit.

Lane continued, obviously keen to get all the information across as efficiently as possible. 'They are very meticulous notes of everything. Well, they show six separate episodes of Christian reburial, over three years. We've only decided to examine one, and so far that's produced eight modern individuals.'

'Are they all non-British?' Alan asked.

'Yes, entirely. Most were young adolescent females.'

'Like the body in the tank, beneath Paul?' asked Alan quietly. That image, of the small foot with the painted toenails still haunted him. Like Sofia's scream, he suspected it always would.

'Yes,' Lane replied quietly, 'like many of the others, in her early twenties, although the bones were mostly disarticulated.'

'Presumably her bones got disturbed when Paul was dumped in, and slightly later when he came round and started struggling?' Alan suggested.

'Certainly that's what our forensic people now think. Anyhow, she was eastern European and we have a record of her on our missing person files. Her name,' he pulled a small notepad from his pocket, 'was Anna Petrova. She can be linked to a Romanian people-smuggling gang, active in Birmingham and the West Midlands. She was thirteen when she arrived here. Soon after she was arrested and warned several times for prostitution. A sex slave, poor girl. No other way of putting it.'

'So this wasn't about "honour killings", then?' Indajit asked.

'No. Far from it. That was a huge assumption on our part, in both cases.'

Lane paused to take a sip from his cup, then resumed.

'Using that café "Mehmet's" as a central point, the Kabuls had established a network which provided a vital service to the sex trade and the general criminal underworld, across most of England...'

'Ali called it "the family business",' Alan added. 'I'm not sure how much he knew, exactly, but he was clearly very angry that Abdul was using his vans at PFC.'

'And I suppose,' Indajit asked, 'that the Kabul Centre at Impingham was going to be its lavish, but logical successor?'

'Yes, you're right,' Lane replied. 'We're still working on it, but there's good anecdotal evidence to suggest that some of the back rooms at "Mehmet's" were used as knocking shops. I don't see why the "corporate facilities" at Impingham couldn't have been for something similar, either.'

Indajit was frowning.

'So they made money from the poor girls' bodies when they were alive, and then when they had no further use for them your fellow archaeologist...'

'Please don't call him that,' interrupted Alan.

Indajit nodded in apology and pressed on.

'So, how much did they make?'

'Our forensic accountants are hard at it,' Lane replied, 'but it looks like each body disposal was worth somewhere around a hundred to a hundred and fifty thousand.'

'And collection was organised by Abdul, using Ali's van service?'

'Precisely,' Lane replied. 'That way they could keep the location of the facility secret, while controlling what was coming in and going out. The entire operation was remarkably well planned and organised.'

There was another pause.

'Yes,' Alan remarked, 'as Ali said, it was quite a family business.'

For a moment or two they sat quietly digesting what had been said.

Alan was the first to break the silence.

'But I still wonder about the underlying motive. What was it that drove... that was so... so... *compulsive* for Mehmet? I can understand why he wanted to be a big man within his family.

And I also understand how competition and rivalries can develop between and within families. That's all fairly standard anthropology. But why did he go so far?'

Alan was thinking of AAC and the Victorian family at Scoby Hall.

'Yes, what made him to do it?' Lane asked.

'I believe,' Alan continued, 'that he was being driven by something beyond him. The only thing I can suggest is some form of internal family dynamic.'

He tailed off, aware that the anthropological jargon didn't say much. Both his listeners were frowning. They didn't follow him. Indajit came to his rescue:

'Is that another way of saying that Abdul wanted to run things? Abdul could see that Ali was brighter than him, but he lacked his ruthless streak. He also realised that his grandfather's great weakness was vanity. So when the opportunity to move into an entirely fresh line of "family business" arose in 2002, thanks to Paul and Flax Hole, he grabbed it with both hands. From the very outset he was the brains behind the body disposal enterprise. But he concealed what he was up to by encouraging Mehmet to pose as the big family man.'

'So,' Lane added, 'it was old man Mehmet who held everyone's attention.'

Alan leant forward, deep in thought:

'Presumably, Abdul believed that if they were ever found out, then Mehmet would be seen as the obvious boss man: the gang leader?'

'Exactly,' Indajit replied.

'But tell me,' Alan asked again, 'what was Abdul's attitude when you started nosing around in the family's affairs all those years ago… Was he obstructive?'

'Now you mention it, he wasn't. I won't say he welcomed my attentions – that would be going too far, but he never once warned me off, nor threatened me. I remember thinking it odd at the time.'

'Yes,' Alan continued, 'it suited him. And of course the agreement the three of them came to…'

Lane, who by this point was taking notes, needed to be quite clear.

'What, the thing Ali told you about. The formal family agreement witnessed by his grandfather?'

'Yes that,' Alan replied.

'So as soon as it became clear that Sofia's death would end up in court, they came to a deal that Ali who had just turned eighteen when the "crime" had been committed, would "confess" and in return Abdul would run his van enterprise for him.'

'Exactly, Richard. It seems to me,' Alan continued, 'that Mehmet's motive had to have more behind it than the simple desire for control. After all, I'm sure he did want to impress the local Turkish community with the strength of his convictions, and an "honour killing" was as good a way to do it as any…'

'And of course,' Indajit broke in, 'Abdul was there, encouraging him all the time.'

'But even so,' Alan said, more to himself than the others, 'to persuade a young member of the family – and somebody at the start of his life – to confess to a crime he didn't commit – a crime that never even happened… I still can't get my head around that.'

'I think I can,' Indajit said quietly. 'Families are about structure and certainty, which you either welcome, or you don't. Personally I find formality can help me relax. You don't need to worry about what happens next, because you know the rules.'

Alan broke in.

'But can't those rules also get in the way?'

'That's for people to decide for themselves.'

'Yes, but surely you would admit that certain rules are rather rigid?'

'Are they? It depends on whether you're inside or outside the system. I don't think there are absolute values here.'

'Even with something like arranged marriage?' asked Alan.

'Yes. Take my brother's marriage. It was arranged by my parents and it works. It always has. They're both very shy people. I won't say there's never a cross word between them, but they're happy together. In fact it makes me very angry when people routinely condemn arranged marriages without knowing anything about them.'

To Alan's surprise Lane came in on Indajit's side.

'Yes. What's the difference between a marriage arranged by well-intentioned relatives who've known you since you were a kid, and some internet introduction agency? I know damn well which one I'd choose.'

'Precisely,' Indajit continued, 'there's a big difference between arranged and forced marriages. Read Jane Austen, read Thackeray: most of those marriages were arranged. Manipulated. Call them what you will. But there was never coercion: they all required couples to consent.'

'Is it unusual for Sikhs to find their own wives?'

Indajit smiled ruefully.

'No. Increasingly it isn't. As you know, I tried…'

He paused for a moment. Then continued half to himself:

'No, but I'll tell you one thing. If my mother were still alive, I'd ask her to find me a nice wife now. I certainly would.'

* * *

Indajit and Lane rose from their chairs. Alan remained sitting, thinking over what had been said. After a while he glanced up at them, standing over by the window, looking out into the garden and laughing at a grey squirrel on the lawn. For a moment he felt a tinge of envy: they had welcomed change into their own lives, and were both the better for it. But had he?

Again he glanced down at *The Times* on Indajit's beautifully carved Indian coffee table. But it wasn't a single report that worried him now. It wasn't like that moment in the site hut when his fag paper slipped through his fingers, onto the wet floor. This time it was the whole of the front page. Most of the stories were about wealth, the rich and the famous. Those pictures said it all. It was the same set of spoiled, primped and perfumed faces, again and again. For a brief moment, the parallels between AAC's lofty portrait, Mehmet's ludicrous statue, and the strutting celebrities of his own time, seemed uncomfortably close.

Then a surge of fury gripped him. Why do these ghastly, self-obsessed people lord it over everyone else – and why do we stand for it? For Christ's sake, he thought, why don't we intervene? Do something. Strike back. Make a fuss. Then he thought back to that piercing scream all those years ago at Flax Hole. He'd had the chance then, but he had done nothing. After all that had happened, that thought still haunted him, day and night.

Epilogue

A bright morning in mid-July. Alan was standing in a small shrubbery with roses and carefully tended lawns. In the distance he could hear the hum of traffic on the Leicester bypass and the occasional cries of children from nearby houses. Schools were now out and the holidays had just begun.

He was observing a small group of five men in the distant Muslim area of the Saffron Hill municipal cemetery. They were looking down at an open grave. After a few minutes they raised their heads and stood still. Then the robed figure shook the hands of the two dark-suited men and slowly returned to the small octagonal Prayer House, behind them. The suited men then turned and walked along the path towards the gate into the car park to Alan's left. The other two men waited a few minutes, then picked up shovels and began to backfill the grave.

The suited men approached the gate and Alan stood back, deeper in the shadows. Their body language was warm. Sympathetic. Alan couldn't be certain, but he thought he detected a glint on Indajit's cheek, of tears. Little Mehmet looked less little now. And stronger. In the car park Indajit produced the keys and unlocked the car as they approached. One car. Alan hadn't expected that. Sofia had brought them together.

As the car pulled away, Alan turned to leave, too. Slowly he walked along a mown path, then found himself sitting on a wooden seat, deep in thought. Why, he wondered was he always on the outside, looking in? Always the observer. He remembered sad little Tiny and that hopeless succession of dead babies and shattered dreams. Then he found those expressionless eyes of the psychopath coldly watching him at that first talk at Blackfen. But most of all he couldn't stop thinking about Sofia's scream. But what were they all telling him, those spectres from the past: to engage? To meddle? To interfere? No, he despised busybodies and people who thought they knew better than others. But surely there had to be a middle way – or was there? Then he realised that his subconscious knew the answer all the time, and for a moment it was as if he was on the other side of that horrible grille, in Ali's place, and looking out at freedom.

Slowly he rose to his feet and headed towards the car park, seeing, feeling nothing, as he allowed the truth to enfold him. He stood stock still beside his mud-spattered Daihatsu, took a deep breath and closed his eyes. He knew now that he was not unusual, that he acted as he did because he had no choice: it was the way he was – and there was no escape. The strongest prison walls are in our own minds.

Like it or not, we are all members of The Lifers' Club.

Acknowledgements

I'm particularly grateful to Martin Kurzik who first encouraged me to try changing tracks, after reading my book *Seahenge: A Quest for Life and Death in Bronze Age Britain* (HarperCollins, 2001). The switch from non-fiction to fiction was expertly overseen by my agent, Bill Hamilton, of A.M. Heath and Co., who made many important suggestions to drafts of the manuscript. This book could not have been written without his help and encouragement. I would normally have suggested to Bill that he find a trade publisher in the usual way, but two years ago I bumped into Justin Pollard at the Hay-on-Wye Festival. I knew Justin from *Time Team* and he enthused about Unbound, which he had just set up with two colleagues. To cut a long story short, a year later I decided to offer the book to them and I have never regretted the decision. Unbound are more an extended family than a publisher and they have helped me master a huge number of new skills. I improved my blog (http://pryorfrancis.wordpress.com) and now Tweet (@pryorfrancis)! Jimmy Leach was the brains behind our campaign to raise subscribers and Liz Garner was my long-suffering, imaginative and diligent story-editor. The copy-editing was ably done by Kate Greig, the proof reading by Hugh Lamb and the book was designed by Green Gate Publishing. Earlier versions of the manuscript were also read and criticised in great and constructive detail by my daughter Amy and by two good friends: Kate Haddock and Iain Kitching. Another old friend, Professor Martin Jones of Cambridge University, helped me with the DNA-speak. I have drawn extensively on his book, *The Molecule Hunt: Archaeology and the Search for Ancient DNA* (Allen Lane, Penguin Press, 2001), a wonderfully clear introduction to a highly complex subject. My brother-in-law Nigel Smith has been a constant source of help, encouragement and practical advice. Finally, I owe special thanks to my wife and plot advisor, Maisie Taylor, who has had to read, reread and discuss no less than twelve versions of this book, over two long and very cold winters.

November, 2013

Subscribers

Unbound is a new kind of publishing house. Our books are funded directly by readers. This was a very popular idea during the late eighteenth and early nineteenth centuries. Now we have revived it for the internet age. It allows authors to write the books they really want to write and readers to support the writing they would most like to see published.

The names listed below are of readers who have pledged their support and made this book happen. If you'd like to join them, visit: www.unbound.co.uk.

Helen Abraham
Carol Ainley
Patrick Alexander
Derrien Allen
Mark Allen
John P Allum
David Alsmeyer
Nyree Ambarchian
Catrina Appleby
Philippa Arthan

Joe Arthur
Fionna and Patrick
    Ashmore
Roberta Ashton
Helen Ashworth / David
    Hillelson
Jacquie Aucott
Edward Bailey
Lyn Baines
Aidan Baker

David Baker
Rita Baker
Nick Balaam & Liz Pye
Peter Baldwin
Michael Bamforth
Phil Barker
Colin Barks
Lesley Barnard
Mark Barnes
Huw Barton
Brian Bassingthwaighte
Kaye Batchelor
Jackie Bavin
Neil Baxter
Alex Bayliss
James Beatty
Bob Beaupre
Pete Beck
Katherine Becker
Bob Beer
Cindy Bennett
Carole Benson
Terry Bergin
Tessa Beukelaar
Robert Bewley
Sarbjit Bisla
Wendi Blair
Thea Bodourian & Jens-
   Kristian Hansen
Peter Boizot
Gill Bolton
Dave Bonta

Ben Booth
Sarah Botfield
Kate Boulden
Corrina Bower
Richard Bradley
Roger Braithwaite
Janey Brant
Melanie Brehaut
Mark Brennand
Teri Brewer
Sarah L Bridge
Mick Bridgman
David Britchfield
Rowan Broadbent
Sharon Brown
Tony Brown
Richard Bunting
Gilbert Burleigh
Andrew Burnett
Bill Busfield
Jenni Butterworth
Peter Calamai
David Callier
Carol Cantrell
Frances Carey
Clare Cartwright
Christopher Catling
John Cherry
Paul Cherry
Tina Chopee
Karen Christley
Lauren Churchill

Rose Clancey

Stephen J Clancy

Philip Clarke

Robin Claxton

Robert Clements

Guy Clifton

Ivan Clowsley

Robert Cole

William Collinson

David Collison

Francesca Compton

Brian Condron

Peter Connelly

Meredith Conran

Joy Conway

Emma Coombs

Tracey-Anne Cooper

Michael Corbishley

Kim Costello

Kerrie County

Charlotte Cox

David Cranstone

Philip & Jane Craske

Mike Craven-Todd

Alan Crawford

Bes Croscombe

Katherine Crouch

Heather Culpin

Current Archaeology

Deborah Curtis

Riann d'Acra

Peter Dalling

James Dalton

Nicola Davies

Sarah Davies

Catherine Davis

Jocelyn Davis

Jonathan Davison

Sue Day

Chloe de Man

Jasja Dekker

Graham Dell

John Dent

Ian Devlin

John Dexter

Eleanor Dickenson

Boyd Dixon

Philip Dixon

DJL

Eleanor Doherty

Kathryn Dolman

Jillian Drujon

Vivienne Dunstan

Sarah Durdin Robertson

Mark Dyson

Frinton Earnshaw

Mark Edmonds

Keith Edwards

Lynn Edwards

Stuart Edwards

Jeannette Elrick

Simon Erskine Crum

Barbara Evans Rees

Mark Everett

Franky Farrell

Harry Faure Walker

Teddy Faure Walker

Naomi Field

John Fields

Ruth Fillery-Travis

Claire Fisher

Marena Fisher

Paul Fisher

Hugh Fiske

Lindsey Fitzharris

Steve Fleming

Will Fletcher

Michael Fogg

Harry Fokkens

Isa Forde

Toby Fox

Katharine Francis

Isobel Frankish

Charles French

Robert Fry

Simon Fuller

Janet Gaden

Daryl Garton

Elizabeth Gass

Lady Elizabeth Gass

John Gater

Dagna Gaythorpe

Helen Geake

Paul George

Don Gibson

Jo Gibson

William Gilbert

Chris Gingell

Philippa Glanville

Peter Glass

Lisa Gledhill

Salena Godden

Ashley Golightly

Denise Gorse

David Graham

Voula Grand

Sue Greaney

Margaret Green

Martin Green

Sandie Green

Tom & Coralie Green

Catherine Greenfield

Dafydd Griffiths

Frederick Grounds

Richard Gunn

Kate Haddock

Rachael Hall

Paul Halstead

Elspeth Hardie

Claire Hardy

David Harford

Jon Harley

Nigel Harper-Scott

Barnaby Harris

Oliver Harris

Richard Harris

Stacy Harrison

Neil Hart

Steve Hartley

Jacqueline Hartnett

Caitlin Harvey

Deborah Hastings

James Hawke

Mark Haworth

Nathan Hazlehurst

Jen Heathcote

Rob Hedge

Polly Heffer

Steve Helder

Anastasia Hellewell

Elizabeth Henton

Gill Hey

Mike Heyworth

Nicholas Higham

John Hillam

Peter Hinton

Holly Hodson

Doug Holt

Sarah Holt

Audrey Horning

Craig Houston

Syd Howells

Paul Howlett

Paul Hudson

Brendan Hughes

Sarah Hughes

Peter Hunter

James F Hutchinson

Keith Hyland

Martyn Ingram

Linda Ireson

Johari Ismail

Isobel

Mark Jackson

Jordan Jacobs

Adrian James

Edward James

Gregory Jennings

Matthew Johnson

Richard Johnson

Pat Johnston

Rhona Johnstone

Sue Joiner

Gail Jones

Phyl Jones

Lesley Keech

Chris Kendrick

Paul Kenton

David Kenyon

Dan Kieran

James Kightly & Bev Laing

Iain Kitching

Becky Knight

Martin Kurzik

Susan Kyle

Cameron & Shirley Laing

Meredith Laing

William Lakin

Anne Lamb

Daniel Lamont

Tom Lane

Jimmy Leach

Alex Lee

Kelley Leffler

Beth Lewis

Claire Lindsay-McGrath

Cassie Lloyd Perrin

Mark Lloyd Price

Spencer Lödge

Andrew and Joy Longmuir

Nick Loweth

Simon Ludgate

Sara Lunt

Heather Mac Archer

Iain McCulloch

Zoe Macdonald

J McHenley

Jim McLaren

Dean MacLennan

David McOmish

Peter Maloy

John Manchip

Jon Martin

Louise Martin

Mary Masson

Kay Mayes

Peter Melkowski

Ute Methner

Deborah Metters

Martin Millett

Ronald Mitchinson

Robert Moody

Camilla More

Harry Marlborough More

Joanna More

Elizabeth Morgan

Jane Morris

Sally Morris

Jim Mower

Nicky Moxey

Jacqui Mulville

Kerry Murrell

Michael Nevell

Kate Nicholls

Taryn Nixon

Robert Noort

Anders Nyman, Uppsala
Sweden

Katherine Oakley

Bryan Oates

Dan Oggly

Peter Olver

Jan O'Malley

Andrew O'Neill

Nick Overton

Claire Owen

Christopher Page

Marilyn Palmer

Edward and Clara Pank

Ian Panter

Mike Parker Pearson

Paul Parkinson LRPS

Rebecca Parr

David Parry

Nick Parsons

Sara Parsons

Simon Parsons

Sarah Patmore

Lucy Payne

Elizabeth Peers

Wiz Pender

David Pendergast

Karl Pesch-Konopka

Mary Peterson

Catherine Pickersgill

Caroline Pierson

Tim Pike

Mike Pitts

Joshua Pollard

Justin Pollard

Sarah Poppy

Bronwyn Louise Potter, NSW, Australia

Dominic Powlesland

Ian Powlesland

Zina Myakicheff Preston

Sian Price

Cameron Prichard

Debbie Priddy

Deborah Priddy

Roger Pritchard

Zoe Propper

Alan Pryke

Amy Pryor

Cressida Pryor

Ella Pryor

Henry Pryor

Mark Pryor

Roddy Pryor

William Pryor

Sylvia Pryor Nicol

Jeremy Purseglove

Huan Quayle

Helen Randle

Hans Rasmussen

Anna Raverat

Rachel Rawlins

Colette Reap

Andrew Rhind-Tutt

Julian D Richards

Ellen Richardson

John Riley

Garner Roberts

Jennifer Roberts

Tony Robinson

Yvonne Robinson

Petre Rodan

John Rogers

Kris Rogers

Margaret Rogers

Andrew Rogerson

Alice Rose

Andrew Rose

Elizabeth Rose, Alice Violet, Andrew Sinclair and Helen Lloyd

Nansi Rosenberg

Sam Ross

Kelly Rourke Fischer

Jim Rouse

George Rowing

Peter Rowley-Conwy

Susan Royce

Zuzu Rug

Chris Rushton

Margaret L Ruwoldt

Marie Ryal

Lucy Ryder

Sally Ryder

Jobim Sampson

Emma Samuel

Rob Scaife

Kate Scarratt

Tim Schadla-Hall

Sebastian Schleussner

Dick Selwood

Dale Serjeantson

Rosie Shannon

Hazel Sheard

Gemma Sherlock

Charlotte Shipley

Jon Shute

Vicki Silcock

Eileen Silcocks

Lee Sinclair

Alison Skinner

David Sleight

Alice Smith

Derek Smith

Dinah Smith

Lucy Smith

Nigel Smith

Samantha Smith

Shelagh Smith

Stuart Smith

Steve Smith, Wimborne

Richard & Victoria Sowerby

William Sowerby

Hayley Steele

Bas Steemers

Bernie Stefan-Rasmus

Jason Stevens

Jason Stewart

Martin Stoermer

Hayden Strawbridge

Sue Strawson

Iain Sutherland

Rosy and Richard Sutton

Kerry Swinnerton

Matthew Symonds

Sarah Talks

Maisie Taylor

Robin Thain

Roger Thomas

Rebekah Thornton

Andrew Thrift

Katherine Toms

Debra Treiguts

Christopher Trent

Michael Turner

Adrian Turnham

Patricia Tutt

Ian Tyers

Simon Tyldesley

Christine Usher
Louis van Dompselàar
Marie-France van Oorsouw
Gillian Varndell
Mark Vent
Dig Ventures
Kellie Vernon
Michelle Vernon
Sarah Voller
Laurence Vulliamy
Clive Waddington
Geoff Wainwright
Geoffrey Wainwright
Stephen Wainwright
Lou Wakefield
Philip Walker
Patricia Wallace
Annie Warwick
Peter Wass
Robert Waterhouse
Stan C Waterman
Caroline Watson
Chloe Watson
Frauke Watson
Howard Webber
Dee Weightman

Nicola Wellband
Steve Whitehead
David Whitehouse
Lindsay Whitehurst
Caroline Wickham-Jones
Gerald Wilkinson
Fiona Williams
Mike Williams
Tim Williams
Justin Williamson
Jane Willmore
Thom Winterburn
Wisbech Grammar School
  Cambs
Emma Wood
Emily Woodburn
Ruth Woodburn
Valerie Woodburn
Stephen Woods
Ray Worman
Daniel Worsley
Richard Wray
Colin and Rachel Wright
Krista Yabe
Katharine Younger

A note about the typeface

Baskerville is a typeface designed in 1757 by John Baskerville (1706–1775). It is considered a 'transitional' typeface, sitting stylistically between historical and modern faces; it was also revolutionary in its time, being designed by Baskerville specifically with paper-making and ink manufacturing in mind as part of experiments intended to improve legibility and consistency in printing.

Contemporaries of Baskerville criticised the stark contrast of the type in its printed form, though many others praised it, including the French type founder Pierre Simon Fournier, Italian typographer Giambattista Bodoni and famous polymath Benjamin Franklin, inventor of the lightning rod.

The original moulds for casting the Baskerville type in metal were sold by Baskerville's widow after his death in 1775 and ended up in the archives of Deberny & Peignot, a French type foundry later absorbed into the Monotype Corporation.

More recently, an American study investigating the effect of font styles on credulity concluded that setting a question in the Baskerville typeface increases the likelihood of a reader agreeing with it by 1.5 per cent.